MASQUERADE OF BONES

J. EMBER HINTZ

MASQUERADE OF BONES
Copyright © 2025 by J. Ember Hintz

Cover & Map Design by MIBLART
Edited by Beth Lawton at VB Edits
Formatting and interior design by Specter Publishing

All rights reserved.

This is a work of fiction. The characters, organizations, and events portrayed in this novel are either fictitious or are used fictitiously. Any similarity to real persons or entities, living or dead, is purely coincidental.

ISBN: 978-1-958602-02-7 (ebook)
ISBN: 978-1-958602-03-4 (paperback)

*For the women tired of being told how to fucking behave,
who also want to be called a good girl by the tall,
dark and morally gray shadow master.*

PRONUNCIATION GUIDE

Aeroc (ay-rawk)

Caron (kair-in)

Cormier (cohr-me-ay)

Craddock (crah-dik)

Crecentis (kruh-sen-tis)

Cyphearus (seye-fur-ihs)

Dagmara (dag-mar-uh)

Gareth (gair-ith)

Grislac (griz-lahk)

Honore (on-er)

Isola (eye-so-luh)

Jo-el (joh-ell)

Krimore (kreye-mor)

Landreaux (lan-droh)

Landry (lan-dree)

Montagnais (mon-tan-yeh)

Perdanth (pur-danth)

Saracen (sair-uh-sin)

Serin (sair-in)

Serros (sair-ohs)

Thale (th-ail)

Tindlestone (tin-dull-stohn)

THE NORTHLANDS
TINDLESTONE
BLOOD LAKES
MARSHWOOD FOREST
DRAGON'S BACKBONE MOUNTAINS
PORT HOPE
SARACEN
DRAKE'S PASS
RED RIVER
PERDANTH
THE WASTES
FORT NETHERTHORN
RED STICK
LAKE LARGEAU
CRECENTIS
N
W
E
S

Chapter One

Nothing stirs the blood quite like watching a witch hang. We're not so scary when we're bound in magical suppression irons and dangling at the end of a rope.

A riot of cheers rolls across the execution yard as I pull my father's old whiskey flask from the leather bag belted to my waist and take a deep swig. The bitter pepper nerve tonic is an acquired taste and the only drug strong enough to suppress the symptoms that would give me away.

Sweat rolls down the back of my knees beneath my skirt as I wait for the guards to drag the next prisoner through the crowd. It's only ten o'clock, and the air is already thick enough to cut with a knife.

I fan myself with my sketchbook. It doesn't fucking help. There aren't any trees to shade the throng of stinking people who've come to throw slurs and rotten vegetables at the men and women being strung up by the neck. Just the long shadow cast by the gallows.

The scents of tobacco and horse shit steep in the early summer heat. I'd give anything to be able to summon a breeze from the river to blow the stench away. I'd need a thunderbird relic to wield a power like that, though. And even if I could afford one, I wouldn't know how to use it. With my cursed luck, I'd end up blowing the entire platform down, getting conscripted into one of the Perdanthian Army's Death Squads, and sent to the Wastes to die defending the crown's assets against reaver attacks—rogue witches who use their magic to terrorize, steal, and destroy. Or worse, I'd be used to hunt down other witches in hiding, like me.

I lift my long hair off my neck and twist it into a low knot, securing it with the hair pin gifted to me by the late queen. The residual magic has been long depleted from the dragon bone it was carved from.

The wrought-iron hitching post digs into my ass as I lean against it and resume sketching the scene in front of me. All the executions scheduled for the next two weeks have been moved up to this morning, ahead of Princess Dagmara's arrival with her royal entourage from the northern kingdom. Wouldn't want to spoil any of the celebrations being held in honor of her betrothal to our *heroic* prince with something as unsavory as daily public hangings.

I tighten my grip on my last nub of charcoal as the executioner's grumpy mule nudges my hip with her nose.

"Sorry, Posey, you already ate all the radishes." I give her graying muzzle an affectionate scrub.

The old mule lifts her head and lets out an annoyed chuff as her master drags the last condemned prisoner onto the gallows. Another mad witch, like all the other dead bodies piled on the cart behind me. This one can't be much older than I am. Twenty-seven. Thirty at most. The goblin-spelled shackles around his wrists and ankles clatter against the scaffold steps, the charmed iron preventing him from channeling magic.

I watch as the hangman secures a rope around the witch's neck.

"For the crimes of arson, murder, and the unsanctioned use of magic by a civilian, you shall be hanged from the neck until dead. Do you have any last words?" the executioner asks.

The convicted man tips his head back and hocks a wad of phlegm onto the executioner's face before letting out a crazed cackle that makes me wonder if he even knows where he is or what's happening to him.

"Fucking reaver scum," the executioner growls as he kicks the lever and the dying man drops through the trapdoor in the platform. The rope snaps taut, creaking under the weight of his twitching body.

My stomach lurches, and I swallow the bile pressing at the back of my throat as I rush to finish the sketch before his life winks out for good.

His feet finally stop jerking, and I force my hand to still. I don't know if he or any of the other reavers I've watched hang these last two years had any involvement in my parents' murder, but I come every week to record their faces just the same. Even though it doesn't bring me closure. It's my fault my parents are dead.

Magic prickles over my skin as I close my sketchbook and drop the suppression ward that helps dull my perception of magic. The gnash of goblin teeth and soft flutter of pixie wings whisper to me from the pockets of men, women, and children in the crowd. Good luck charms tied up in little cotton sachets. Most aren't strong enough to protect their owners from a mosquito bite, much less a string of bad fortune.

Except for the lucky bastard in possession of a dragon scale.

The hair on my arms rises as the powerful dragon relic demands my attention, creating a wave of phantom sensations—the huff of hot breath cascading down the back of my neck, and the eerie feeling that I'm being watched.

I scan the crowd in search of its owner. The air around the guards protecting the perimeter of the square ripples with a mirage of invisible heat only I can see. Which tells me they're channeling their power from firebird relics. Not rare dragon scales.

If I could get my hands on a dragon scale, I could pay off my debts to Madam Faye and have enough left over to stash away for treatment as my condition progresses. Not even the royal army can afford to outfit its conscripted witches with such an expensive weapon. One that could be used to torch the entire square. Its current owner is either the wealthiest relic collector in Crecentis or a thief. I'd bet good money on the latter.

Posey brays loudly as I shove off the hitching post.

"Don't worry, old girl. I'll bring more radishes next time. I promise."

The grumpy mule bucks her head to tell me she's still annoyed I didn't bring enough treats.

I shoulder my way through the mob of desperate souls pressing toward the gallows. They wave silver coins in the air, hoping to bribe the executioner into letting them stuff letters and messages to loved ones who have passed into the dead man's pockets, hoping he'll carry them with him to the Otherworld.

"I bet he shit himself. They all do," a husky, pockmarked teen says as he flashes his friend a conspiratorial grin.

I have no interest in learning whether the man evacuated his bowels when he died. I am, however, interested in getting to the *Penny Press* building on the other side of the city before anyone else sells them sketches of the dead to print in their weekly circular. The newspaper pays fifty cents per image, and they're the only press in Crecentis that doesn't halve the commissions paid to women.

The money I make selling death sketches is the only thing keeping a roof over my and my brother's heads. I've got over thirty drawings today. The fifteen dollars I'll make for just two hours of work is more than I earn in a week at the Menagerie.

I take a shortcut through the alley behind the prison that will shave ten precious minutes off my race across the city. The streetcar and carriage fares are no longer in my budget.

"Why the rush?" a sultry feminine voice asks behind me.

I throw a hurried glance over my shoulder, expecting it to land on one of the courtesans the Riverside District is known for. Instead, I'm staring down the length of a thin blade.

The woman pointing a knife in my face is dressed like the rest of Madam Faye's hired muscle. She wears a fitted vest over a cotton shirt with a pair of men's trousers. Tight coils of dark hair hang down her back beneath a bowler hat. A silvery mirage ripples around the black and red plume tucked into the band. Firebird feathers are a popular good luck charm among the elite and wannabe well-to-dos who want to show off.

"I don't want any trouble," I say, raising my hands, my sketchbook gripped tight in my fist as I back away. "I'm on my way to see her and pay this week's interest right after I sell my sketches."

It's not the first time Madam Layla Faye has sent one of her private security goons to threaten me. At least this one's not as brutish as her usual debt collectors. I take another step back.

"That's far enough, girl," the woman says in a melodic accent I can't quite place. My gaze snags on the fake relic dangling from her long neck. A beautifully intact snapping turtle skull sold to her by a charlatan as a southern horned pixie skull, no doubt. Everyone around here knows the difference and wouldn't be caught dead wearing such an obvious fake. Which means the woman isn't from Crecentis or anywhere else in southern Perdanth. Definitely not one of Faye's goons then.

"I like your necklace. Is that a pixie skull?" I ask, feigning ignorance. If I can distract her, I might be able to sneak my hand inside the secret pocket of my waist pouch where I keep what's left of my firebird relic. I can't weave a protection ward around myself without making physical contact with the feather.

"Thank you. It was a gift," the woman says, flashing a smile at something behind me.

"More of an inside joke, but we can call it a gift if you like." A deep voice drags over me like a gust of hot air, setting my senses ablaze. Every nerve in my body is fully aware of the dragon scale somewhere in his possession. His entire body emanates with the relic's raw power.

He's annoyingly tall and ruggedly handsome, with broad shoulders and dark hair that curls at the nape of his neck. Stubble lines his upper lip and jaw, softening the sharp angles of his perfectly symmetrical face. My fingers twitch with the urge to draw him.

Bursts of gold give his molten brown eyes a deceptive warmth. There's nothing warm, however, in the predatory way he rakes his gaze over me from head to toe like a man who's used to taking what he wants.

His clothing matches the woman's—fine quality and tailored to hug his lean, muscular form, but crumpled from long wear. The sleeves of his white shirt are rolled to the elbow. He wears a set of pearl-handled pistols holstered under his arms. The kind of guns one wears for show more than actual shooting. I scan the pockets of his waistcoat and trousers for the sharp outline of a dragon scale.

"What do we have here?" he asks, snatching the sketchbook from my hand.

"That doesn't belong to you." The words hiss past my clenched teeth as I grab for the book.

He towers above me. The man has to be part giant. Threads of magic trail the onyx ring on his thumb as he raises his arm and holds the sketchbook out of my reach. Who needs a goblin-spelled good luck charm when they possess a dragon scale?

He takes a step back and flips through my illustrations of the extinct magical creatures on display at the Menagerie. My unofficial bestiary of bones. His dark eyes flick to mine when he gets to the death portraits at the back.

I'm overcome with the sudden urge to run, but I'm rooted to the ground like a stunned rabbit caught in a snare.

"It's disrespectful to make pictures of the dead." He rips out the death sketches with one hand.

There's no chance I'm letting this pretty thug and his friend steal my work so they can sell it to the nearest newspaper and run off with my commission.

"Give them back." I lurch for the pages. The woman grabs me from behind, pulling me against her chest in a fierce grip, the tip of her knife pressed to my ribs.

The thief stares at me like he's trying to work something out before glancing at the sketches again, as if he's considering returning them. My stomach flutters. Maybe this asshole has a conscience after all.

Heat flashes across my face as he summons a black flame and torches the pages. All that's left are the bits of glowing ash that float to the ground between us.

I fucking hate reavers.

I'm not sure if I say it out loud or just think it.

He crowds into my personal space and grips my jaw with his soot-covered hand. The faint scent of wood smoke and clove stuffs up my nose as he turns my head from side to side, studying my mismatched eyes—one brown, one blue.

I jerk away from the bruising strength of his fingertips. It's no use. Sandwiched between the two of them, I have nowhere to go.

"There are fifty guards in the execution yard." The words fight to get out through my squished lips. "All I have to do is scream."

"You could certainly try," he says. Dark shadows crawl over his shoulder and down his arm, then coil around my throat as he flashes me a seductive smile that promises the kind of trouble that could make a woman forget she's sworn off cocky witches for good.

Heat pools low in my belly as he slides his thumb over my bottom lip. There is definitely something wrong with me. I should not be imagining all the things I would let this man do to me in the dark. My brain is definitely creeping toward madness. Inhibitions are among the first to go when the sickness takes hold.

"If you give me the sketchbook and let me go, I won't tell anyone I saw you. You have my word." My heart slams against my ribs as I unclench my sweaty fist and slowly slide my hand into the pouch at my waist.

"If you want to negotiate, you'll need to offer something more enticing than your word."

I stroke the tattered firebird feather hidden in my pouch, drawing the residual magic into my body and breaking the promise I made to my mother. My chest tightens with guilt, knowing how disappointed she'd be if she were still alive, if she knew how many times I'd broken my promise and summoned magic in the last two years.

"I don't negotiate with reavers," I say with as much disgust as I can muster while he's squeezing my face. My ability is raw and untrained, but he's not the only one who knows how to play with fire.

"Is that your final offer?" he asks, dropping his gaze to my mouth.

"By the Mother of Fire," the woman behind me says, tightening her grip around my chest. "Stop toying with the girl and snap her neck already."

I can't compete with a witch summoning power from a dragon scale, but there's just enough magic left in my pitiful firebird feather to shoot a flare into the sky. This close to the prison and gallows, the two witches will have no choice but to run.

No one would believe the explosion of magic had come from me. There were only two people in this world who knew my secret, and they both took it with them to the grave.

"Let her go," he commands, releasing his grip on my face.

I suck in a desperate breath as his shadows recede.

"So she can sketch our faces for a wanted poster? I don't think so," the woman says behind me.

"I said let her go," he repeats, cutting his partner a dark look.

She mumbles an obscenity as she shoves me away from her. "You heard him, girl. Get the fuck out of here."

I fight the instinct to run, squaring my shoulders and ignoring the thudding sensation in my chest.

"Do you have a death wish?" the woman asks with an incredulous grunt.

"Depends on the day." I hold out my hand and plaster a pleasant smile on my face. "I'll be on my way as soon as he gives me my sketchbook."

There's no fucking way I'm letting them steal it. My father gave it to me along with a set of fine charcoals when I was admitted into the Royal Academy of Science. Quality paper and art supplies are a luxury I can no longer afford. Not when there are more pressing debts to pay.

"I think I'll hold on to it for a few days. As collateral." Wisps of shadow circle the leather-bound book. It disappears with a flick of his wrist. "Keep your mouth shut, and I'll pay you a visit before I leave this cesspit of a city to return it."

"The next time I see you, reaver, it'll be at the end of a rope."

"Perhaps." The corner of his mouth pulls up as he backs down the alley with his arm slung over his companion's shoulder. "Until we meet again, *Miss Thorne.*"

Chapter Two

"What in the Otherworld happened to your face?" Wallace asks, keeping her voice low as I drop into the wooden chair at the worktable we share in the Menagerie's archive wing. "You look like you fell headfirst into the coal box."

"Nothing worth mentioning." I swipe my hand over my cheek. It comes away with a smear of sweat and black soot.

My best friend slaps her palms on the wooden surface between us, earning daggered looks from half a dozen other curators working at stations spread around the silent room. "Please tell me you're late because you were romping in the boiler room with the chimney sweep again," Wallace whispers as she leans toward me. "It's the perfect place for a secret rendezvous. The guards never patrol there."

"Not this time," I say. The only reason I lured the handsome sweeper into the boiler room the first time was to ensure that the coal chute was unlocked so I could sneak in and out of the Menagerie at night when the museum is closed. All the other times were because he proved to be *very* good with his hands.

Her amber eyes glint with excitement. "Who was it, then?" she asks. "The new guard built like a tree trunk, or the skinny one with nice teeth?"

"A cocky witch who likes to show off." Anger gnaws at my insides as I lift the corner of my white smock and use it to scrub the shadow summoner's sooty fingerprints from my skin.

Without the money from my death portraits, I don't have enough to pay the weekly interest I owe Madam Faye. Maybe he and his companion work for her after all. It's not uncommon for her to hire extra muscle during Festivalla, when the city turns into a nonstop party for two weeks to celebrate the consolidation of the southern clans under the Krimore crown. It would explain how he knew my name.

Dammit. If I can't make my interest payments, there's nothing stopping her from taking my house, since I put it up as collateral against my debt. I need to get my hands on some cash before Faye sends more of her goons to collect. I only have one option. I have to sell my firebird feather.

The old-timers say the magical birds gave us the gift of fire, and with it, the ability to drive away the darkness. One doesn't need to be a witch to benefit from the residual magic in their feathers. The black and red plumes are a powerful repellent against evil intent the same way a torch protects its bearer from the wolves that stalk the swamp at night.

Without the relic, I won't be able to weave a suppression ward to block my perception of magic, but the extra coin will buy me more bitter nerve tonic and a few months' grace from the woman who holds the deed to the only home my brother and I have ever known. The last connection we have to our parents.

"Are you going to spill the details or not?" Wallace asks. "You know I live vicariously through you, right? My overprotective brothers aren't like Adrian. They escort me everywhere like it's their job to scare men away. I haven't had sex in over a year."

"There are worse things than having people who want to take care of you."

"I never get a moment alone. Between working here and at the Duck, my love life is as dry as a bone. Now tell me everything about the witch who made you late for work. I want all the juicy details. Please"—she leans closer—"be *very* specific."

"I'm done with witches," I say as I set out my ink pots. "They're not worth the trouble."

"Mm-hmm," Wallace hums in agreement as she picks up her paintbrush and returns to layering in the fine details of a thunderbird shooting lightning out of its eyes in the midst of an aerial battle with a dragon. "The kind of trouble that leaves big, sooty man prints all over your face."

"I'm serious."

"I've heard that before. We both know you're drawn to men with magic like a moth to a flame. When are you going to give yourself permission to admit what you really want?"

"And what's that?" I ask, rolling my eyes.

"The same thing we all want. The thing that stirs your soul and fills you with joy. Whatever it is, only you can answer."

"What do you want?"

"I don't know," Wallace says with a shrug. "To see the world, adventure. Something more exciting than painting exhibit murals or sweating my ass off cooking and cleaning up after other people for the rest of my life. This isn't exactly what I thought I'd be doing when my clan offered to pay for me to go to the academy." She waves her paintbrush at my nose.

"I thought you loved the Whistling Duck. It's been in your family for generations. It's where you were born."

"I love my family. *They* love the inn," Wallace says. "If I don't get out, I'll die there as well. Now spill the beans. Where did you meet this witch you *don't* want to talk about?"

"He was a guard on duty at the gallows." I hate how easily the lie rolls off my tongue. Better she assume I was making out with one of the conscripted military witches instead of pushing my luck in a back-alley standoff with a handsy reaver.

Aside from my brother, Wallace is the closest thing I have to family. She knows everything about me. Everything except my crippling debt, my debilitating illness, and what I am. I'm a shit friend, but I can't ever share the burden of my secret with her, or anyone else I care about. Knowingly harboring a witch is punishable by death. I refuse to put her life at risk.

"What panel did you pull for me today?" I ask as I drag the instructions toward me, eager to change the subject.

"Just an old legend for the new exhibit." A copper curl springs free from the front of her bonnet as she crinkles her freckled nose and scowls at her work. "I hate that we're stuck painting pretty pictures of extinct creatures instead of working on an active relic excavation."

I pull a linen bonnet over my hair and secure the ties as a pair of newly conscripted witches in purple military tunics float a sealed crate of unicorn relics past us. The rumble of galloping hooves assaults my senses. No one else can hear the deafening thrum coming from the wooden box.

I've never met another witch who can sense magic without touching a relic. It's the reason I went into paleontology instead of medicine like the rest of my family. I wanted answers. I wanted to make the noise stop. All I've gotten for my efforts is the early onset of the burning disease that takes all witches in the end.

"It's not fair that these kids will get to work at a dig before we do," Wallace says, cutting the young witch conscripts a withering glance. The two boys can't be older than fourteen or fifteen.

"I don't envy their fate," I say once the teens are out of earshot. "Most of the army's conscripts who get deployed to dig sites and other assets in the Wastes never make it home."

"The ones that do tear up the tavern with their rowdy antics and drunken brawls," she says. "Like they're entitled to do whatever they please just because they can wield magic. They're worse than the Lakeside elites who slum it down in Riverside during Festivalla to throw their money around. No offense."

She doesn't need to add the last bit. I know she doesn't mean me. My parents were elites once favored by the queen. I was raised at court, but royal connections aren't worth much when your last name is synonymous with being a reaver sympathizer.

"Being a witch is a curse I wouldn't wish on anyone," I mumble as I mix my paints.

"Someone needs to teach them to have a little respect for the people who clean up their mess after a night of debauchery. It's like they forget all their home training when they come back from the Wastes."

There's never been a witch in Wallace's clan. She doesn't understand what it's like to survive the fever, only to wake up cursed with the knowledge that you'll only live a half-life. That you'll never grow old or meet your grandchildren, or why most witches live fast and hard and squeeze everything they can out of life before it's taken from them.

I was sixteen and traveling with my parents deep in the forests of Saracen when my witch fever started. They hid me for months, waiting for me to die or recover. The only thing I remember is the nightmare of a beast clawing me open from the inside.

When I finally woke, drenched in sweat in the back of my parents' covered wagon, I could hear the relics whispering to me. I haven't had a moment of peace or been able to sleep soundly since. My parents made me promise to never tell another soul about my curse. Not even my brother, Adrian, who was eighteen at the time and stayed behind in Crecentis to attend the Royal Medical Academy.

"I met a lot of sick witches while traveling with my parents," I say. "Despite their reputation as reaver sympathizers, most of their patients were conscripts kicked out of the military when they started getting sick. Once the symptoms start, witches have five years, ten if they're lucky, before they can no longer take care of themselves. Very few have families willing or able to care for them as they decline."

Unfortunately, my plan to build my medical fund at the gaming tables so I'm not a burden to my brother backfired. Now I owe Madam Faye more than I can ever repay.

"Your parents were good people," Wallace says, offering me a soft smile. "I'd give anything to travel the way you did when you were young. It seems so exciting and glamorous. I've never been farther than Red Stick, where most of my clan comes from."

"Sleeping on the hard ground all summer is the opposite of glamorous. We spent most of those trips stopping at every dusty and dilapidated border town along the edge of the Wastes while my mother and father conducted tests on all the sick witches they could find in their desperate hunt for a cure. Look where that got them. Slaughtered by the people they were trying to help. Trust me, we're much safer here building exhibits for the Menagerie than we are digging up relics in the Wastes."

I read the instructions for the next art panel—a depiction of Gideon Krimore, First King of Perdanth. The man who tamed the last living dragon two hundred years ago and rode it into battle against Saracen. The victory earned him the Perdanthian throne. His lineage has held it ever since.

"I saved that one just for you," Wallace says, biting back a mischievous grin.

"Seriously?" I glare across the table at her.

"What? It's not my fault your princely ex-fiancé was named after his heroic ancestor."

A sudden dropping sensation sends my stomach plummeting as another group of young witches floats a crate of thunderbird fossils past our table on a cushion of air.

I pinch the bridge of my nose and exhale slowly to ease the dizziness.

Wallace squeezes my hand. "I'm sorry. You've been so nonchalant about Gideon coming home. I... I don't know what I was thinking. Here, we can switch." She pushes her canvas toward me.

"It's fine," I say, picking up my blank canvas before she can snatch it away from me. "It's been four years."

"Are you sure?" Wallace asks skeptically.

"Why are they emptying the vault?" I ask, eager to change the subject again. I haven't heard from Gideon Krimore since he left me to play soldier in the Wastes—aside from the royal missive delivered to my doorstep two years ago, the day after my parents died, informing me that our betrothal agreement had been dissolved.

Apparently, the crown was no longer obligated to honor the promise made by the queen to my mother once both women were dead. King Serros announced Gideon's betrothal to the princess of Saracen the following day.

"To make room for Princess Dagmara's dowry. The Menagerie's warded vault is the only one secure enough to keep it safe."

"The king of Saracen paid his daughter's dowry in relics?" I ask.

"The delivery is arriving this afternoon."

"No, that can't be right. Gideon would never accept such an obvious offense."

Before he took his military commission, Gideon had been extremely vocal about his views on banning the conscription of witches and the use of magic entirely. He loathed relics and anything to do with the magic that slowly ate away at his mother's mind. When she passed, he was inconsolable and lashed out at everyone who tried to placate him with soft words. I was the only one who recognized his rage for what it was. Anger at himself for being powerless to stop death from taking the person he loved most.

I understood because I felt it too. Queen Marlayna had been like a second mother to me. She took care of me when I was too young to travel with my parents during their summer missions and lavished me with gifts fit for a princess on my birthday and during Festivalla. I'd loved her too, but she was Gideon's entire world. Her death cut him deeply, and I couldn't bear to see him suffer. So I did the only thing I could think of to help him take back control. I convinced him to help me destroy the most famous magical relic in Perdanthian history—the dragon his namesake brought down with a bolt of lightning.

The beast's skeleton had stood guard in the great hall behind the Krimore throne since the time of the first king and queen. We'd just turned fourteen and could barely swing the ax between us. All we managed to do was knock one of its forelegs loose and topple the massive relic over. It made a thundering noise when it tipped forward and smashed his father's throne to splinters, earning Gideon the nickname Throne Breaker. I'm pretty sure the king saw me as a bad influence from that point forward. Gideon started his military training the next day, and the king had the skeleton moved to the Menagerie to avoid any future accidents.

"People change," Wallace says. "He commands an army of witches and wields a goblin-spelled blade that ensures every deadly strike hits its mark. He can't be that averse to magic. Besides, you never know what someone is willing to sacrifice for love."

My gut tightens in a way it hasn't in years. Like I need to vomit and destroy something at the same time.

I bite the inside of my lip and blink back the hot pinch tugging at the corners of my eyes. *Fuck.* I promised myself I would never cry over the man who cut me out of his life with a royal decree two days after my parents' murder. He didn't even bother with the courtesy of sending me a personal letter explaining himself. Even though we were born on the same day and slept next to one another in the same cradle while our mothers bound our hands in a foolish promise. Even though Gideon and I were each other's first friend, first confidant, first... everything.

He doesn't deserve my tears. I'll never let another man hold that kind of power over me again.

"Are you sure you're good with painting that particular panel?" Wallace asks again. "I don't mind switching."

"It's fine," I insist, unsure of who I'm trying to convince. Her or me.

Wallace and I spend the next hour working in silence. I'm nearly finished painting the background on my canvas when the steam whistles begin to blow up and down the river.

My spine goes rigid. The crown prince is home.

Chapter Three

"Aren't you coming?" Will, one of Wallace's flame-haired younger brothers, asks me as she removes her smock and bonnet.

"I still have a bit of work to do," I say, gesturing to my unfinished canvas.

"Wally said the Menagerie gave everyone the afternoon off to watch the royal parade. Don't you want to go?" Whitt, his identical twin, asks, genuinely confused as to why anyone wouldn't want to watch the war hero prince ride past with his battalion of battle witches.

"Everly doesn't like crowds." Wallace shoots me an apologetic look. "Do you want me to stay with you?" she asks, concern wrinkling her brow.

"Go, have fun," I say, fisting my right hand to hide the slight tremor. The bitter nerve tonic is wearing off. "I'd prefer to finish up alone."

"Come on, you mongrels. Let's let Everly finish her work in peace." Wallace ushers her brothers toward the exit.

"Will and I will catch some pretty beads for you," Whitt says as he tussles his brother's hair. He flashes me a wide grin, giving me a glimpse of his slightly pointed canines.

I pull the flask from my bag once they're gone and take a swig of the bitter tonic to steady my nerves. The day will come when I can't hide my symptoms anymore. That day is not today. I pack up my box of paints and canvas, tuck an easel under my arm, and make my way to the exhibit wing. The light is better there in the late afternoon, and I need a dragon in front of me while I paint to make sure I get the proportions right. I can't afford to have my pay docked if it isn't finished before I leave.

During Festivalla, the Menagerie is usually packed with children wearing dragon masks and pretending to spit fire and roar at their exasperated parents. I'm thrilled to find it blissfully empty for once. The entire city is outside, lining the street in front of the museum that stretches from the port in Riverside all the way to the palace, everyone eager to get a glimpse of the royal caravan as it parades past.

Everyone except me. I have no desire to see Gideon or the princess who will become his queen. I plan to spend the next week right here, surrounded by the bones of extinct beasts. Safe from the sneers and fake smiles that follow me when I show my face at court.

I can handle the withering looks and wagging tongues. It's the pity I can't stand, especially from the few friends my parents had among the elites. The ones who go out of their way to tell me how sorry they are that my mother and father are dead every time they see me. Or how unfair it is that I'll never sit on the throne as Queen Marlayna intended. Like I need a fucking reminder.

I'd rather break out in boils than set foot in another ballroom. Fortunately, the Thorne name fell off the royal guest list two years ago. Though sometimes I wish it hadn't, for Adrian's sake. I'd do just about anything to see my brother's face light up like it used to when he lost himself to the music, dancing through the night during the Festivalla ball.

I banish the memories of the past and focus on the massive dragon skeleton snarling at me with its sharp teeth. I run my fingertips over a curved talon as long as my arm, its surface worn smooth by thousands of curious hands. If I stand on my tiptoes and stretch, I can almost touch its ribs.

"How are you today, my majestic friend?" I ask the dusty replica of a long-dead dragon as I set up my easel. There's no phantom whisper of hot breath on the back of my neck. Like every extinct creature on display in the Menagerie, this one is silent. The magic depleted from its bones centuries ago.

Even before they were extinct, dragons were a rare sight. To fall under one's shadow meant certain death. The predatory beasts plagued farms and villages, eating livestock and humans alike.

Some say the dragon Gideon the First summoned into battle had black scales that shone deep purple in the moonlight. Others insist they were more blue. The only constant among the descriptions were the dragon's crimson eyes and lust for carnage. The first king of Perdanth was a monster-hunting witch beloved by the southern clans. How he managed to summon the last living dragon to do his bidding, I haven't a clue.

The new exhibit is meant to tell his story, to convince us that we're the most powerful species to walk the earth, despite our lack of innate magic. That we're somehow better than the magical beasts that were here long before us. That our superiority is synonymous with our right to control and subjugate. What a load of crap. Humans wouldn't have survived this long without the magic we steal from their decaying bones.

I planned to make the ancient dragon slayer resemble King Serros, with his olive skin and dark hair shot through with streaks of silver, but he came out looking more like Gideon the last time I saw him. All golden curls and shining armor. I bite back a petty smile as I go over the face again and give him a bulbous nose. It doesn't help. He's still annoyingly handsome.

A shiver crawls down my spine, making my skin pebble as the room temperature plummets. The sensation is too sudden to be anything other than a relic. One I've never felt before.

I shove my hands beneath my armpits and lumber to the wall of arched windows, my feet may as well be blocks of ice for how heavy they suddenly feel. The crowd parts, allowing an armored wagon to enter the Menagerie's gated courtyard. The princess's dowry.

Dozens of Saracen soldiers on horseback make a protective circle around the wagon as six witches in green and gold tunics drop to the ground from the roof.

The Saracen witches seem unaffected by the chill that's pulsing from the wagon in debilitating waves and making my teeth chatter. They raise their hands, contorting their fingers in a way that tells me they're unraveling the protective wards around the wagon. I watch each of their movements, memorizing the patterns.

A biting wind howls past me when the wards fall. I groan as I reach beneath my smock and fish around in the pouch at my waist. It's no use. I can't feel a thing with my numb fingers. I shove my stained paint smock aside and grab the firebird feather, siphoning some of its magic to weave a protective ward around myself to block the bone-chilling cold. I don't care that the feather is now almost useless. I have to get closer to the mysterious relic before it goes into the vault. It's like nothing I've ever felt before. I *need* to know what it is.

The Saracen witches float three large crates toward the east entrance that leads to the archives. I curse my decision to work on the opposite side of the building as I duck behind a tapestry into the secret passage designed as an emergency escape route for staff in the event of a reaver attack.

Wearing a shield woven with firebird magic is a bit like standing too close to a raging bonfire. My skin radiates with heat as I sprint through the narrow corridor, clearing it of cobwebs. My hair comes untied and flops with my bonnet behind me. Sweat soaks through the armpits of my high-necked blouse.

I'm panting for breath as I burst through the hidden door in the archives and stumble into the workroom. The curators and guards are gone, replaced by a sea of soldiers clad in the green and gold regalia of the northern kingdom. Several of whom have swords or guns pointed at my chest.

I raise my hands instinctively.

"State your business," one of the soldiers demands as he takes a step in my direction.

"I work here," I say, a bit breathless. "And I'll thank you to take your weapon out of my face."

His eyes dart to the open wall panel behind me. "The Menagerie's staff were sent home hours ago. That either makes you a liar, a spy, or both." He uses the tip of his gleaming sword to gather a clump of spider silk from my shoulder.

"Lower your weapon, Gareth." There's a hint of amusement in the familiar voice that sends my heart into a gallop. I don't need to look to know who I'll find. "Everly Thorne isn't a liar or a spy."

"Welcome home, *Your Royal Highness*." I dip my head, refusing to make eye contact with the man who ripped out my heart.

"She can't be in here. We have strict orders from Princess Dagmara. No civilians," the soldier says, keeping his sword pointed at my chest.

Gideon reaches out and lowers the tip of the man's blade. There's a burn scar on the back of his hand that wasn't there the last time I saw him. The knotted flesh continues under the cuff of his dark purple uniform coat. He gives me a practiced smile that doesn't quite reach his blue eyes. "Carry on, Gareth. I'll see that Miss Thorne is escorted out of the Menagerie personally."

The soldiers part as he leads me toward the gardens. I pretend to casually glance at the Saracen witches as they begin weaving a complicated ward to seal the vault. Three witches. Three different wards. Gareth—the soldier who held his sword to my throat—shifts his wide shoulders, blocking my view as he orders one of his men to search the secret passageway for more spies.

Gideon places his palm against the small of my back and turns me toward the sprawling gardens that separate the Menagerie's peeling gold dome and the gleaming white columns of the palace that sits like a crown overlooking Lake Largeau. I glare at him, and he immediately removes the offending appendage.

We move in a choreographed silence toward the secluded east wall, tracing the familiar crushed-shell path past fountains, manicured hedges, and marble sculptures. A path I could follow with my eyes closed, even after all these years.

"Everly, please. Say something." There's a pleading edge in his voice as we duck under the thick arms of the gnarled oak that was once our sanctuary. I turn my back to the stone bench where we made desperate promises to one another the day he left four years ago.

"Your new friends seem a little uptight." I lean against the shaded brick wall and stare up at the dangling fingers of gray-green moss hanging from the tree. The cool brick is a welcome relief against the invisible inferno of magic licking at my skin.

"They're not my friends," Gideon says with a disgusted grunt. Something in his tone makes me wonder if I was right about the dowry of relics being an insult, after all.

I lift my gaze and allow myself to take him in. His shoulders are broader than they were when I last saw him. His boyish good looks and carefree gait have morphed into something more rugged. Tense. Given the injury to his hand, it's obvious he's done more than play at being a soldier. I hate the way the realization softens a little of the anger seething inside me.

I force my gaze away from where he fists his goblin-spelled sword before I give in to the urge to ask about the scar. I don't need sympathy clouding my emotions. Not with him.

"Your future subjects, then? Already thinking like a king. You've certainly changed."

"Not in any of the ways that matter." Gideon rakes his hand through his sun-bleached curls as he paces in front of me. "We don't have much time. Gareth will come looking for me soon. I had a plan. A whole list of things I wanted to say. I wasn't prepared to see you yet."

"That makes two of us. I was hoping we could avoid seeing one another altogether." He flinches at that. Good. "Go ahead and spit out whatever it is you need to get off your chest so we can get this over with."

"I need to ask you something, and I need you to be honest with me. I'm pretty sure I already know the answer. I can see it all over your face," he says, gesturing to my magic flushed skin. "I just... I need to be sure. I need to hear it from you."

Fuck. He knows. Of course he knows. He's spent the last four years surrounded by witches. Why else would he lure me out to our spot where no one can see or overhear our conversation? I've managed to hide the truth from Adrian and even Wallace, but Gideon always knew me better than anyone. Before he left, hiding my curse from him was the hardest thing I'd ever done. I've lost track of the number of times I came close to telling him. Giving up that part of myself to anyone, especially someone who vehemently loathed magic, never felt safe. It feels even less so now.

"I don't have time for this." I shove away from the wall, ready to leave.

"Are you with someone? Is that why you stopped writing to me? Is it because you met someone else?"

I ball my fists as I spin toward him. "That's not any of your business."

"So the rumors are true?"

"It's been four years, and that's the first thing you ask me? If I've fucked anyone besides you?"

He drags a hand down his face. "This conversation isn't going as I planned. I'm asking if you have someone. If you're happy. Tell me the truth. You owe me that, at least, after all we've been through."

I'm struck speechless. The scab I've built over the wound in my chest cracks, and my rage seeps out.

"All we've been through?" I ask, surprised by the steadiness of my voice. "Our history doesn't entitle you to anything from me, Gideon. I'm not your soft place to land anymore, not the way I was when we were children. I'm jagged and broken and I will cut you with my sharp edges. So don't ask me to help you tie up the loose ends of your conscience so you can get the closure you need to move on with your royal engagement guilt-free. Go back to your princess and leave me alone." I step around him and move toward the crushed-shell path, refusing to give him the answers he needs to be at peace with what he did to me. Fuck Gideon Krimore and his stupid, handsome face.

He catches my wrist. "Closure is the last thing I want with you, Everly."

I squeeze my eyes shut and give myself the length of a breath to smother the fire rising in my gut. "No. You are not allowed to say things like that to me. Not after the way you ended it."

He turns me toward him and cups my face in his gentle grip. "I know. I'm sorry."

"I didn't hear from you for nearly two years, and you sent a royal messenger to my door with a note to break off our engagement two days after my parents were murdered." I can't stop the angry tears that roll down my cheeks. He swipes them away with his thumbs. "I needed you, and you cut me out of your life with a piece of perfumed fucking parchment."

He slides his hands to my shoulders. "My father sent the notification without my knowledge. That's not how I wanted you to find out. I tried to leave Fort Netherthorn as soon as I heard about your parents. I had to see you, but we were attacked by reavers. They cut off the fort's access to water and the outside world for weeks. We wouldn't have survived if the king of Saracen hadn't sent his army to aid us. By the time it was over, the entire world knew about the alliance and my betrothal to Dagmara, and it was too late."

Not the heir of Saracen or even Princess Dagmara. Just Dagmara. The casual way he uses her given name sticks like a bone in my throat.

"Why didn't you write to me before that?" I ask.

"Correspondence from Crecentis arrives every other week with the regiments of new recruits that come to replenish the witches we lose. We send riders disguised as reavers back home with supply requests, death logs, and mail. They don't always make it. I wrote to you every damn day for six months. Even after your letters stopped coming, I kept writing, hoping some of them would make their way through to you."

"I never got them." My chest tightens.

"When your letters stopped coming, I assumed you'd met someone else, and as much as it killed me to imagine you with another man, I wanted that for you. I prayed to the fucking gods for it to be true. You can't imagine what it's like in the Wastes. I didn't think I'd make it home, and I told myself it'd be easier for you if you moved on. That if you had someone to comfort you, it might not hurt as much if I never came back."

It's been a shit day, and I can't help the way I lean into the familiar comfort of his touch, even though I hate myself for still craving it. What am I supposed to say to the man who shattered my heart and waited until I'd fused all the bleeding shards back together before stepping back into my life to reclaim it?

"I never stopped thinking about you, Everly." He drops his gaze to my mouth, and for a moment, I'm afraid he might kiss me. I don't know whether my throat goes dry from the heat of the firebird's magic coursing through me or the realization that I might let him.

It's all too much. I pull away and drop the invisible shield protecting me from the call of cold magic pulling at my senses from the Menagerie's vault. The fine hairs on my arms stand at attention as my skin pebbles and the chill creeps over me. Now that I'm farther away from the mysterious relic, the sensation isn't as intense. All that remains is the pocket of cold air that follows me like a living thing as I put space between myself and Gideon.

"I'm sorry. I can't do this with you right now."

Shells crunch along the path as someone approaches.

He steps closer and brushes a cobweb from my hair. "Dagmara's man watches me like a hawk. I won't be able to come to you. Meet me at Nymph's Wager tonight. I'll play a few rounds. Once Gareth is lost in his cups, I'll meet you upstairs and we can finish our conversation. There's something I need to discuss with you before the ball. Do you still have the key?"

"Yes, but—"

Gideon's hand goes to the hilt of his sword as he backs away to a socially appropriate distance. The Saracen soldier who held a sword to my chest strolls around the corner before I can tell Gideon that I've been banned from all seven of Madam Faye's gambling houses, including Nymph's Wager, where he kept private rooms for the nights when he was too drunk to travel back to the palace. The key to which I couldn't bring myself to throw away, no matter how many times I tried.

Chapter Four

The hazy gray light streaming in through the Whistling Duck's front window doesn't do my ratty firebird feather any favors.

"See, there's plenty of life left in this little beauty," I say, twisting it between my fingers and holding it closer to the candle on the polished wooden table.

The stout woman sitting across from me tips the brim of her black top hat back and leans closer to inspect the pitiful relic.

"I've seen firebird feathers as long as my arm. What you got there is nothing but a bit of used-up down." She shoves away from the table with a grunt and hoists herself up from the chair.

"Size and appearance don't matter when it comes to magic," I say in an attempt to salvage the sale. "A bit of wear and tear won't make it any less effective at warding off bad energy."

"That may be true, but I ain't sticking no unsightly feather in my lucky hat." She dismisses me with a wave of her wrist.

I grit my teeth as she disappears out the front door. She's the fifth person to scoff at my pitiful relic. It's been two days since the cocky reaver stole my sketchbook and the crown closed the Menagerie to anyone other than the Saracen witches.

I haven't been able to work, and I'm past due in my arrangement with Madam Faye. Her thugs haven't chased me down yet, but I'm not foolish enough to believe she's forgotten about me. The city's population has swollen with the influx of Festivalla revelers partaking in the music, food, drink, and gaming available all hours of the day and night. They'll come to collect as soon as things settle down.

"If you keep clenching your jaw like that, you're gonna crack a tooth," Wallace says as she sets two glasses and a bottle of watered-down rum in front of me, along with a plate of fried dough dusted with sugar.

"A little early," I say, eyeing the shot glasses. "It's not even lunchtime."

"When has that ever stopped you?" She pours two double shots of watered down rum and drops into the chair across from me. "Drink that before you scare all my paying customers away with your sour face."

Who am I to argue with that logic? I tip my head back, savoring the slight burn as the rum slides down my throat. It's not as strong as the bitter pepper nerve tonic in my flask, but it's enough to take the edge off.

"Wanna talk about it?" she asks.

"No." I slap the glass on the table.

"The ball is in three days."

"I wasn't invited, and I'm certainly not going to humiliate myself by crashing a party being thrown in honor of Gideon's fiancée."

I grab the bottle and pour myself another double shot before gulping it down and waiting for the alcohol to dampen my senses.

The Whistling Duck sits in the heart of Trader's Square, about as far from the Menagerie as you can get without jumping on a steamer and leaving Crecentis. I can still feel a whisper of the mysterious relic all the way from the Menagerie's vault. I've scoured through every bestiary I own and can't figure out what kind of relic would attack me with frostbite.

"Aren't you even a little curious about what the prince has to say?" Wallace asks. She only met Gideon once. He came to the Menagerie the day before he left for the Wastes for one more "goodbye" romp in the gardens, even though we'd spent the entire night fucking away our fears and uncertainty in his rooms at Nymph's until we'd both collapsed from exhaustion.

Things with Gideon had always been like that. If we were in the same room, he had to be next to me, with a hand, shoulder, thigh, or foot touching mine in a way that made me feel like I was the center of his gravity. Like I was the only thing keeping him from spinning out of orbit, especially after his mother died. I didn't mind back then. We both needed the comfort of being in each other's presence, even if we didn't talk about our pain. Everyone knew I'd been hand selected by the queen herself to be his soft place to land. It was my duty as his future wife and queen.

The man who led me into the gardens two days ago might be a battle-hardened version of the boy I used to know, but I can still read him as easily as I can read a relic from across the room. Gideon's anxious about something and needs an outlet for all those uncomfortable emotions.

"If he wanted to talk, he wouldn't have suggested I sneak into his old rooms so we can fuck out our feelings the way we used to."

"Would that be so bad?" Wallace asks. I cut her a sharp look as I pour another round.

"Whose side are you on?"

"Everyone is saying he's a hero for the way he held Fort Netherthorn against the reavers. He could have any woman in Perdanth, and he still wants you. That has to count for something."

I down the rum and stand a little too quickly.

"Where are you going? You haven't even touched the fried dough."

"I'll see you later. I need to visit the bone broker." I grab two of the pillowy confections and stuff them in my mouth before heading for the door.

———

A string of sun-bleached gator teeth and shells clatters against the door as I shove it open with my shoulder and step over the sandbags piled in front of the threshold. The old witch most people know as Guy Maynard always could predict when it was about to rain, and the last place you want to get caught in a storm is downriver where the manure-covered streets are the first to flood.

I flinch at the blast of magic that washes over me as I enter his shop. The crowded space hasn't changed since the last time I visited with my parents right before they left on their last medical mission. They were in high spirits that day, hopeful it would be the summer they finally found a cure. Little did they know they would never come home. I bite the inside of my cheek to stop the sting pressing at the inner corners of my eyes.

Wooden death masks and straw medicine dolls cover the walls. Bunches of sage and other dried herbs hang from the ceiling. A cone of ground cloves burns on the counter. I forgot how much I love the smoky, spicy smell. My mother used to throw them into the campfire at night to keep the mosquitoes, gnats, and pixies away while we slept.

I pay my respects to the stuffed swamp wolf in the corner, letting my fingers glide over the rougarou's coarse, copper-tipped fur along its human-like forearm. The beautiful creature's elongated snout and sharp teeth terrified me as a child. I had nightmares about it stalking me in the woods when I camped with my parents. I convinced myself I'd seen yellow eyes blinking at me from the dark, just past the glow of our campfire.

Now, the stuffed creature just makes me sad. No one has ever seen a rougarou outside the swamps surrounding Crecentis. That doesn't stop parents from telling their children they'll be snatched from their beds and eaten by one of the snarling beasts if they misbehave.

I ignore the desiccated black hole in the wolf's chest where a bounty hunter brought it down with a bullet to the heart. Hunters go out looking for them every full moon. Legend says the swamp wolves were once a clan of humans cursed with insatiable hunger after consuming human flesh during a famine.

It's nonsense, of course. The only curse the creatures suffer is from the men who hunt them for their pelts and the traces of magic in their bones. When ground up into a powder and administered for a full lunar cycle, it's said to improve libido and cure infertility.

Fragments of relics whisper to me from beneath the counter. None are strong enough on their own to yield much magic, but combined in the right way, they could make powerful charms to protect against curses and illness or prevent an unwanted pregnancy. All illegal, of course. Witchcraft is strictly forbidden outside the military.

I ring the brass bell on the counter. A cot creaks behind the heavy curtain that separates the shop from the bone broker's small bed chamber.

"Go away, we're closed," Beaux calls with the deep rasp of a man who lives on a diet of tobacco and rye.

"Is that any way to treat an old friend?" I ask cheerily, unable to suppress my smile. His cantankerous recluse act never worked on me.

Another creak of the cot is followed by the soft shuffle of footsteps and the slow tap of a cane. I've met more sick witches than I'd care to count, but I'm not prepared for the way my chest tightens at the sight of how much he's declined in the last two years. The man bears little resemblance to the gangly teenager who hid in my parents' wagon for an entire summer when I was six. The usual scowl is missing from his haggard face and has been replaced by a dropping, expressionless stare. His once broad shoulders are bony and a bit off kilter.

I can still remember him as the swarthy young man who taught me every vulgar word I know. He had a different name then—and a price on his head for deserting the royal army.

Recognition flashes across his glassy eyes as he pushes the curtain aside.

"You're wandering a bit far from the clean streets of the upriver elite," he says dryly.

"When have you ever known me to be afraid of a little dirt?"

I wait for the skin around his eyes to crinkle with a hint of amusement like it used to when he teased me for being happier than a pig in mud when I would bury sticks behind my parents' medical wagon, then dig them up and pretend they were dragon bones.

His deadpan expression remains as frozen as the death masks on the wall. The happy memory deflates, leaving my stomach in knots. Seven years. That's the difference between us. The amount of time I have left—maybe less—before the burning takes me.

"What are you doing here, Thorne?"

"What can you give me for this?" I fish the firebird feather from the secret pocket in my waist pouch and set it on the counter.

He leans on his cane and runs his trembling fingers along the frayed plume. "Where'd you get this?"

"Found it in the mud at Gallows Square." I've told the lie so many times it rolls off my tongue like second nature.

"The magic is nearly used up," he says. "Barely enough left to weave a simple ward or light a few candles. I can give you ten dollars. It's more than it's worth in this condition."

"You can add it to one of the illegal dark-charm bags you keep under the counter and sell it for ten times that."

His gray eyes flick to mine. "I'd be curious to know who told you about those so I can thank them for the referral."

"I overhear things... at the gallows." Another lie.

He grips the edge of the counter. Whether it's to keep his balance or stop his hand from twitching, I can't tell. "I can give you twelve dollars on account of what your parents did for me back in the day. But not a lick more."

I lower my voice and whisper his real name. "Beaux, please. I wouldn't ask, but I'm in way over my head with Madam Faye. I really need the money."

"It's the best I can do." He bolts the shop door with a flick of his wrist. He's never given me a reason to fear him, but my back stiffens all the same. The burning does terrible things to witches in the late stages. They become more prone to violence as the disease eats away at their bodies and minds. "There is something you might be able to help me with," he says. "I got a client looking to acquire a dragon scale. Rumor has it there are a load of rare relics in the fair princess's dowry. If one happened to go missing from the Menagerie's vault and find its way to me, I'd be mighty grateful."

"Curators don't have access to the vaults. Besides, stealing from the crown is a guaranteed way to get a date with the noose," I say with enough indignation to make him believe I've never even contemplated such a thing—or spent the last two years teaching myself how to break through the wards securing the army's emergency stockpile.

Stealing a relic from one of the Menagerie's vaults wouldn't be as easy as pickpocketing a firebird feather off a drunk reaver, but it isn't impossible. Given enough time, I can unravel just about any magical lock. It's the guards that are the challenge.

"If I were to stumble across a dragon scale—"

"In the mud?" he asks. I can't tell if he's teasing me, questioning my story about the firebird feather, or both. His flat affect makes him difficult to read.

"What kind of commission would something like that fetch?" I ask, purely out of curiosity.

"I pay a two percent finder's fee."

My shoulders slump as I do the mental math. Two percent isn't enough to pay off a quarter of what I owe Madam Faye. But it's more than nothing, which I currently have. If I can't keep up with the interest payments to the gaming queen, she'll take my house.

I slide my palm over my firebird feather, letting the lingering magic kiss my skin. "I'm sure you overhear a thing or two yourself, being the fine, upstanding citizen you are."

"I hear a lot of things, but I forget real easy these days. My memory improves in the presence of good coin."

Apparently, the man's gratitude to my parents for helping him start over and hide in plain sight for the last twenty years only goes so far. I suck the inside of my lip and try a different approach.

"Hypothetically, if a person was interested in locating a shadow summoner, where would she start?"

"What kind of business would a nice girl like you want with a shadow-wielding witch?"

"Shadow summoners wield their magic from dragon relics, do they not?"

"A witch would need access to a dozen dragon scales, maybe more, to summon shadows. It's an expensive skill to fuel. The Saracen army is the only outfit with those kinds of resources these days."

"What about black-market traders?"

"There was one, back in the day, before the market dried up. Depleted the supply by buying up every damn dragon relic he could get his hands on. Never met him myself, but they say he worked for someone with deep pockets, went by the name Drake."

"As in Baby Face Drake?" I ask. Every witch my parents treated had a tall tale about the infamous outlaw born and raised in the Wastes. Some of the stories stretched so far back, they couldn't possibly be attributed to the same person. He'd have to be over 200 years old to be responsible for all the ghastly deeds committed during his reign as the unofficial king of the Wastes.

Despite his nickname, no one could say what the real Baby Face Drake had actually looked like. During their raids, he and his crew wore death masks painted with human blood, a tactic still used by reaver raiding parties and every two-bit witch looking to strike fear in the hearts of their victims. A red mask was found on the ground next to my parents' ransacked wagon and their bodies.

"Haven't heard his name mentioned in near a decade," Beaux says, raising a shaking hand to rub the back of his neck.

"I'm looking for someone younger, around my age. He's traveling with a woman who wears a snapping turtle amulet."

"Try Chopping Bottom. All the up-and-coming crews hang there. If there's a shadow summoner in the city, someone there will know." He nods to the counter. "You best hold on to that feather. You're gonna need whatever luck it has left if you go there looking for trouble."

"Thanks, but I need money more than I need a good luck charm." I slide the feather toward him. "I'll take the twelve bucks."

Beaux shakes his head as he reaches beneath the counter. He slaps several bills onto the smooth surface and slides them toward me with the feather. "Keep the feather. I got no use for a mangey, used-up bit of down."

I shove the relic into my pouch, eyeing the money. "I can't afford any more debts."

"Consider it an advance for the next time you find something special in the mud."

My stomach knots as I take the cash and stuff it into my pocket. We both know it's a handout. "Thank you. I'll pay it back all the same."

"You know where to find me." He twists his wrist, using magic to unbolt the door.

I nod and give the stuffed rougarou another pat as I make my way to the exit.

"Everly." Beaux's unsteady voice betrays his emotionless expression. "Be careful mucking about in the mud. Dealing with rogue witches ain't no child's game. I'd hate to see you end up like your parents."

CHAPTER FIVE

"What am I supposed to do with a trunk full of moth-eaten stage costumes?" I ask as my brother sets a wooden trunk on our kitchen table where Wallace and I are finishing the lunch she brought over from the Duck.

Adrian runs a hand through his honey-colored curls. "I'm sure you'll figure something out. You know about these things better than I do."

"Yesterday it was a bucket of crawfish. Last week it was radishes. Now this? You can't keep accepting whatever your patients offer you in exchange for your services."

"Are you suggesting that I refuse to treat the sick just because they can't pay in cash?"

"Of course not," I say with an exasperated sigh. My brother's soft heart and lack of business sense are so much like our parents' I want to kick him sometimes. Neither of them kept track of the finances either. The only thing left when they died was this crumbling house and its furnishings. Now we don't even have that small bit of security. I can't tell him how dire things are without explaining how they got that way. Adrian will want to know *why* I cheated at the gaming tables and lost the deed to our home. I can't tell him about my condition without putting him at risk. It's safer for him if he doesn't know I'm a witch.

Fortunately, Adrian never asks to see the ledgers I keep locked in our mother's desk. If he did, he'd see how deep in debt we truly are. Madam Faye isn't the only one I owe money to. The druggist that provides the medicines Adrian uses to treat his patients—including the large quantity of nerve tonic that never makes it into his supply cabinet—has cut off his line of credit until I can pay off the balance.

"My folks are still more than happy to buy whatever food you receive as payment," Wallace says, flashing my brother a lovesick smile before opening the trunk. "I can probably sell a few of these items to the ladies who work in the brothel across from the Duck. Everyone in Trader's Square is obsessed with Honore Landreux. I bet they'll pay extra if I tell them this stuff used to belong to her."

"I apologize for the confusion," Adrian says with a serious look. "I treated Miss Landreux for a fainting spell. She paid in cash. These were given to me by a young woman whose baby I delivered this morning. Not Miss Landreux. My patient was kicked out of her traveling theater troupe three months ago when they found out she was pregnant. She's a washer woman now and says she no longer has need of the costumes."

I place a hand on his arm. "Wallace is suggesting we lie about the costumes' origins."

"Why would you lie about that?" There's no judgement in Adrian's his tone, only curiosity. It would never occur to my dear, trusting brother to lie about anything.

"To fetch a higher price when we sell them."

"I see," he says, glancing at Wallace, whose face has gone crimson.

"It's just that Honore Landreux is the most famous burlesque performer in Perdanth," she adds quickly. "Everyone knows you treated her on opening night at the Festivalla showcase. It wouldn't be difficult to convince people that she gave you her old costumes as a token of her appreciation."

Adrian gives her a curt nod and retreats to his study.

"Did I say something wrong?" Wallace asks, looking deflated.

"Adrian doesn't care what we do with the clothes. He doesn't care much about anything aside from his work. Other than the occasional game of cards after supper, he spends all his time with his head buried in our parents' old casebooks. The ones we still have, anyway. Here, help me carry this up to my room so we can sort through it." I close the lid while Wallace peeks around the corner to catch another glimpse of my brother. "Can you be any more obvious?"

"I have no idea what you're talking about," she whispers as she grabs her side of the trunk with an innocent grin.

"Adrian doesn't see you like that," I remind her. I'm not sure Adrian sees anyone like that.

Wallace shrugs. "I know. I just really like his—"

"Don't even think about finishing that sentence." I cut her a warning glance as we trudge up the stairs.

"What? I was going to say smile. He has lovely teeth."

"What is it with you and teeth?"

"I'm just saying, if he wanted to bite me, I'd let him."

"I hate you right now." If I'm being honest, I'd be thrilled if Adrian showed an interest in my best friend. In anyone, really. I worry about what will become of him when the burning finally takes me, and he's left all alone. He needs someone to look out for him.

We drop the chest onto my bed and separate the clothing into piles. One for corsets, others for wigs, skirts, and overdresses. There's even a pile of clothing that Adrian's patient must have used to play the role of a young boy.

"You should keep this one," Wallace says as she holds a red lace dressing robe to her chest. The sun streaming in through the open balcony doors catches her hair, turning the copper locks into burnished flames as she spins around my room.

"Everly," Adrian calls from the foyer. "There's a royal messenger at the door for you."

My hands freeze in the middle of folding a pair of boy's trousers as panic takes hold.

There's a royal messenger at the door.

It's the same phrase my brother used two years ago when a palace guard arrived to tell us our parents had been brutally murdered, and again, two days later, when I got the letter notifying me that my engagement to Gideon had been nullified.

"I can't." The words croak out of me like a broken whisper.

"I got it." Wallace helps me sit on the bed before hurrying down the steps.

Heat creeps up my neck. My ears go hot. I take a deep breath in through my nose and out through my mouth. I tell myself I'm being irrational. There's nothing to fear. The only two people I care about are here with me. Unless something bad happened to Gideon. But they wouldn't bother telling me, and surely the city bells would be ringing.

I dig out my flask and unscrew the metal cap with trembling hands. The bitter tonic quells my nerves, and I'm no longer shaking when Wallace reenters my room.

"Do you want the honey first, or the bees?" she asks.

"Bees. Bad news first, always." The sting is always worse after you've been seduced by the sweet. Better to pay for the pleasure up front with pain.

"The Thornes have received an official invitation to the masquerade ball being held in honor of the future queen, Princess Dagmara Montagnais of Saracen."

The tension drains from my body, and I can't help but laugh. "Is that all? I thought you were going to tell me something awful, like the Menagerie burned down and we were out of a job for good."

"I wasn't finished. Adrian has already accepted for you both."

"Fuck." I plop down in the cane-seat chair at my dressing table.

"You can make an excuse," she says. "Feign a headache or something. You don't have to attend. Let Adrian put in an appearance for both of you."

"No, I can't leave him to the vultures alone. What's the good news?"

Wallace disappears into the hall and comes back a moment later carrying a flocked lavender box tied with a black silk bow from the royal modiste. She uses the box to push the piles of costumes aside as she places it on my bed. "At least you have something to wear."

I open the lid and run my hand over the gown. The dark purple bodice and matching mask are embroidered with metallic gold thread in a pattern that resembles dragon scales.

"The colors of Clan Krimore," she says as she pulls the shimmering dress from its silk-lined box. "I thought they were reserved for the royal family."

"And the king's mistresses."

Her head snaps up. "Does this mean what I think it means?"

"That Gideon thinks he can still have me?"

"Or that he's still in love with you."

"If Gideon loved me, he wouldn't humiliate me in front of the entire fucking kingdom by parading me around like I'm his property." I yank the gown out of her hands, wad it into a ball, and throw it toward the musty costume trunk. It misses and slithers down the side of my bed onto the floor.

"Are you still in love with him?"

"It doesn't matter. I don't want to be anyone's second choice."

"Are you sure he's not trying to send you and the entire world the message that you are, in fact, his first choice? That he'd rather have you at his side than her?"

"The only thing I know is that I'm not wearing that dress. Can you imagine how it will make Princess Dagmara feel?"

"Then we need to figure out what you *are* going to wear." She hunts through the pile of toppled clothes until she finds the red dressing robe and a matching corset, tossing them to me. "Try these on."

CHAPTER SIX

I grip my mug and lean against the wrought-iron railing outside my bedroom doors. The metalwork is bent and broken where the heavy jasmine vine has strangled it into submission. The delicate white blossoms fill the air with a sweet, heady scent.

Thunder rumbles in the distance. I make a mental note to fetch a pot from the kitchen to catch the rain that will inevitably drip from the crack in the ceiling.

Wallace wiggles her fingers at me before crossing the cobbled street in front of the house to board the streetcar bound for Trader's Square with her brothers. Whitt winks at me, the trunk of costumes perched on his broad shoulder.

As the only girl in a brood of five siblings, Wallace knows her way around a needle and thread. She's determined to transform my crepe mourning dress into something less dower, even though I'm perfectly content to wear the simple black frock to the ball. Let the high-nosed elites gossip about my terrible fashion sense instead of my family's tarnished name for once.

I take a sip of my rose hip tea, savoring the fruity zest. My mother used to prepare it with honey—a luxury I can't afford. I've learned to enjoy it this way, bold and a little tart, not hiding behind a sweet shield and pretending to be something it's not.

I set the mug on the small table next to my bed and add a shot of nerve tonic. I'll need a clear head before heading to the Downriver District tonight to find the bastard who stole my sketchbook. There's only one problem. Chopping Bottom is one of Madam Faye's gaming houses. I've been banned from all seven, even the ones I've never set foot in, including the notoriously rowdy shithole popular with reaver crews.

Even if I manage to get inside without being recognized by one of Faye's goons, twelve dollars isn't enough to buy me a seat at any of the gaming tables. Milling about close to the players, where I can eavesdrop on their conversations, and their hands, is a guaranteed way to get me kicked out on my ass. A lesson I learned the hard way. I need to find a way to blend in.

I lift the wrinkled ball gown from the floor and scrape my short nails over the delicate embroidery. Custom pieces from the royal modiste cost hundreds of dollars and take weeks to complete. Which means Gideon didn't send it on a whim.

The mixture of tea and tonic churns in my empty stomach. The fact that he put thought into this and still came to the infallible decision that he could convince me to be his mistress with a pretty apology and an obscenely expensive dress is proof of how little he cares about what I've been through.

Between Gideon and Adrian, I don't know who's more clueless when it comes to women. They both have the dogged sense of logic that makes them good at soldiering and doctoring, but neither has ever seemed to understand the same reasoning can't be applied to my feelings. I can't just erase all my problems with a ballgown and a trunk of moth-eaten costumes.

I pad along the threadbare rug and hold the purple satin up to the dying light. A smile creeps across my face. There is one problem this dress can solve. Information doesn't come cheap, and I need more money before I go poking around Chopping Bottom, asking questions about a six-and-a-half-foot-tall shadow-summoning asshole with perfectly symmetrical features.

My toes graze something soft and fluffy, and I jump back, waiting for Pig's telltale hiss. The feral cat has a habit of sneaking into my room and sleeping under the bed when rain is coming, and I have a habit of leaving my balcony door cracked so he can come and go as he pleases.

I scoop the fabric aside, expecting to find the grumpy tabby, and discover a wig and the pile of boy's clothing that must have toppled from the bed when Wallace made room for the modiste's box. I set the dress aside and pick up the linen shirt, trousers, and long blond wig.

Maybe Beaux was right. There might be a little luck left in my firebird feather after all.

———⬦———

I keep a hand on the wad of cash in my pocket as I slide into line behind a group of wannabe reavers entering the notorious gaming house. The sixty bucks I got for the ballgown is a quarter of what it was worth, but my story about it belonging to Honore Landreux was shaky at best. So I didn't haggle with the madam who was willing to help me part with it earlier this afternoon.

The money in my pocket could pay two weeks' interest on my debt to Madam Faye. It could also buy the information I need to get my hands on a dragon scale and pay off a much larger chunk of my debt.

My disguise doesn't earn me a second glance from the bouncers guarding the door as I follow the group of teenage boys inside. I used a wooden bowl to trim the wig the same way I saw Wallace cut her brother's hair once. It makes my already round face appear even plumper, and it's a bit lumpy over the mass of dark hair I've managed to stuff underneath, but it does the job well enough. The narrow-cut trousers are a bit tight over my wide ass, but the shirt fits loose enough to cover my tightly bound breasts without hinting at my curves.

The gambling hall reeks of sweat, sour ale, and tobacco. A smoky haze hangs in the air, giving the gas lamps an ethereal moon-like glow. It's rundown and dirty, but the gaming floor is set up the same as the ones I'm familiar with in the Upriver and Lakeside districts; dice tables in the center and card tables circling them, all under the watchful eye of Faye's security men patrolling the interior gallery a level above.

Women selling cigars and clove-infused hotpicks make their rounds. Their wares are displayed on wide trays secured with a strap around the neck that keeps the merchandise at eye level for seated customers—right below the women's low-cut bodices. Scarred tavern tables that have seen more than one brawl sit beneath the gallery and are separated from the gaming floor by an ornate wrought-iron railing like the one that lines my balcony.

The group of boys I've been shadowing takes a table, and I make my way to the bar at the back of the room. I've spent enough time at the Duck to know the barkeep is my best bet for information. If the shadow summoner has been here, they'll know. They see and hear everything in a place like this.

I drop the suppression ward blocking my perception. The phantom flutter of pixie wings tickles my skin. Never a good sign in a place like this. They should put a sign at the bar telling ladies to watch their drinks. The territorial little creatures reproduce prolifically, and the dust from their wings is a potent aphrodisiac or sedative, depending on the dose.

The hair on my arms rises as a rumble of thunder rolls through the room. It's too close to have come from outside. I glance behind me, looking for the source.

A witch with dark skin and arms as thick as tree limbs enters the hall. He looks around and scowls when he catches me staring. Thunderbird relics aren't as rare as dragon bones, but they're just as powerful and fetch a good price on the black market, since most are in possession of the military, reserved for the army's deadly Storm Squad.

I'm not likely to find a relic on this bruiser, even if I was brave enough to trip into him and slip my hand in his pockets to investigate. Like most reavers who spend any time in the Wastes, this man has gone to great lengths to prevent someone like me from liberating him of his source of magic. He's covered in reaver tattoos from neck to knuckle. A beautiful canvas of storm clouds and lightning shoots down his bare arms where he's forgone wearing a shirt beneath his waistcoat. Probably couldn't find one to fit around his enormous biceps. The man is huge. From the amount of power crackling around him, it feels like he's ground up an entire thunderbird skeleton and added it to the ink.

He approaches the teenage boys I followed in, and they give up their table immediately. I avert my gaze when he catches me staring again and scan the room as I lean against the bar and rest my boot on the copper rail. There are dozens of firebird feathers and a unicorn tooth somewhere in the crowd, but not a single dragon scale.

"You gonna keep standing there holding up my counter, or are you gonna order something, kid?"

I slide a copper coin out of my pocket and set it on the sticky wooden surface. "A shot of the house special," I say, forcing my voice lower.

He takes the coin and pours me a shot of rye. "This will help you put hair on your chest."

He lets out a grunt of amusement when I choke on the whiskey as it burns its way down to my belly. It's stronger than the watered-down rum I'm used to at the Duck. I pay for another shot and give myself a few minutes to let the heat in my chest settle before I take out another copper and tap it on the counter. When I have his attention, I lie and tell him I'm searching for a tall shadow-wielding witch who hurt my sister and likes to corner girls in alleys and choke them with magic.

He eyes the coin in my hand. I slide it toward him, and he nods to the stairs, where several women and a few men in low-cut corsets and painted faces beckon from the railings. "Ask for Cass. She caters to clients with special requests. Rumor has it she had a customer a few nights back matching that description."

I mutter my thanks and push away from the bar. My knees wobble more than I'd like as I make my way toward a stick-thin man wearing a peacock-blue corset.

"Hello there, handsome." He drops his eyes to the bulge of folded bills in my pocket and smiles. "You looking for a suck or a fuck?"

"Is Cass working?" I ask, forcing my voice down an octave.

"Cass is always working, baby. Follow me." I grip the railing and let him lead me up the steps and down a dark hallway. Moans and wet slapping sounds bleed through the closed doors. He points to a narrow bench outside the last room on the left. "Wait here," he says and gives the door a firm knock. "Cass, you got a fresh one out here."

Ten minutes later, a full-figured woman around my age calls me in. Dark hair falls over her rounded shoulders in soft waves that barely hide the mottled bruises around her throat.

"It's ten dollars for every half hour. I charge extra for choking, biting, bondage, and rough stuff. You prepay or no service. No refunds if you finish before your time's up or if you can't get off. That's your problem, not mine."

"I... I just want to talk. How much for ten minutes of your time?" I ask, forgetting to disguise my voice.

"We can do anything you like, honey. It's still gonna cost you ten dollars."

I pull the sum from my pocket and set it on a small table by the door. She holds the bills up to the oil lamp to inspect them. Satisfied, she stuffs them into the slot of a safe built into the wall, flips a sand timer, and sits on the bed.

"Don't be shy." She pats the space next to her. "I'm all ears. What would you like to talk about?"

I stay where I am. "I'm looking for a witch you may have encountered in the last few days. Tall, black hair, likes to choke girls with magic." Her back stiffens, telling me she knows exactly who I'm talking about. My blood boils as I clench my fists and nod to her neck. "Did he do that to you?"

"I don't kiss and tell for free."

I hold up another dollar and drop it into the slot.

She laughs. "You're going to have to cough up more than that. Our mutual friend paid me sixty bucks to keep my mouth shut about his unique fetish."

"Sixty dollars? To let a man choke you with shadows?"

Her mouth curls at the corner. "He did a lot more than that, honey. If you want to buy the details, you'll need to drop sixty more dollars."

Seventy-dollars? I'm in the wrong fucking business. It's nearly everything I have from the ballgown and the money Beaux lent me.

"Before I pay, I need to know that we're talking about the same person."

"Black hair, big brown eyes, sexy as sin, with a face and body like chiseled marble, onyx ring on his right thumb, and a big, beautiful—"

"That's enough." I don't need any help picturing his big, beautiful anything. "Do you know where I can find him?"

She smiles and nods to the slot on the wall. I admire her shrewd business sense, but it doesn't stop my stomach from twisting into hard knots as I shove the bills in the slot one by one. I tell myself it'll be worth it if I can get my hands on his dragon scale.

"He didn't hurt me," she says once my pocket is empty. "Just the opposite. That man knows his way around a woman's body. The things he can do with his—"

"Stop." I close my eyes and wave my hand in front of me as if it can erase the picture my imagination is all too happy to paint of the two of them together.

Cass stands and plucks a piece of candied ginger from a dish on her nightstand and hands it to me. "This will help."

I pop the sweet into my mouth and pull my shit together.

"I'm sorry if he's your husband or something. This is just a job. I don't ask, and they usually don't tell. If they do, it's because they want me to do something their wives won't."

So much for my disguise.

"How'd you know I'm a woman?"

"Aside from your voice? Your stance, for one. It's all wrong. You keep jutting your hip out. You need to stand straight with your feet apart like you're trying to air out a set of sweaty balls, like this."

I copy her posture.

"Better." She places her hands on my waist and gives me a gentle shake. "Now loosen up and pretend you own the fucking world, and you got it." Her hazel eyes meet mine. "Witches run hot. Men like yours need constant physical release to balance all that power burning up their insides. It don't matter if it's fucking or fighting, they gotta let it out, or they'll go mad. You're paid up for the night. I'd be happy to teach you some things that will keep him coming back to your bed instead of mine."

"Maybe another time." I don't bother correcting her assumption. "Just tell me where I can find him."

———

Rain drips off the tip of my nose in the dark alley. The barrel I'm crouched behind doesn't offer much relief from the downpour that chased me from Chopping Bottom up to the Lakeside District. At least I have a clear view of the brick-paved street that runs in front of the elegant inn. I pull another clove-infused hotpick from the box Cass gave me and clench it between my teeth. The name and address of the restaurant occupying the bottom floor is printed on the paperboard lid. She said the shadow summoner left it behind three nights ago.

It's a piss-poor lead. Every restaurant in the city gives out complimentary toothpicks soaked in clove oil to customers who need to clean their teeth or freshen their breath. He could have picked them up after a meal while passing through. It doesn't mean he's staying here. This particular inn caters to wealthy merchants and traveling elites. It's not the kind of place I'd go to find a reaver.

My feet have gone numb from squatting in one position for too long. It's been three hours, and my senses haven't picked up even a hint of dragon magic.

The clock tower at the end of the street chimes twice. Two a.m.

I stand and stretch, ready to give up and go home to my bed, when a huff of hot breath slides down the back of my neck. *Finally.*

Goose flesh pebbles my wet skin as I plaster my back against the alley wall just past the dim glow of the buzzing streetlamp. I take a deep breath to slow my galloping heart. Hushed voices float toward me as two cloaked figures stop to argue in the middle of the street. My dead feet prickle as I inch closer to the light.

"We need a better plan. There's no way to get in or out without attracting attention." I recognize the sultry accent of the woman with the snapping turtle amulet. Heat waves radiate around her like a silvery mirage. Definitely a fire summoner.

The tall figure next to her pushes the oilskin hood off his head, running a hand through his wet hair, and my heart skips a damn beat. His face is a symphony of hard lines and dark shadows—a kind of mesmerizing beauty that's difficult to look away from. My fingers twitch again with the urge to draw him.

"We have a limited window of opportunity, and I won't waste it. Let me worry about the plan. Thale is already rounding up a distraction. Tell Tiny to be ready to ride as planned."

Pain shoots down my leg. My eyes water as I bite down on the hotpick between my teeth to keep from crying out. Of all the times to have an episode. I slide the flask out of my back pocket and give it a shake. Nearly empty. *Fuck.*

"Fine, but we'll need to leave soon to get there and back before first light."

The rain picks up, and they duck into the lobby. I spit out the toothpick and down my last dose of bitter tonic. I don't have any money left to buy more. That gives me twelve hours before the tremors give me away. I shove a finger under the blond wig and scratch my scalp, wishing I'd checked it for lice before putting it on.

What would the late queen say if she could see me like this? The dutiful protégé she handpicked to take her place hiding in an alley, dressed as a street rat and contemplating how to steal a powerful relic from a reaver.

The rough brick wall scrapes against my back as I sink to the ground and scrub my hands over my face. Sometimes I feel like there's someone else living inside my skin. A being that takes the reins when I get like this. When I obsess over something and can't let it go. It isn't the first bad decision I've made in the last two years, but it's definitely the most impulsive. At least I had a plan when I tried to beat the system by cheating at the gaming tables. It even worked for a little while.

I should have kept the money from selling the gown. It would have given me a few more months to figure something else out. I don't know what I was thinking. That I'd waltz in there and take on a shadow summoner and fire witch by myself? I stroke the pitiful relic in my pocket as two cloaked figures exit the inn.

Maybe I won't have to. I can't see their faces with their hoods up, but there's no mistaking the mirage of heat radiating off the smaller witch. She's carrying a large leather bundle under her arm, given the heat radiating around it like a bonfire I know it's stuffed with firebird feathers.

What she needs with that many relics, I couldn't begin to guess. It's enough to arm an entire squad of fire summoners. Whoever these witches are, they have plenty of money.

Lady luck might be on my side tonight. The dragon scale is still somewhere inside. Once they're out of sight, I duck behind a wagon making an ice delivery to the service entrance and slip into the building unnoticed. I let my senses guide me up five flights of creaking stairs to the warded attic room where the shadow summoner thinks he's secured the relic.

It's the only room on this floor. Smart. Wallace's family charges double for their attic room. The windows under the eaves on both sides offer better ventilation. No balcony for thieves to climb in or out of and no nosy neighbors to overhear conversations about whatever it is they're planning.

Still, I can't shake the feeling that I'm being watched. I glance down the dimly lit hallway to ensure I'm alone before sinking to my knees in front of the door and pulling the firebird feather from my pocket. My fingers tingle as I stroke the plume and draw the remaining magic into my body.

My vision shifts, and I focus on the glowing threads of magic protecting the door. It's a complicated ward woven by a skilled hand.

I may not have any formal training, but I've spent the last two years studying the Menagerie's warded vaults and teaching myself how to unravel them. They change daily, giving me a new puzzle to unlock and rebuild.

"Hello, gorgeous," I whisper, unable to dampen the pleasure in my voice as I study the elegant knots and lines. "I promise I'll be gentle if you let me in." I spend a few minutes memorizing the pattern so I can recreate it when I have what I came for without leaving a trace of my presence. It takes longer than usual to dismantle. The firebird magic coursing through my veins has me sweating through my muslin shirt by the time I'm done.

The hair on the back of my neck rises as I crack the door and slip inside. Unlike the hallway, the room is pitch black. I don't have enough magic left to light the candles *and* rebuild the ward when I leave. I have no choice but to search in the dark. I squint and give my eyes a moment to adjust and ignore the niggling voice in the back of my head warning me that I shouldn't be here. If the reavers come back and catch me in the act, I'm as good as dead.

CHAPTER SEVEN

I curse under my breath as my shin collides with a wooden chair in the middle of the floor. Something cold and clammy greets my hand as I steady myself against it. Someone's rain-soaked clothes. One of them must have changed before going back out.

Without the moon or a candle to light my way, the room is a maze of dark shapes. I squint, but it only makes it worse. My pulse quickens as I inch toward a large object on the left wall that could be a narrow armoire or maybe a rougarou waiting to devour me. I shove down the childish fear and stretch my arms out in front of me.

My fingers meet solid wood, and I sigh in relief as I find the handle and open it. A dry shirt and pair of trousers hang from the rod. I feel the pockets. No sign of the dragon scale hiding somewhere in the room. A pair of holstered revolvers hang from a peg on the side wall. Odd that he'd leave every weapon at his disposal behind.

I continue along the wall and come to a washstand with a porcelain bowl and pitcher of water. My fingers glide over a towel and a bar of soap. I lift it to my nose and inhale the crisp peppermint scent. Past the washstand is a small writing table. I skim my palms over a stack of ledgers and smile when my fingers meet the cold metal of a cash box with the key still in the lock.

My heart races as I open it and scoop out the thick wad of bills and stuff it in my tight back pocket. It's too dark to waste precious time trying to count it. Anyone with the resources to buy a dragon scale won't miss a few hundred dollars.

The shadow-wielding bastard stole from me first.

I keep a hand on the wall as I round the corner and take a few quick steps until my knees collide with the bed. I pat the unmade surface and feel my way around the edge of the plush mattress.

"Where are you?" I whisper to myself as I search the other side of the room. A kiss of hot breath against the back of my neck tells me I'm getting closer.

There's a candlestick on the small stand next to the bed. The wax is still warm at the tip. Spider feet crawl down my spine, and I ignore the overwhelming instinct to flee. I've come this far. There's no way I'm leaving without what I came for. I open a drawer in the bedside table and shove my hand inside. My heart leaps as my fingers collide with the familiar feel of supple leather.

I pull out my sketchbook and kiss the cover before tucking it into the rear waistband of my wet pants. "Thank you, Cass. You can keep the sexy-as-sin asshole and his big, beautiful man parts. I just want to get my hands on his dragon scale."

Even though it's dark, I close my eyes and open my senses wide, letting the magic have its way with them. My entire body buzzes with a rush of fear and excitement as I turn toward the dark corner behind the door. *There.*

"You're mine." I barely recognize my own voice as the words crawl out of my throat on a soft growl.

An inky black form rushes at me from the shadows. It grabs me before I can scream and shoves me face-first against the wall.

"Say it like that again, princess, and I'll be yours all damn night if you like." His warm, clove-scented breath glides over my ear from behind. "I love a woman who isn't afraid to take what she wants."

He has one of my hands twisted behind my back and the other pinned above my head.

"Unhand me, asshole." I buck against the heavy body pressing me to the wall.

"If you keep thrusting your incredible ass against me like that, my big, beautiful man parts are gonna make this more amusing than it already is, Miss Thorne." He rips the wig off my head and drops it onto the floor.

I force my body to go still.

"Good girl." He practically purrs the words as he slides his hand over my backside and digs the wad of cash and flask out of my pockets. "If I let you keep the sketchbook, do you promise not to scream?"

I nod. Every candle in the room lights as he releases me and backs away. I watch as he pads barefoot across the room in a pair of half-buttoned trousers and places the cash back in the box. His broad shoulders and naked back are covered in dragon scales.

The reaver tattoo extends past his elbows and across his shoulders and chest like plate armor, fading out at the edges. So much for stealing his relic. How many ground-up dragon scales did it take to cover that much skin? A trail of dark hair disappears beneath the low-slung trousers that he must have thrown on in a hurry.

I file the image away for later and drag my gaze back to his face.

"How do you know my name?"

"Let's just say we have a mutual acquaintance." He unscrews the cap of my empty flask and sniffs the contents with a scowl. I ignore the way his muscles flex as he twists to set it down. "More than one, apparently. Sixty bucks doesn't buy as much silence as it used to."

"Have you been hiding in the corner watching me this whole time?"

"You broke into *my* room, witch. I'll be the one asking the questions."

The wards. He knows. I'm going to be sick. This can't be happening.

"No one, not even my crew, has ever been able to unravel one of my wards. I have to weave recognition into the spell so they can pass through without getting hurt. Tell me how you did it."

My gaze flicks to the door. I need to get out of here. My feet are moving before I take my next breath. I grab the knob and yank it open. Shadows whoosh around me and slam it shut.

"You're mine now."

I shoot a flare at him. It misses and hits the bed, setting the sheets on fire. The cocky bastard doesn't even flinch. Dark shadows curl behind him and smother the flames, filling the air with the acrid scent of scorched horsehair.

"Sit down," he demands, using his shadows to slide the chair toward me.

"Go jump in a lake," I say, holding up my hand again, even though I've burned through all my magic. He doesn't need to know that.

A rope-like tendril wraps around my wrist and forces my arm behind me. Before I know what's happening, my backside slams down in the chair, and my hands, mouth, and ankles are bound by his shadows.

My chest heaves as he crouches in front of me so we're eye to eye.

"Layla said you were feisty. She failed to mention the bit about you being a rogue witch. She knows everything about everybody in this stinking city and does very well for herself, selling that information to men like me. If she'd known you were a witch, she would have sold you to the army a long time ago. You've done an excellent job keeping your gift a secret. Until now."

The chair legs tip back as I thrash against his restraints. He reaches forward and grips my knees to hold me still.

"This is how it's going to work. You have a debt to be paid and a secret that needs keeping. I have a job that requires a witch with your unique set of skills. Now, you can keep lashing out at me like a pissed-off pixie, or you can listen to my offer. Nod when you're ready to have a civilized business conversation."

I grunt and roll my eyes at the irony of being told to act civilized by a fucking reaver, but I nod reluctantly. He holds all the cards here, and I'm fresh out of luck.

The shadow rope around my mouth evaporates. "What kind of job?"

"We'll get to that once we agree to a few terms. You clearly don't trust me, and I don't trust anyone outside my crew. The only way to fix that is with a blood oath."

I bark out a laugh. "There's no way I'm binding myself to you." I've read about blood oaths between witches. The wording needs to be very specific. Once the oath is sealed, it can't be canceled or altered. The only way to get out of the agreed terms is by fulfilling them. If either party fails to hold up their end of the bargain, they forfeit their life.

"It's the only way to guarantee your secret goes to the grave with me. I'll also pay off everything you owe Madam Faye. All you have to do is agree to help me with one little job."

He must think I'm mad. No one in their right mind would enter a blood oath over a little job. If this reaver is willing to bind himself to me to guarantee my cooperation, it has to be something big. Something only I can do. The sketchbook stuffed into my pants digs into my back as I lean against the chair.

"You've seen my drawings of the Menagerie."

"They're very good."

"I'm guessing you paid Madam Faye for information on someone on the inside who would be easy to blackmail or manipulate, and she sent you sniffing in my direction, knowing I was financially compromised enough to agree to help you break into the biggest stockpile of relics in Perdanth."

"Layla also said you were smart." The corner of his mouth twitches with the hint of a smile.

Not as smart as her, apparently. She gets paid twice in this scenario. He pays her for info on me, and I pay her off when the job is done. It's brilliant, really.

"You didn't offer me a job when you ambushed me in the alley. If you know my history, you know about my connection to Gideon Krimore. You hesitated because you're not sure where my loyalties lie."

"The prince *was* a problem." He stands and stretches to his full height, forcing me to crane my neck to look up at him or stare stubbornly at his crotch.

"Was?" I ask, keeping my gaze on his face.

"Rumor has it the royal modiste made a gown fit for a queen. A gown that was delivered to your home and somehow found its way to a brothel. I'd say your loyalties to the prince are unsteady at the moment."

"How do you even know about that? I just sold the dress this afternoon."

"Like I said, Layla has eyes and ears everywhere, and I pay her extremely well to keep me informed." He picks up my flask. "How much tonic do you drink a day to keep your symptoms in check?"

"That's none of your business."

"If we're going to work together, I need to know how much of a liability you're going to be. How bad is it?"

"Stage one. Just the headaches." I force my shoulders to slump, softening the lie. If he figures out how far gone I am already, he might not offer me a deal and I might not get another chance to wiggle my way out of this.

Up close, his tattoo has a slight iridescent shimmer from the dragon scales ground up in the ink. I'm reminded again of how much money this man must have at his disposal. If I were him, I wouldn't risk entering a blood oath with a sick witch to steal a crate of firebird feathers or unicorn hooves. This reaver isn't interested in just any old relics. He's going after one very unique prize.

"You want me to help you steal Princess Dagmara's dowry?"

He traces a finger along my jaw and tips my chin up to face him. "Do we have a deal or not?" His refusal to acknowledge my accusation is proof enough.

"Stealing from the crown is a hangable offense."

"It's the least of my crimes."

I swallow hard. "The people who work there have families who depend on them. I don't want any bloodshed."

"You don't have to kill anyone, but I'll make no such promise."

"And if I don't agree to your terms?"

The shadow restraints evaporate as he takes a step back and gestures to the door. "You're welcome to walk out of here right now and enjoy your last few hours of freedom before I turn you in and collect the army's bounty for new conscripts. You'll be sent to the Wastes with the next deployment, and your brother will be sentenced to hang for harboring a witch."

"Adrian. Has. Nothing. To. Do. With. This." I spit the words out like daggers. "My brother has no idea what I am."

The cocky bastard shrugs. "Then his death will be all the more unfortunate."

I calculate the distance between his head and the footboard. If I can knock him over, he'll hit his head, and I can escape. Adrian and I can go into hiding. We can leave for Saracen tonight. I lunge forward.

He anticipates the move and sidesteps my attack. He shoves me back into the chair, binding me to it as it flips backward. I brace myself for the inevitable impact of my skull against the hard floor, but it never comes. Instead, my head rests on a cushion of shadows.

"Are you always this feral?" he asks, staring down at me with a smirk.

"Maybe you bring out the beast in me." I plaster a sweet smile on my face, refusing to concede that I'm completely at his mercy.

"Perhaps." His brow furrows as he studies me. "Do we have a deal?"

"I have demands."

He leans forward and casually props his foot on the front edge of the seat between my knees. "I'm listening."

"I'll help you steal the dowry, and in exchange, you'll pay off everything I owe Madam Faye, plus a two-thousand-dollar advance so I can buy the supplies I'll need to break the wards. If something happens to me, you'll pay my brother an additional fifty thousand dollars as a death benefit."

"You drive a hard bargain, Miss Thorne." The hint of a smile pulls at the corner of his lips.

"I'm not finished." He cocks a brow and lets me continue. "You won't kill anyone, unless it's to save my life or your own, until the oath is fulfilled." He starts to protest, but I keep going. "You don't tell anyone what I am, including your crew, and you tell me what's so special about Princess Dagmara's dowry that's worth risking my neck over. Those are my terms. Take them or leave them."

"You're a shrewd negotiator." He studies me intently, as if he's working out a counteroffer.

"Getting cold feet, reaver?" I ask, trying to force the panic out of my voice. It's a lot of money, and I hit him intentionally high with the death benefit, knowing I'll have to negotiate down or give it up entirely to protect my secret and wipe out my debts for good. I'm not above offering him other things to seal the deal if I must.

"I'll agree to all your demands except the last two. You don't need to know anything about the dowry to help me steal it, and I don't keep secrets from my crew. You'll swear the same oath they did when they bound themselves to me. I'll keep your secret too and protect your life as if it were my own. You won't reveal anything you learn or witness while working with us to anyone on the outside."

I blink back in astonishment. He didn't even flinch at the price and is offering me everything that matters. If I agree to help him steal the relic, he keeps my secret and pays off everything I owe Madam Faye. I'm sure I'm missing something—a loophole that will allow him to use me and leave me with nothing. This is why Cass makes her clients pay in advance.

"I have one more demand. I want all the money up front. In addition to my advance, if you pay Madam Faye everything I owe her and post the fifty-thousand-dollar death benefit with the bone broker of my choice first thing tomorrow morning, you have yourself a deal."

I squawk as the chair rights itself and he pulls me to my feet with his shadows.

"Show me your palm," he demands.

I mimic his stance and raise my left hand so it's facing his. He interlaces his long fingers with mine as dark tendrils seep from his tattoo and crawl down his arm. They tickle my skin as they coil around my wrist and invade the space between our joined hands.

I flinch as something sharp lashes across my palm. He tightens his grip as warm blood trickles down my wrist, staining the cuff of my shirt crimson.

"It hurts." I groan as a burning sensation builds in my chest like an inferno fire ripping through my lungs.

"Then I suggest you repeat your demands quickly." He doesn't take his eyes off mine as we repeat our terms.

I grit my teeth as the fire spreads through my body, flaring in my left palm and searing the bond between us. He drags me to the washbasin and plunges our hands into the bowl. The cool water blooms red as he gently glides his thumbs over the sealed wound that matches his own.

"Why does my chest feel like it's on fire?" I ask, all too aware of how close we're standing.

"Dragon fire," he says, using the towel to wrap my injured hand. "If you betray me or refuse to complete your part of the oath, it'll burn you alive."

"And if you fail to deliver on your terms?"

"Don't worry, princess. I always keep my word."

"My *name* is Everly," I say, glaring up at him.

"I know exactly who you are, Everly Marlayna Thorne." His deep voice curls around my name like it's a forbidden secret between us. "You can call me Silas."

Chapter Eight

The pine floors creak under my bare feet, still swollen with the lingering humidity of last night's storm, as I pad into the kitchen. The kettle is still on the table where I left it—next to a plate of cinnamon toast Adrian has left out for me. I cradle my wrapped hand against my chest as I pour myself a cup of cold tea.

It's been eight hours since my last dose of tonic. My head is already blooming with the promise of pain. If I don't get to the druggist soon, I won't be able to function by the end of the day. The inferno in my chest has settled into a glowing seed behind my sternum. There's something seductive and a little terrifying about the pulsing warmth. Part of me wants to test its limits, see just how far I can push the boundaries of the magic holding me to the oath. Fortunately, the other part of me—the one that keeps that mad witch in check—is in control today.

"Did that vicious flea-infested beast bite you again?" Adrian asks, jolting me from my thoughts.

"Pig isn't vicious. He just doesn't like to be touched," I say defensively. My feral cat and I have an understanding. I don't attempt to hold him down and comb out his fleas anymore, and in return, he doesn't bite me.

"Let me see."

There's no point trying to hide the injury from my brother. I can't cough or sneeze without him noticing and insisting on doctoring me. I hate that I'll be a burden to him someday.

As my only family, he'll be responsible for me when I start to decline and can't take care of myself. My attempts to build a nest egg to help pay for the medicine and assistance I'll need failed. It will all fall on Adrian now. My only consolation is that my debt to Madam Faye will be paid, and he won't lose the house.

"It's just a little burn," I say. My left hand throbs as I unwrap the towel, revealing the raised welt of angry flesh that stretches across my palm like a brand. "I may have been a little drunk when I got home last night and tried to make a pot of tea." It's not a complete lie. I did make a pot of rose hip tea to help me sleep after the reaver bandaged me up and threw me out with instructions to meet him at Nymph's Wager at noon to collect my advance.

"You shouldn't use the cookstove when you're intoxicated. You could have burned the house down." It's more a statement of fact than a reprimand.

"I know. I'm sorry." I brush a blond curl away from his face as he inspects the wound. "I'll never do anything to risk losing the house again. I promise."

Adrian lifts his clear blue eyes to mine, and every emotion I've strangled into submission for the last four days—the last two years—breaks free and streams down my face. The headaches and tremors aren't the only things I can't control without the tonic. My emotions are far too close to the surface when I don't have it.

"Does it hurt that much?" Adrian asks.

"Sometimes it does," I say, even though we're not talking about the same thing. I throw my arms around him. His body goes rigid for a moment before he relaxes and hugs me back. "Everything's going to be okay," I add, even though I won't allow myself to believe it until I finally have the deed to our home in my possession.

"You need to keep your hand covered and clean while it heals." Adrian pulls away. "Let me get a few things from my study."

I slip the soft towel off the table and tuck it under my robe. The linen is too white and missing the tattered edges and yellowed stains to match the ones we own. Adrian didn't ask me where it came from or who bandaged me up. He never asks about anything I do. Sometimes, I wish he would. I chew on a piece of dry toast and tell myself it's better that he doesn't. It's easier when I don't have to lie to him.

"I'll need to change the dressing daily," he says when he returns with his supplies and applies iodine and a few drops of liniment to my palm. "It needs to stay wet while it heals. I'm out of burn salve. The druggist is late with their delivery again. I'll have to go between my afternoon appointments."

"Don't trouble yourself." The words rush out too fast as he rewraps my hand with gauze. I clear my throat and force the panic out of my voice before continuing. "I'm spending the afternoon with Wallace so she can put the finishing touches on my dress for the ball. Make a list of everything you need to restock your medical cabinet, and I'll pick it up on my way home."

———————

Feminine laughter floats down to the street from the open windows of Layla Faye's private apartment above the casino. The iron railings lining the second and third floor galleries drip with hanging ferns as green as the emerald the woman wears around her neck.

"Move along, Miss Thorne. Thieving card cheats aren't welcome here." The doorman is dressed better than the ones outside Chopping Bottom, but he's not fooling anyone with his fine clothes. Threads of magic poke through the fabric of his topcoat around the bulge under his armpit, giving away the goblin-spelled gun he's carrying, the one likely charmed to hit its mark. Just like Gideon's sword.

"I have an appointment with someone inside." The sensation of hot breath on the back of my neck tells me Silas is already here.

"And I have standing orders to bounce your ass onto the street if you try to come through this door."

"Can you please let her know I'm here to settle my accounts," I say with as much patience as I can summon in this heat.

"Madam Faye is indisposed with a gentleman caller and has asked not to be disturbed."

"She'll see me now." My vision flashes red, and I'm vaguely aware of a phantom fire flaring inside my chest as I take a step toward the doorman.

"It's all right, Nelson. Please escort Miss Thorne to my rooms," a woman's melodic voice says above me. Madam Faye's chin-length silver hair falls forward, glinting like sunlight on water as she leans over the railing. Silas watches me from the shadows behind her, leaning against the redbrick wall, arms crossed. He's wearing a pair of black gloves. Is it to hide the blood oath scar? Does she know he's a witch?

I don't miss the way Faye casually glides her hand over his shoulder as she sashays back into her rooms. An unusually intimate gesture between business associates.

"Apologies, Miss Thorne. Right this way." The doorman's gruff voice is anything but apologetic.

Unlike Chopping Bottom, The Nymph's Wager is Faye's crown jewel. No expense was spared in its creation, from the opulent furnishings covered in rich velvets and brocades in soft shades of blue and green to the gold leaf trim and crystal chandeliers dripping from the muraled ceiling depicting water nymphs at play.

Games run day and night inside Faye's gambling houses. Nymph's is no different. It just caters to a higher end crowd—wealthy merchants, the idle rich, and royalty. I scan the card tables as we pass through. No sign of Gideon or his Elite Guard. I don't know if the butterflies in my chest take flight in relief or disappointment.

Nelson ushers me up three flights to Faye's office. She's perched on the corner of a large desk, fanning herself with a piece of parchment that's yellowed with age. The deed I put up as collateral against the fifty thousand dollars I owe her.

"I suppose you'll be wanting this back now that your debt is paid in full." She pulls the paper back as I reach for it. "Of course, I'd be happy to hold on to it and open a line of credit in all of my gaming houses for you."

"I'll just take the deed and be on my way." The woman has me all wrong. Cards and dice hold no enticement for me. The odds are stacked against players. That's the real game. I took my thrill from breaking her system and making it work in my favor. Until she caught me cheating and threatened to have me thrown in prison if I didn't sign a loan note.

"As you wish." She hands it over reluctantly. "You're very fortunate to have such a generous benefactor. I must say, I was surprised when the prince purchased your debt and chose to stay in his old rooms here instead of the palace on his first night home."

"What?" My stomach plummets.

"Gideon Krimore paid off your account three days ago," Faye says.

"What is she talking about?" I glare at the man leaning casually against the balcony doorframe, filling it completely, hands stuffed in his pockets.

Silas smirks around the hotpick clenched between his teeth. "I told you the prince was a problem."

He knew. The bastard knew my debt had already been wiped out when he forced me to swear a blood oath to help him steal the dowry. That's why he didn't balk at the high cost of my demands.

I'm overcome with rage.

"And you didn't think to mention it before—" The rest of the words turn to ash in my throat as the fire in my chest flares, threatening to make me self-combust.

Madam Faye says something about not having enough time or resources to track down all the people who don't owe her money.

My vision goes red again, and it takes every bit of composure I have not to stomp across the room and strangle the reaver where he fucking stands.

"Princess Dagmara is certainly beautiful," Faye continues, but I don't process the words. "They say she's quite frigid. Given your history with the prince, I suppose it makes sense that he would prefer your company over hers. When soldiers come home from the Wastes, they crave the comfort of familiar things."

I'm such a fool. The reaver agreed to my terms too quickly, and I ignored the warning in my gut. He knew my debt had been cleared and he let me believe I had no other choice—that binding myself to him was my only option. I try to swallow, but it's like hot glass scraping down my throat.

Silas flexes his left hand as if it's causing him pain. Good. I hope it hurts. I hope it gets infected and it has to be amputated. If they cut off his hand, will I be free of the oath?

Sweat dampens my armpits as my skin heats. What's happening to me? I've never been this angry before. My entire body feels like it's about to burst into flames.

"*Keep it together.*" His deep voice is louder than it should be—like it's floating inside my head as he pushes off the wall. Faye keeps talking as if she doesn't hear him. Silas pours a glass of water from a decanter on a small table.

I stare at his unmoving lips as he crosses the room and hands me the glass with a scowl.

"*If you self-combust and burn the building down in a fit of rage, the entire city will know your little secret, and this will have all been for nothing.*"

The burning started six years ago with headaches. The tremors came shortly after. Hallucinations aren't supposed to take hold until stage four. Why can I hear his voice inside my head? How am I supposed to take care of Adrian if I lose my mind?

I gulp the water. The relief it brings as it slides down my throat makes me whimper.

Madam Faye helps me sit on a tufted chair. "It's all right," she says. "Being a kept woman is a perfectly honorable profession."

I nearly choke on the last sip. "Excuse me?"

"A bit of advice, though, woman to woman. Don't underestimate your value. Your debt was pocket change for the prince. You need to think bigger. Ask for a mansion on the lake with a stable full of horses, a fine carriage, and a grotesque monthly allowance. You're a smart girl. Save whatever he gives you and invest it in a business of your own. The attention of powerful men is as fleeting as a summer bloom. Set yourself up for the future, and you won't be left wilted and penniless when he's bored with you."

"Miss Thorne already has a job." Silas's gloved fingers brush mine, lingering a moment too long as he hands me another glass of water. "*You belong to me now.*"

I stop breathing for a second when he flashes me a seductive smile.

"*And to answer your question, no, you can't get out of the blood oath by cutting off my hand.*"

⸻ ❖ ⸻

"What did you do to me?" I demand as Silas drags me into the alley across from Nymph's. "Why can I hear your voice inside my head?"

"It's a side effect of the dragon fire holding us to the terms of the oath. It'll go away once all the terms have been fulfilled. You almost lost control back there. Have you never channeled magic from a dragon relic before?"

"Have I channeled from a relic that costs more than most houses?" I don't even try to hide my annoyance.

"What did you use to unlock my wards?"

"A firebird feather I stole off a drunk reaver."

He arches a dark brow. "A rogue witch, a card cheat, and a thief? If you're not careful, you'll become one of us." He pulls a thick envelope from the inside pocket of his waistcoat and hands it to me. "Your advance."

"I'll turn into a reaver the same day you transform into a gentleman," I say as I attempt to count the money with my shaking hand.

"You'll find it's all there."

"There's only two thousand dollars in here. What about the forty-eight thousand you still owe me?"

"I vowed to pay your existing debt to Madam Faye. Seeing as you no longer owe her anything, that part of the oath is technically void."

"You lied to me, you unscrupulous bastard."

"Like you said, I'm no gentleman. Get your supplies and meet me at the gates of the Dead City District at midnight."

"You can't just order me around like one of your crew."

Silas takes a step toward me. "If you want to survive, you'll obey every order I give you. The ball is tomorrow night. We need to go over the plan."

"You're doing it tomorrow, during the ball?" My stomach drops. I thought I'd have more time.

"Don't be late," Silas says, turning to walk away. "And get yourself some more nerve tonic. I need your mind sharp."

CHAPTER NINE

My head is drenched in sweat three hours later as I enter Beaux's shop. Turns out carrying a wooden crate of medical supplies around the city in the sweltering heat isn't much fun. The druggist was more than happy to sell me everything on Adrian's list, including the four large bottles of tonic I added at the bottom, but refused to reinstate his account after I paid it up to date. No more free deliveries or open tabs.

I set the heavy crate at the rougarou's feet and wait while Beaux haggles with a young woman over a contraceptive poultice of ground herbs and water wraith venom—the lake monsters who get their name from the infant-like cry they use to lure their victims to the water's edge. I slide my gloved fingers over a warded glass case while I wait.

Adrian accepted my tea kettle lie without question, and Madam Faye didn't seem to notice my bandaged hand. Beaux won't be fooled so easily. Fortunately, lace trimmed day gloves are still fashionable, despite the summer heat. Even if they cost me a sizable chunk of what was left of my advance after paying the druggist.

Two exquisite goblin-spelled amulets—one set with a black stone, the other white—rest inside the case. An arc of mesmerizing light flows from the milky white pendant and is absorbed by the darker gem.

"Compulsion stones," Beaux says as he shuffles over to the case. "Just came in this morning. The moonstone gives the wearer the power of suggestion over the person wearing the onyx."

"How much does something like that cost?" I ask, wondering if they could compel someone to release a person from a blood oath. It would serve Silas right after he manipulated me into bonding myself to him under false pretenses. I'd do anything to keep my secret, but I'm not sure it's worth risking my neck to steal from the crown. If they find out I'm a witch, I'll be conscripted and sent to the Wastes. If I'm caught stealing from the crown, I'll be sentenced to hang. Either way, my already short life expectancy just went down.

"More than the death bond a woman with a snapping turtle amulet posted on your head this morning. She put these up as collateral against your life and didn't seem like she had high expectations that she'd be coming back to claim them."

I open my mouth to answer. The words die in my throat as my chest flares with heat—the magic of the blood oath ensuring I don't talk about Silas or his crew.

I pull a wad of cash from the leather pouch at my waist and set it on top of the case.

"What's that for?"

"Everything I owe you from the other day. Plus my gratitude for your tip about Chopping Bottom. How much for a firebird feather with all of its luck still intact?"

Beaux flicks his wrist toward the door, and the bolt slides into place before he answers.

I count the cash and lay it on the glass. He reaches beneath the counter and pulls out a crimson-tipped black firebird feather. The extinct creature's magic hums against my fingers, sending a phantom flame licking up my arm. Its magic is significantly stronger than the tattered old feather I'm used to. I tuck it up my sleeve until the quill rests against my shoulder and the plume is completely hidden.

I pull out twenty more dollars and put it down. "How would a reaver go about canceling a blood oath?"

"What kind of trouble have you gotten yourself mixed up in, Thorne?"

I ignore the question and put another twenty on the pile with a gloved hand.

He shakes his head and pockets the stack of cash.

"There are only three ways a witch can get themselves out of a blood oath. Fulfill the terms. Betray the terms and let the magic burn them alive. Or set themselves free by killing the witch they're bound to."

I swallow past the dry lump in my throat. The first two options are likely to end in my swift death. The third... I don't think I could kill anyone, not even a reaver.

The Duck's summer kitchen is hot enough to melt lead in the late afternoon. The massive cast-iron cookstove coughs up woodsmoke from sunup to sundown, even now, during the break between their lunch and supper rushes. My armpits are stained with sweat and my hair and clothes smell like a campfire, but there's no place I'd rather be when the Cormier clan sits down to eat.

I'm thankful for the breeze that sweeps through the three open sides of the covered outbuilding as Wallace and the very pregnant wives of her two older brothers set food on the table. Half a dozen flame-haired children chase chickens out of the way.

Whitt and Will stroll around the corner, each carrying an armload of stove wood. They're three days shy of being a year younger than Wallace. With Walker and Warren—also twins—just eighteen months older, the five siblings are as tight as stair steps.

Wallace's mother plops down on the bench across from me. "Wally tells us you're going to the Festivalla Masquerade tomorrow night." Her golden eyes glint with excitement. I don't have the heart to tell her that attending my ex-fiancé's engagement party is the last thing I want to do. Especially after her daughter has spent days working on my dress.

"The invitation was a bit of a surprise," I say instead. At least I'll have an alibi. The more people who see me at the ball and remember me being there, the better, even if I have to endure their fake smiles and vicious whispers before I sneak across the gardens to the Menagerie.

"I'm sure you'll have a splendid time. So many unmarried gentlemen to dance with. I believe your parents met at a ball," her voice lifts suggestively at the end as she waggles her eyebrows at me.

I fist my hands in my lap to hide the tremor as I force a practiced smile. Marriage and a family are things I'll never have, things I've never allowed myself to even consider. I have five, maybe ten years before the burning destroys my body and devours my mind. It would be cruel to trap someone in a relationship based on a lie and expect them to care for me as I decline. It's bad enough knowing I'll be a burden to Adrian.

"Everly isn't going to the ball to hunt for a husband," Wallace groans.

"What's a ball for if not to find a mate? If I can convince your friends to settle down, there's still hope I can convince you. You broke your poor cousin Henri's pride when you refused his proposal last year. The man has a good job at the prison."

"He's my cousin." A shudder rolls across Wallace's shoulders.

"Twice removed and he has excellent teeth. It's tradition to marry within the clan. He's as fine a choice as any."

"Why don't you pester the twins about finding wives?" Wallace asks.

"Because we come as a matched set," Whitt says as he and Will stack the wood in a pile by the detached kitchen's door. "Haven't met a woman who can handle both of us at once."

I bite back a smile as Wallace's mother swats a hand in their direction.

"There's a pretty blonde on Desire Row who might disagree," Wallace whispers as she sets a plate in front of me.

"What are you girls chittering about?" her mother asks.

"I was just telling Everly that I already have two jobs. I don't have time to train a husband or raise a litter of yapping children."

"At the end of the day, we all serve the future of the clan in our own ways. Do not discredit the duty others have chosen because it is different from your path, dear." Wallace's mother deposits an oversized portion of crawfish pie onto my plate. "Raising the next generation of Cormiers is just as important as the work you have committed yourself to doing. Duty often calls us to serve where we least expect it. Like our ancestor, Seffian Cormier, who was called to serve the first queen of Perdanth as captain of her Elite Guard. His descendants still proudly protect her legacy to this day."

"You never told me that," I say to Wallace as she takes a seat next to me.

"She's talking about my cousin who works in the palace kitchens," Wallace says, rolling her eyes. "He's one of King Serros's food tasters."

"It's an important job," Wallace's father says, coming out of the tavern's rear door with a pitcher of ale in each hand. "Five of the thirteen Krimore kings have been poisoned over the last two centuries. The other seven sent to an early grave thanks to the burning. Their bloodline is cursed, if you ask me. They say Serros is half mad too, even though he's not a witch and never went through the fever."

"Hush your mouth, Bertrand," Wallace's mother chides. "You'd have gone off your rocker too if you lost your wife and had to run the inn and raise these feral beasts all alone."

"I reckon that's true," he says as he bends down and nuzzles the back of her neck.

My father used to kiss my mother the same way. I force my gaze away and watch Will and Whitt as they take turns rinsing their heads under the spicket pump. Whitt uses an old flour sack to scrub his short auburn curls and neck dry. He brings a finger to his lips and winks at me as he twists the damp cloth into a rope and whacks Will on the ass while he's bent over.

Will gives him a wide grin and wrestles his twin into a headlock.

"Enough roughhousing, you two. Can't you see we have company?" Wallace's father says, sliding into the seat next to his wife. "My apologies, Miss Everly. Those two aren't completely house-trained yet. How's the good doctor getting on? He still treating the residents at the Downriver Home for Wayward Children?"

"Yes, Adrian is well. His work keeps him busy. We live in the same house and hardly see each other most days."

Wallace groans as a dripping wet Whitt squeezes in on her other side and tells his older brothers about something he read in the newspaper about the increasing number of people that have gone missing along Saracen's border with the Northlands, where giants hunt humans for sport and keep them as slaves, despite the peace treaty.

I eat quietly, content to absorb the chaos. Wallace's father peels an orange and hands the segments to his wife one by one while she talks out the pros and cons of upgrading the inn to indoor plumbing and how much more they could charge if each room had a self-filling copper tub and flush commode. Apparently royal betrothals that coincide with Festivalla are good for business. Walker's wife Frannie and Wallace discuss how many more people they'll have to hire if the Duck stays this busy all summer.

The Cormiers have always made me feel welcome at their table, and they've treated me like one of their own. Still, I feel like an outsider floating at the edge of the beautiful chaos swirling around me. What will they say when the papers report the theft of the princess's dowry or the capture of a reaver crew and their inside accomplice? Will they come to watch when I hang?

I blink away the tears pricking at the inner corners of my eyes. Wallace and her family have been nothing but kind to me. I wish I didn't have to lie to my best friend. I want to tell her about the shadow summoner and the oath. About all the times I seduced the Menagerie's night guards to let me inside and drugged them with pixie dust to knock them out while I experimented with the wards.

The warmth in my chest flares, sending a burning sensation up my throat, reminding me of my vow to never speak of Silas or his crew. I pour myself a glass of ale and gulp it down, quelling the thoughts before they spiral out of control and I self-combust.

Dinner is over too soon, and Wallace drags me up to her room after we help Frannie clear the table. I don't protest when she insists I take off my sweaty undergarments before trying on my altered dress—not that they'd fit under the form-fitting gown she's pieced together from my demure mourning dress and the blood red corset she found in the old chest of clothes.

"When I said you could cut up my dress, this wasn't what I had in mind," I say as I step from behind the dressing screen.

"You look like a goddess." Her eyes gleam as she motions for me to spin so she can inspect her handiwork.

"It's borderline indecent. People will talk," I say, gliding my hands over the black silk gown. The high neck, poufy sleeves, and voluminous overskirt of my demure mourning ensemble have been ripped off, leaving the form-fitting bodice that barely contains my breasts and matching under slip that falls straight to the floor, clinging to the curves of my soft stomach and wide hips. Flame-like cutouts backed with sheer red lace lick their way up my sides from my thighs to my ribcage.

"They're going to talk about you no matter what you wear. At least this way it will be about how stunning you look."

"Everyone will be able to see my undergarments." I run my fingers over one of the lace panels that flares over my stomach, revealing my belly button.

Wallace cuts me a wicked smile. "I designed it to be worn without a corset or drawers. Every fashionable elite in Crecentis will be wearing a statement piece to the masquerade. You'd have stood out like a sore thumb in that hideous high-necked mourning dress."

She picks up a flounced bustle and ties it around my waist. It's made from the cut layers of black tulle from my old petticoat and scraps of silk from the red dressing gown. She's cut and pieced the fabric together in a way that makes the flowing train resemble a firebird's singed tail.

"What statement am I supposed to be making with this?" I ask as I pull the black satin gloves up past my elbows.

"That you're a survivor." She pushes my hair back from my shoulders and ties the ribbons of the matching black mask at the back of my head. The starched lace curls around the left side of my face and forehead, leaving the right side open.

I barely recognize the woman staring back at me in the mirror. The costume is a masterpiece.

"It's perfect." The words rasp from my dry throat.

Wallace grips my shoulders, pulling them back and correcting my posture. "You're Everly Marlayna Thorne. The strongest person I know. Don't ever forget who you are."

Tears stream down my cheeks for the second time today. My best friend can't be more wrong. I'm not strong. I've just perfected the art of pretending. My body and mind are already betraying me, and I can't be honest with her about any of it. I'm a terrible friend. I don't feel like a survivor. I feel like a fucking fraud.

"None of that," she says. "You'll ruin your mask."

"I'm sorry." I untie the black ribbons and swipe at my tears. "Thank you for this. For everything. If anything happens to me, promise you'll look after Adrian. Take him to Guy Maynard's in the Downriver District to collect the bond on my life. Adrian is the beneficiary. Help him use the money to set up a free clinic where he can treat patients regardless of their ability to pay."

"Nothing is going to happen to you. Why would you say something like that?"

"My parents didn't think anything would happen to them either. I just want to make sure Adrian is taken care of. That's all. Will you do it?"

"Of course," she says, pulling me into a hug. "You know my family and I would do anything for you. Now take that dress off before you ruin it. You stink almost as bad as Will and Whitt when they come back from a hunt."

Chapter Ten

The buzzing streetlamps always seem louder when I'm walking alone at night. I can't shake the feeling that I'm being watched as I approach the sprawling cemetery, better known as the Dead City District, with its high walls and winding rows of marble mausoleums lined up like miniature mansions along manicured streets.

Silas leans against the scrolling iron gate, one foot propped on a rung behind him. A dark flame dances in his hand. Shadows swirl around him and bleed into the fog creeping in from the river.

"You're late," he says, annoyance tightening his deep voice.

"I was washing my hair." My fingers graze the packet of pixie dust hidden in the deep pocket of my skirt.

His eyes track the movement, and I force my hand away. I don't know how much of my mind the reaver can read through the blood bond, and I'd like to keep that little trick a secret. It might be my only defense if things don't go well.

The tasteless, odorless powder has a slow sedative effect on humans when ingested. My parents gave it to me so I could sleep through the constant call of magic. I've taken it so much it no longer has an effect on me. A pinch is all it takes to knock out a man Silas's size. Two pinches, and he won't remember what happened when he wakes.

"Were you worried I'd self-combusted and turned into a pile of ash?" I say to distract him.

"I'd know if you'd betrayed the oath." He extinguishes his dark flame and shoves off the gate.

"What's the plan? The sooner we get this over with, the sooner I can get back to my life." I rub my sternum. "I need this inferno in my chest to go away. It's been making me sweat profusely all day."

"Not here." Silas glances around, as if he's picking up the same eerie feeling that we're not alone. "Follow me."

The only way in or out of the cemetery is over the brick wall or through the iron gate, which he unlocks with a flick of his wrist. The metal groans as he pushes it open just far enough for me to squeeze through under his arm.

"Do you use magic to do everything?" I ask as we trudge through the knee-deep fog that's settled between the long rows of stone mausoleums. Their white façades reflect the moonlight, making a lantern unnecessary.

"Yes."

"You're not worried about going mad? The more you channel, the worse the symptoms are when the burning takes hold."

"That won't be what kills me." He glances around as he guides me between the tombs to the next row. The crunch of shells from the path beneath our feet is the only sound. There's not even a chirp from the tree frogs or crickets that keep me awake most nights.

"What about your family?" I ask to fill the heavy silence.

"Gone."

"How many people are in your crew?"

"Six, including me."

"Are you always such a charming conversationalist?"

"Are you trying to wake the dead with your incessant fucking chatter?" Silas growls, keeping his voice low as he moves me in front of him and glances behind us.

"I'm just trying to make conversation. Cemeteries are built for the living. Not the dead." I gesture to the tight row of marble mausoleums. "Their rotting corpses might be bricked up inside these monuments, but their souls don't reside here."

"Not everyone has the luxury of moving on to the Otherworld." He checks behind us again, as if he's waiting for something to jump out of the dark.

"Don't tell me the big, bad shadow summoner is scared of ghosts," I tease, waggling my fingers at him.

Silas crowds into my personal space. I scramble back toward one of the tombs. My ass bumps into the stone façade. He presses his palms to the wall on either side of my shoulders.

The hairs on the back of my neck rise, my senses telling me I should run. A little too late for that now. Where were those instincts when I thought I could steal a dragon scale from a reaver and not get caught? If I'd just waited, my only problem would be figuring out how to avoid a prince at a ball.

"I was speaking about myself. When I die, my soul will be bound to these bones, wherever they fall."

"Everyone goes to the Otherworld," I say, heart pounding, "even reavers and murderous thieves."

"The Otherworld isn't meant for monsters like me, princess."

I'd seen my parents treat enough sick witches to know the ones who survive their conscription don't come home whole. They never get over the things they were forced to do to survive. Silas wears that same darkness like a shield. I can only imagine the terrible things he must have done to believe himself unworthy of entering the Otherworld.

"I'm not scared of you." I'm not sure why I say it or why I feel the need to stand my ground every time this brutally beautiful man corners me.

"Then you're not nearly as smart as Faye says. Fear is the only instinct that will keep you alive. Stay quiet and try to keep up. The locals get restless this close to a full moon, and it would be very *inconvenient* for me if you got yourself killed before fulfilling your part of the oath."

He shoves off the wall and stalks away, forcing me to jog to keep up with his long strides.

A tremor runs through me as he stops in front of a crumbling tomb. The cracked slab that once sealed the entrance lies in two pieces on the ground. They've been there for some time, if the weeds growing up around them are any indication.

A lantern flickers inside, spilling golden light onto the steps. Magic prickles my skin as I approach the warded threshold. Silas disappears through the door unscathed, joining four others. Three of them are channeling powerful relics. The woman with the turtle skull necklace flexes her fingers on the handle of her sheathed dagger. Heat waves ripple around her like a silvery mirage, betraying the firebird feather hidden somewhere on her body.

I recognize the hulking storm summoner standing behind her from Chopping Bottom. He's a head taller than her and twice as wide. His bright blue eyes stand out against his dark skin. Static rolls off his bulging arms in waves. I don't want to know how many thunderbird skeletons it took to concentrate that much power in his body. Relic tattoos cover every visible inch of his massive frame from knuckles to neck. He isn't carrying a gun. Not that he'd need one.

A man with long white-blond braids leans against the back wall. He watches me with the same detached interest one would expect from a person watching grass grow as he sips from a flask.

I don't see any tattoos on his pale skin, but the rumble of hooves tells me he's carrying a unicorn relic, making him the crew's healer. Unicorn magic isn't much good in a fight, but it comes in handy if someone gets injured.

He passes his flask to the last person in the tomb. This one can't be older than eighteen, maybe twenty. Reddish-brown curls brush his shoulders. He isn't carrying a relic, but the long cane knife hooked in his belt looks sharp enough to take off a limb. A sheepish smile breaks across the young man's face as he gives me a little wave.

Silas said there were six in his crew. I scan the cemetery behind me for the missing member—not that I'd be able to see an attacker lurking in the dark.

"What's this?" I ask, gesturing toward the invisible wards.

"A test," Silas says.

"You've already seen what I can do, reaver."

"They haven't, and how do I know it wasn't a fluke? That you didn't get lucky? If you can repeat what you did in my room, it'll help convince my crew that I didn't make a huge fucking mistake bonding myself to you. They have a lot to lose if you're not up to the task. Each one of them gets to choose for themselves whether they want to work with you."

"And if they decide I'm not up to their standards?" I glance at the woman who's been watching me like a hawk. "I'm not used to working in front of an audience."

"Then it's a two-man job. Just me and you."

"Two witches against dozens of guards?" I plant my hands on my hips. "Have you lost your mind? That's practically suicide."

"More like me against thirty-seven armed Saracen guards and sixteen of the most well-trained summoners I've ever seen. I've had worse odds, but your defensive skills are pathetic. Since I don't have time to teach you how to fight, our chances of making it out alive without their help aren't promising."

"I'd like to know what's so special about this dowry before I risk my life over it."

Everyone on his crew shifts slightly, their subtle movements betraying their masks of indifference. Whatever they're going after is important, and they're all willing to die for it.

"That's not part of the deal," Silas says. "If you want to increase your odds of fulfilling the oath without getting caught or killed, I recommend you try real hard to convince my crew you're not a liability."

The woman with the turtle amulet smirks at that. Something tells me this *test* was her idea, and she expects me to fail.

Silas's voice slides along the bond between us. "*If any of them could do this, you wouldn't be here. Do not disappoint me.*"

"*Stay out of my head, reaver.*" I roll up my sleeve and run my fingers along the silky plume hiding under my shirt. The firebird's residual magic prickles across the scar on my palm, leaving a tingling sensation in its wake as I pull what I need into my body. I don't miss the way Silas fists his left hand impatiently. I make note of the little tell. The reaver is putting all his cards on the table by introducing me to his crew. This is all or nothing for him. Good to know.

"Can you move the lantern closer?" I ask as the threads of his elaborate ward shimmer to life. The kid with auburn curls lurches forward and places one of the lanterns on the floor near the threshold.

"Thanks," I say, offering him a sweet smile as he sits cross-legged in front of me on the other side of the ward.

"You're welcome. I'm Bastian, but you can call me Bas. Everyone does." His accent has a local lilt, and I wonder if he's a recent addition to the crew.

"Are you from Crecentis?" I ask.

"No, ma'am. I was born upriver, in Red Stick." I drop my gaze to his big hands and catch a glimpse of a faded scar on his left palm. Not so recent, then.

"Bas, let the woman concentrate." Silas's deep voice softens with the gentle command.

"Sorry, boss," Bas says as he scoots back on the dusty floor toward Silas's feet.

I swallow past the dry lump in my throat. If I can't unravel this ward, the odds that they'll let me walk out of here aren't great, blood oath or not. Silas vowed to protect my life. I don't remember the exact words, but I'm pretty sure he left himself a loophole. The manipulative bastard has already proven he can get around the terms. The only thing keeping me alive right now is my ability to break this fucking knot.

My blouse clings to my back under my still damp hair as I squat down and focus on the shimmering threads in front of me. It's even more complicated than the one guarding his room.

The sharp prickle radiating from the ward tells me this lock has teeth. What did Silas say last night? That he had to weave recognition into the pattern to keep it from attacking his crew when they pass through it?

The trick to unraveling a ward is recognizing the relic used to cast the threads. A firebird feather or dragon scale—whatever the witch who created it has on hand. The problem is guessing what kind of relic they used. Getting it wrong can be fatal, especially if they wove in a nasty surprise.

I don't have to guess. Silas wove this one with three relics, tied and knotted together in a way that appears random. Each thread sends a different sensation through me when I tug it. The hair-raising prickle of static against my skin tells me the first string was cast from a thunderbird talon. The phantom vibration of hooves pounding against the ground in a stampede means the second came from a unicorn relic. The third thread is obviously from a firebird feather. No dragon scales.

The tricky bastard. He has no intention of making this easy for me.

"*Where's the fun in that?*" he asks across the bond.

I glare up at him. Amber light flickers across half his face, leaving the other side cast in shadow. The seductive smile on his lips makes my pulse skitter. Silas might be the monster he claims to be, but he also respects every person inside this tomb. If he didn't, he wouldn't be giving them a choice. He also gave me a choice, shitty as it was, to take the oath or expose my secret.

I twist my damp hair into a knot and drag my gaze back to the ward. The longer I stare at the pattern, the less chaotic it appears. After each seemingly random knot, it twists and doubles back on itself like a hunter covering his tracks. *I see you, reaver.*

My fingers glide over the vibrating threads in front of me, tugging and untying. The firebird magic I'm channeling radiates against my skin. A bead of sweat rolls down the side of my face. I don't risk letting go of a single strand and wipe my head against my shoulder instead.

I'm not sure how long I've been at it, but the muscles in my arm burn with fatigue when it's done. I sit back on my knees, fully spent.

"Time?" Silas asks without taking his eyes off me.

"Seventeen minutes, eight seconds," Bas says, glancing at a pocket watch. A toothy smile breaks across his face. "I vote yes."

"Seventeen minutes is too long," the woman with the turtle skull amulet says. "We need to get in and out in under ten."

"I watched the Saracen witches seal the vault after the dowry came in," I say. "They used three wards stacked on top of one another. They're nowhere near as complicated or elegant as this one. It'll take me three minutes, tops, to unravel each layer."

"It's still too long, girl. That only leaves one minute to secure the—"

"Serin. We'll have to make it work," Silas says, cutting her off. He shifts his eyes to the storm summoner covered in thunderbird tattoos. "Can you stretch out the distraction for fifteen minutes?"

He grunts in response as I pull myself to my feet.

"That's a yes for Thale," Bas says as he bounds out of the vault to stand next to me.

"Count me in," the man with long white-blond dreads says, a cold gleam in his gray eyes. "It's been a while since I've had a good excuse to waste some lead."

"That's Val. He and Tiny are our sharpshooters. Tiny holds the record for the most kills, but Val has a faster draw."

"Bas," Silas says in a warning tone.

"What? You said she swore the oath like the rest of us. She can't repeat anything we tell her."

"That doesn't mean she needs to know every detail," Silas says.

I glance over my shoulder again. Tiny must be the missing sixth member of his crew.

"Mother of Fire. She wouldn't know anything if you hadn't bound your—"

Silas cuts Serin a dark look. "We had a problem. I solved it."

She clenches her fists as they have what looks like a silent conversation.

He places a hand on her shoulder. "None of us will hold it against you if you sit this one out."

"And let you take all the credit? I don't think so."

The one called Thale wraps a reassuring arm around her and plants a soft kiss on the top of her head. They're together. I'm not sure why that knowledge sends a wave of relief through me.

"Let's go over the plan." Silas pulls a stick of charcoal and a folded piece of parchment from the inside pocket of his waistcoat, then smooths the paper over the stone slab in the middle of the vault. Our fingers brush as he hands me the stick of charcoal, sending a rush of warmth up my arm. "Miss Thorne is going to draw us a map of the Menagerie."

<hr>

"The coal shoot is the only way in that doesn't involve bloodshed," I say, tapping the rough sketch. "The guards don't patrol the boiler room this time of year, and it's close to one of the secret passages between the walls." I drag my finger along the map. "We can take it all the way to the archive room, which has a clear view of the vault."

"We've been watching the building for five days," Serin says. "Saracen military guards are stationed at each entrance, with more on the roof. We won't be able to take the dowry out through the coal shoot. We need a distraction to get out without being seen. That's where Thale comes in. While the ball is in full swing, he'll swim out and cut one of the dragon boats rigged with fireworks from its mooring in the middle of the lake. He'll stir up a gentle breeze to push it under the palace's south terrace. When everyone gathers on the terrace at midnight to watch the floating parade and fireworks show. The crowd will erupt into chaos. Everyone knows the Palace Guard will focus on protecting the king. With so many visiting dignitaries and elites, the Saracen military guards will be called from the Menagerie to extract the northern king and princess. That's when we go in."

"Explosives?" I wheel toward Silas. "You can't just blow up part of the palace. You agreed you wouldn't kill anyone."

Serin lets out a sultry laugh. "You've definitely gone mad, girl. Silas would never—"

"I agreed I wouldn't kill anyone unless it was necessary to defend her life," Silas says, cutting her off before swinging his gaze back to me. "I made no such promises on behalf of my crew."

My body tightens with anger. "Adrian will be on that terrace."

"Then I suggest you find a way to convince him to leave early."

"What about everyone else? Every elite family in Crecentis will be there."

"All you need to worry about is getting yourself to the Menagerie before midnight without being followed. We'll handle the rest."

I turn and walk out of the tomb, fisting my hands to hide the tremor. "We're not done here."

"You got what you needed from me," I say, testing how far I can push the magic binding me to the oath before it starts to burn.

"We still have details to discuss. Get back in here and draw a map of the palace."

"If you wanted me to follow orders, reaver, you should have been more specific with the terms of the oath. I agreed to unlock the wards protecting the dowry. Nothing more. I'm certainly not going to help you put innocent lives in danger. I'll be waiting for you in the Menagerie's boiler room at midnight."

My chest doesn't flare as I stalk into the dark, proving my point. By this time tomorrow, the blood oath will be fulfilled. I'll never have to see him or his band of thieves again.

That leaves me less than eighteen hours to convince Gideon to cancel the dragon boat parade.

CHAPTER ELEVEN

The royal carriage Gideon sent to pick Adrian and me up for the ball jolts to a stop in the middle of the street. A mob of pedestrians flows around us like water, everyone pushing to get closer to the fence, a ten-foot-tall monstrosity decorated with wrought-iron roses and flesh-shredding thorns to discourage anyone from climbing over.

Not that they'd make it far. An entire regiment of conscripted witches in deep purple uniforms line the perimeter of the palace grounds. A storm summoner stationed at the gate sends a warning shot of lightning over the people's heads. The road clears as they scatter. The gate opens, and our carriage lurches forward.

Golden light spills from the floor-to-ceiling windows along the palace's front façade. Four sets of double white columns stacked three stories high frame the curved front entrance. Gideon's Elite Guard, dressed in their black military uniforms, flank either side, keeping watch over the festivities.

I tug Adrian around fire-eaters and jugglers on stilts as we make our way past the great lawn. Masked revelers lean over the railings of the upper galleries to get a better view of the who's who as they arrive. The marble balustrades drip with garlands of dusty green moss and wild roses, an homage to the first queen of Perdanth. Her ghost is rumored to still haunt the halls.

I tighten my grip on Adrian's arm as we enter the foyer. We've managed to escape any real notice, thanks to our masks and the completely unnecessary cloak I threw on over my costume. A servant guides us to the line of people waiting to enter the receiving room to be announced. I've already seen four other women and two men dressed as firebirds. Their costumes are ridiculously over-the-top, with towering headpieces and trailing tails of dyed feathers. None are as audaciously revealing as mine, though.

"Are you sure you're prepared to see the prince?" Adrian asks, as if it just occurred to him that attending the party thrown in honor of Gideon's engagement to another woman might not top the list of things I want to do tonight... or ever.

"A bit too late to worry about that now." I can't blame my brother for not realizing it earlier any more than I could blame Wallace for assuming I was long over Gideon. Which I am. Mostly.

I spent the first six months after my parents' death drinking myself into a stupor and pretending Gideon had been killed by reavers too. I entertained macabre visions of him dying in battle, drew death portraits of him engulfed in flames. Allowing the anger to fuel my imagination was easier than giving in to the pain.

When news of the attack on Fort Netherthorn and Gideon's injury inflicted by a fire-summoning reaver made its way back to Crecentis, the guilt almost killed me. I buried all the pictures I'd drawn of him in a shallow grave under our tree and left him there.

I've spent the last year and a half filling that empty space left by my rage with noise—if you can call getting myself banned from every gaming house in the city and fucking my way through the night guards at the Menagerie noise.

Adrian never questioned where I'd been when I came home at all hours of the night, if I came home at all. My confidence grew with every ward I successfully unraveled and rebuilt. I wasn't sleeping all day or dressed in all black anymore.

"I'm fine." I give my brother's arm a reassuring pat. "I'd like to find him right away and offer my congratulations."

Adrian accepts the lie at face value and hands his calling card to the witch stationed at the ballroom's grand entryway. He channels magic from the thunderbird talon in his hand to project his voice over the crowd like a slow-moving storm.

"Doctor Adrian Thorne and Miss Everly Thorne."

A servant removes my cloak before I can protest. My stomach drops as every masked face swivels in our direction and the din quiets. The only sound is the thud of my heart in my ears and the brassy tune being played by the full orchestra at the back of the room.

It takes eight infinitely long seconds for the chatter to begin again. I take a deep breath and scan the ballroom for Gideon. My gaze lands on a stunning woman in an unadorned emerald gown and a simple gold crown. No mask. No costume. No pretense.

Princess Dagmara dips her head in my direction. There's an undeniable challenge in the bold act of recognition. Good. She has a backbone. She'll need it in King Serros's court, where sharp tongues cut to the bone.

I steer Adrian toward the bar. The sooner I appear to start drinking, the sooner I can make an excuse to leave early and sneak across the gardens to the Menagerie. Before I do, I need to find Gideon.

"Shall we check out the games?"

"The gaming rooms are too smoky for me," he says. "I'm content to stand here where there's a breeze."

Adrian takes the mint julep from my outstretched hand and glances around the room. Everything's been redone in cream and white, from the diamond pattern on the painted wood floors to the velvet couches and heavy drapes held back by gold cord to reveal the moonlit lake through the open terrace doors. Outside, fifty-three Festivalla barges, one for every major battle won by the first king and his dragon, wait to set the night aflame.

"Are you sure you'll be all right on your own?" I ask, placing a gloved hand on his forearm.

"I'm a grown man, Everly. I don't need a babysitter. Go have fun with your dice." He leans against a plaster column, half tucked behind a large plant. "I'll wait here for you."

"You know where to find me if you change your mind." My heart aches as I leave him. My brother isn't spared the withering looks and wagging tongues any more than I am. Our parents' reputation as reaver sympathizers clings to both of us like a foul odor. Adrian is brilliant and handsome, with his honey curls and striking blue eyes. Still, he won't find a willing dance partner aside from me, and I don't have time for revelry. I only have three hours to find Gideon and convince him to cancel the dragon boat parade before I feign a swollen head and make my exit.

I trade my full glass of wine for a nearly empty one atop a discarded tray and pretend to sip as I stroll through the parlors that have been converted into temporary gaming rooms. I'll need a clear head and steady hand to break through the wards protecting the princess's dowry.

Peanut shells crunch beneath my slippered feet. Players are only permitted to gamble with nuts inside the palace. A tradition started by the first queen of Perdanth to keep the southern clan leaders from turning on each other in the early days of the Krimore reign.

Gideon always preferred cards to dice, so I keep moving through the rooms until I spot his golden crown of curls. He's wearing a royal purple suit with a dragon scale–embroidered waistcoat made from the same fabric as the gown he sent me. His matching mask is tucked into the breast pocket of his jacket.

He doesn't see me. I take a moment to get used to the sight of him again, hoping it will loosen the knot in my stomach. There's a rigidness to his posture that wasn't there before. The kind every soldier has when they return from the Wastes. Like they're holding everything they've done and seen tight because they know letting it out will be the thing that breaks them.

"Care to make the night more interesting with a wager?" Madam Faye says next to me. I've been so focused on Gideon I didn't notice her approach.

The rich taffeta of her turquoise gown sparkles under the gold net-like overlay like the glint of sunshine on Lake Largeau. Gossamer blue-green lace fans away from either side of her mask like fins, giving her the appearance of a water nymph plucked from the deep, ready to grant her lucky captor a wish.

"I'm through with wagers." I return my gaze to Gideon as he tosses a handful of peanuts into the center of the table, upping the ante.

She tracks my line of sight. "So have you taken my advice and chosen the safe bet instead of chasing your luck with our mutual friend?"

"Luck isn't something you can chase. It either smiles on you or it doesn't." I know better than to confirm or deny anything with Faye. If I told her I had no intention of taking Gideon up on his offer, she'd use the information to set odds on how long it would take for me to change my mind. Which I'm not going to do. Not today. Certainly not while I'm in debt to him.

She plucks the mostly empty glass of wine from my gloved hand and replaces it with a shot of whiskey from a passing tray.

"A toast, then. To forging our own paths." She clinks her glass to mine, and I copy her as she takes a dainty sip of the amber liquid. "You have a lot of moxie, Miss Thorne. I always thought you'd make an excellent queen. It's unfortunate King Serros has other plans. There are whispers the nobles are divided on the prince's betrothal to the heir of Saracen. They worry an alliance with the northern kingdom will bring undesirable changes to Perdanth."

"Like allowing witches to live free and making it illegal to hunt magical creatures?" I say sarcastically.

"Our friend said the same thing the other day. He hates Perdanth and rarely comes this far south without a *very* compelling reason," she says, cutting me a sidelong glance.

I take another slow sip of my drink, ignoring her pointed stare. Does she expect me to thank her for holding my home hostage and sending Silas sniffing in my direction, knowing I was compromised and couldn't say no?

"A bit of advice," Faye says, leaning closer and lowering her voice. "Whatever your business is with him, end it quickly. Silas enjoys taking trophies from his enemies. Once he sets his mind on something, he won't let anything stand in the way of possessing it. Not even a prince. He's been playing this game a long time, and he always wins."

"I have no interest in Silas or his games." I tip my head and knock back the whiskey. I'm not sure what burns more, the lie or the alcohol as it slides down my throat.

I hand her the empty glass and make my way to the table where Gideon is playing cards with the Saracen guard who followed us into the gardens.

Gideon's eyes widen with surprise before he schools his response and takes in my firebird costume with a scowl. He tugs his ear. Our old code to meet in the one place no one will come looking.

Fuck maintaining my faculties. I can't do this sober. I pluck a glass of rum punch from the edge of a gaming table as I pass and suck it down to steady my nerves. It's been four years since I made my way to the abandoned second floor in the east wing.

I glance over my shoulder to make sure I'm alone before squatting down and running my hand under the edge of the heavy carpet that runs the length of the dark hallway. My stomach drops as my fingers brush against the cold metal key.

It's still there. Right where I left it the last time I used it to unlock the door to Marlayna Krimore's private chambers.

The musty room is a maze of ghostly shapes, the furniture still covered in white sheets. I run my fingers along the silky plume tucked into the half-up, half-down masterpiece Wallace managed to make of my hair.

Firebird magic prickles up my arm as I create a spark and light an oil lamp on the mantel. It flares and smokes as I replace the glass chimney and turn the wick down as far as it will go without snuffing out. The windows are shuttered, but I'm not taking any chances. One of the guards patrolling the grounds could look up and see the glow between the louvers if I turn the light any higher.

Dust billows into the air as I tug the sheet off the portrait hanging above the fireplace. Queen Marlayna stares back at me with a warm smile that makes my chest tighten. I stare at the dragon bone comb peeking out from her chestnut hair as I blink away the wetness. It had belonged to Tula Krimore and was passed down through the centuries from queen to queen. Marlayna was like a second mother to me, and it's all I have left of her. Fuck tradition. There's no way I'm giving it up. It belongs to me.

"I miss you." I stare up at the woman who doted on me as a child. My memories of her have gotten fuzzy. She was so frail at the end. The constant tremors left her bedridden. A shell of the woman she'd been. She couldn't sit up or even hold a book on her own at the end. Only a few years older than I am now when she died. I hate that that's how I see her in my mind. I prefer to remember her like the portrait. Beautiful in the purple gown that brought out the warmth in her brown eyes and chestnut waves. So vibrant and full of life before the burning destroyed her body and mind.

"I'm told she was kind," a woman's voice says behind me.

Princess Dagmara's silk skirts whisper against the thick carpets as she approaches the fireplace.

"What are you doing in here, Miss Thorne?"

The woman is everything I'm not—tall, slender, and poised—and looks every bit the queen, with an onyx crystal the size of my fist set in the center of her gold crown. The air around it vibrates with the same pattern as the goblin-spelled amulets in Beaux's shop.

"Forgive me, Your Royal Highness. I was just paying my respects to the queen. My mother was her personal physician."

"I was very sorry to hear about your parents. I understand they were close to finding a cure for the burning."

"Then you know more than I do, I'm afraid. Their casebooks and personal belongings were stolen by the reavers that killed them. We didn't even get to lay them to rest properly. I don't know if they received a funeral pyre to send them to the Otherworld or if their bodies were left on the ground to be picked apart by animals in the Marshwood Forest. It's difficult to accept that someone is gone when you don't get to say goodbye."

Dagmara lets out a heavy sigh as she studies Queen Marlayna's portrait. "We have that in common. I lost my mother to the red plague three years ago. She wasn't just my mother. She was my best friend. My father was ill too, and he ordered my uncle to take me to his country estate so I wouldn't contract the disease. I never got to say goodbye either.

"People say things they think will help—that she's in a better place, that she's no longer suffering. Everyone wants you to move past the grief like it's a sickness that needs to be cured." Dagmara brings her hand to her chest, digging her fingers into the soft flesh above her bodice. "The pain isn't an affliction. It's proof that I loved her with my whole heart. That I carry her with me in everything I do." Her voice cracks a little at the edges. "I will hold on to this pain as long as I live. It's the price I choose to pay for loving her and knowing I was loved in return."

I nod silently, not trusting my voice. Princess Dagmara glances around the room, as if assessing how she'll redecorate the space once it's hers, before dragging her gaze back to me.

"You're not wearing the dress." The softness in her voice a few moments ago is gone.

"I... I'm not sure what you mean." Heat creeps up my neck to my cheeks. Of course she knows. The whole city probably knows about Gideon's gift, thanks to Madam Faye. I need to get out of here. This is not a conversation I want to have with his future wife.

"You're not wearing the dress I had delivered to your home with an invitation to the ball. You're here as my guest, Miss Thorne. Surely you read the invitation."

My fidgeting body stills. "You sent the dress? Not Gideon?"

"Your prince would never do anything that bold. King Serros touts his son as the hero of Fort Netherthorn while hiding the fact that his army has taken catastrophic losses. There aren't enough witches left to protect your kingdom's assets in the Wastes *and* your western border. That hasn't stopped him from trying and failing miserably at both. Serros can secure the border against reaver raids by pulling his army out of the Wastes. But without the mines, your economy would collapse. If he sends all his resources to protect them, it will leave the border open to invasion. Your king needs my army. Gideon wouldn't dare do anything as rash as flaunting a mistress in front of my father and risk jeopardizing the alliance."

"But you would. That's why you sent the dress. You don't want the alliance."

"I have a powerful army of witches at my disposal and an army King Serros desperately needs, in addition to our timber and steel. Perdanth has the bitter pepper, sugar cane and tobacco we can't grow in the north. I'm not against an alliance negotiated on fair trade. What I don't want is a husband. My father's health is failing, and he seems to think I need a man to help me rule Saracen once he's gone. I've been running my country just fine on my own in the three years since his recovery from the red plague. I have no desire to share my throne with anyone, especially a power-hungry Krimore prince. I'm willing to pay you handsomely to keep Gideon out of my bed and my country once we're married."

I bite my tongue to keep from asking how much she might be willing to pay. It doesn't matter. I would never do that to Gideon. He may have ripped my heart out, but he was also my best friend once. Gideon may not deserve my tears, but I won't let his future wife make a fool of him.

"You're wrong about Gideon. He cares about the future of Perdanth, but he isn't power hungry. Not like his father. I can't imagine how low your opinion must be of me to presume I would accept money in exchange for manipulating and lying to the man I was betrothed to for twenty-three years."

She raises her hands in surrender. "You have my sincere apologies, Miss Thorne. It appears I've misjudged you. Thank you for your candor." She looks up at the painting of Gideon's mother again. "It's a shame you won't sit on her throne. Your country could benefit from a queen who isn't afraid to speak her mind. A woman like that would make a strong ally."

Princess Dagmara isn't at all what I expected, and I'm not sure how to respond to the odd compliment. She opens the fan dangling from her wrist to cool herself, even though it isn't the least bit warm. I wrap my arms around my body to stave off the chill creeping through the room.

"I should go back to the ball. My brother will be wondering where I've disappeared to," I say as my teeth start to chatter and I realize the cold sinking into my bones isn't normal. The relic in the princess's dowry is no longer in the vault at the Menagerie.

It's here.

Chapter Twelve

"I'm sorry. I have to go." I rush out of the room and down the hall, letting my overactive senses guide me. If I can steal the relic and deliver it to Silas before midnight. His crew won't have a reason to create a distraction. No one has to die.

My feet prickle toward numbness as I stumble past the gaming rooms like a drunk pixie. I shove my freezing fingers under my armpits and follow the phantom sensation toward the guest wing. I brace a hand against the wall for support and will my legs to keep moving toward the Hall of Kings, where eleven solid gold busts enshrined in dark alcoves honor each of the former rulers. The self-aggrandizing display lines the hall to the guest wing and serves as a reminder to visitors of the Krimores' legacy. Never mind that more than half of them ruled for fewer than five years before their untimely demise. Wallace's father might be right. Gideon's family is cursed.

A hazy memory of playing hide-and-seek with his mother overlaps my present perception. My hand is tucked in the queen's as she leads me from one sculpture to the next, pretending to look for Gideon, even though we can hear him giggling from the last alcove. Voices float toward us that are not part of the memory.

"Hide," Queen Marlayna says as she turns to me and evaporates like steam. A burst of icy air slams into me. My brain and body are too sluggish to move, and I feel myself falling backward as my vision goes black. Or maybe I'm floating. It's hard to know which way is up when I'm surrounded by a darkness so complete it blocks out all light and sound as it coils around me.

"Are you drunk, little firebird?" His deep voice wraps around me like a velvet cloak.

"Silas?" My teeth chatter as he cradles me against his chest. Heat seeps into me everywhere our bodies touch, and I can't resist the urge to nuzzle into his warm neck. This close, he smells like peppermint soap, woodsmoke, and cloves. The discordant notes should clash, not make me want to press my cold nose against his skin and breathe him in.

"Fuck. You're freezing." His voice goes tight with rage as he pulls me closer. "Which one of the Saracen witches attacked you?"

"No one attacked me." A shudder rolls through my body. That's not entirely true. Something attacked me. "The relic from the princess's dowry. It's here."

"I'm aware," he growls as he pulls his shadows back enough so I can see him glaring down at me. "How do *you* know about the relic?"

Shit.

"I overheard the guards talking. They said—"

"Don't lie to me."

"I'm not lying." The ember of dragon fire in my chest burns as I shove against him. "Put me down."

"Your heart rate says otherwise. I can hear your pulse racing. You're either scared, turned on, or lying. You've already told me I don't frighten you, so it must be one of the other two. Or perhaps a bit of both." The corner of his full mouth curls into a smirk.

"You can't hear another person's heart beating without a stethoscope."

"We share a blood bond. I'm acutely aware of the way your body reacts in my presence." He keeps a firm arm around my back as he releases my legs slowly.

I slide down the front of him. The thin silk of my dress rides up, causing the high slit to gape open at my hip. My insides go molten as his fingers brush my bare flesh. A low, guttural sound vibrates through his chest as he bends down and brushes his lips against my ear. "Tell me how you know about the relic."

"Not until you release me."

"I'm afraid I can't do that. I swore an oath to protect your life. If I let you go, the Saracen guards walking past us right now will assume you're a spy. They'll arrest you immediately." He tilts my chin up. "When they put their hands on you, I'll have no choice but to slit their fucking throats. Since you insisted that I keep the bloodshed to a minimum, I won't be letting you out of my grip until it's safe, so start talking."

I try to peer over his shoulder, but I can't see or hear anything beyond the boundary of his shadows. I have no idea if he's telling the truth or just trying to intimidate me. It doesn't matter. He can read my mind. There's no point in lying to him.

Silas relaxes his grip around my waist, allowing a little space between us as I heave a sigh of defeat.

"I knew you were carrying a dragon scale in the crowd that day at the gallows." My palms are still pressed against his chest.

"How?"

"The same way I know Serin uses firebird feathers as her source, that Val carries a unicorn relic, and that Thale has the remains of an entire thunderbird tattooed on his body. The bones whisper to me."

His body tenses. "Magic speaks to you?"

"Not with words, just phantom sensations."

"Explain."

"I feel things. The gentle flutter of wings when someone strolls past me with a vile of pixie dust in their pocket. A phantom gust of wind from witches channeling thunderbird relics. I can see heat waves radiating off anyone wielding firebird magic." I rub my thumb back and forth over the edge of his silk waistcoat. "The dragon scales inked on your skin announce your presence before you enter a room, sending a huff of hot breath down the back of my neck."

"And you can't turn this unpleasant awareness off?" Silas dips his head closer to mine like he's trying to read something in my eyes.

"I can block the worst of it with a shield when I'm awake. If I have a relic."

"And when you don't have a relic?"

"Alcohol helps. Rum, whiskey. Anything strong enough to knock me out for a few hours of silence so I can sleep. The pull of magic is difficult for me to ignore. It hurt when they brought the princess's dowry into the Menagerie. I was overcome with a debilitating sense of cold. Like my body was slowly turning to ice. It was the same tonight. I *know* there's a relic in her dowry," I say, daring him to deny it. "I just don't know what kind."

He slides his hands up and down my arms to warm them. "Did you sense anything else besides the cold?"

"No." I don't tell him about the hallucination I had of Queen Marlayna's ghost before I fainted. It isn't the first symptom of madness I've experienced. It certainly won't be the last.

"Do you have enough energy left to summon another shield?"

"Yes."

"Good. You're useless to me if you can't protect yourself from another attack."

"What kind of relic can attack a person?"

"A frost dragon."

My heart skips a beat. "I've studied every bestiary of magical creatures ever written, even ones from kingdoms on other continents. I've never heard of a frost dragon. Where was the relic excavated from?"

"Giants in the Northlands beyond Saracen's borders tell stories of an ancient dragon whose breath could freeze anything it touched."

"Why haven't I heard of such a thing? Surely if it's true, the royal academy would know. They're the foremost authority on dragons."

"Giants are protective of their cultural knowledge. They don't share it with humans. It's not surprising the story hasn't made it into any of your historical records."

"Where did *you* learn about it?"

"I spend a lot of time in the north. How familiar are you with the layout of this wing of the palace?" he asks.

Silas switches thoughts so quickly it takes a beat for my mind to register that he's waiting for me to answer. "It's... used for visiting royals. I've never had a reason to go beyond the Hall of Kings."

His body goes rigid as his gaze snaps to something over my head. "What is it?"

"Your prince is headed this way." Silas shoves me out of his embrace. "Keep him out of the guest wing."

"He's not *my* anything," I whisper-yell at his shadow as it creeps along the wall, leaving me standing alone in an alcove behind one of the gold busts as the last of his warmth evaporates from my body. The bone chilling cold returns as I run my fingers along the feather in my hair and throw up a heat shield to block the frost dragon relic's pull on my senses.

A frost dragon? My fingers twitch with the need to commit the image I have in my mind to paper. I suddenly understand Wallace's eagerness to go on a dig. I would give just about anything to be the first to study the remains of an undocumented magical species.

My chest flutters with excitement. The first bestiary to include such a creature would be printed in every language and sold on every continent. The author's name would be associated with the foremost authorities on magical creatures.

I shove the feeling down with a sigh as I straighten my dress and bustle. King Serros would never approve an exploratory mission in the Northlands, where humans who wander across the border are hunted like game by giants traveling in large hunting parties. Not when you can spit in any direction in the Wastes and hit a relic.

I peek left and right before stepping out from my hiding place a moment before Gideon strides around the corner. How Silas heard him approach, I don't know.

"Everly. What are you doing here?"

"Waiting for you, like you asked."

"You were supposed to wait for me in my mother's chambers."

"You weren't there, so I came here instead." He and I have shared more than one stolen moment in the alcoves behind the sculptures during a ball. The memory brings a flush to my cheeks.

"This hallway is crawling with Saracen guards. You're lucky you weren't caught. Especially wearing that." He takes in the sheer bits of my costume as he slips out of his jacket and moves to wrap it around my shoulders.

I step out of his reach. "What's that supposed to mean?"

"That dress shows nearly all of your skin."

"It's not a dress. It's a masquerade costume."

"What are you even supposed to be?"

"A firebird."

"Well, it doesn't suit you."

"You haven't seen me in over four years. You have no idea what does and doesn't suit me anymore," I say as I plant my hands on my hips.

"You're right. I'm sorry." He raises his hands in surrender, allowing me a good look at the gnarled scar on his hand. "In my head, you're still the same girl you were when I left. I'm caught off guard every time I'm confronted with the woman you've become." He reaches for my hand. I ignore it, and he fists the jeweled hilt of his ceremonial sword instead. "A woman I don't seem to know at all. But I'd like to. I miss my friend. Tell me what I can do to rebuild her trust."

I steel myself against the raw honesty in his blue eyes.

"Do you pay off all your friends' debts, or just the ones you used to fuck?" The words come out harsher than I intend.

"I was trying to help." He doesn't flinch at the wrath in my tone this time, which tells me he's prepared for my reaction. He knew I wouldn't be happy about it, and yet he did it anyway. "I asked around. I know things haven't been easy for you and Adrian these last two years. Settling your debt with Madam Faye was the least I could do after what I put you through."

"You should have asked me first."

"I would have if you'd have shown up at Nymph's like we agreed."

"You mean like you demanded? We didn't agree to anything. You have no authority over me. Besides, you're engaged to another woman. If I meet with you anywhere outside official palace functions, people will talk."

"If it's Dagmara's reaction you're worried about, don't bother. She's made it abundantly clear our union is to be a political alliance and nothing more."

"She said the same to me earlier when she offered to pay me to be your mistress."

The muscle along his jaw flexes. I don't know whether he's angry at the princess's impertinence or because she got to me first. "Everly—"

"I told her no."

Gideon opens his mouth to speak, then shuts it again, like he's not sure what to say. For better or worse, he and the princess are stuck with each other. They may dislike one another right now, but at some point, both kingdoms will require an heir. They'll have children together. A family. I won't be the thing that sabotages any chance they might have of finding happiness.

"I told her my affection isn't for sale. Which is why I'm going to pay you back. With interest."

"I don't care about the damn money. I've wagered and lost more than double that in a single night at Nymph's." There's an edge in his voice that I've never heard before.

"Clearly my pride is as meaningless to you as your father's money." I cross my arms over my chest. "I'm not a wager to be won or lost, Gideon. You say you want to regain my trust, but all you've done is insult me since you came home."

He scrubs his face with both hands. "For fuck's sake, Everly. They say you've been selling death portraits to make ends meet. Paying off your debt was meant as a gift, not an insult."

"I didn't ask for your charity. Madam Faye is a gossipmonger, and now she thinks there's something going on between us. It won't be long before the rest of the city is whispering lies about us being together."

He reaches for my hand again, and this time I let him take it. "I'd be lying if I said I didn't want you at my side. Even though you hate me, you're still the only person I trust."

My stomach tightens into a hard ball. I want to scream at him, tell him I'm the last person he should trust. I've been lying to him for so long I don't even feel guilty about it anymore.

"I don't hate you." It's the only truth I can offer.

"Will you forgive me if I have the royal treasurer send you a promissory note so you can make payments to the crown?"

"It's a start."

Voices float toward us from the guest wing.

"Fuck. That's Gareth, Dagmara's storm summoner. You should go back to the party ahead of me." He grips my hand and drags me down the hall. I'm getting sick of men telling me where to go and what to do.

"Wait, there's something I need you to do." The fire in my chest flares, but I keep pushing. "You can't ask any questions. I just need you to trust me, and I'll explain everything tomorrow."

"Make it quick," he demands as the voices get louder.

"Cancel the dragon boat parade and fireworks show," I say quickly, hoping I don't self-combust. I don't know if Silas will go through with the distraction plan now that the relic is here and not the Menagerie, but I can't take that chance.

"I'll see what I can do."

"Thank you." Guilt twists my stomach as I press up on my toes and kiss his cheek.

Gideon turns and presses his forehead to mine. "You need to go. Gareth can't find us alone like this."

Chapter Thirteen

My faux feather train drags through the peanut shells covering the game room floor as I down my second shot of whiskey and make my way to the dessert cart. I grab a fluffy white divinity and shove it into my mouth before grabbing two more.

The terms of the blood oath were clear. I promised to unlock the wards protecting the dowry. Unfortunately, I neglected to specify *which* wards—the Menagerie's vault, a room in the palace, an armored fucking wagon. There must be at least two hundred conscripted witches patrolling the grounds. That doesn't even include the Saracen soldiers guarding the damn thing.

I stuff two more sugary treats into my mouth at once and wash them down with a glass of champagne from a passing tray. My stomach gurgles as I take a gold-dusted macaron from the display and make my way to the ballroom to find my brother so I can convince him to go home without me. I have no idea what's going to happen now that the plan has changed.

Unfortunately, Adrian isn't where I left him. I spin toward the dance floor and almost lose my balance. Champagne always goes straight to my head. He's not there either. My gaze darts to the terrace doors. I release a slow sigh when I find him engrossed in deep conversation with a middle-aged gentleman wearing an emerald suit and holding an oversized fan made of peacock feathers that matches his mask. His shoulder-length blond hair is pulled back at the nape of his neck.

"My gold mine has been in operation for over a decade without any issues," the man says as I approach. "Now every human sent down the shaft suffers convulsions and temporary paralysis within minutes. I've had to shut down operations, but I'm still contractually obligated to house and feed all the workers. As you can imagine, I'm very eager to find a solution."

"It could be something they're breathing in. I couldn't be sure without studying their symptoms."

"Are you going to introduce me to your new friend, Adrian?" I hook my arm through his to steady myself.

"Everly, yes, sorry. Ambassador Caron, this is my sister. Everly, this is Edgar Caron. He traveled all the way from Saracen with the king."

"That's quite a long journey to make only to attend a ball."

"The late queen was my sister. Princess Dagmara is my niece and relies on my council as the only remaining family on her mother's side. Where she goes, I follow." The goblin-spelled moonstone ring on his pinky finger snags my attention as he flicks his fan. Is it paired with Dagmara's crown? Did she compel her uncle to occupy Adrian so she could corner me alone? Why else would a royal ambassador seek out my brother to discuss a disease outbreak? Surely they have doctors in Saracen.

The phantom kiss of dragon's breath cascades down my neck, commanding my full attention. I resist the urge to glance over my shoulder, knowing exactly who I'll find.

"How are you finding Crecentis thus far, Ambassador?" I ask a little too loudly. "I trust you've received a warm welcome?"

"Warm, indeed." He fans his face. "I feel like I'm standing next to a blast furnace in one of my factories every time I step outside. One can barely escape the oppressive heat even when the sun fades."

"I hope you won't judge us too harshly based on our heavy air." I focus on enunciating each word. "Crecentis is a wonderful city once you acclimate to the heat and humidity."

"I don't understand why you don't jump in the lake to cool off." He waves a manicured hand toward the terrace overlooking Lake Largeau.

"I imagine their reluctance has something to do with the alligators that lurk beneath the surface," Silas looks like a dark god in a black-on-black suit that must have been tailor made.

It's not fair for a man to be this fucking beautiful.

"They say," he continues, "that alligators are the descendants of dragons who fell from the sky and lost their fire when they plunged into the swamps."

"I'm afraid you've been egregiously misinformed, sir. There's no fossil evidence to suggest that alligators had an ancestor with wings or magic in its bones."

Silas raises a dark brow. "Then I shall have to defer to your expertise on monsters, madam, since it seems to be far greater than mine." He drags his dark gaze over me before turning toward the ambassador. "Everything is prepared for your departure tomorrow, Ambassador Caron."

"Excellent. Thank you, Mr. Drake."

"Drake?" I ask, glancing between them.

"Where are my manners?" Ambassador Caron says. "Allow me to introduce you to Silas Drake, my private security consultant. This is Dr. Thorne and his sister, Miss Everly Thorne."

"It's a pleasure to meet you." Silas nods politely to my brother and takes my offered hand, pressing a kiss to my satin-gloved fingers. "Miss Thorne."

"Drake, was it?" I ask with an incredulous grunt. "As in Baby Face Drake, infamous outlaw and a self-proclaimed king of the Wastes?"

"Every orphan born in the Wastes takes the name Drake," Silas says as he slides his thumb over my knuckles before releasing my hand.

"A lucky moniker, if you ask me." The ambassador plucks four crystal champagne coupes from the servant's tray and hands one to each of us. "I haven't had a single shipment go missing in the two years since I hired him."

"That hardly seems possible," I say as I roll the stem of my glass back and forth between my fingers. "The Menagerie loses nearly half of our relic deliveries coming in from the dig sites, and they're escorted by the royal army."

"The army convoys would suffer far fewer losses if they stopped sending their shipments by rail on a predictable schedule and route." Silas's goblin-spelled ring catches the light as he takes a sip of his champagne.

My chest burns as I open my mouth to ask how he knows the Perdanthian Army's shipment schedule, but the words turn to ash in my throat. I take a gulp of the bubbly wine instead.

Ambassador Caron leans in conspiratorially. "Mr. Drake travels under the cover of darkness and never takes the same route twice. He and his crew have yet to lose a single haul from a reaver raiding party."

"You must sleep well at night knowing your assets are so well protected from thieves, Ambassador." I glare at Silas over the rim of my glass.

"Indeed," Ambassador Caron says. "Though I find my sleep troubled of late by how much the mining blight is costing me."

The music slows its boisterous pace. Adrian and the Ambassador resume their conversation about the mystery illness.

"Dance with me." Silas holds out his hand.

I shift closer to Adrian and slip my arm through his. "My apologies, Mr. Drake, but I'm afraid my brother and I were about to leave."

"*It wasn't a request,*" Silas says through the bond.

I open my mouth to tell him I don't take orders from reavers, but the words stick in my throat.

"You can't steal your brother away just yet, Miss Thorne," Ambassador Caron says. "We're discussing the consulting fee I'm willing to pay if he can advise me on how to solve the epidemic plaguing my mine workers." He flashes Adrian a warm smile.

"What kind of consulting fee?" I ask.

"A considerable one. I hemorrhage money every day the mines remain closed. I'm eager to—"

"Protect the health and safety of your workers?" I plaster a sweet smile on my face.

"That is the primary concern, of course," Ambassador Caron replies.

"Before I can make a recommendation, I'll need more information." Adrian extracts his arm from my tight grip. "Can you tell me more about the symptoms?"

The only thing he loves more than music is puzzling out the cause of rare afflictions. At least he comes by it honestly. In some ways, it's a blessing my parents' mission casebooks were never found. If Adrian had them, he'd never leave his study.

Silas plucks the glass of champagne from my hand and deposits it on a passing tray.

"*I wasn't finished with that,*" I say in my head.

"*You've had more than enough.*" Silas presses his wide palm against the small of my back. "*We have work to do, and I need you sober.*"

Only a handful of couples remain on the dance floor. The rest have taken advantage of the shift to softer music and gone in search of refreshment.

Silas isn't the kind of man that goes unnoticed in a crowd. Whispers and curious gazes follow us to the center of the dance floor, where he turns me toward him and slides his arm around my waist.

The last man I danced with was my father. Three years ago, in this very same room, during the winter solstice ball. I bite my lower lip to keep it from quivering. I promised myself I wouldn't fucking cry tonight.

"*They're all watching.*" I'm not sure if I say it out loud or just think it as I glance at the crowd.

"Eyes on me."

I lift my gaze to his at the command.

"Let them stare. You're the most beautiful woman in this room, and you're mine tonight, not theirs."

My body flushes with heat. "I don't belong to you, or anyone else."

"We all belong to someone or something."

"Who do you belong to?"

He studies my eyes as if he's checking to see how drunk I am before answering. "The one thing I can't walk away from."

"Let me guess, money? Power?"

"Vengeance."

Silas twirls me around the dance floor with surprising grace. Our bodies move in unison, like he knows exactly how and when I'm going to move. It's hypnotic. I resist the urge to melt into him like I did in the hallway. He's a reaver, a liar, and a thief. He's killed people. I can't allow myself to be lured in by the beautiful façade, especially when he's staring at me like there isn't another person in the room.

"Where are the others?" I ask, a little breathless.

"Thale and Bas are preparing the diversion. Follow my lead and stay close no matter what happens. I need to keep you safe when the masks come off."

He tightens his grip around my waist, holding me in place as I twist to find Adrian.

"Your brother is safe." Silas spins me so my back is against his chest, his hand splayed across my soft stomach, holding me against him as we sway with the music. He nods toward a couple standing near the terrace doors behind Adrian and the ambassador.

I recognize Serin and Val, the fire summoner and healer from Silas's crew, despite their elaborate costumes and feathered masks. Serin glares at me with a vicious smile while Val keeps his eyes on the room.

"They won't let anything happen to him. You have my word."

He spins me around, and we're dancing again.

"You ordered them to protect my brother?" The alcohol has definitely gone to my head. "I don't understand."

"Ambassador Caron pays me a small fortune to ensure his safety when he travels outside Saracen. He and your brother have common interests. It took very little to convince him to seek out Dr. Thorne's company during the ball. Serin and Val are protecting them both."

I stumble over my feet and step on the hem of my dress. Silas pulls me against him to keep me from falling as we stop in the center of the dance floor. I stare up at him as the band continues to play and the other couples swirl in a blur around us. The relic was moved without warning. There hasn't been enough time for Silas to alter his plans or for Val and Serin to find costumes. Which means protecting my brother was part of his plan all along.

"Thank you," I whisper.

"I didn't do it for you. If you can't hold up your end of the bargain, we're all screwed, and I'll lose the most valuable haul of my life. I need your complete focus on the task at hand. You're useless to me in your current state of distraction."

"So it's all about the money for you, after all?"

He leans down and brushes his lips over my ear. "Don't even think about wandering off before midnight. You and I have a date with a warded crate in the guest wing." The music stops, and Silas releases me slowly.

The slurry of alcohol and sugared sweets churns in my stomach as I glance around the room to count the number of guards. My gaze lands on Gideon instead. He's standing to the left of his father's throne, jaw tight.

King Serros stands and steps to the front of the dais and lifts his glass of champagne. "I'd like to propose a toast to the future king of Saracen and his lovely bride-to-be."

Dozens of waiters snake through the crowd, passing out more champagne. The thought of drinking or eating anything else makes my stomach lurch.

Silas takes a glass from a tray as the king addresses the crowd.

"You were all invited here today to celebrate the upcoming union of my son, the Crown Prince of Perdanth and Savior of Fort Netherthorn, to the heir of the Saracen throne."

"She has a fucking name," I murmur under my breath.

"I receive weekly reports from the border," Serros continues. "You know what my generals tell me? They tell me about the growing reaver problem in the Wastes. About the horrible, terrible things that don't get printed in the papers. How they attack our mines and our relic research convoys. Trust me, no one knows more about reavers and the situation in the Wastes than I do."

A few grumbles of agreement roll through the crowd as the king grabs Gideon's burned hand and holds it up to show off the puckered scar.

"My son nearly lost his life in the siege at Fort Netherthorn, and he bears the scars to prove it. Your prince may not be a powerful storm summoner like the first king, but he's proven himself to be just as brave and cunning as Gideon the Great, whose name he bears."

Gideon resumes his military stance when his father finishes using him as a prop—legs apart, shoulders squared, hands clasped behind his back, face and eyes forward. The image of obedience his cruel father demanded and used to beat into him every day. Gideon's jaw flexes over his clenched teeth, the only outward sign of the hatred he bares for his father. How can Dagmara have spent any time with him and not know that Gideon and Serros are nothing alike? They don't even look alike. Where Serros is short in stature with dark hair, Gideon is tall and fair.

"Thanks to my foresight in arranging this marriage and strengthening our ties with our allies in the north," Serros says, "we were able to send those nasty reavers running for their lives. My generals tracked them down, and let me tell you, they aren't so scary without the cowardly death masks they hide behind."

"That's because your men slaughtered every witch they could find in a hundred-mile radius," Silas says under his breath. "Most of whom were too feeble from the burning to have participated in the attack."

A shiver crawls over me as I turn to ask how he knows so much about it. But as I do, I come face to face with the ghost of Tula Krimore, First Queen of Perdanth.

"You're fourteen," she says.

My hand trembles as I pull off my mask and stare at her.

"Fourteen," she repeats frantically. "You need to leave."

I'm definitely going mad. This isn't a memory like the one I had in the Hall of Kings. This is a full-on hallucination. She reaches for me. I take a step back and bump into Silas. The apparition vanishes.

Silas's fingers graze my wrist. "Your heart is racing."

"It's just a little warm in here." I press the back of my hand to my cheek and drop my heat shield.

He grips my elbow and guides me to one of the marble columns that separates the ballroom from the receiving area, where a cross breeze sweeps in from the front entrance.

"Better?" he asks. I'm not naive enough to think he's concerned about me. He's just worried I'm not up to the task.

"Yes," I lie, forcing my attention back to the king's rambling speech.

"Without strong allies, what's happening in the Wastes will seep into our cities. The number of reavers in our midst will continue to grow and threaten our safety and the safety of our women and children."

Silas crosses his arms and leans against the column.

"*I think he means you,*" I say in my head.

Silas cuts me a dark look. "*Would you like me to point out all the moral high ground you're not currently standing on? Put your shield back up.*"

"This is Crecentis. There is no high ground." The words come out of my mouth louder than intended.

The room fills with the soft shuffle of taffeta and silk as annoyed elites turn to scowl in my direction.

King Serros's cold gaze lands on me before continuing to sweep over his audience. "Miss Thorne is right. We need to get tough on these nasty reavers. Show them that crimes against the innocent people of Perdanth will not be tolerated inside or outside our borders. Crimes like the brutal attack on her parents. Now, I know some will say they asked for it, doing business with dangerous criminals, and I won't argue with that. But imagine what the good doctors might have accomplished if the reavers who killed them had been stopped at the border."

I clench my fist, crushing the starched mask in my hand. He has no fucking right to use my mother and father as propaganda. Heat flares in my palm. The acrid scent of singed satin assaults my nose.

Silas moves so quickly I don't realize he's dumped his drink on my hand and hooked my arm around his to hide my ruined mask and glove until he's ushering me toward the terrace doors.

"Everly, are you all right?" Adrian asks as we approach.

"She's fine. Just needs a bit of air," Silas says as my brother takes a step toward us.

Adrian's eyes glisten. He doesn't care for the king's speech any more than I do, he's just better at hiding it.

I touch his elbow with my free hand. "I'm okay. Mr. Drake offered to escort me to the terrace, and I promised to bore him with more facts about ancient beasts and their bones." I add the last bit to keep Adrian from pressing his concern. We don't ever talk about our parents' deaths. In fact, we avoid it at all costs and distract ourselves by obsessing over medicine and relics.

Adrian nods, and Silas shuffles me outside to the empty terrace overlooking the dragon boats. Some have already been lit in preparation for the parade.

Val and Serin shift positions to block the doors behind us. My palm throbs as Silas peels the ruined glove down my arm. His featherlight touch makes my skin pebble.

"When was the last time you took the nerve tonic?" He runs his thumbs over the outside of my palm, careful not to touch the tender scar.

"This morning."

Silas sets my hand in my lap and reaches into his pocket. He pulls out a glass vial like the ones in Adrian's medicine cabinet. "You've overdosed yourself on firebird magic. You're lucky you didn't self-combust. Drink this. It'll dampen the power until you can burn it off." There's an annoyed edge in the demand.

I take the bottle and sniff the contents before tipping my head back. The tonic is stronger than the one I'm used to. It burns my sinuses and makes my eyes water.

"Now reset your fucking shield."

"How can you tell it's not up?"

"Because I can hear all your damn thoughts. I have to work harder to block them when you're not using a shield."

"Why can't I hear yours?" I lean against the marble balustrade as the gentle waves of Lake Largeau slap against the sandy beach. My chest tightens as I fill my lungs with the faintly fishy air that reminds me of digging for clams with my parents and steaming them over a campfire every summer when we traveled up the Red River that separates Perdanth's western border from the Wastes.

Silas crosses his arms. "You hear what I choose to project through the bond. The rest are warded."

"Against me?"

"Against everyone I share a blood oath with."

I nod at Val and Serin's backs. "I thought you didn't keep secrets from your crew."

"No one should ever have unfettered access to your mind. To see the dark, twisted truths that fuel your fears and desires. The ones you can't even name. The temptation to use them to manipulate you and take what they want is difficult to deny."

"A thief with trust issues? How surprising."

I suck in a breath as Silas closes the distance between us and cages my throat with a gentle grip. He drops his gaze to my mouth. "It's not about trust. It's about greed, and I'm a very greedy man. There's no limit to the things I want to take from you."

A fire ignites low in my belly as he bends until our lips are nearly touching. His warm breath is laced with the sweet scent of cloves. I part my lips, anticipating the decadent taste of him.

"I could steal a kiss right now, and you wouldn't do anything to stop me because you're already thinking about it, aching for it, aren't you, little spark? Even after everything I've told you."

I lean forward and capture his bottom lip, letting it drag between my teeth as I call his bluff. "*How far are you willing to go to make your point, reaver?*" I ask in my head.

"Don't tempt me. You have no idea what I want to do to you right now."

"Enlighten me."

Silas tightens his grip on my throat, sending my pulse into a gallop as he brings his mouth to my ear. "If I snap your neck, no one will hear you scream."

"Do it. Put me out of my misery," I taunt, knowing he won't. The manipulative bastard wouldn't have sworn a blood oath to me if he didn't need my unique set of skills. I'm safe until it's fulfilled.

He shoves away from me. "Pull up your fucking shield and stay close to Ambassador Caron." Silas stalks back into the ballroom, leaving me alone in the dark.

I rebuild my wards and wait for my pulse to settle before venturing inside.

Serin gives me a murderous look as I brush past her to join my brother and Ambassador Caron. My gaze drifts to the opposite side of the room, where Silas leans casually against the wall near the exit to the Hall of Kings. The corner of his mouth curls with a triumphant smirk, as if he didn't just threaten to kill me. I force my attention back to Serros, who's still rambling on.

"Three months from today, you're all invited back to this room to witness Gideon and the princess of Saracen exchange vows and unite our kingdoms."

Gideon's head snaps toward his father in surprise as guests clap excitedly. Princess Dagmara leans down and whispers in her father's ear. He nods in approval and pats her on the hand. If she's surprised by the announcement, she doesn't show it.

King Serros motions for the crowd to settle down. He's clearly not done talking.

"That windbag can't possibly have any more to say," Ambassador Caron mutters before holding up his empty champagne glass and raising his voice. "To Dagmara and Gideon, long may they reign." The crowd cheers. Crystal glasses clink throughout the room.

Dagmara helps her father stand from the throne that will soon be hers. Pox scars speckle his round face, marking him as a survivor of the red plague. They say he was a powerful storm mage in his youth. His gray eyes are clouded and his body hunched like an elderly man's, even though his blond hair hasn't yet gone completely gray. He's lived longer than most witches cursed with the burning.

"Before we begin the celebrations, my father would like to say a few words."

All eyes are on the northern king as he proposes another toast. I follow the princess's gaze to her guard, Gareth. She gives him a subtle nod, and he disappears through the door to the guest wing.

"*Stay close to Serin,*" Silas says through the bond as he follows Gareth into the hall.

Chapter Fourteen

Adrian makes room for me at his side as King Otto thanks Serros for hosting the ball during Festivalla.

"I've always been curious about the spectacle," Otto says. "We don't have anything like it in Saracen."

"Perhaps we'll bring the tradition to the north once our countries are united." Serros raises his glass.

Dagmara smiles sweetly at Serros. "With all due respect, Your Royal Highness, as queen, I would never dishonor my people by forcing them to participate in a month-long spectacle of drinking and debauchery to celebrate the dragon who reduced our armies to ash and burned every farm and village along our southern border."

An uncomfortable silence blankets the room. Serin and Val shift closer to the ambassador. They're both focused on the ballroom's grand entrance, as if they're waiting for something to happen.

Two Saracen soldiers stand guard at every exit. Dozens more clad in green tunics and gold masks linger casually throughout the room. There isn't a single purple uniform in the crowd. All the palace guards are outside, patrolling the grounds and keeping the throngs of gawkers from breeching the gates.

"Princess Dagmara is right," Gideon says. "Our shared history is bloody. While I won't apologize for the actions of my ancestors, it is my belief that we're stronger standing together as one against our enemies."

"I think you mean *your* enemies," Dagmara says. "Saracen doesn't need help protecting its borders. Our country hasn't been attacked in over two centuries. Our last enemy was a Krimore king and his fire-breathing beast."

"A rift we are eager to rectify," Serros says. The twitch of muscle along his jaw is the only evidence of his seething rage. "When our countries are unified, we can eradicate the reaver problem for good."

One of the masked Saracen guards coughs to cover an incredulous grunt. The gold buttons on his tunic strain over his middle. I glance at the other guards. None of their uniforms seem to fit properly. Something isn't right.

"While I appreciate the sentiment," Dagmara says, "my people need assurances that the past will not repeat itself."

"Is my son's promise to make you his wife and future queen not enough of a guarantee?" Serros asks.

"Betrothal agreements aren't exactly binding here in Perdanth." Dagmara's gaze swings toward me. "I'm afraid the people of Saracen require proof of the prince's commitment before we exchange vows. As do I." She gestures to the grand entrance.

Gareth clears a wide path through the center of the ballroom. Three witches float a goblin-spelled iron crate large enough to cage a person.

Where the fuck is Silas? My new firebird feather is much stronger than the pitiful bit of down I'm used to. The heat shield blocks every phantom sensation, including the tickle of hot breath along the back of my neck, making it impossible to pinpoint where the shadowy bastard is lurking without dropping my protective ward.

My gaze slides over a head of copper curls. I do a double take as the lanky man in a wolf mask nudges his companion. Bas lifts his mask and flashes me a wide smile. His companion's reaver tattoos are hidden beneath the high neck of his tuxedo, but there's no mistaking Thale, Silas's storm summoner.

They're supposed to be outside setting up the explosives. Why are they wearing tuxedos? Silas's entire crew is here. In the ballroom. Waiting for something.

One by one, the Saracen guards in ill-fitting uniforms take off their gold masks. I recognize several of their faces—the want-to-be reavers I followed into Chopping Bottom. Where I saw Thale that same night.

Silas's words from earlier ring through my head. *I need to keep you safe when the masks come off.*

They're not Saracen guards. They're fakes, and I'm pretty sure they're the distraction.

My stomach drops. I need to get Adrian out of here.

"I'm not feeling well," I say to my brother, hating myself for the lie I know will get his attention. "Can we take a stroll in the gardens?"

"Of course." Adrian makes his apologies to the ambassador. I ignore the warning flare in my chest as I tug him across the empty dance floor. It's the shortest distance to the receiving area where we came in. We just need to make it outside. The grounds are crawling with real palace guards. All I have to do is scream fire, and they'll come running.

"Create a perimeter," Gareth shouts, pushing people out of the way with a wall of wind as the witches carrying the armored crate set it down in the center of the room, blocking our path. "No one crosses this line."

Adrian and I are forced back with the crowd craning their necks to get a look at Princess Dagmara's dowry.

"Everly Thorne, is that you?" Something sharp pokes my ribs as I turn toward the sultry feminine voice. Serin pulls me into a hug, pressing the tip of a knife into my bodice. "I hope you're not trying to leave. The party is just getting started."

She keeps her arm around me as I pull away, holding the knife to my back.

"We were just headed to the garden to take some air."

"Come, stand with me by the terrace. There's an excellent view and a steady breeze."

"That's very kind, but—"

"I insist," Serin says.

"Adrian, you don't mind if I skip the stroll to catch up with my friend, do you?" I scratch my scalp, letting my fingers graze the feather in my hair, pulling the latent magic into my body.

"I thought you weren't feeling well."

"I'm fine. You know how champagne goes straight to my head." The only other living thing I've ever built a shield around, aside from myself, is Pig. Unlike my feral cat, Adrian doesn't hiss or try to bite me as I squeeze his arm and weave a protective ward around his body.

The hasty shield won't stop a stray bullet, but it will deflect one or two direct attacks from a fire or storm summoner before fizzling out. It's the only protection I can give him.

He presses the back of his hand to my forehead. "Are you sure? You're quite warm."

"It's just the excitement. You should finish your conversation with Ambassador Caron. He seemed disappointed when I dragged you away.

I'm sure it will be far more interesting than listening to us catch up on court gossip." Manipulating my brother is the last thing I want to do, but it's the only way to keep him safe. "It would be nice to have at least one client who can afford to pay."

"He did seem keen on discussing a fee."

"I'll come find you when I'm ready to leave," I say.

Serin tucks the small dagger between her breasts as Adrian walks away.

"Was that really necessary?" I ask.

"Just following orders to keep you alive."

"You and your boss need to get your stories straight. He told me he wanted to snap my neck not thirty minutes ago."

"What we want and what we need are often different things, girl." She grabs my arm. "Let's go. You can't see anything from the back of the room. Silas wants you up front where you can study the wards around the crate."

Serin elbows her way to the front of the crowd until we're standing at the edge of the perimeter near the dais. The iron crate sits alone in the center of a thirty-foot circle.

"I would like to offer a gift to the crown prince," Dagmara says. "It was given to me two years ago by the queen of giants at Saracen's bicentennial as a symbol of her commitment to continued peace between our people. They don't cross the border to hunt, and we don't dig for relics on their land without permission.

"I will give you the same warning Queen Isola gave me along with this gift. When exceptional power is laid at a man's feet, he will do one of three things. Protect it, use it to his own advantage, or destroy it." The princess nods to the witches who brought in the crate. "Gideon

Krimore, this is not a dowry. It is my betrothal gift to you. What you choose to do with it will tell me everything I need to know about the kind of ruler you have the potential to be and whether you are worthy of sharing my throne."

The Saracen witches raise their hands to unlock the wards. I watch closely, memorizing the patterns. They float the lid off, revealing a soft blue glow from the open top. Whispers echo through the room.

I glance over my shoulder to check on Adrian. The way Ambassador Caron smiles proudly at his niece and doesn't seem the least bit surprised tells me he's seen this treasure before. Is that why Silas sought him out, or did he learn about the frost dragon relic after Caron hired him?

Where are you, reaver?

Part of me hopes Silas got caught and is being hauled away in irons. Though that won't release me from the oath, not unless they kill him. The fire in my chest flares at the thought. I wish I was that lucky.

The Saracen witches unlock the final ward, and all four walls of the crate clatter to the floor. My heart skitters. The room goes silent in collective shock.

"It's an egg," someone yells as snow falls in the column of air above the dragon egg.

It doesn't look like any petrified relic I've ever seen. The egg is nearly the size of the rum barrels in the Duck's storeroom. Three feet high and thicker around the middle. Pale blue overlapping scales the size of my hand shimmer with an iridescent sheen where they catch the light.

"It's not a relic." My voice is barely a whisper. "It's a dragon."

"Kill the Krimore king," one of the fake guards in an ill-fitting uniform shouts as he pulls a reaver death mask over his face and charges across the dance floor.

The sound of cracking ice cuts through the room. The fake guard's cry of pain chokes off as he freezes mid stride. His body shatters like glass. Bloody red shards spill outward across the floor, and the room erupts into chaos.

"Seize the guards. They're impostors," Gareth shouts.

Elites scream and shove each other out of the way to get to the exits as the rest of the fake guards charge toward the dais.

"Stay down." Serin pushes me out of the way as a flare flies past my head and slams into the magical shield protecting the king.

My knees smack the floor. I scoot back against the front of the dais on my ass.

Gideon draws his sword and steps in front of his father.

"That man is stealing your glory," Serros says as he sips his champagne. I track his line of sight to the back of the room, where Silas is cutting down one fake guard after another with a pair of shadow blades. "Get out there before you lose your reputation as the hero of Crecentis to a fucking shadow summoner."

Gideon leaps off the left side of the dais and guts a fake guard before he can launch a flare at the throne. Static crackles over my head as Gareth strikes three at once with a bolt of forked lightning.

"You're not where I left you. Do I need to teach you a lesson in following orders?" Silas's voice fills my head, dimming the clangor of screams and clash of weapons. Tendrils of dark smoke trail behind his ebony blades as he crosses them, lopping off a guard's head. The dead man's severed neck sizzles like meat on a hot spit as his body crumples to the floor.

"You promised not to kill anyone," I say in my mind. *"How are you getting around the oath?"*

A cocky smile breaks across his face as he shoves a dark blade through another fake guard's gut. The man's flesh catches fire where Silas drags the weapon through muscle and bone, splitting him open from stomach to shoulder.

"*I promised not to kill anyone unless it was to save your life. These reavers have orders to kill your king. You're the one who placed yourself between them and the throne.*"

My hands twitch with the urge to strangle him.

"*Serin dragged me over here on your orders. Why did you change the plan without telling me?*"

"*This was always the plan.*" The bastard smiles as he cuts through another fake guard. "*Layla told me about your ingenious little gambling scheme. How it took her months to figure out how you were cheating her system. She warned me not to trust you with anything I couldn't afford to lose, and she was right. Feeding you a fake plan was the real test. You failed when you asked your prince to cancel the fireboat parade.*"

"*How do you know about that?*"

"*I told you. I can read every fucking thought that runs through your mind, princess.*"

"Who is that man?" Serros asks, taking another sip of his champagne as if this is all part of the evening's entertainment.

"I believe he's in Ambassador Caron's employ," King Otto says, equally unconcerned atop the warded dais.

"Summoning magic is a hangable offense for civilians in this country."

"As part of the royal family, my uncle and anyone in his employ have diplomatic immunity," Dagmara says. "I'll make sure my uncle compensates the crown for any damages caused by his private security team."

Two more fake guards cross the perimeter around the dragon egg and make a run for the dais. Their bodies freeze and shatter like the first.

"That's the real ward you'll need to unravel." Silas's voice cuts through my mind again as he kicks a smoldering body off his blade. *"What do you make of it?"*

Frost creeps across the floor surrounding the dragon egg, stopping a few inches from my feet. My fingertips prickle with cold as I reach out, searching for the threads. There's nothing there. No discernible pattern to unravel. Just pure, undiluted magic.

"I've never seen anything like this before. I don't think I can break it. Not without studying it."

"Study quick, before they reseal the crate."

"I think you've overestimated my abilities, reaver."

A flare slams into the floor next to me. My feathery train ignites. Fire consumes the gossamer fabric as I struggle to untie the ribbon securing it to my waist. The flames singe my legs as I kick it off. I scramble to my feet and back toward the dancefloor, away from the dais.

The frost dragon's magic hums against my skin, eating through the heat shield protecting my body. My movements slow as the cold sinks into my bones. The skin and muscles along my bare back freeze. I can't move my shoulders or arms. Something crunches beneath my foot. I don't have to look down to know I'm standing on top of the frozen and shattered remains of three bodies.

I crossed the perimeter. A skin-splitting pain lashes my back, accompanied by the soft sound of cracking ice.

I'm going to die. I'm going to shatter like the others.

My chest tightens with the realization. How many nights did I lie awake and hope for this over the last two years? Beg the gods of the Otherworld to take the pain away when I didn't have the courage to do it myself?

Shadows rip through the room, killing the remaining fake guards.

The ballroom goes quiet.

"Everly, please. I'm begging you. Don't take another step."

"Gideon?" My breath freezes in the air.

He reaches for me from the edge of the perimeter. "Come back this way. It's just a few steps."

It's no use. I can't move.

"Tell Adrian I'm sorry." My voice trails off as frost burns its way down my throat. Sharp tears crystallize at the corner of my eyes.

"Close the fucking crate," Silas growls as he shoves his way to the frost line and stops. Snow catches in his dark hair, melting instantly.

The Saracen witches lift their hands. Metal clangs together behind me, enclosing the egg in its warded iron casket, suppressing the deadly magic.

It's too late. The damage is already done.

"Don't you dare die on me, little spark. I'm not finished with you yet." Shadows explode across the space between us and coil around me. He reappears in front of me.

"Fix her. Now." Silas barks the order at someone over my shoulder as my knees give out and I collapse against him. Heat radiates from his body as he sweeps my hair away from my back, cradling my head against his chest.

The color drains from Gideon's face as he approaches from the side, staring at my back. "I'm going to enjoy destroying that fucking egg."

"No, don't hurt it." I try to reach for him, but my body refuses to cooperate. I scream as it jerks the wrong way, sending another skin-splitting pain across my shoulders.

"Hold her still," Val says. "You know how fucking painful this shit is to come by. I don't have enough to dose her twice if her frozen flesh keeps cracking open."

"Is that alicorn powder?" Adrian asks from somewhere behind me.

"This is gonna hurt like a bitch. Make yourself ready."

"Just fucking do it," Silas growls, tightening his grip around me as his voice softens, filling my head. "*Take a deep breath for me and hold it while I count backward from ten. By the time I get to one, it will be done. I promise.*"

A shallow breath is all I can manage before my back explodes with a fiery pain. I claw at Silas's back as my vision closes in.

"*Ten. You asked me about my family last night.*"

It feels like Val is rubbing hot glass into my open wounds.

"*Nine. I don't remember my father.*"

I grit my teeth against the burning sensation crawling across my skin. It's a thousand times worse than the flame that seared the blood oath into my veins.

"*Eight.*" Silas's voice is strained, as if this is as painful for him as it is for me. "*I watched a storm summoner murder my mother.*"

"Make it stop," I hiss through my teeth.

"*Seven. I was young and hadn't come into my magic yet. There was nothing I could do to save her.*"

Silas strokes my hair.

"*Please,*" I beg silently, no longer able to form words.

"Six. I've spent a long time exacting my revenge on the people responsible for her death."

"It's working." Val pulls his hand away. The pain flares as my skin knits back together.

"Five. It never feels as good as you hope it will, taking someone's life."

I groan as I grind my face against his chest.

"Four. You do it over and over again, hoping things will change. That you'll fucking feel something other than rage so you can finally stop."

Tears spill down my cheeks. I'd give anything not to feel any of it.

"Three. No matter how many years go by, nothing ever changes. So you hunt down the biggest, scariest beast you can find and pick a fight. Maybe it will be your last. After you beat the shit out of each other, he makes you an offer you can't refuse. He swears a blood oath to put you out of your misery the next time you lose yourself to the darkness. In exchange, you have to help him with a little job."

The fire lessens to a throbbing ache.

"Two. I learned to be more specific with the words I chose when swearing blood oaths after that. Thale still likes to zap me with a little lightning and bring me back to myself when my shadows take control."

A tingling sensation spreads across my skin as the pain recedes. My body floods with decadent warmth as I take a deep breath and melt into the beautiful nightmare holding me.

"It's done," Val says. You've impressed me, Miss Thorne. I've seen battle-hardened warriors with less devastating wounds who couldn't take the pain as well as you."

Silas brushes the hair away from my face as his voice caresses my mind. *"Pain deserves to be rewarded with pleasure. Any time you want me to show you how good magic can feel, all you need to do is ask."*

"Let me go."

Silas releases me reluctantly. He's right. No one should have access to a person's deepest held secrets and desires. He's seen mine and knows how to use them against me. Like distracting me with that little story about losing his mother to make me think we're the fucking same. Or tempting me with all the depraved things I've imagined him doing to me in the dark.

"How does it feel?" Adrian asks, gently inspecting my back.

"Itchy." My voice is still raw from the frost that burned my throat.

Serros, Dagmara, and the king of Saracen are all watching me. Everyone except Silas, who's having a quiet conversation with the ambassador, as if nothing out of the ordinary just happened. As if he didn't just save my life.

My brother tests my newly repaired skin. "It's remarkable. I've read about the healing power of unicorn horns to treat contagions and combat poison, but I've read nothing about its ability to do this. The fissures split through muscle right down to your bone. It didn't even leave a scar."

Gideon sloughs off his jacket with a scowl and drapes it around my shoulders as if he can't bear to look at my back without seeing the damage. I allow it. There's a familiar comfort in having him close, and I'm too exhausted to protest.

"Remarkable indeed," King Serros says, descending the dais as he surveys the room, his tone deceptively light. Never a good sign. His audience of elites has fled. The once pristine ballroom is littered with dead bodies. A dark stain creeps across the white floor where the frozen and bloody shards of three people are starting to melt. "How fortunate we are to have had a royal healer on hand to save Miss Thorne. Though I don't recall King Otto giving the order. Alicorn powder is an extremely rare commodity and reserved for the emergency treatment of the royal family only. Would someone please explain to me why it was wasted on this woman with common blood?"

"It's my fault, Your Majesty," Ambassador Caron says, stepping forward. "The healer works for me. I assumed Miss Thorne was on the list as the crown prince's mistress. I gave the order."

Why does everyone in this city assume I'm fucking Gideon?

"Because I paid Layla Faye to spread the rumor. Thought you might need a plausible alibi when this is over."

"Stay out of my head, reaver."

The corner of his perfect mouth curls.

"An understandable mistake, Ambassador." Gideon gives Dagmara a pointed look. "What I want to know is how the attackers got their hands on Saracen uniforms. And why the fuck did we open that monstrosity in a ballroom full of people?" He swings his arm toward the iron crate.

"It's not a monstrosity," I rasp. "It's a frost dragon from the Northlands."

"It's a weapon that needs to be destroyed."

"What? No." The words scratch out of my throat. "You can't. Gideon, please. Dragons have been extinct for over two hundred years. Now we have evidence that there might still be a mating pair out there somewhere. We need to study the egg. Figure out if it's viable, and if so, why it hasn't hatched. You can't destroy it."

"That thing killed three people. It almost killed you."

"How many people did you kill today, Your Royal Highness?" Dagmara asks.

"That's not the point," Gideon growls.

"*Seven. To my thirty-three.*" Silas smirks and I ignore the unwanted intrusion of his voice inside my head.

"The young woman is right," King Otto says. "There are many in the north who oppose this alliance due to old wounds and our history with Perdanth. We revealed the egg publicly to ensure that history doesn't repeat itself."

"*The only thing that stunt ensured is that every damn reaver from here to the Wastes will be coming after it,*" Silas says across the bond.

"If you would like to secure the alliance, I require proof that your son is worthy of my daughter's hand in marriage and all that comes with it," King Otto says. "The prince must travel to the Northlands and hunt down the beast that laid this egg as a gesture of good faith that a dragon will never terrorize Saracen again."

My stomach twists. The alcohol and sugary treats I consumed earlier threaten to come back up. This can't be happening.

"You want to send me on an expedition into the Northlands, where humans are hunted for sport?" Gideon asks Dagmara.

"It seems we finally understand each other, Your Royal Highness."

"This is just another delay tactic," Serros barks. "We need to solidify the alliance now. They should have been wed two years ago when the betrothal papers were signed."

I'm still processing the northern king's outrageous demand when Silas steps forward.

"I'd be happy to offer my assistance with the hunt, Your Majesty." Silas bows to the king. "I've spent a great deal of time in the Northlands. I know it well and have considerable experience tracking down things that don't want to be found. If you allow me to use the relic as bait,

I can ensure the crown prince completes his quest before his wedding three months from now.”

“And take all the credit, of course?” Serros asks. “The first king of Perdanth was a monster hunter. His ruthless ambition earned him the people’s adoration and a throne. Yet you ask for nothing in return. It makes me wonder what you hope to gain.”

Silas dips his head with a smirk. “I have no interest in fame. I prefer my quiet life. But I’d be lying if I told you I don’t have my sights on something bigger.” His gaze flicks to mine. “The prince can take credit for the kill. I want the beast’s carcass as payment.”

Greedy fucking bastard. He wants to steal the egg and take the dragon’s bones for himself.

I open my mouth to protest, but the words stick in my throat as the ember in my chest flares. Fine. I steal Silas’s words instead. The ones he put into my head.

“You’ve just revealed the existence of a new species of dragon to the world. Every reaver from Perdanth to the Wastes will come after the dragon egg. It’s safer here, in the Menagerie’s vault, where it can be protected and studied.”

“*Not helpful.*” Silas pins me with a murderous glare.

“She’s right.” Gideon runs a hand through his hair the way he does when he’s thinking about doing something foolish. Like trying to live up to his ancestor’s fucking heroics. “Only half of the relic convoys we send back from the wastes make it. I’ll need an army to move that thing safely.”

“An army convoy is too conspicuous,” Silas says. “I recommend a small crew that can travel quickly and quietly under the cover of darkness so they don’t attract attention from reavers or parties of hunting giants. Of course, the prince would need to pay his respects to Queen Isola to gain permission to hunt on her land. I understand she's invited many foreign dignitaries to the opening of Prince Aeroc's new Menagerie next month."

Serros folds his hands behind his back. "I understand this man is currently in your employ, Ambassador Caron?"

The ambassador flicks his fan open, stirring the threads of magic around his goblin-spelled ring. "Drake has been with me for years. He oversees the shipments from my mines in the Wastes. I've never lost a convoy under his protection. There's no one I trust more with my gold or my life."

My throat goes dry. The ambassador—uncle and adviser to the future queen of Saracen and possibly Perdanth—is clearly under Silas's control. I don't know what kind of game the shadow summoner is playing, but there's no way I'm letting the bastard win. Heat flares in my chest. I'll let the blood oath burn me alive before I help him hunt down and kill a magnificent beast.

"Your Majesty?" I soften my voice and slip on the mask of obedience I wore for most of my life inside these walls. Don't be too loud. Don't speak until spoken to. Smile and pretend to be a pretty accessory. It's what Serros expects. What his fragile ego won't feel threatened by.

"Yes, Miss Thorne?" Serros says, a thread of exasperation hardening his voice.

"It occurs to me that this is a historic moment. One that should be recorded for posterity. Would it not be wise to send a scribe to record the prince's quest? Someone close to the crown to ensure Gideon's heroism is portrayed *favorably* when the story is printed in every newspaper in Saracen and Perdanth?"

"Are you volunteering yourself, Miss Thorne?"

"It would be an honor to serve the crown in any way that I can, Your Majesty. I must admit that my motivations are somewhat selfish as well," I say, forcing a submissive posture, head down, gaze fixed on the tattered and singed remains of my hem. "It would give me time to study the dragon egg and prepare a full report on what it's capable of."

"*What do you think you're doing, princess?*" Silas growls through the bond.

"*Stop calling me that. I have a fucking name.*"

King Serros smooths his short beard as he studies the smoldering carnage on the ballroom floor, the majority of which was caused by Silas and his shadow blades.

"Your witch is a skilled fighter, Ambassador Caron. I'll give him that. If he's as good as you say, I'm surprised you're willing to part with him."

The ambassador clears his throat. "I've been forced to shut down my mining operations indefinitely due to unforeseen circumstances. The issue will take some time to resolve. I don't have any shipments that need protection at the moment. I have no work for Mr. Drake and would be willing to loan him out temporarily."

"Queen Isola invited me to attend the unveiling of the new Menagerie next month," Serros says. "Gideon, you'll go in my place. Find out where she got the egg. Give the shadow summoner a temporary commission in your Elite Guard and put him in charge of securing it during the journey. And take Miss Thorne with you. I want to know everything about my new weapon."

CHAPTER FIFTEEN

The new skin across my back feels too tight as I pull a pillow over my head and attempt to fall back into the shadowy caress of my dream.

Pig meows, telling me I forgot to leave my balcony door open a crack so he can escape and hunt for his breakfast. The grumpy tabby can wait. There's no fucking way I'm getting out of my bed before noon. Not after the night I had.

He starts to purr loudly. I've never heard the feral beast purr. I force my eyes open.

"I like your pet," Serin says from the chair in the corner of my room where Pig is curled up on her lap.

"How did you get in here?"

"The door was open." Her lazy gaze swings to the balcony.

"What do you want?"

"To lay in bed with my lover all day, but I must have angered the Mother of Fire because I'm stuck babysitting you for the duration of the journey north. Silas blames me for your dimwitted stumble into the egg's deadly ward. I have orders to escort you to the docks within the hour. Now get your ass up and start packing."

"Tell your boss I don't answer to him or you. The military transport doesn't leave until sunset. The only way I'm getting out of this bed is if Silas shows up and drags me out of it himself."

"That shouldn't be difficult to arrange, seeing as he's downstairs with Ambassador Caron and your brother."

"What?" Pig hisses and scampers under the bed as I bolt upright.

"Apparently, the ambassador has made your brother an offer of employment at his mining outpost in the Wastes. They're negotiating terms as we speak."

My feet thump against the wood floor as I barrel out of bed and down the stairs to my brother's study, only to find Silas standing guard outside the door.

"Move."

"Why would I do that?" Silas crosses his arms. The all-black battle witch uniform marking him as a member of the Elite Guard stretches over his shoulders as if it's a size too small. It would look comical on another man. On Silas, it just enhances his muscular physique.

"I need to speak to my brother. He and I are partners. I advise him on all business matters."

"Are you in the habit of conducting business in your nightclothes, Miss Thorne?" Silas asks as his gaze skims over the thin fabric of my shift.

"It boggles the mind how you were able to convince the ambassador that you're a gentleman."

He leans down and whispers in my ear. "I'm very good at pretending. Now, go back upstairs and start packing."

"This is my home. I'll not let a cocky—"

Silas scoops me up and throws me over his shoulder like a sack of potatoes. Shadows coil around me, choking out light and sound as he marches up the stairs.

"Put me down, or I'll scream," I demand, kicking and twisting to get out of his arms.

Silas tightens his grip, digging his fingers into the back of my thighs. "Scream as loud as you like. No one can hear you when you're inside my shadows."

"I hate you."

"Trust me, princess, the feeling is mutual."

"I have a name, you oversized brute."

"You wouldn't have anything if I hadn't pulled you away from that egg last night. You've been nothing but a pain in my ass since I bound my life to yours. We'd both be dead right now if Val hadn't been there to heal your wounds."

"What are you talking about?"

"You still don't understand how this blood oath works," Silas says as he drops me on my bed. "I swore to protect your life with mine. If you die before the oath is fulfilled, I'll have failed to uphold my end of the deal, and the magic will burn me alive."

"Wait, what are you saying?"

"If you die, I die."

"That wasn't part of the deal. Why would you do that?"

"A regrettable mistake. I told you to keep her on a tight leash," Silas growls at Serin.

"She's as headstrong as a mule."

"Don't let her out of your sight again."

Serin summons a flame to her fingertips as Silas stalks away. "You have thirty seconds to get out of that bed and start packing before I light it on fire and drag you to the docks with nothing more than the clothes on your back. If you want to wear something besides that thin shift for the next three months. I suggest you make haste."

Serin wasn't

<hr>

kidding when she said she'd be watching my every move. She doesn't even bother to turn her back while I relieve myself in the chamber pot and wash up at the basin before changing my clothes.

She follows me to the kitchen and remains silent while I lie to Adrian, telling him it's protocol for the royal historian to have a bodyguard, even in her own damn home. I'm not sure if it makes him feel better or worse about me studying a relic that tried to kill me.

"Are you going to tell me about your visit from Ambassador Caron this morning?" I ask, dropping my overstuffed carpet bag on the kitchen floor.

"He offered me a job."

"When do you leave?"

"I have a house call to make this afternoon," he says as he puts the teakettle on the stove.

"I mean for the Wastes. How much did Ambassador Caron offer to pay you?"

"Not enough to convince me to abandon my patients... or this house. I could never leave Crecentis."

Relief spreads through my body as I grab the edge of the table to steady my shaking hands.

"Before you get angry, you should know he paid me a generous consulting fee to correspond with him by mail."

"I'm not angry, Adrian. I'm so overjoyed I can barely breathe. I don't think I could survive if anything happened to you too."

"How long will you be gone?" he asks, glancing at my bag.

"It's only three months. I'll be back before you have a chance to miss me."

Adrian's brow wrinkles as the words settle around us like a heavy weight.

It's only three months. That was the last thing our parents said to us before they left two years ago.

He stiffens as I throw my arms around his middle and hug him tight. "I'm coming back. I promise. They didn't have a regiment of soldiers to protect them."

"I miss them," he whispers as he relaxes and folds his arms around me. Neither of us has ever said the words out loud. I still can't. Not without ripping the wound open.

"Keep an eye on Pig for me. He likes toast." It's all I can manage to push past the lump in my throat. We both know saying "I love you" is a bad omen. It was the last thing we both said to our parents before they left.

"Toast?" Adrian raises an eyebrow.

"I share mine with him every morning."

"Then I'll share mine with him until you come home." Adrian begrudgingly tolerates Pig, but he knows I adore the contrary beast. His promise is his way of telling me he loves me too.

"I'll write to you when I can."

"We should go, Miss Thorne." There's no impatience or irritation in Serin's tone for once. Just a firm reminder that I have obligations to fulfill—to a ruthless outlaw who owns my body and blood, to a king who won't hesitate to execute me if I betray the crown, and to a brother who can't survive another loss if I fail to keep my promise to come home.

CHAPTER SIXTEEN

A wall of cold air scrapes over my skin as our carriage approaches the river and passes through the outer limit of the frost dragon's power. I pull up a thin shield to dampen the overwhelming sensation. I can't afford to numb my awareness completely. Not while I'm stuck on a boat with two reavers, three hundred battle witches, and a deadly relic that almost killed me.

The horse slows its trot and bucks against its reins, as if it senses the danger. Our driver flicks the lines gently and clucks a soft command, urging the animal forward as it huffs in protest.

White steam billows into the air from the whistle of an elegant six-story cruise ship announcing a boarding call. A flag bearing the Saracen crest flaps above the pilothouse. Its dual black smokestacks and top deck are all that's visible above the grass-covered levee.

I can't see the flat military transport barges that will take us north, but I know the relic is sitting somewhere on the bank, waiting to be loaded.

Serin hops out of the carriage before it comes to a full stop and grabs the worn burgundy carpet bag that has accompanied me on every excursion I've ever taken outside Perdanth. I follow her as she jogs up the steep hill.

She cuts me an annoyed look as I crest the top of the levee, sweaty and out of breath. "You're slower than molasses. We'll need to work on that."

I ignore the comment and scan the muddy riverbank.

Porters scurry up and down the steamship's gangplank, loading crates of supplies. There isn't a military barge or Perdanthian soldier in sight.

"Where's our boat?" I ask.

"You're looking at it."

"I thought we were traveling with the army."

"We are. Your king took Silas's concerns about protecting his new weapon to heart. A unit of palace guards is transporting the empty iron crate to the Menagerie as we speak. No one will suspect Perdanthian soldiers to sail under the Saracen flag or that we're carrying the egg on board."

"And Princess Dagmara agreed to this?"

"I believe it was her idea, at the behest of her uncle after last night's reaver attack. They left an hour ago, disguised as civilians on a merchant barge headed north, escorted by Thale, Val, and Bas. It's a ruse to minimize the risk of reaver attacks as we move upriver."

"Would those be real reaver attacks, or ones staged by a showboating shadow summoner? I'd like to know so I can practice my look of shock and surprise for next time."

Serin grips my arm, digging her nails into my flesh. "Silas saved your life last night. You could at least pretend to be grateful."

I yank away from her and march down the hill. If what Silas said about the blood oath is true, that his life is tied to mine, he didn't pull me away from the dragon egg to save me. He did it to save himself. Everything he does is a calculated manipulation—feeding me a fake plan, the mind games, and the seductive flirtations he has no intention of following through with. Now that I know what I'm dealing with, it'll be easier not to stumble into his little traps.

A porter leads us to our shared room. The narrow space is only slightly larger than the stacked bunks that fold down from the wall. We can't move around it without squeezing past each other.

"I'm taking the top." Serin tosses her bag on the upper bunk. "Let's get back down to the main deck before they load the relic."

I set my bag on the mattress and pull out my nearly full sketchbook before following her into the hall. I'll need to find more paper to record what I learn about the egg.

We make our way to the fifth deck, where three storm summoners in Saracen uniforms float a barrel of rum over the side of the ship. The goblin-spelled iron hoops around the middle ripple with the charm that keeps the deadly magic contained inside.

I wish I'd paid more attention to the metal crate last night to determine whether the entire container is warded or just the locks keeping the walls in place. If these witches drop the barrel and it breaks, everyone within thirty feet will be dead.

We follow the summoners at a safe distance as they move the barrel into the chart room overlooking the observation deck. Glass-front bookcases line the back wall. Gold stars dot the pale blue ceiling. A wall of windows looks out over the front of the ship, giving navigators an arcing view of the river and wide main deck, where a group of conscripted witches in green tunics are clearing the lounge chairs away.

A polished round tabletop missing its base leans against the bookshelves. The storm summoners set the rum cask in the center of the room and place the round tabletop on it, then file the chairs in around it.

"Hiding in plain sight? Whose idea was that?" I ask, rolling my eyes. Everything about this ruse reeks of Silas.

"Mine," Gideon says as he steps through the door on the opposite side of the long room, looking like a dandy in the dark green Saracen uniform with its shiny gold buttons, braided epaulets, and slouchy feathered hat. "When reavers attack our supply trains in the Wastes, they take everything of immediate tangible value, weapons, relics, food. Not once have they bothered to steal a piece of furniture."

"Aren't you going to ward the room?" I ask as the witches file out.

"That would only draw more attention to the fact that we're hiding something," Gideon says. "You'll complete your work here. This chart room is the closest thing we have to an archive, and with its proximity to the deck where the Elite Guard will be running combat drills, it's one of the most secure rooms on the boat. You'll be perfectly safe from reavers if we're attacked."

Serin's mouth twitches like she's trying hard not to smile as Gideon takes an assessing loop around the room. He has no clue the outlaws he thinks he's hiding the egg from are already on board. There has to be a way to warn him without violating the blood oath and getting myself killed.

"How am I supposed to study the egg when it's stuffed inside a barrel?" I fold my arms over my chest.

"Your research will have to wait until we're done with the first leg of our journey north." He fists the hilt of his sword. "I'm not opening that thing until we're back on land and have room to set up a safe perimeter."

"What am I supposed to do for the next three weeks?"

"You'll be spending your time here training with the other new navigators. I've had your uniform delivered to your room."

"Uniform?"

"This is a military deployment, Private Thorne. Once you're changed, report to Major Mattern in the pilothouse. She'll be your commanding officer for the duration of the journey."

I flinch at the stern tone. Gideon has never spoken to me that way. I can't tell whether he's angry with me or attempting to establish some kind of boundary in front of his soldiers.

"Thank you, Your Highness." I bow my head and play along.

"I'm not a prince here, Private Thorne. Call me Colonel Krimore. Get to work. We push off in six hours."

I blink at his retreating form. Two witches, who I assume are his aides, follow as he makes his way to the training deck and gives someone an order before descending the stairs.

"What in the Otherworld just happened?"

"I believe he just gave you an order. Welcome to the army, girl."

⁂

The familiar kiss of hot breath slides down the back of my neck as I follow Serin through a maze of interior stairs and corridors, telling me Silas is somewhere on board.

Everything he does is calculated. He doesn't leave anything to chance. Why would he leave himself vulnerable by binding his life to mine? It wasn't one of my terms. Silas was meticulous about the wording regarding my debts to Madam Faye. It doesn't feel like the kind of mistake he would make.

He's not the only one who regrets our little bargain. I hate the way my gaze drifts to every dark corner, searching for his shadowy presence as we make our way back to our room. I hate the pang of disappointment that washes through me when we don't run into him even more.

As promised, a sleeveless Saracen military tunic and leggings are waiting in a neat pile on my bunk, next to a new sketchbook and full set of colored charcoals. I run my hand over the red leather cover and open it to the first page.

For your research.

The handwritten inscription reminds me of the scrolling calligraphy Gideon and I were forced to practice and perfect by our tutors. His lettering was always impeccable, and I can't help but smile at the thoughtful gift.

"What's that?" Serin eyes the book skeptically.

"Just the supplies I need to record the journey for the historical archives. Would you mind waiting outside while I change?"

"Yes."

"Where am I going to go?" I gesture around the room. "Even if I wanted to escape, I couldn't fit my ass through the tiny porthole window."

"Make it quick. I'll be just outside."

I strip down to my undergarments and tuck my firebird feather into my corset between my breasts before shaking out the green and gold tunic, hoping it will fit.

A letter flutters to the floor, along with a peanut shell. I glance over my shoulder before picking it up and breaking the wax seal.

E—

This letter is an apology for what I've done and for what I must ask you to do. I'm not happy with my father's decision to send you on this deployment. The selfish part of me is thrilled to have you where I can see you every day, even if we can't speak. The other half of me is close to dragging you off this boat and leaving you behind where I know you'll be safe.

As commanding officer, I can't show favoritism to any of my soldiers. Especially you. If the others think I'm taking it easy on you because of our history, they'll haze you all the harder. I can't step in. They'll resent you if I intervene. Fortunately, the navigation squad isn't as brutal as the other units with their initiation tactics. It's a shitty tradition, but it's the only way to maintain control of the chaos.

Watch your back with your bunkmate. I believe she and the shadow summoner are Dagmara's spies. I wouldn't have agreed to bring them on if my father hadn't forced them on me. My future wife would rather see me dead than complete this quest. I fear they'll attempt to sabotage or assassinate me somewhere along the way.

I need you to be my eyes and ears. If you see or hear anything unusual, don't come to me directly. We can't be seen together outside of our normal duties. There's a clerk in the post room they call Hardy. If you need to contact me, give him a letter addressed to your brother without the honorific before his name. The clerk will make sure it gets to me. When you want to write to Adrian, include the Dr. before his name, and it will go out with the mail at the next port.

If you need to speak to me in person, give Hardy the peanut shell, and he'll give you instructions.

Destroy this letter. No one can know that we're communicating.

—G

My heart leaps into my throat as Serin pounds on the door.

"Just a minute."

I slide my fingers over the firebird feather between my breasts and quickly summon a flame. The flare nearly touches the ceiling before it shrinks back. I lean away from the ball of fire in my palm. Black smoke and the acrid stench of burning flesh fills the small room. The letter chars and curls, but it doesn't light right away. Because it's not fucking paper. Gideon's royal stationery is made of high-end vellum.

The door bursts open as the letter finally goes up in flames.

"Burning the boat down won't get you out of the oath," Silas says as his shadows engulf me, sliding over my skin like warm silk before retracting, taking the fire, smoke, and stench away with them. "Care to explain why you're torching your room, princess?"

"I'm practicing so I can throw a flare at your head the next time you call me that." I scowl at my sooty fingertips. When Silas doesn't respond, I glance up and find him staring at me. At my corset and knee-length drawers. I hug my arms over my chest.

"Get out."

"No."

The door lock clicks behind him, and he leans against it.

"I need to change into my uniform."

"Don't let me stop you."

"A gentleman would give me privacy."

"We've already established that I'm not one of those."

"Well, enjoy the view because it's the last time you'll ever see it, reaver." I yank the green tunic off the bunk and pull it over my head.

"I think we both know that's not true either."

I curse the way heat pools low in my belly and remind myself that he's just pretending as I give him my back and tug the tight leggings over my backside. If Silas means any of the seductive things he says to me as anything other than the manipulations they are, he wouldn't have backed down when I called his bluff and dared him to kiss me at the ball.

Chapter Seventeen

Major Mattern's short, tight twists of dark hair don't move as she hefts three oversized chart books onto the round table—each one three feet tall and two feet wide—and flops them open.

"All right, rabbits, can anyone tell me what these are?"

Her voice carries an unexpected air of authority for someone so young. The gold sextant embroidered on her green tunic marking her as a member of the Navigation Squad matches ours. She can't be much older than me, which makes her ancient compared to most of the soldiers onboard.

"Maps?" This comes from a stick-thin girl with frizzy straw-blond curls standing in front of me. Her head barely reaches my shoulder. She, Serin, and I make up the Navigation Squad's newest members.

"Anyone else? Private Thorne? You're supposed to be some kind of scholar. Tell us why she's wrong."

I rack my brain for the trick answer she's looking for. My parents had map books of Perdanth and Saracen, but none that included the towns that would pop up and disappear overnight along the border of the Wastes. Traveling without the security of a map to follow always put my father on edge.

"They're the difference between death and survival when traversing unfamiliar territory?" It's a terrible guess.

"Exactly. These books are the most valuable tool a regiment has. If we're attacked and need to take evasive maneuvers, the commanding officers rely on us to chart a safe course. Every soldier's life on this boat depends on our ability to choose the right path. These books are now your responsibility to preserve and protect. You will carry them with you day and night. Do not leave them unattended. Other squads will attempt to steal them over the next few weeks. Anyone who outranks you is permitted to punish you as they see fit if they catch you without your book. Any questions?"

The girl's hand shoots up.

"You don't need to raise your hand, Private Roy. Just spit it out."

"The books are really big. Can we use magic to carry them?"

"You may carry them any way you like, as long as they remain clean, dry, and free of damage. However, I suggest you become accustomed to their weight. You won't always have a relic to rely on. Once we're off the ship, you'll be marching with the books on your back with the rest of your gear."

The teenager raises her hand again.

"Yes, Private Roy," Mattern says, closing her eyes in exasperation.

"What about when we need to use the privy, or when we're in the training ring practicing with our relics? What do we do with the books?"

"You're a squad. Figure it out." Mattern hands us each a slip of paper with two sets of map coordinates. "Your job this afternoon is to chart a course from the first location to the next. Have a detailed itinerary with step-by-step troop movements to me before we launch at sunset."

"This is so exciting," the young teen says as soon as the major exits the chart room. "Can you believe we actually get to carry these around?" Her big doe eyes give her round face a doll-like appearance as she beams at Serin and me. "My name's Nellie."

Serin scowls at her and takes one of the books to a desk in front of the window.

"It's lovely to meet you, Nellie. I'm Everly, and that's Serin."

"What relic did they give you?" Nellie asks.

"Everly isn't a witch." Serin doesn't bother looking up from her book. "She volunteered for this. Practically signed her name in blood to be here."

"I got a firebird feather," Nelli says, not missing a beat as she pulls a six-inch piece of fire down form her pocket. "I was hoping to be assigned to Fire Squad, but they stuck me here instead. Major Mattern said I need to start out slow since I just got over my fever last week. My sister got hers at fifteen. I got mine right after I turned thirteen. Ma says it's on account of me being an overachiever."

"Last week?" I ask, surprised. It took me months to regain my strength after my fever broke.

"I would've volunteered too, but Ma insisted on reporting me so she could claim the bounty." Nellie lifts her book and stumbles two steps backward before weaving sideways with it gripped to her chest. It's almost as big as she is.

"Here, let me help you." I grab the book before she topples over and help her slide it back onto the table. "Do you know how to read a map?"

"I never learnt to read. My ma said there was no sense wasting her money on schooling my sister and me when the army would do it for us. She said I was better served learning a more useful skill."

"What would you have done if you hadn't come down with the witch fever?" I ask.

Nellie shrugs. "I was a chimney sweep before I got sick. It's one of the better-paying jobs for someone my size. I didn't like it much, being that high off the ground," she says with a shudder. "I preferred working at the farmyard down the road with my feet in the dirt. They raised rabbits and chickens and hogs. There's not a lot of work for small farm hands though. I wasn't strong enough to control the horses when they got ornery. I'd probably have stuck with the sweeping or become a washerwoman like my mamma."

It takes a few hours, but I manage to show Nellie how to recognize topography symbols and match the numbers on her strip of paper to the latitude and longitude lines in her book. Together, we successfully plot a course through a valley between two steep mountains. My coordinates are different, and I only have thirty minutes left to draw a path around a deep canyon that cuts through the Wastes.

Serin snores softly, her boots propped up on her desk, while Nellie watches a crew of lightning summoners burn three large rings into the deck boards outside the chart room. The scent of charred wood reminds me of my summers in Saracen with my parents. My mother kept a fire going day and night when we made camp, steeping batches of rose hip tea for her patients.

The sun disappears behind a cloud as a shrill scream splits the air. My gaze snaps up to the deck as a young boy falls from the sky and lands on the boards with a bone-cracking thud. No one else bothers to move as I race out the door.

My stomach lurches at the angle of his twisted body—legs and arms bent all the wrong ways. I bolt to the railing and vomit over the side of the boat.

"We're not even moving yet, and this rabbit is already feeding the fish," a snide voice says, eliciting a riot of laughter from the other storm summoners on deck.

I drop to my knees next to the dead boy. He isn't wearing a uniform. His face and clothing are covered in black soot. I glance up at the dual smokestacks towering above the pilothouse as Serin, Nellie, and Major Mattern rush out of the chart room.

"Was he cleaning the smokestacks?"

"Who are you talking about?" Mattern asks.

"Him." I gesture to the lifeless body staring blankly at the blue sky.

"Are you feeling unwell, Private Thorne?" Major Mattern's brow creases with concern.

"We can't leave him like this. Serin, help me move the body."

"I think your rabbit is a bit touched in the head, Mattern." The Storm Squad witches snicker again at the man's comment as he adjusts his white gloves. His dark hair is neatly cropped. Uniform starched and pressed. Boots polished to a blinding shine.

Victor Landry. Youngest son of the wealthiest family in Perdanth. He had a reputation for being cruel to animals and running underground dog fighting rings before his conscription. They say his father donated a gold mine to the crown to keep him out of the military for five years after he recovered from his fever.

"What kind of asshole laughs at a dead child?" I swipe my sour mouth on my arm and glare up at him.

"Be careful with that sharp tongue, Thorne. Someone might try to cut it out." There's a lieutenant's patch sewn above the gold lightning bolt on his lapel, marking him as a member of the infamously brutal Storm Squad.

"Last I checked, you had your own conscripts to harass, Lieutenant Landry. Back off and let me deal with mine," Mattern commands.

"Until we meet again, rabbit." Landry saunters away with a smirk.

Serin steps in front of me. Her boots pass through the boy's body as if he's made of smoke, and the hallucination dissipates. She grips my face and studies my eyes. "She's still recovering from the trauma of last night's reaver attack and the injuries she sustained from the egg. She needs to rest."

"Colonel Krimore insisted Private Thorne not receive any special treatment. She can rest when she's completed her duties for the day. The next time you leave the chart room, take your books. That's the first and only warning you'll get." Mattern turns on her heel and heads back to the pilothouse above the chart room.

"What the fuck was that?" Serin hisses as she helps me up.

"Nothing. It's like you said. I just need to rest." I straighten my uniform and stalk back to the chart room to finish my work.

Serin doesn't push the issue, but I can tell by the way she watches me that she's trying to work out how much of my mind has been devoured by the burning.

I finish plotting my assigned route around the canyon and close the oversized map book. It's too big to tuck under my arm or carry with one hand.

"It would be easier to carry these things around if we had some rope," I say to Nellie, who's been oddly quiet since my episode.

She darts out the door and comes back with one of the cork flotation rings that hang on every section of the boat's railings.

"Will this work?" she asks as she hands one to me.

"Yes, I think it might." I remove the attached rescue rope and truss it around Nellie's book the same way we do at the Menagerie to lift heavy dragon bones into place when there are no witches available to help us move the displays.

"Try this." I help her slide her arms through two of the loops so the weight of the book rests on her back and shoulders.

She leans forward instinctively to counterbalance the load as she takes a few steps.

"Do you think you can manage that?"

Nellie nods with a grin. "Will you show me how to tie knots like that?"

"Here, help me make one for Serin."

"Don't waste your time," Serin says. "I have no intention of carrying a book or anything else on my back." She reclines in her chair and kicks her feet up on the counter. "I'm here on loan from Ambassador Caron and have no obligation to participate in the Perdanthian Army's hazing rituals. Any of these children playing at being soldiers who has a problem with that can have a conversation with my blade."

———◆———

Serin wakes me up before dawn so she can run. When I refuse to get out of bed, she threatens to summon Silas to babysit me. The idea of suffering his presence again in the small room seems like the worse choice, so I agree. How bad can it be?

After ten laps around the perimeter of our second-level deck with the book strapped to my back, I'm sweating from every crevice. Each heaving breath comes with a sharp stab of pain in my side.

"Why would any sane person do this for fun?"

"When you have unused magic in your veins, you have to burn off the excess energy before it seeks an outlet of its own. Most witches fight or fuck it off. I prefer to run. It keeps my head clear so the other two things don't bleed into one another. That's why they make new recruits do physical things like carrying around heavy books and sparring twice a day. A commitment to physical discipline helps keep the mind and magic in order."

Her words stick in my brain as we make our way to the dining room on the first deck for our morning rations. Gideon said something similar in his letter. I've experienced my fair share of lust since I started summoning two years ago. But the urge to fight with someone? That's more recent.

I sigh with relief as I slide the rope from my blistered shoulders and lean the map book against a table draped in white linen. The deep cushioned chair feels like a dream as I sink into it. Every part of my body aches, and I haven't even gotten through breakfast yet.

The dining room rivals the one in the palace. Heavy green and gold drapes frame the windows, and the curved ceiling drips with fancy electric lights powered by the ship's steam engine.

"Good morning." Nellie beams as she flips the armless chair backward, straddling the seat so she doesn't have to take her book off to eat her ration of beans, bread, and black tea.

Serin scowls in her general direction, but it has zero effect on Nellie's chipper demeanor. If anything, it makes her smile all the wider in a way that reminds me of Wallace's perpetual good mood.

My chest tightens. I didn't have time to say goodbye to my best friend. I make a mental note to write to her as soon as I get back to my room.

"Are you excited about starting combat training?" Nellie asks around a mouthful of bread. "I can't wait to see who our instructors are. I hope it's Colonel Krimore. They say no one has ever bested him with a sword."

Before I can respond, someone grabs my book and runs away. My legs protest as I jump up to chase after him.

"Not so fast, rabbit." Victor Landry steps into my path, blocking my pursuit of the thief. Static crackles around him, telling me he's carrying his Thunderbird relic. "You'll get your maps back after I've had my fun."

Serin stands, a hand on the hilt of her knife.

Everyone is watching.

You need to earn their respect. I can see the line of scrolling script from Gideon's letter in my mind as I grit my teeth.

"Get on your knees." The six new conscripts behind him snicker at the command.

"Careful, Lieutenant," Serin says. "Private Thorne was your future queen once."

"And now she's nothing but a destitute reaver-sympathizing elite who's fallen so far she's not even good enough to be the prince's whore. Get on your knees and lick my boots, rabbit."

Serin steps between us.

"It's fine, Serin. I just want the book back."

A blast of heat rolls down my neck as I drop to my hands and knees. The dining room doors swing open, and Silas stalks toward us wearing a predatory smile, followed by Gideon and the rest of the Elite Guard in their black uniforms.

"*Get up, little spark. This asshole is about to lose his fucking head.*" His voice fills my mind as he summons a pair of shadow blades.

"Stand down, Drake." Gideon's order is loud and clear. "This is between Lieutenant Landry and Private Thorne."

Silas keeps coming like a dark, deadly nightmare. He's going to kill Landry.

"*Stop.*" I yell the word in my head. "*Don't even think about interfering, reaver. I can fight my own fucking battles.*"

Silas halts in the middle of the room, glaring at Landry as black tendrils curl around him.

"What are you waiting for, rabbit? Let me see how well you use that pretty mouth I've heard so much about from the guards at the Menagerie."

I lean forward and drag my tongue over his polished boots, one at a time. They're so clean I can see my reflection in the surface.

"That's a good little rabbit." The Storm Squad officer orders the kid who snatched my book to return it. "Now scamper away and don't let me catch you without those maps again. You might not enjoy the next thing I make you lick, but I can guarantee I will."

My left palm singes the dark carpet where it presses against the floor. It's all I can do to control the firebird magic coursing through my veins as I stand.

"In that case, I certainly hope the guards warned you about my teeth as well. I like to bite, Lieutenant."

Landry smirks as I heft the book onto my back.

Silas's deadly gaze narrows on the storm summoner as Serin ushers me out of the room.

CHAPTER EIGHTEEN

*D*ear Wallace,

I'm sorry I didn't say goodbye. Joining Gideon's quest to hunt a dragon wasn't on the list of things I thought I'd be doing when I went to the ball. I wish you were here.

My roommate is a bitch.

I scratch out the line and re-write it.

My roommate made me run. For fun. Who does that?

Gideon is pretending to be a cold-hearted asshole and acting as if he didn't ask me to meet him in his private rooms at Nymphs the minute he returned home.

Will the mail clerk read the letter before sending it? I scratch out the line just in case.

I have to carry a fucking thirty-pound book of maps around day and night. If I let it out of my sight, the officers are allowed to punish us any way they'd like.

I scratch that out too. I don't want Wallace to worry.

As the royal historian, I've been tasked with keeping track of the regiment's library of maps and important documents.

I made a new friend who's young and eager and will probably die if we're attacked.

No. That will definitely make her worry.

There's a young girl on the Navigation Squad with me. She reminds me of you, and it makes me feel less alone here. I hope you get to meet her someday.

And there's this shadow summoner with impeccable teeth.

Fuck. I rip the page out of my new sketchbook and light it on fire. No matter how many times I try, I can't seem to find the right words to convey to my best friend what a disaster this deployment is turning out to be.

Serin pauses her incantation prayer to the Mother of Fire and glares up at me from where she's seated cross-legged on the floor. "Are you having a problem, girl?"

"No."

She waves her hand over the black candle in front of her, extinguishing the flame. "Good. Get your book. We're going to the training ring early. You need to warm up."

———◈———

All the new conscripts stretch and size each other up as they take pointers from their commanding officers on the wide deck in front of the chart room.

Lieutenant Landry and his six new storm summoners are the only missing squad. The whispers and curious glances aimed in my direction tell me I'm not the only one who's noticed.

"What did you do, reaver?" My shoulders burn where the ropes of my trussed book dig into the raw skin under my tunic as I stretch my arms.

Part of me wants to strangle Silas for drawing more attention to Landry's disgusting hazing stunt. The other part of me—the one that's getting harder to keep in check—thrills at the thought of Silas running that asshole through with one of his shadow blades.

"Your height makes your head a perfect target," Major Mattern tells Nellie. "Keep it covered and use your petite stature to your advantage. Dart and duck around your opponent. Keep them moving long enough, and you'll tire them out."

"Got it. Move quick, like a rabbit." Nellie throws three punches at an invisible foe and topples backward under the weight of her book.

Serin grabs the ropes and yanks her upright as I shift back and forth on my feet.

"On second thought," Mattern says, "there's no shame in taking a hit right away and ending the round by passing out."

"That won't help the girl survive a real fight," Serin says. "You have to be stronger, faster, or smarter than your enemy. Better to be all three. When you're up against a larger, more skilled opponent, you need to catch them off guard. Aim for their lower body. It won't take much to knock most of these kids on their asses if you lunge for their legs. The lower, the better. They won't be expecting it the first time. The shadow summoner is twice my size, and I took him down with that move once."

"Speak of the shadowy bastard and he shall appear." I turn as the phantom kiss of heat tickles the back of my neck. Serin follows my line of sight to the stairs with a confused look.

Everyone stands at attention as Gideon strolls up the steps a moment later, followed by five members of his Elite Guard. Silas's gaze finds me immediately, then flicks to Serin.

She curses under her breath.

"What's wrong?"

"Nothing you need to worry about. Just try to avoid getting your bell rung on the mat," she says, glaring at Silas's back. "We don't need any more unexpected complications."

Gideon's guards take their place behind him. Silas swore a blood oath not to kill anyone unless my life was at risk. He's already found a way around that part of the deal once. My pulse quickens as I conjure all the terrible things he might have done to Victor Landry.

"*I love your wicked imagination.*" The corner of Silas's mouth curls as his voice slides across the bond.

"*Stay out of my head, psychopath.*" I glare at him from the opposite side of the deck.

"*I'm not the one imagining a hundred vicious ways to maim a man. Revenge looks good on you, little spark.*"

"*Did you hurt him?*"

"*Would that please you?*"

I force my attention back to Gideon, refusing to let Silas bait me into another one of his traps.

"Welcome to your first round of combat training," Gideon says. "In the next few weeks, you'll learn how to defend yourself against a physical attack. Our enemy has become more sophisticated. Don't be fooled by their unregimented approach to warfare. Chaos and the appearance of disorganization have been their most effective weapon. They use it to distract and disorient their victims during an attack."

Gideon's voice is confident and commanding, and I'm struck by how different this version of him is from the person I used to know. He seems more like himself here among his conscripted soldiers than he ever did at court.

The sound of heavy boots draws everyone's attention to where Lieutenant Landry leads all three Storm Squad units onto the deck. I'm not sure whether I'm relieved or disappointed that he's still in one piece. Phantom tendrils of static crackle softly like loose glowing threads in his wake, raising the hair on my arms as he passes.

"Thank you for joining us, Lieutenant Landry," Gideon says. "I hope our posted training schedule hasn't inconvenienced you."

"I apologize for our tardiness, Colonel Krimore. Our... squad meeting ran late."

"To ensure it doesn't happen again, Storm Squad will take latrine duty for the duration of the journey."

Landry cuts Silas a dark look.

Silas's cocky smirk remains unfazed as Gideon continues.

"We'll be leaning heavily on hand-to-hand combat and weapons training. Reaver crews don't have the luxury of moving in large groups within the borders of Perdanth or Saracen. They'll wait until we're off the boat and attempt to pick us off one by one. If at any point you find yourself separated from your unit and its ration of relics, you need to know how to defend yourself. My Elite Guard has been chosen for their unmatched fighting and survival skills. They'll be your instructors. Their orders supersede all others, aside from mine, inside these rings. The first person to knock the other out of the circle wins. There are only two rules. No magic and no fatal wounds."

The witches gathered on deck grumble.

"I know you're itching to begin duels. If this were a fireproof military barge, we'd be starting today. But I promised your future queen that we wouldn't destroy her pretty boat. Anyone who breaks the rules will earn themselves a goblin-spelled suppression collar. Good luck."

The Elite Guard splits the new conscripts between the three circles. Serin and I are the only ones who aren't in our teens. Silas doesn't even try to hide his satisfied smirk when he's assigned to oversee the first ring, where Storm Squad's six recruits have been paired with ten from Fire Squad. The second is all Fire Squad. Nellie, Serin, and I are sent to the third with the nine Medic Squad trainees as if we're an afterthought. The kids in our group are younger than the rest, just like Nellie.

Jo-el Sanchez, the captain of Gideon's Elite Guard, stands at the center of our circle, his cropped obsidian hair gleaming in the morning light. He and Gideon went through their training together, long before they left for the Wastes.

I resist the urge to roll my eyes. I shouldn't be surprised. Of course, Gideon would assign his personal healer to my section. So much for not showing me any favoritism. The last thing I need is another babysitter.

Jo-el makes a point of looking directly at me when he asks for the first volunteer. Thankfully, Nellie's hand shoots up next to me. Serin takes her book as he waves the grinning teen into the ring.

Sweat drips down my back as I watch him use her to demonstrate the proper fighting stance and several defensive blocks. He repeats the process with each member of our group, working his way around the circle.

My attention drifts to the first ring, where Silas is demonstrating the same techniques by sparring with one of the other elite guards. The way he moves is mesmerizing. Graceful and deadly. It's downright annoying how fucking beautiful the man is.

"Thorne."

I startle at the sound of my name.

"You're up," Jo-el says.

Heat creeps up my neck as I hand my book to Serin. I copy Jo-el's stance and pivot my body sideways, with my right hip and foot forward, raising my hands to protect my head. I'm rusty and out of shape, but the muscle memory is still there from years of practice with Gideon in his apartment above Nymph's Wager.

Jo-el demonstrates a combination of slow-motion strikes that don't actually touch me, explaining how to block each one as I slowly retreat in a circle around the ring.

"Are you teaching them how to dance or fight, Captain Sanchez?" There's an amused lilt in Silas's voice. I hate the way my insides flutter as he approaches our group. "We only have a few short weeks to train them before we lose the warded safety of the ship. They need to be able to do more than dance around each other before we hit reaver territory. Mind if I have a go?"

Jo-el shoots Gideon a questioning glance before responding. "You're welcome to step in if you think you can do better, Drake."

Silas makes a show of reaching behind his head and pulling off his black tunic with one hand, revealing the wide expanse of taut muscle and dragon scale tattoos that cover his torso.

"*I'm growing weary of your games, reaver,*" I say in my head, keeping my gaze focused on his face as he tosses the tunic aside and circles around me, wearing a cocky smirk. It's a distraction technique, and I refuse to let him unnerve me.

"You're the one who insisted on fighting your own battles. Since my life is tied to yours, I need to ensure that you can do that without getting us both killed."

Silas stops in front of me and laces his fingers behind his back. "Go on, then. Take your best shot."

"I think it's someone else's turn." I drop my guard and step around him. Silas sweeps my feet out from under me. My back slams against the wooden deck, knocking the air from my lungs. I struggle to suck in a frantic breath, vaguely aware of the cushion of shadow protecting my head as the blazing sun burns spots in my vision.

"Breathe in through your nose and out through your mouth. Just like that. Slow and deep."

"Fuck you."

"Help her up and get her something to drink. She's dehydrated."

"Come on, girl. On your feet." Serin pulls me up and hands me a canteen.

I chug the lukewarm water as Silas addresses the crowd.

"Never turn your back on the enemy," he says, giving me his back to prove he doesn't see me as a threat.

I hand Serin the canteen and wipe my mouth. I'm done with this jackass underestimating me. I may not be able to take him down, but if I catch him by surprise, I might be able to push him out of the ring and end the session.

I sprint toward his broad back, groaning as my legs burn from the effort, my muscles still aching from Serin's predawn torture run. Silas pivots as I raise my hands to shove him into the crowd. He sidesteps my advance as if he's got eyes in the back of his damn head. The momentum sends me barreling into Serin's waiting arms at the edge of the circle. She spins me around and sends me back toward the middle.

"Can anyone tell Private Thorne the mistake she just made?" Silas asks.

"Thinking she could take on an opponent twice her size," Lieutenant Landry says with a smirk.

"Wrong. Her plan to use my size and weight against me by catching me off guard was a good one. It would have worked if she hadn't growled at me as she attacked, giving away her intent and her position." His dark eyes land on me. "You need to keep your head cool in a fight. Giving in to fear and rage will get you killed. Don't let your opponent use them against you. Now, try to hit me. I'll even keep my hands behind my back."

"What are you trying to prove, reaver? That I'm weak and useless in a fight?"

"You're doing that just fine all on your own, princess. Your reflexes are pathetically slow. Sanchez wasn't doing you any favors by taking it easy on you."

I ball my fist and aim for his smug fucking face.

Silas twists away, and I miss him by a mile.

He takes a step closer. "Again."

I swing and miss.

"You're telegraphing each move before you make it. Like this." He punches toward me, stopping an inch before he hits my chin. "Watch my shoulder. See how it cocks back before I swing? Concentrate on getting rid of the excess motion. Don't pull your arm back and wind it up. Your power doesn't come from here." He pokes my shoulder. "It comes from here." He presses his palm against my stomach. "Keep it tight. Keep your elbow close to your body and strike straight on like this."

My hair flutters when he punches through a nonexistent target next to my head.

"Try again."

I copy his stance and tuck my elbow. This time, I aim for his stomach instead of his face.

Silas turns sideways, and I miss. Again.

"It's not a fair fight when you can read my mind."

Everyone is watching us now.

"Better, but you're still telling me exactly where you're aiming," he says to me before raising his voice to carry over the crowd. "You don't need to be able to read your opponent's mind when they tell you exactly where they're aiming by staring at their target. I knew Private Thorne would go for my gut because she couldn't keep her eyes off my abs."

"Care to guess my next target, jackass?" I drop my gaze to his crotch and take a step back.

He advances as I retreat. *"Is your prince watching?"*

I glance over his shoulder at Gideon and nod.

*"Good."*Silas smirks as he stalks toward me. *"Does he look pissed enough to kick me off combat training duty yet?"*

"Is that what this little demonstration is about? You trying to get out of a duty assignment?"

"Among other things."

"If I help you, what's in it for me?" I take a jab at his chiseled jaw and miss.

Silas grabs my wrist and twists my arm behind my back. *"Are we negotiating terms again?"*

"*Tell me why you bound your life to mine?*"

He shoves me away from him. "*I already told you. It was a mistake.*"

"*I don't believe you.*" A bead of sweat trickles between my breasts.

"*Then pick something else. There has to be something you want from me.*" He drops his gaze to my mouth.

"*Teach me how to weave a mind ward to keep you out of my head.*"

Silas stretches his neck from side to side as he circles me. "*Fine. Help me get out of training duty, and I'll show you how to set a mind ward to keep me out. You have my word.*"

"*I'm afraid I'm going to need something a little more reliable than that. Order Serin to do it. Make her agree now or no deal.*"

He backs off. "Get some more water, Thorne. You're panting like a damn cat."

Serin glares at him as she hands me the canteen.

I take a deep swig and wipe the corner of my mouth. "Did he tell you what I want?"

"You're playing a dangerous game, girl."

"Will you do it?"

Serin gives me a tight nod.

"Swear it on the Mother of Fire."

She grabs the back of my head and brings her face close to my ear. "I swear by the god of life, death and rebirth, the mother of light and darkness, the queen who rules the Otherworld, that I will teach you how to protect your mind."

Serin snatches the canteen from my hands and shoves me back into the ring.

"Come on, Thorne. Show me those sharp teeth," Silas says as I stumble toward him.

"Get in line, Drake," Lieutenant Landry says behind me. "That filthy mouth of hers is mine."

Silas throws the Storm Squad commander a daggered glance. I use the distraction to my advantage and lunge for him, aiming low like Serin suggested.

It's like hitting a brick wall. The man is immovable. Silas presses his palm between my shoulder blades, shoving me down. I sprawl flat on my stomach. He straddles my back, knees braced on either side of my ass, a hand firmly on the back of my head, holding my face against the deck.

I let my body go slack. *"If you're trying to get a reaction out of Gideon, you're going about it the wrong way. He already told me he won't step in to stop anyone from torturing me. You need to make him jealous."*

Silas loosens his grip. *"What do you suggest?"*

"Kiss me."

I twist onto my back beneath him. He captures my hands, holding them above my head and covers me with the full weight of his body. I buck against him to make it look real.

He ghosts his lips over my ear. "Careful with that."

Heat coils low in my belly as I angle my face to his. Silas's brown eyes are mesmerizing this close, a mix of gold, orange, and russet tones. The way he drags his gaze over my mouth kicks my pulse into a gallop.

"Say please."

I close the distance between us and bite his bottom lip. Hard.

Silas's chest vibrates against mine with a low, guttural sound. And then his mouth is on mine. The kiss isn't brutal or demanding or at all what I imagined. He's slow and methodical and takes his time teasing me open as the deck erupts into hoots and sharp whistles.

When Silas sweeps his tongue into my mouth, the rest of the world disappears. I don't remember him releasing my wrists, but my hands are skating over his bare shoulders. His sun-bronzed skin is decadently warm beneath my palms. He inches his fingers up my side to my ribs. Heat floods my core as he shifts his weight and presses his thigh between my legs. The uninhibited part of me awakens and I arch against him.

"That's enough, Drake," Gideon says, stepping into the ring.

Silas breaks the kiss and stares down at me, wearing a strange expression.

"What do you call that move, shadow summoner?" someone shouts.

"Looks like a draw to me," someone else yells as Silas springs to his feet, leaving me breathless and on my back for the second time today.

"There are no draws when it comes to battle." His tone is deadly serious, completely unfazed, while I'm still trying to muster the stamina to peel my throbbing body off the floorboards. "There are only the dead and the ones who survive to fight another day. I'd like to thank the Storm Squad for their help with my little demonstration." Silas gestures to the chart room, where Lieutenant Landry and three other witches are floating the frost dragon egg in its warded rum barrel over the side of the ship. "While all of you were watching me, they could have gotten away with precious cargo. Fighting isn't always about the opponent in front of you. If you want to survive, you need to be aware of your surroundings at all times."

Gideon claps, and the rest of the crowd follows suit as he leans close to Silas. "Don't ever pull a fucking stunt like that again without running it by me first."

"Apologies, Your Highness. The king brought me on as a security consultant. I was merely demonstrating our current weaknesses so they can be improved."

"Are you all right?" Gideon asks me.

"Where was your concern, Colonel, when Landry made me lick his boots?" I ignore Gideon's outstretched hand and push to my feet.

"*Was Landry's disgusting behavior in the dining room part of your little performance too?*" I ask in my head.

Silas's jaw ticks. "*I needed to focus the prince's attention on you this morning. That sick fuck took it too far.*"

I ball my fists. "*And the kiss?*"

He runs his thumb over his swollen bottom lip with a dark smirk. "*That was your idea. Not mine.*"

"*Stay away from me, reaver.*"

CHAPTER NINETEEN

The black candle on the floor flickers between us as Serin holds her hand above the flame, letting it lick her palm and curl around her hand.

"My clan believes the Mother of Fire is a god with two forms. One benevolent and kind who breathed magic into the world. The other cruel and vengeful who cursed humans with the burning."

"What does your god have to do with keeping Silas out of my head?"

"I invoked her name for you today. We must make an offering to avoid her wrath."

"What kind of offering?"

"Blood." Serin pulls her dagger from its sheath. "Give me your hand."

"Why does it have to be my blood?"

"Because there aren't any live chickens or rabbits on this ship to sacrifice. If you'd rather wait until we make port in two weeks we can—"

"Just do it." I give her my hand.

Serin pricks the tip of my middle finger with her knife. "Write your name," she says, handing me a scrap of paper. I sign it in blood, and she holds it over the flame. The paper curls and ignites.

"Your name is known to her now."

"What does that mean?"

"You may call on her in a time of need. How she chooses to respond is for her to decide. Which version you get is never guaranteed." Serin waves her hand over the candle and snuffs out the flame.

"How do you put your faith in a deity with two forms, one good, one evil?"

"Because we're all more than one thing. The gods aren't the only ones with two forms. We all have one side we show to the light and another we hide in the dark. Secrets no one should have access to without permission."

"Is that why you agreed to teach me how to block Silas from my mind?"

"He should have shown you how to do it from the start."

"Why didn't he?"

"Silas doesn't trust easily. It took him two years to trust I wouldn't betray him, even with the blood oath I swore to keep his secret. I'm going to drop my mind ward and rebuild it. Put your hands on my head."

I shove my hand in my waist pouch and brush my fingers over the firebird feather hidden there. Magic races up my arm, over my shoulder, and down to my other hand until they're both tingling.

"If you singe my hair, I will cut you."

"Understood." I place my palms on either side of her head. She closes her eyes, and the ward comes to life. The pattern moves around her like a living flame. Phantom heat pulses against my skin. It's like standing too close to a bonfire. If I wasn't accustomed to my own heat shield, I don't know how long I could bear it.

"If you want to speak with Silas through the bond, you'll need to create a warded room in your mind with two doors that you can lock."

I memorize the patterns as she unravels the layers and rebuilds them.

"Do you need to see it again?"

"I've got it." I pull my hands away. "How will I know if it works?"

"You'll feel a pulse of magic over your scalp when he tries to read you. Whether you let him in or keep him out is up to you. Either way, the mind ward will ensure he doesn't get past the second door."

"Have you ever read him?"

Serin places the candle back in its feather-lined box. "Silas never drops his wards."

"Not even in his sleep?" I ask.

"Do not attempt to enter his mind, girl. Even if he invites you in. You may not like what you find."

"What's that supposed to mean?" I ask, leaning against the edge of the bunk and taking a swig of bitter tonic from my flask.

"I've seen the way you look at him. The way your attention drifts in his direction when you're in the same room. You have a thing for stray cats and even more so for feral people. Some are sweet and harmless and just looking for a new home, like Nellie. Silas might let you pet him, but he isn't the kind of beast that can be tamed."

—⁂—

My side seizes with a sharp cramp. I double over to rest my hands on my knees until it passes. Sprinting up six flights of stairs with a thirty-pound book strapped to your back is a whole new level of torture. It's been nearly two and a half weeks, and I still can't keep up with Serin during our predawn runs. Every time I stop to catch my breath, she makes me do fifty push-ups.

We stretch and practice my sparring stance when I'm not transcribing coordinates or sweating my ass off in the ring.

Silas has been doing his best to avoid me. The only time he deigns to speak to me is during the afternoon combat training sessions, where he scowls down from the shadows of the twin smokestacks above the pilothouse, arms crossed.

When I lose, which I always do, my scalp tingles with the soft caress of magic. I unlock the door to the warded room in my mind, and he projects the same three words across the bond. *"Drink some water."* No more. No less.

The only other time we cross paths is during dinner. He eats with the Elite Guard and doesn't bother acknowledging my existence now that he's gotten what he wanted. After Silas's theatrical stunt, Gideon came to the realization that the shadow summoner's talents were better served on night watch duty, keeping an eye on the egg. He played right into Silas's plan.

Part of me wishes he and Serin would just steal it already and let me get on with my life. The other part of me waits for Silas's shadowy presence to stand guard outside my door every night while he gives Serin an hour's reprieve from babysitting me. It's the only time I allow my imagination to run free. To picture all the things he could do to me as I slide my shift up my thighs and slip my hand between my legs, imagining my fingers are his as I coax out my pleasure. It's become a ritual I can't seem to fall asleep without.

He didn't relieve Serin last night for her break. I felt him leave when the boat docked to resupply. I tossed and turned for hours, unable to sleep until the familiar kiss of hot breath caressed the back of my neck before dawn.

"Where did Silas go?" I ask as Serin backtracks toward me, the thin sheen of sweat on her brow the only evidence that we've been at this for over an hour. "He left the boat at midnight and didn't return until three."

"How do you know about that?" she asks, jogging in place.

"I felt his presence leave and return just before the ship started moving upriver again."

She jolts to a stop and stares at me. "You can sense his presence?"

"Of course I can sense him." I hold up my scarred palm. "I'm bound to him, just like you."

Serin drags me away from the long row of cabin doors to the back of the ship, where the red paddle wheel churns. "That's not how blood oaths work."

"Maybe it's different with me because of the way magic speaks to me. I can tell you exactly where he is on the ship. Well, not him exactly, but the ground-up dragon scales in his tattoo."

"Can you sense my firebird feathers when we're not in the same room?"

"No. Firebird magic gives me visual cues. I see a phantom ripple of heat around you. Unicorn and thunderbird relics are more auditory. Dragon scales, and, well, actual dragons, I suppose, are the only magic I've ever been able to sense when it's not in the same room. The egg is the most powerful thing I've ever been drawn to. In Crecentis, it called to me from the other side of the palace."

Serin stares as if she's taking me in for the first time. "Does Silas know?"

"That relics speak to me? I told him everything I just told you."

Serin runs her hands down her face.

"The burning hasn't driven me completely mad yet, if that's what you're worried about."

"I wish that was our only problem."

Serin doesn't explain what she means as she drags me to the women's showers. There are too many others around to ask her to elaborate. I'm getting tired of being left in the dark.

We take turns babysitting my book and getting cleaned up. Hot water powered by the ship's steam engine cascades down my body, soothing my aching muscles and pallet of colorful bruises.

They say Princess Dagmara invented the bathing system herself and spared no expense having it installed on the ship and the Saracen palace. Gideon could do worse. I'd marry her myself if it meant I could take a shower like this every day for the rest of my life. It's so decadent, I don't even care that it stings every cut and abrasion on my knuckles and knees.

The soft scent of rose fills my nose as I scrub the sweat and grime from my hair, then my face and body, careful not to open the scabbed rope burns on my shoulders. I swipe the sponge between my legs last. It comes away with the first smear of my monthly courses.

Fuck. I rinse off and cross the room to where Serin sits in front of a small mirror, twisting her damp hair into tight braids. The book is propped against the wall in front of her. The steam can't be good for the paper, but I'll be damned if I'll let Lieutenant Landry or any of his Storm Squad goons catch me without it.

"Can I borrow your knife?"

Serin gives me a withering look. "No."

I glance around at the other women in the shower room and lower my voice. "I need to cut my towel into rags. I got my period, and I forgot to pack my menstrual bell."

She fishes around in her bag and hands me a small cotton pouch.

"Won't you need it?"

"I have my own. That one is new. It's for you."

"Where did you get it? We've been stuck on this boat for weeks."

"Do you want the bell or not?"

I take the soft bundle and thank her.

"Is there something else you need, girl?" She eyes me impatiently in the mirror.

"I'm not putting it in right here, in front of everyone." I glance around the steam-filled room again. "I need to go to the latrine."

"Make it quick."

I get dressed and grab my book before she changes her mind.

The storm summoner on duty inside the women's latrine glares at me in the mirror above the washbasin as she stuffs her long black hair into a bonnet. I slip into one of the private toilet stalls and insert the soft rubber bell-shaped cup as quickly as I can. It's the first time I've had the freedom to move about on my own without a chaperone. There may come a time when I need to slip my leash. I need her to trust me. I finish and hurry back.

———✦———

Nellie works diligently beside me in the chart room as I draw the training deck in the red sketchbook Gideon gave me. The expensive vellum takes the charcoal better than my old book. Nellie sounds out each place name on her map as she transcribes them. The girl is tenacious and never gives up. She's learned to read and write in a matter of weeks.

It's been two days since Serin sent me to the latrine alone. She hasn't let me out of her sight again—aside from the hour Silas spends guarding my door every night—and I haven't pushed.

"Dragon's Buh-ack-buh—"

"Backbone," Serin says, eyes still closed, feet kicked up on the table where she pretends to sleep every afternoon while *not* teaching Nellie how to read.

"Back-bone." Nellie's head bobs as she sounds out the syllables, committing the word to memory.

A smile tugs at the corner of Serin's mouth, and I'm reminded of what she said about the Mother of Fire. How we all wear two faces. One we hide and one we show to the world. Serin may be prickly on the outside, but under that thorny shell, she has a soft, pliable heart, and Nellie has melted her way right into it.

My knee bounces under the table that hides the frost dragon egg. Some of us have three faces. The mask we let everyone see, the face we hide from the world, and the one we bury deep because we're too afraid to look at it ourselves.

I sit here and pretend I'm not a thief and traitor to the crown that might have been mine. That I never wanted it. That I don't hate the people who took it from me just a little. That I don't hate myself for lying to everyone I care about. For cowering behind a mask instead of taking what I want like Silas does.

A shiver runs down my spine, pebbling my skin as I use the tip of my finger to smudge the charcoal on my sketch of the chimney sweep, recreating the soot stains on his clothes. I've tried drawing Nellie and

Serin—even the egg—but I can't seem to finish them. Not while I'm in the chart room. I keep coming back to the boy's ghost.

I glance at the brass clock enclosed in the glass bookcase behind me. Almost noon.

He's here.

I close my eyes and wait for the now familiar scream that comes at the same time every day. A shadow passes over the boat. The boy falls from the sky, slams into the deck at all the wrong angles, and disappears exactly seven minutes later. I don't know why his ghost haunts me or what message he's trying to convey, but it feels like another warning.

The first time I saw him, I assumed he was a hallucination induced by the burning. My parents treated dozens of witches afflicted with disturbing visions. Not once did they ever mention them coming on like clockwork—like a ghost stuck in a loop, haunting the place where it died.

Maybe the others were ghosts too. Maybe I'm not losing my mind.

I saw Gideon's mother right before Silas pulled me into the shadows so the guards wouldn't catch me in the Hall of Kings. Tula, the first queen of Perdanth, appeared to me right before Silas's fake reaver attack. I was in danger both times.

The boy's scream splits the air, causing me to flinch, even though I'm expecting it. I swear the thud and awful crack of bones get louder each day.

The first two warnings were clear, even though I didn't understand them at the time. Marlayna spoke directly to me when she told me to hide in the Hall of Kings. Queen Tula was clearly distressed, shouting at me to leave. The boy doesn't interact with me. He just screams. Is he trying to tell me not to climb the smokestacks? I couldn't if I tried.

I already know I'm in danger. It's a constant undercurrent on the ship. One conscript has already died. The young fire summoner succumbed to heat stroke after he got caught without his relic and was forced to run laps around the ship for two hours in the full sun.

Landry and his minions lurk around every corner, waiting to catch me without my book. The irony that the scariest person on the ship is the only one who can't hurt me isn't lost on me.

"Is that the shadow summoner?" Nellie asks, leaning across the table to see my sketch.

I don't remember flipping the page and drawing Silas, but his half-finished face stares back at me all the same.

Serin opens her eyes and raises a brow.

I stuff the sketchbook into the pouch at my waist. "We should go down to lunch. I'm starving."

CHAPTER TWENTY

"**Y**ou need to work on controlling the distance between you and your opponents today," Serin says as I flip my chair around and sit backward like Nellie does so I don't have to remove my book to eat. "Step into the attack so your body isn't at the apex of their swing. Remember, they can move forward faster than you can retreat. If you step in, you take most of the power out of their punch. Grab their blocking arm, get behind them, and aim for the kidneys like I showed you."

I take a deep swig from my flask, hoping it will help drown out the phantom sensations assaulting my senses in the packed dining room. The rumble of thunder and flashes of static that follow the storm summoners around. The head-numbing pound of hooves from the Medic Squad seated at the table next to us. Everything is always brighter and louder when I'm on my period.

"Are you listening, girl?" Serin kicks my chair.

"Yes." I bite out the word as I stand.

"Where are you going?"

"To get some coffee to wash down this rock-hard bread."

"Take Nellie with you and stay where I can see you."

"Are you and Serin having a lover's tiff?" Nellie asks as we approach the coffee cart.

"Serin and I aren't lovers. What gave you that impression?"

Nellie shrugs as she pours herself a cup. "You're always together. I never see either of you with anyone else. She doesn't take her eyes off you, and she snarls like a guard dog at everyone you go up against in the ring."

I smile as I fill my mug with the black brew. The ember in my chest flares at the thought of telling her Serin is, in fact, my bodyguard. Her only job is to make sure I don't die.

"I think she feels obligated to protect me since we're bunk mates. I can't defend myself with magic like everyone else, so she's teaching me how to fight."

"It must be nice to have a friend like that, someone who always has your back. My bunk mate is a storm summoner who hasn't said three words to me. But that doesn't stop me from trying. I'll wear her down eventually."

The girl's positivity is effervescent. She could charm a smile out of snake if she put her mind to it.

"I'm sure you will." I glance over Nellie's head at Serin, who's watching us like a hawk. I have no misconceptions about her motivations for keeping me alive. I'm not naive enough to fool myself into thinking we're friends, but it makes sense that Nellie would see it that way. She sees the best in everyone.

"Serin reminds me of my older sister. She was a grumpy bitch too, but she had a good heart, just like Serin."

My shoulders shake with laughter as I turn back toward the table and collide with Landry. Scalding coffee sloshes out of my overfull mug, hitting him in the stomach and dripping down his perfectly pressed uniform.

Landry swipes at the dark brown stain on the front of his otherwise pristine clothing, spreading it to his white gloves.

"Watch where you're going, Thorne. Do you know how hard it is to keep a uniform clean without a fucking laundress on board?"

"You should definitely soak those before it sets," I say, biting back a smile. "Wouldn't want anyone to think you didn't have the decency to wash up after your latrine duty shift."

"You're going to regret the way you speak to me with that filthy little mouth, rabbit." Landry takes a step toward me.

"I don't think she will," Serin says, stepping between us and holding her dagger to his crotch. "You can't touch her as long as she has her book."

Landry backs away with a smirk. "I'm coming for your skin first, Thorne."

"That asshole has a serious death wish," Serin hisses.

"He's talking about the rabbit hunt," Nellie says. "His squad is ranked as the favorite to win. Payout is two to one."

"What the fuck is a rabbit hunt?" Serin asks as we head back to our table.

"It's a team-building game the new conscripts play. The squad that collects the most skins at the end of the night wins."

"Skins?" I say, more than a little horrified.

"It's like hide and seek, only when someone finds you, they get to take a piece of your clothing. If I had money, I'd put it on Storm Squad. They're favored to win."

"Someone's taking bets on the game?" I ask.

"It's tradition. The winning squad gets twenty-four hours of shore leave when we get to Port Hope."

Serin's cheeks dimple with a wide smile. "Who's holding the purse on the bets?"

"You can't be serious. We're not participating in this," I say.

"All the rabbits have to play. It's the rules. If you want to make a wager, you gotta see a civvy called Hardy in the post room."

"Come on, girl. We need to go back to our cabin."

"I haven't finished eating."

Serin grabs a hunk of hardtack off the table and shoves it into my hands. "Take it to go. I have a bet to place and need to get some money from my bag."

"We need to find Gideon and make him stop this," I say, trailing after her.

"We'll do no such thing."

"Why not?"

Serin glances around. "Because we have a rendezvous in Port Hope, and I'm not letting Silas go alone this time. The Navigation Squad is going to win this game."

———⚬———

Dear Adrian,

I hope this letter finds you in good time. I'm happy to report that I have accepted your challenge to make new friends. We're getting on well. The journey has been quiet thus far, and I haven't had anything noteworthy to report.

We dock in Port Hope in a few days. There's a competition to win a day of leave to explore the city. My friends are determined to win. We've been cooped up on this ship for weeks with no connection to the outside world. They're desperate for some free time to regroup before setting out on the next leg of our journey.

I'm not sure if I'll have time to post another letter. Give Pig extra attention for me. It's storm season. He'll do anything to be let out, but he can't be trusted. It might be best to keep him locked in.

Your dutiful sister,

—E

I tear the page out of my sketchbook and blow on the wet ink. Serin extinguishes her candle and hops up from the floor.

"We only have twenty minutes left to make our bets before combat training. Give it to me."

"Wait, that's private."

Serin grabs the letter and holds it under her glowing palm. The glossy ink slowly turns matte, drying from the heat. My pulse jumps as she scans the coded message addressed to my brother but intended for Gideon. I have no doubt that Silas will find a way to punish me if he finds out I'm feeding information to Gideon, but I have to do something to warn him about my suspicions of their plans to get off the ship.

Serin's gaze settles on me.

I swallow past the hard lump in my throat.

"You have lovely script, girl. It's almost as pretty as Silas's. Let's go. I'm not getting stuck with latrine duty for being late."

I release a slow breath and grab my book.

The line to place bets spills out of the post room and wraps around the corner. A group of Fire Squad conscripts in front of us debate the best strategy for winning the game. One thinks they should find a hiding place and defend it. Another disagrees, saying it's better to go on the offensive and hunt the other groups like the Storm Squad always does.

The rabbit hunt begins at sunset tomorrow. I have twenty-four hours to convince Gideon to cancel this ridiculous game.

"Twenty-five dollars on the Navigation Squad," Serin says, handing the clerk called Hardy a wad of cash.

"You can't be serious."

"Always bet on yourself. It increases the odds of winning."

Hardy eyes the wad of cash. "Twenty-five bucks is a lot of money, little lady. You sure you want to throw that much away? Storm Squad never loses."

"I don't recall asking for your opinion."

Hardy records her bet and looks at Nellie.

The girl beams as she hands him a silver coin. It's probably all she has. "Fifty cents on the Navigation Squad."

"The crown appreciates your donation, kid." He drops it into the till and looks at me. "What about you? Care to make a wager?"

"All I have is this." I place the peanut Gideon gave me on the counter.

He raises an eyebrow and makes a show of swiping the peanut into the trash. "Is there anything else I can do for you, or are you going to keep standing there and wasting my time?"

"I'd like to post this." I hand him the letter addressed to my brother without the honorific in front of his name.

The mail clerk glances at the address and drops it into a canvas sack as he waves us away to help the next person in line.

—⬩—

"Come on, girl. I know you can move faster than that," Serin yells from the sideline during our afternoon combat training session.

The game starts in four hours. I haven't gotten a response from Gideon since posting the letter yesterday afternoon. Serin has kept Nellie and me up late, laying out our strategy to win the game. She's even skipped her nightly hour-long reprieve from guard duty. Silas hasn't had a reason to come to my door and I haven't been able to sleep. I'm exhausted, and every part of my body aches. Whether from Serin's brutal training routine or getting my ass handed to me by a storm summoner during our morning combat training session, I can't be sure.

"Remember to keep your weight off that front foot," Serin says.

I adjust my stance and block as Grace LeMay, Landry's star pupil, swings for my head.

"Don't disappoint me, rabbit. It's not a win if you don't leave a mark," Landry yells.

The girl's body tenses. "I heard about what happened to you at the ball." Her tone carries the familiar combination of practiced disdain and apathy of the elite.

She shifts back and forth on her feet, sending her blond ponytail swinging behind her. Her arms are covered in lace-like burns cause by lightning—evidence that Storm Squad hasn't been following the no-dueling rule.

I have no illusions about my ability to win this round. She's taller, faster, and in better shape than I am. Her long arms give her the advantage of reach. I won't be able to get close to her without taking a hit. I watch her shoulder, waiting for her to signal her next move so I can block and avoid another bruise.

"Quite the bold move to show up at your ex's betrothal party dressed like a harlot." Grace plants her weight on her front foot and takes a swing at my face. I step into the attack like Serin showed me, hugging her as I reach around and hit her with a weak shot to the kidney. She doesn't even flinch.

"It was a firebird costume," I say, shoving her away.

"Good work, Thorne," Serin shouts. "Put your weight into it next time."

"Stop dancing around, LeMay. Go for the throat like we talked about," Landry demands from the sidelines.

Grace glances warily at Landry as she retreats. "I heard it was a bunch of shredded lace you sewed together in your kitchen. Good for you, making do with what you have. Such a shame your parents left you destitute. I suppose they got what they deserved for fraternizing with reavers."

I swing for her head.

Grace uses the opening to go for my gut. I drop my elbows to block, and she cracks me in the mouth with her opposite hand.

"Fuck." I bend over and spit blood on the deck.

"Break." Jo-el steps between us, stopping her advance before she can hit me again.

I step to the side of the ring and wince as Serin inspects my split lip.

"You have to be stronger, faster, or smarter than your opponent," Serin says. "That girl is beating you on all three. Stop planting your feet when you block. Keep moving. Block and dodge, block and dodge." She lifts her hands in front of her face and twists her body sideways to demonstrate.

A huff of hot breath slides down the back of my neck, making my pulse leap. I lift my gaze to the smokestacks as Silas steps out of the shadows. He crosses his arms and leans against the black column.

"You all right, Thorne?" Jo-el asks.

"It's just a scratch." My scalp tingles with Silas's request for access to the warded room in my mind. I ignore him and grab my canteen. I don't need another reminder to drink more water.

"If you need to go to the medic, we can call the round."

"Call the round, Sanchez. Grace drew first blood," Landry demands.

"Get in there and kick that storm bitch's ass." Serin spins me around and shoves me back into the ring toward Grace.

She comes at me again.

I step in and block the blow, but as I twist away from her, she sweeps my feet out from under me. My shoulder slams into the deck, knocking the wind out of my lungs. Magic prickles over my scalp again.

"*I don't need any more fucking water, reaver.*"

"*She leads with her left foot. Kick her knee out as soon as she places her weight on it.*"

"*Are you speaking to me now?*"

"*Focus on your opponent, Thorne.*"

I grit my teeth. "*No more princess? You finally learned my name.*"

Silas doesn't respond.

"Don't drink too much tonight," Grace whispers as she helps me up. "You'll want a clear head if you want to survive the game." She advances on me again. As soon as she plants her weight on her left leg, I kick her knee. She shrieks like a water wraith and drops to the deck with a thud.

I glance up at the smokestack as the bell rings.

Silas is gone.

"Gray, you're up next," Jo-el says, pointing at Serin.

She grins as she enters the ring. Watching her fight is like watching a bird dive in and out, taking vicious bites of her opponent. He's bigger and stronger, but only half as fast. She makes him chase her around in circles until he's drenched in sweat and panting for breath.

"That all you got, Dunlow?" someone yells. "Stop dancing and hit her already."

He cocks his thick arm back and swings wide. Instead of retreating, Serin steps into him and grabs the back of his neck with both hands. His powerful punch misses its mark, and his forearm grazes off her shoulder. She brings her knee up and catches him in the groin. He drops his hands to cover his crotch. Serin punches him in the throat as he goes down.

Nellie squeals and pumps her fist in the air as the bell rings, ending the round.

"Where did you learn to fight like that?" Nellie asks as Serin rejoins us.

"Prison."

Nellie's jaw goes slack. Serin gives us both a look that doesn't invite any more questions.

"You didn't have to go that hard on him," I murmur.

"Just giving everyone a preview of what they can expect if they try to come after us tonight."

The bell rings again, and Jo-el drags a gangly kid whose face is gushing blood out of the ring.

"Thorne, you have medical experience. Get over here and hold him still while I reset his nose."

The crowd parts as Jo-el walks him toward the chart room, away from the gawking spectators. "This isn't break time, people," he says, pointing at Nellie and Serin. "The two of you, in the ring."

The injured kid jerks away as Jo-el lifts his hands to inspect the damage. The poor kid's nose is on the wrong side of his face. I school my expression and place my hand on his arm.

"Hey, look at me. You're okay. I'm going to give you a big hug. We're going to take a deep breath and count backward from ten together while Captain Sanchez checks to see if it's broken. Okay?"

He whimpers as I hug him from behind, trapping his arms against his trembling body. He copies my deep breath as Jo-el places his fingers on the teen's face.

"Ten." I nod to Jo-el.

There's an audible crunch, followed by a scream as he forces the kid's nose back in place. The kid goes limp in my arms.

"Gideon is waiting for you in the infirmary." Jo-el pulls a bottle of smelling salts out of his pocket.

I glance toward the training ring.

"I'll keep your friends occupied." He pops the cork, and the kid jolts awake as he passes the bottle under his nose. "Thorne, take Private Guidry to the medic on duty and get back before anyone misses you."

Gideon glances up from where he's seated on the edge of the infirmary bed as I shoulder my way through the door, the still woozy teenager leaning heavily against me.

"Looks like you have another customer who needs your attention more than I do," Gideon says to the medic who's massaging ointment into the bunched and twisted flesh that extends from his hand, up his arm, and onto his bare chest.

"That's the third broken nose today. Let's get you cleaned up, Private." The medic takes the boy into the washroom at the back of the infirmary.

"Does it hurt?" I ask, nodding to Gideon's burn scars.

"It looks far worse than it feels." He shrugs his shirt on quickly and locks the door. "I received your message. What have you learned about Dagmara's plan?"

"That's not... did you not read my letter?" He clearly didn't understand the metaphor about not letting my feral beast of a cat out of the house. "I need you to cancel the game. It's not wise to let anyone off the boat unsupervised."

"The last time you asked me to cancel something, the palace was attacked. What do you know that you're not telling me?"

"Nothing. I just feel like something bad is going to happen."

"I'm sorry, Everly, but I'm going to need something more concrete than your gut feelings this time. Tell me why you were so adamant about canceling the dragon boat parade."

"It would have been an insulting gesture to the king of Saracen and your future wife to force them to watch a celebration glorifying the devastation we did to their country two hundred years ago."

"Did Dagmara pay you to manipulate me into canceling the parade?"

"How could you even think that?" I ask, drawing back.

"You said she offered to pay you to be my mistress. Her shadow-summoning spy almost killed one of my officers for insulting you. Then you help him pull off that stunt with the egg to make me look like a fool in front of my soldiers. You should have told me what they were planning."

"I didn't know anything about that. You can ask Landry. He and Silas planned it together."

"I have. Landry said the shadow summoner has been seen sneaking off to your room when he's supposed to be patrolling the decks with the night watch. If you're not plotting with my fiancée's spy, why would he visit you every night?"

Heat creeps up my neck at the thought of Silas standing guard outside my door while Serin takes her break. Landry and his minions watch me like a hawk. Anyone could have seen him coming and going. If I deny he was there, Gideon will never trust me again.

"Do you really want me to go into detail? Why does it baffle you that another man would seek out my company."

"Are you saying you're sleeping with Silas Drake?"

"You asked me to get close to him." My gut wrenches with the lie.

He runs his scarred hand over his face. "I didn't ask you to fuck him."

"I make my own choices, Gideon." My chest flares as I grab his hands. "You have to cancel the hazing game. Someone is going to get hurt. Landry has already threatened me twice."

"It's a tactic the senior officers use to intimidate the conscripts so they'll take it seriously. The rabbit hunt isn't a game. It's a training exercise. As soon as we're off the boat, these kids have to be able to communicate effectively and depend on each other. You saw what happened at the ball. It was chaos. Reavers aren't the only danger we'll face. We're heading into the heart of the Northlands, where humans are hunted for sport. The only way these soldiers will survive is if they learn to work together as a coordinated unit. I'd rather they figure it out in a controlled scenario before we're in real danger."

"Please, Gideon. I feel like something bad is going to happen."

He presses the peanut into my hands and pulls away. "I can't stop the rabbit hunt, but I'll do what I can to make sure no one gets seriously injured. Don't risk coming to me again unless you have something important to report." Gideon slips out the door as the medic ushers Private Guidry out of the back room.

Chapter Twenty-One

"No one is gonna mess with us tonight. Not after you wiped the floor with those storm summoners," Nellie says, catching up to Serin and me as we exit the showers.

I can't shake the heavy feeling in the pit of my stomach. We're the smallest squad by far. The odds of us getting through this game unscathed are slim, even with our unconventional plan.

The lines to enter the dining room extend all the way into the main deck's lobby with its grand wrought-iron staircase. There's an excited hum in the air as Serin cranes her neck to see what's causing the back-up.

A huff of hot breath slides down my neck, making my pulse do a traitorous little kick as I stretch my aching arms.

"This way," Serin says, pushing me to the line on the far left, where Silas and Jo-el are patting everyone down before they enter.

"What's this about?" a storm summoner asks ahead of us.

"New rule," Jo-el says. "The Colonel doesn't want you fools destroying his fiancée's pretty boat tonight. Hand over your relic and any weapons you have."

The tightness in my gut loosens a little. *Thank you, Gideon.*

Tendrils of phantom static hover around the storm summoner's feet as he hands Jo-el a dagger. "I left my relic in my bunk."

"*He's lying*," I say, unlocking the door in my mind. "*Check his left boot.*"

"Make him take his shoes off," Silas says to Jo-el, patting down a gawky teen.

"You heard him, Private. Take off your boots."

The storm summoner shoots Silas a dark scowl as he pulls the sliver of a thunderbird talon out of his boot.

"Gray, over here," Jo-el says as Serin steps up to Silas.

"Hand over your weapons and relic."

Serin reaches up her sleeve and pulls out a piece of firebird down. Her body still ripples with heat as she hands it over, telling me she's still carrying several more.

"Any weapons?" Jo-el asks.

"I don't need a weapon to kill you, boy."

"Turn around."

Serin grits her teeth as Jo-el pats her down and pulls the dagger from the back of her waistband and waves her in. "Next."

Nellie already has her feather ready. She hands it to Silas as I stop in front of Jo-el.

"Keep moving, Thorne."

"Aren't you going to pat me down, Captain Sanchez? I could be hiding a dangerous weapon too."

He motions for me to turn around. I slip the book off my back and smile at Silas as Jo-el runs his hands over my ribs, down my sides to my hips and over my backside. Silas's jaw clenches as his gaze tracks the man's roving hands.

"Don't forget my bag, Captain Sanchez." I hold it open, knowing he won't find the firebird feather that's coiled up in the warded pocket.

Jo-el gives my belted bag a cursory glance before waving me into the dining room.

The usual buffet line serving rations of beans and hardtack is closed. Each table is set with fine china, polished silver, and sparkling crystal. The plates and cloth napkins all bear the Saracen crest.

"Is this all for the game?" I ask as Mattern approaches our table.

"This is likely the last formal meal we'll see for a while. Once we leave the ship, you'll be living on whatever rations you can carry and what we can forage or hunt as we march north. Leave your books in your room. Everyone gets a reprieve from their responsibilities tonight. There are only a few rules. If you're caught hiding in your cabin, your entire team forfeits. The infirmary, chart room, and the pilothouse are off limits. Squad officers cannot offer any assistance, protection, or advice once the game begins. Good luck and try to enjoy yourselves. This is supposed to be fun."

I can't help the indignant snort that escapes me. Being hunted and forcibly stripped of my clothing by a band of feral teenagers isn't exactly my idea of a good time.

"I don't eat fowl," Serin says as a witch with long black hair sets a platter of what looks like squab or maybe roasted duck with white potatoes in the center of the table. Her face is familiar, but I can't place her. Her server's smock covers the squad emblem on her uniform, and she isn't carrying a relic.

"Then I recommend you fill up on bread," Mattern says as the server places a basket of biscuits and cornbread on the table. "It's likely to be a long night. Have you talked about your strategy?"

"We're going to hide with—"

"Never share your plans with anyone outside your circle of trust. That's rule number one," Serin says.

"And if someone asks you the plan, you lie. That's rule number two," I say, biting back a smile.

"You don't have to tell me anything," Mattern says as Serin cuts me a sidelong look. "There's no dishonor in hunkering down in a storm. We dock in Port Hope at dawn. Morning duty and combat training are canceled tomorrow. Report to the chart room for your new assignments at noon."

"What if we win?" Nellie asks.

"I recommend you go straight back to your rooms after dinner and layer on every piece of clothing you have," Mattern says as the server fills our glasses with champagne. "I'll see you all tomorrow at noon."

"I don't think Mattern bet on us," Nellie says as she takes a gulp of her fizzy wine.

"Rule number three. Keep a clear head before going into battle." Serin reaches across me and takes Nellie's glass. A fluttering sensation tickles my face as the wine passes under my nose.

"Wait." I grab Serin's wrist. "Don't drink that." I swirl my finger in the wine to dissipate the bubbles. The phantom pulse of wings beats against my finger. "It's laced with pixie dust."

My stomach drops as I glance around the room. Almost everyone has sucked down their champagne. Storm Squad are the only ones who haven't touched their glasses.

Silas sits with Gideon's Elite Guard at the long head table. His gaze flicks to Serin over his half-empty glass as they have a silent conversation. His nostrils flare as he sniffs his champagne and holds it up to the light.

I grab the bottle off our table and take a deep swig as I make a meandering circle around the room. Ripples of heat radiate from the fire summoner Serin kneed during combat training.

"*This one's still carrying a relic,*" I say across the bond.

"Hello, handsome. You took the pain so well today. I think you deserve a reward." I stick my finger in his wine and trace the liquid over his lip before giving him a quick kiss. No flutter.

"Are you my prize?"

I twist away from him before he can grab my ass with his meaty hands.

"*What the fuck do you think you're doing?*"

"*Checking to see if all the wine is laced with sedative, or just mine.*"

I take another long pull from the bottle, savoring the burst of bubbles in my mouth as I move to another table.

"Private Guidry," I say, frowning at his blackened and swollen nose. "You're not supposed to have that." I pluck his glass from his hand and knock it back in one gulp. "Doctor's orders."

"*Stop drinking it.*"

I yawn widely as I pick up a glass from one of the Storm Squad's tables, taking a small sip.

"*Everly.*" The way Silas slowly growls my name across the bond sends a flush of heat through my body.

"*Relax, reaver. I know what I'm doing.*" I lock the door in my head, kicking him out.

Silas scowls as I run my fingers along the length of the head table, setting the wineglass next to Gideon's, knocking it over. It sloshes over my fingers, soaking the white tablecloth.

"Everything all right, Private Thorne?" Gideon asks.

I force another fake yawn, ignoring the prickle of magic across my scalp. "I just wanted to thank you for keeping us all safe," I say, plucking a piece of duck off his plate and popping it into my mouth.

"You're drunk."

"I think you might be right. You know how champagne goes straight to my head. I should probably lie down."

"Captain Sanchez, take Private Thorne back to her quarters so she can sober up before the game begins."

Silas shoves his chair back, grabbing a loaf of bread off the table. "I've got it, Sanchez. Stay with the colonel. I'm headed out for watch duty anyway."

I hiccup and sway on my feet the way the Menagerie guards did after I drugged them. Silas grabs my book by the ropes and leads me out like a horse by the reins.

He doesn't let go until we're in the hall outside my room.

"Do you think toying with my life is some kind of game?" Silas backs me against the warded door.

"One of you want to explain what the fuck that was back there?" Serin asks, coming up behind us.

"Not here." Silas unravels the ward and shoves me inside the tiny room that is definitely too small for two people and an angry six-and-a-half-foot-tall slab of carved muscle. "Drink this." He takes the champagne bottle and shoves his canteen into my hands.

"What is it with you and water?"

"You just drank an entire bottle of drugged wine. You need to start flushing it out of your system."

"Why did you keep drinking if you knew it was drugged?" Serin asks.

"My parents prescribed pixie dust to help me sleep through the incessant call of magic after I woke from my fever. I built up a tolerance. It doesn't work on me anymore."

"Who would want to drug you?" Silas asks, jaw tight.

"Landry," Serin says. "He threatened her yesterday. Said he was coming for her during the game."

"I think Grace may have been trying to warn me. She told me not to drink the wine when we were sparring. That I'd need a clear head to survive the game."

"Can you prove that sick fuck was the one who dosed the wine?" Silas asks.

"What does that matter?"

"Because the blood oath won't let me kill him unless I know for a fact that he tried to hurt you."

"It may not even have been meant for me. They could have been targeting Serin. She's the only real threat on our team. Besides, you can't just kill one of Gideon's officers."

"I'll make it look like an accident." Black shadows curl around Silas's shoulders.

"I'm serious. You can't touch a hair on that asshole's head. If you start killing Gideon's senior officers, it will only confirm his suspicions that you're a spy."

"Why would he suspect that?" Silas asks.

The room suddenly feels too warm with the three of us packed in the narrow space between the bunks and the wall. Him at my front, Serin at my back, just like in the alley the day we met.

"Answer me," Silas demands.

"He suspects that the two of you are Dagmara's spies and asked me to keep an eye on you and let him know if I noticed anything suspicious."

"What did you tell him, girl?"

"Nothing, I swear. The blood oath wouldn't let me even if I tried. You're not the only one who doesn't want to burn alive."

"How are you communicating with him? You haven't left Serin's sight since you boarded the ship."

"Gideon left a letter in my bunk the first day, asking me to be his spy. You burst into my room while I was trying to burn it."

"Ward the door behind me and don't let her fucking leave," Silas says to Serin.

"What about the game?" she asks. "We need those passes."

"Someone tried to sedate Everly to make it easier to catch her and relieve her of her clothing. If anyone so much as touches her, I'll relieve them of their fucking hands. She stays here for the rest of the night, and so do you."

Silas slams the door on his way out, leaving Serin to weave a protection ward over it.

"What is his problem?"

Serin shoots me a withering look. "Please tell me you're not that daft."

"Apparently I am."

"Silas is extremely possessive of his things."

"He doesn't own me. He can't just order me to stay in here like a prisoner."

"So long as his magic burns in your chest, you belong to him, and Silas Drake does not like to share."

"He doesn't act like that with you."

"One, because I can defend myself. And two, I would never let anyone bind their life to mine, not even my mate. Agreeing to a life bond is the most powerful form of control someone can give you. It makes him vulnerable and comes with certain side effects. The longer you're bound to him, the more intense they'll become."

"What kind of side effects?"

"The kind that make him want to cut off a man's hands for touching you. Why do you think he was so desperate to get out of combat training duty? It would have been difficult for him to watch other men put their hands on you without overreacting."

I shrug the book off my back and drop it on my bunk.

"No, I don't accept that. He's an expert at manipulation and misdirection. He controls everyone and everything around him."

"Everything except you. You shouldn't have let him kiss you."

"Because it brought out his homicidal tendencies?" I roll my eyes. "I'll not take the blame for his bad behavior."

"Trust me, he doesn't blame you. Blood oaths are powerful magic. He knew the consequences of binding his life to yours, and he did it anyway."

"Why?"

"You'll need to ask him that yourself. I can't tell you that without violating my oath to him. I'd rather not self-combust either. It's not my time yet."

"He won't tell me."

"No, I don't suspect he will."

"Did you just agree with me? Nellie will never believe this." I grab Serin's arm. "Shit. She drank the wine, and we just left her out there to fend for herself."

CHAPTER TWENTY-TWO

"That's not going to happen, girl. Silas will kill me if I let you out of this room."

"Then leave me here and go find Nellie. I promise I'll stay put."

"No."

"Please, Serin. She's just a kid. She can't defend herself without a relic."

Serin sputters a string of curses as she unlocks the wards. "Lock yourself in."

I weave one of Silas's patterns over the door, then pace the room. I lie down. I sit up. I kick off my boots and do push-ups. Anything to get the awful images out of my head. All I can see is Nellie dropping from the sky and landing on the wooden deck at all the wrong angles.

Was this what the boy's ghost was trying to tell me? That Nellie's life was in danger? She was there, sitting right next to me every time he appeared. She even said she worked as a chimney sweep.

What if Landry makes her climb the smokestack, and she slips? If she dies, it will be my fault. Just like my parents. They took more risks and traveled farther into the Wastes in their search for a cure after I got the fever. They did it for me. Now Nellie's a target too. Because of me.

I sit on the edge of my bunk as my thoughts spiral. I wish Wallace was here. She'd know how to talk me down. She'd tell me Serin knows her way around the ship better than anyone, thanks to our predawn runs. That she's fast and she'll find Nellie in no time.

Fuck. I swipe the tear from my cheek. I miss Wallace. She'd handle all of this so much better than I have. She certainly wouldn't sit around waiting for something to happen. She'd be out there looking for Nellie herself.

Serin isn't the only one who knows her way around the ship. If Silas catches me, he'll be furious. He might punish me, but he won't hurt me. His wrath, I can live with. If something happens to Nellie, I'll never forgive myself.

The hallway outside our room is empty. So is the internal staircase as I creep up the steps in my bare feet. Serin won't think to check the smokestacks. She'll have gone straight to the women's showers on the bottom deck, where we agreed to encamp for the night with the medic squad conscripts. The one door and dog-legged entrance is easy to defend and is the perfect place to ambush intruders. The plan was to offer refuge to anyone else looking for a safe place to hide in exchange for two pieces of clothing.

"Did you see which way she went?" someone asks from the landing below me.

"You go down; I'll go up," Grace LeMay says in her unmistakable haughty tone. "Make sure you get all her clothing if you find her. We can't go back empty-handed."

I race up the cold metal stairs, hoping her sprained knee slows her down. A twinge of guilt twists in my gut. She'll be limping for weeks with the injury I inflicted in the training ring. The march into the Northlands will be painful. She'll be vulnerable if we're attacked.

A breeze tugs at my long hair as I exit the stairwell and slide along the wall. There's no telling who's keeping watch from the pilothouse. I don't know what Silas will do to Grace if he catches her chasing me. If what Serin said is true, I need to be careful with the lives around me. I can't be responsible for anyone else's death.

I slip into the chart room and hide under the counter that lines the bank of windows.

"What are you doing up here, LeMay?" Landry says. "You're supposed to be keeping an eye on that mouthy whore. Did you not understand your orders?"

I grip the edge of the counter and peek out the window.

Static crackles at his fingertips. Grace winces as he summons a coiled whip of lightning. "You know how disappointed I'll be if I don't win, Gracie."

"Of course. I'm sorry, Victor." She hugs her own chest, covering the burns on her arms with her hands as she stares at her feet. "I watched her like you said. She left her room alone a few minutes ago. I... I thought I saw her come this way."

"You leave her to me." Grace flinches as he brushes a strand of hair away from her face. "Now get the fuck downstairs and skin as many rabbits as you can. Whoever brings me the most clothing at the end of the night will be generously rewarded."

Grace swipes a stray tear from her cheek as she runs toward the external staircase.

I duck as Landry turns toward the chart room. If he comes in here, he'll see me. A tremor quivers through my body, making my muscles go weak as I crawl across the floor and duck into the shadows under the round table.

"Come out, come out, wherever you are, little rabbit." Landry knocks on the window as he makes his way around to the door.

My pulse pounds in my head. I'm not sure how much he can see from the outside or what he'll do when he finds me. Grace was clearly afraid of him.

Silas was right. Landry is a sick fuck.

The door clicks open. My body stiffens.

"I know you're in here, Thorne." He pulls the chairs out one by one. "You might as well come out and accept your punishment for ruining my uniform. I'm going to enjoy silencing your filthy little mouth."

Static crackles in the air. I can't reach my belt pouch without shifting and giving my position away. Landry can wield lightning, wind, and rain. I can barely shoot a flame.

Chair legs scrape across the wooden floor on the opposite side of the table.

He's going to find me.

My heart pounds in my ears. I make myself as small as possible behind the thick table base that hides the egg. If I try to fight him off, he'll only hurt me more. I just need to endure whatever vicious punishment he thinks he's entitled to enact.

He pulls out the chair in front of me. All he has to do is crouch down.

I squeeze my eyes shut and curl around the ember of magic binding me to the oath and to Silas. I cling to it as it flares. Landry can't hurt me if I let it consume me. I want it to consume me. To erase every trace that I was here. I want it to make me disappear.

Fire spreads through my chest. It stretches into my limbs like an ancient beast waking from a long slumber. The dragon's magic surges through my body and explodes around me like a dark flame. The shadowy tendrils lick at my skin and envelop me like a shield.

"What the—" Landry's voice cuts off. The chair clatters to the floor. The port-side door slams open. Heavy footsteps move away.

Minutes pass. It's eerily quiet. Darkness clings to me like an impenetrable blanket of night. It's so thick I can't even see my own shaking hands. There's no light, no sound, no whispers of magic. I'm alone.

I crawl out of my hiding spot and drag my aching body up to my feet. The delicate brush of shadows against my skin is disorienting. They swirl around me like a warm breeze waiting for direction as I feel my way around the room. I try to shake them off, but they won't go away.

I bend over and reach for where I think the toppled chair lies on the floor. My forehead smacks against the enclosed glass bookcase instead.

Shit. How am I supposed to search for Nellie if I can't even find my way out of the damn room? I drop my shield and open my senses.

Nothing. Not even the cold call of the dragon egg, and it's right next to me.

I've spent the last ten years suffering through the constant onslaught of magic. The complete absence is strange and beautiful. I press my cheek against the cool glass and let the silence seep in. My mind hasn't been this quiet in over a decade. I almost forgot what it feels like to be at peace in my own skin.

The ember of dragon fire in my chest throbs, but it doesn't burn like all the times before when I tested the limits of the oath. When I channel power from a firebird relic, it feels foreign. Like it doesn't belong to me.

The dark magic flowing through me now feels familiar—like a part of me that's always been there. The one I keep buried deep. The one that tried to claw its way out of my chest during my witch fever and still haunts my dreams. It scares me. Because all I want to do is sink into its power and let it devour me whole.

I'm not sure how I summoned shadows from the residual dragon magic binding me to the oath. Or how to give them back. And I *need* to give them back. They're as seductive as a lover's caress. A caress that will go cold as soon as the oath is fulfilled.

"You're very bad at following orders, little spark."

"Silas?" I spin in the direction of his voice.

"Do I need to start tying you to the bed to get you to stay put?"

"How did you get in here?" The shield blocked his magic. I didn't feel him approach.

"I think the more pertinent question is why you're not in your room. How did you sneak out without Serin noticing?"

"It's not Serin's fault."

"I asked you a question." His scent washes over me. An intoxicating mix of the peppermint soap he uses and the lingering sweet spice of clove on his breath. He's right in front of me.

"You asked me two questions."

"What are you doing in here, Everly?"

If I reach out, I know he'll be there. Waiting for me in the dark like he is every night in my imagination as I pleasure myself.

I press my back against the bookcase.

"Did you think it would be fun to make me chase you around the ship."

"Your ego is truly unmatched." I can't help the incredulous grunt that escapes me. "I was looking for someone."

"You used the bond to summon me." Silas pulls the darkness back just enough for me to see his brutally beautiful face.

"I summoned the magic binding me to the oath. Not you."

"We're one and the same. When you summon my magic, you summon me. My shadows got here first." He raises his fingers to my swollen lip like he wants to touch me, then decides against it.

"How do I unsummon it?" I say, unable to mask my rising irritation.

"Are you asking me to leave?" Silas smirks as he pulls away.

"No." I fist his tunic, hating the thread of panic in my voice. "I didn't mean to summon you. I was looking for my friend Nellie. When I got up here, Landry was on the deck. I hid, but he found me."

"I know." A phantom growl resonates through the dark.

"Did you kill him?"

"Tell me how you got past Serin."

"She thinks I'm still in the room. Nellie drank the wine. I'm worried she might be in trouble. I begged Serin to go find her and promised I'd stay put, but she'd been gone a long time, and I couldn't just sit there and wait. Now I'm stuck inside your shadows, and I don't know how to release them."

"Shadow magic is an extension of the dragon fire in your chest. All the power comes from here." Silas presses his palm against my sternum. "It responds to your base instincts. If I want someone dead, the shadows become my blades. If I want to touch something, they become my hands."

A dark caress glides over my cheek.

"How do I make them go away?"

"The magic is reacting to your fear. If you want to drop them, you need to convince yourself you're not afraid of me."

"I'm not afraid of you, reaver."

Silas presses his thumb to the side of my throat. "So you keep insisting. Your racing pulse says otherwise."

He pushes off the bookcase and reels in the darkness around us.

A chill sinks into my bones. Without the protection of his shadow shield, the egg's cold magic drives the warmth from my body. I stuff my hand into my waist pouch and draw magic from the firebird feather hidden inside, then pull my wards back into place.

"I'll take you back to your room."

"What about Nellie?"

"Serin is an incredible hunter. She'll find her. Take my hand."

"Why?"

"Because your muscles are fatigued from training and you drank an entire bottle of wine without eating anything. Not to mention summoning me through the bond depleted most of your energy. I can't have you falling down the fucking stairs and breaking your damn neck."

Rough calluses scrape against my palm as I accept his outstretched hand. I'm perfectly capable of walking on my own; I just don't feel like arguing about it.

My legs tremble like they're made of wet mud as he leads me down the tight interior stairwell. I hate that he's right. How does he always seem to know what my body needs before I do?

A blast of heat hits me as we enter the second-floor landing. A group of fire summoners blocks our path.

Silas glares down at them. They part so he can pass. One of them grabs me, yanking me into the center of their little team, and summons a circle of flame around me.

"Take off your clothes, and we'll let you go, rabbit."

My gaze meets Silas's. "*Don't. It's just a game.*"

His eyes flash crimson, reflecting the ring of fire, and the world goes dark.

Their bodies drop to the floor with soft thuds.

Silas's hand covers my mouth, stifling my scream as he pulls me back against him.

"They're not dead. But they'll have a vicious headache when they wake." The shadows recede, revealing the unconscious teens slumped on the floor.

"They're just kids, you overprotective ass. You didn't have to hurt them."

"Let's go." He grabs my hand and drags me out of the stairwell and down the hall.

Serin is waiting outside our door.

"Where's Nellie?" I ask.

"Sleeping soundly in the infirmary. Sanchez is looking after her. We have a bigger problem." Serin gestures into our tiny bunk room.

Silas pushes past her and utters a rumble of obscenities.

My map book is lying on the center of my bunk with a goblin-spelled dagger plunged through the cover—the Landry family crest engraved on the jeweled hilt. Subtle threads of magic ripple around it.

"I should have killed that sick fuck when I had the chance."

"He's not dead?" I ask, my voice breaking over the words.

"You asked me not to kill him. I gave him a warning instead."

"Since when did you start listening to her?" Serin asks.

"You left her alone." His voice turns into a low growl as he turns on Serin.

"If she'd been in here when he came looking, you'd both be dead."

"You're right." Silas grabs my carpet bag and starts stuffing my things inside.

"What are you doing?"

"You're not safe here."

"Are you sending me home?"

"Letting you leave before you've fulfilled your end of the oath would be suicide. If you die, I die." His dark gaze darts to mine. "From now on, you sleep with me."

Chapter Twenty-Three

"You can't be serious." I stop in the doorway and glance around his tiny cabin. It's even smaller than the one I shared with Serin.

"It's only two nights," Silas says, dropping my bag on the floor with a thud.

An alarm clock ticks out the seconds from a narrow writing desk. A wooden stool and large armoire are the only other furniture.

"There's no bed."

"It folds out of the cabinet." He opens the armoire built into the far wall to reveal a mattress as wide as the room.

The image of Silas and me squeezing into the small bunk together makes my pulse skitter. The man is huge. We'll be on top of each other.

"You should get some sleep. I'll be spending the night in the hallway, where I can keep watch."

My chest deflates. I'm not sure if I'm relieved or disappointed.

"If you're doing this to punish Serin, you can stop. It's not her fault. I forced her to go find Nellie. I'm the one who broke your order to stay in the room."

"No one forces Serin to do anything she doesn't want to do."

"She said you forced her to babysit me as punishment for not keeping me safe at the ball."

"Did she?" The corner of Silas's mouth lifts as he pulls a dark cloak from a hook in the cabinet.

"Is it not true?"

"I assigned the duty to Val, but Serin thought you'd be more receptive to a woman and volunteered."

"Serin? The woman who's been torturing me for three weeks?"

"You mean the woman who's been watching your back, teaching you how to defend yourself, and helping you build up your strength and stamina?"

"I didn't think about it that way." I drop my gaze to the wooden floor.

"Do you truly believe I'm the kind of man who would punish one of my crew for making a mistake?" Silas folds the cape into a pillow-sized square and sets it on the desk.

"You're liar and a thief with murderous tendencies. I've watched you slaughter thirty men and knock half a dozen children unconscious when you thought my life was in danger. What else am I supposed to think?"

"You might be grateful for my murderous tendencies the next time Landry comes looking for you."

My stomach drops.

"Look at me." Silas cups my face. "Whatever you think of me, I need you to trust that I won't let anything happen to you."

"Until the blood oath is fulfilled."

"Yes." His brow furrows as he studies my eyes.

I jerk away from him. "Why did you tie your life to mine with the oath? That wasn't one of my conditions. And don't tell me it was a mistake. I've seen the way you work. You don't make mistakes."

"You shouldn't ask questions you won't like the answers to."

"I'm risking my life with this oath too. I deserve to know the truth."

He leans against the edge of the desk. "Do you remember the day we met, when I promised to pay you a visit to return your sketchbook before I left Crecentis?"

"I wish I could forget."

"You were a loose end I couldn't afford to leave untied. Faye said you were smart. Two reavers attack you and steal your sketchbook with drawings of the Menagerie's layout days before the dowry goes missing. I couldn't have you putting it all together and drawing our faces for the wanted posters."

I swallow past the lump in my throat. "You were going to kill me?"

"I would have made it quick and painless."

"Why didn't you do it the night I came to your room?"

"You broke through my wards, and I realized you were more useful to me alive."

"That still doesn't explain why you tied your life to mine."

"So I wouldn't be tempted to kill you when you became an inconvenience." Silas reaches out and brushes a strand of hair from my face. "And you are *extremely* inconvenient."

"Inconvenient?"

"You asked for the truth. Now get some rest." Silas reaches for his folded cape.

"You can't sleep in the hall."

The corner of his mouth lifts. "And why is that?"

I fold my arms over my chest.

"Answer the question, little spark. Why don't you want me to sleep in the hall?"

"I may have led Gideon to believe that we've been sleeping together so I can spy on you. If you start acting like a gentleman and spend the night in the hall while I'm in your bed, he'll know I lied and kick us both off the ship."

"He can certainly try." Silas smirks.

"If you touch a hair on his head, you'll find out just how much of an inconvenience I can be, reaver. All I have to do is ask, and Gideon will put me on a boat back to Crecentis. What happens to you if I choose not to fulfill the oath and let the magic burn me alive?"

"Are you threatening me?"

"I'm suggesting a mutually beneficial solution to our predicament. If we both pretend that we're having sex, he won't have any reason to doubt me or kick us off the ship."

Silas raises a brow. "You want to *pretend* that we're fucking?"

"Exactly. As long as you and I can put on a convincing act, no one will question why we're suddenly spending so much time together or why you're acting like an overprotective jackass."

"It's a dangerous game, pretending. You can't drop the mask. Ever. No matter how much you might want to. They'll be watching everything we say and do. Especially Krimore. Are you sure you can handle that level of scrutiny?"

"I've been living a double life and lying to the people I love since the day I woke from my fever. I know how to pretend better than anyone."

He places his hands on my shoulders and moves me out of the way.

"What are you doing?" I ask as he winds the alarm clock and folds the mattress out of the armoire.

"Getting ready for bed." Silas tugs the black tunic off over his head and climbs into the single bunk. He props himself up on his side and pats the empty space next to him. "See? Plenty of room."

If he's going to torture me by sleeping half naked, it's only fair I do the same. I pull my shift out of my bag. I don't bother asking him to avert his eyes as I give him my back and pull the nightdress over my head. Once it's covering me, I slip out of my uniform and unlace my corset, letting it drop to the floor.

Silas watches me as I climb onto the bed.

"Stop staring at me like that."

"Like what?"

"Like I'm a decadent confection in the bakeshop window waiting to be devoured."

"Would you like to be devoured?" He drops his dark gaze to my mouth, making my stomach do a traitorous little flip. "This doesn't have to be pretend."

"Let's get something straight, reaver. If you try anything, I'll set your cock on fire while you sleep." I yank the pillow to my side of the bed and lie down next to him.

"You're stunning when you threaten me with violence."

"Save your flattery for when we have an audience."

"We need to set the rules for this little game before tomorrow. What's your definition of convincing?"

"How do you normally behave with the women you sleep with?"

"Before or after I pay them?"

"Have you never courted a woman?"

"Why don't you tell me what you like, and we'll start there?"

"Are you asking me to give you instructions on how to seduce me?"

"I don't need instructions, little spark. I just need you to lay out the rules."

"No kissing."

"I'm afraid we've already set the precedent for that. Everyone saw me kiss you in the training ring. Gideon will expect it."

"Fine. I'll allow the occasional kiss and affectionate caress."

"What kind of touch am I permitted?"

"The usual sort of things."

"Show me."

"You want me to touch you?"

Silas's gaze darkens. "What I want is irrelevant. I can't read your mind anymore. I need you to tell me your limits so I don't cross them. Show me what I'm allowed to pretend with you."

I brush a lock of hair away from his forehead.

"Is that all? This needs to be convincing."

I ghost my fingertips over the contours of his face. Silas closes his eyes as I trace his brow and the perfect bow of his lips. His throat bobs as I drag my nails over the day-old stubble along his jaw and down his neck. I trace the tattoo that covers his arm and fades onto his chest. His skin pebbles beneath my light touch.

"How many relics did it take to create your tattoos?" The magic contained under his skin hums against my fingertips.

"Just the one."

"It feels like more."

"Does it?" The way his stomach tightens as I flatten my palm against his taut muscles sends a thrill through me.

Touching him is addictive. My fingers ache to trace the dark line of hair that disappears beneath his trousers. I pull my hand away before I'm tempted to explore further.

"I don't have much experience with dragon scales," I say, clearing my throat. "But I can tell you how many witches there are in a room by the phantom sensations I receive from their relics. That's why my parents hid me when I got my fever. They feared the king would use me to hunt down deserters and rogue witches if I was discovered."

"I met a storm summoner who sensed things the way you do."

I prop up on my elbow. "How old was he? My parents searched for another witch who suffered from the same affliction in hopes that it would help them determine how long I might survive the burning. In their decades of travel, they never found one."

"He was a hunter a few years past his fever. He tracked my mother and me to a cave, waited for her to leave, and dragged me back to his village. We skipped rocks on a lake, and he told me all about his power and how it worked. I was young and hadn't come into my fever yet. I didn't realize he was using me as bait. When my mother came looking for me, he struck her down with a bolt of lightning right in front of me."

My heart aches at the image in my head of him as a boy, watching as his mother is murdered, knowing how terrified and helpless he must have felt. I didn't see my parents die, but I've imagined it a thousand times, unable to stop it. It's the feeling of helplessness that sticks with you the longest. It cracks you open, leaving a gaping hole in your chest.

"I'm sorry that happened to you." I blink back the sudden wetness threatening to blur my vision.

"Don't be. I've spent my life enacting my vengeance." Silas's brow furrows as he studies my mismatched eyes. "Your parents were wise to hide you."

"For all the good it did. They'd be disappointed if they could see me now. Sleeping with the enemy and betraying the crown."

"Are we enemies?"

"We're not friends. Our arrangement is purely transactional. You keep me alive, I help you steal the egg. Once you have what you're after, we'll never have to see each other again."

"Good to know you don't have things confused."

"No confusion here, reaver. I won't forget that I'm nothing more than an *inconvenience* to you." I roll onto my side and face the wall, ignoring the tightness in my chest.

"We need to talk about how you're going to handle Gideon's reaction tomorrow. You'll need to hurt him a little. That may be difficult for you."

"Good night, Silas."

Chapter Twenty-Four

Pebbles skitter over the cliff as I peer down into the canyon. The river looks like a silvery ribbon from this height. The steep walls are painted in layers of red and black rock. I've never been this far into the Wastes before.

My hand swats at the fly buzzing around my head. But it's not my hand. Someone else is in control. I feel like I'm looking out through their eyes as we back up. My heart lodges in my throat as we run and leap off the edge. I try to scream, but no sound comes out.

I squeeze my eyes shut and count backward from ten as I fall.

Ten. Wind whips at my skin.

Nine. Shadows wrap around me like a cocoon.

Eight. Bone-cracking pain rips through my body.

Seven. My limbs twist at all the wrong angles.

Six. I feel like I'm being ripped apart

Five. The ember in my chest ignites.

Four. Fire licks its way through my veins.

Three. The pain evaporates everywhere but my shoulder blades. It feels like they're holding a tremendous weight.

Two. The shadows evaporate as I open my eyes. Everything is brighter and more vibrant. Layered rainbows of rock whip past as I dive along the cliff face. I can see things I couldn't before. Small animals skitter across the ground far below. A school of fish trawls the bottom of the deep river as if the murky water has suddenly gone crystal clear.

A low, rib-shaking rumble vibrates my chest chasing dozens of birds from their nests and hiding spots in the canyon wall.

My body feels heavy and strong. I glance at my aching shoulders. A pair of leathery wings protrudes from my back. Wings. I have wings.

I pull them in and shoot toward the canyon floor. An exhilarating thrill zips down my spine. I can't remember the last time I felt this free.

The air warms as the ground rushes up to meet me. I throw my wings out at the last moment. The force tears at my back as I shoot out across the river. I glance down at my reflection on the surface. A massive beast with ebony scales and red eyes stares back at me.

I startle awake in a tangle of limbs and shadows. My cheek rests in a puddle of drool on Silas's bare chest. I listen to the steady beat of his heart and slowly extract my leg from where it's draped over his thigh. His shadows stir as I slip out of his arms and scoot my back against the wall.

Silas rolls onto his side to face me, and I force my body to still. His eyes move rapidly beneath his lids, hinting that he's still immersed in his own dreams.

He's utterly beautiful like this—one arm folded behind his head, all the tension in his jaw relaxed. The man is a work of art. My fingers twitch with the urge to draw him.

I watch his eyes move beneath his lids. What does a man like Silas Drake dream about?

If I could get inside his head, I might be able to figure out what he plans to do with the egg. Will he let me go when the blood oath is fulfilled? Or will he follow through on his original intent to kill me?

I reach out and touch his temples, using the remaining firebird magic in my system to bring the glowing threads of his mind ward to life. It's different from his other wards. There's no elaborate puzzle to unravel. The threads are knotted together like a tapestry depicting the map of a mountain range.

A tendril of shadow catches my wrist as I attempt to memorize the pattern, making my heart pound against my ribs. The shadow curls around my hand, tugging it away from Silas's face. I don't know how he's controlling the magic while he sleeps, but I desperately need him to teach me. If I could maintain a ward in my sleep, I'd never have to go to bed drunk again.

His alarm clock goes off from the desk under his bed. The mattress shifts next to me as Silas wakes and retracts his shadows.

"Sleep well, little spark?" His voice is rough and laced with an annoying smugness. I force my gaze away from the bulge in his trousers as he stretches lazily.

"No." I lie as I climb out of his bed, eager to be anywhere but here in this too small room. It was the first night in two years that I wasn't plagued by nightmares or the call of relics.

"Unpleasant dreams?" He folds the mattress back into the armoire and retrieves his black tunic from where he left it, folded neatly on his desk.

"I dreamed I was a dragon, soaring over a canyon in the Wastes." Silas pauses with one arm half in his tunic.

"How do you maintain your wards when you sleep?" My stomach growls as I retrieve my leggings from my pile of clothes on the floor and pull them on under my nightdress.

"Practice." He lets out a breath and tugs the tunic over his head.

"Will you teach me?"

"You need to master keeping them intact while you're awake first. Once you're dressed, we'll get some breakfast."

"What time did you set the alarm for?"

"Quarter after eight."

"Why would you do that? You know I run every morning at dawn with Serin." I shove my feet into my boots and scoop up the rest of my clothes from the floor. "She's going to make me do triple laps for this." I open the door and stumble into the hall. Strange that it's not warded.

Silas reels me back with his shadows. "Serin can wait."

He backs me against the doorframe.

"What are you doing?"

"Pretending." He leans down and captures my mouth. I let him tease me open as voices approach in the hall. He slides his hand to the back of my neck, fisting my hair and tipping my head back for better access. The mix of pain and pleasure is the best kind of torture. I grab his waist and tug him closer because I'm a fucking masochist, and all I want to do right now is melt into him.

"We missed you at breakfast, Drake."

Silas pulls away slowly, smiling down at me as he projects his voice across the bond. "*Right on time.*"

"As you can see, Captain Sanchez, I had more pressing matters to take care of." Silas steps away from me and dips his head. "Colonel Krimore."

"Everly." Gideon's face flushes as if he's the one who just got caught sneaking out of someone's room.

"Colonel Krimore." I lower my gaze to the floor.

"Was there something you needed, Your Royal Highness?" Silas asks.

"Since you missed most of your shift last night, Drake. You're on babysitting duty for the day. You'll accompany last night's game winners into Port Hope and ensure they make it back to the ship safe and sound tomorrow morning."

"Congratulations, Private Thorne. The Navigation Squad's plan to protect as many assets as possible won the training exercise."

"What?"

"Enjoy Port Hope with your new *friends*."

"As you wish, Colonel."

Gideon gives me a curt nod and stalks down the hall.

I yank Silas back into his room and slam the door.

"You set that up, you bastard. You knew exactly when he'd be walking past." I summon a flame to my hand.

"Your prince allowed Landry to force you to your knees. He deserved a gut punch. Now put your flame away before you hurt yourself."

"I didn't swear my life to yours in the oath. I could turn you to ash and walk away from all of this right now."

Silas reaches out and presses his palm to mine. The flame curls around his wrist and crawls up the dragon scales on his arm. Shadows flow over his shoulder like a wave and smother the flame.

"I've seen inside that wicked imagination of yours. If you want to destroy me, I know you can come up with something more creative than fire. Now get dressed. I can't wait to get off this fucking ship."

Silas keeps a hand on me as we make our way back to my room. Discarded clothing and hungover witches litter the ship. I kick a pile of green tunics to the side as we enter the stairwell.

"How did Serin manage to single-handedly win the game?"

"By being faster, smarter, and stronger than her enemy."

"Did you teach her that mantra?"

"She taught me."

"How long has she been in your crew?"

Silas glances down at me. "Since Thale made me swear a blood oath to help him break her out of prison."

"Wait... was the story you told me at the ball, about Thale offering you a job, true?"

"I've never lied to you."

"Is that your attempt at making a joke?"

"Name one time that I've lied to you."

"You lied to me about your plans for the ball."

"I withheld information to protect my crew. How is that any different from you pretending to be a spy or acting like you don't want me to make your body quiver with pleasure until you beg for release? Acting like you haven't imagined what it would feel like to be touched and teased by my shadows."

Heat creeps up my cheeks. There's no point in denying it. He's been inside my head. "Fantasizing about something and wanting it aren't the same," I say as we approach Serin's room.

"Just like lying and withholding the truth?" Silas taps out a quick cadence on Serin's door with his knuckles.

"You were supposed to meet me at dawn." Serin scowls as she ushers us inside.

"Take it up with Silas. He's the one who decided it was more important to stage a performance for Gideon." I squeeze past her and work Landry's dagger out of my map book. The goblin-spell magic pulses up my arm.

"I tried to talk to you about the plan last night. You're the one who refused to discuss it."

"You didn't tell me you were going to ambush him in the hallway while you were sticking your tongue down my throat." I wave Landry's blade in the air. The subtle magic creates a phantom trail of shimmering black threads behind it. Encrusted with rare black opals mined in the Wastes, it must have cost Landry a fortune. It's strange that he would throw away something so valuable to send me a message. Maybe he has so much money it doesn't matter.

"Pretending that we're fucking was your idea," Silas says.

"What did you just say?" Serin's head swivels back and forth between us.

Silas explains the ruse, and I have to admit it sounds less brilliant in the light of day than it did last night.

"The two of you are like dynamite and a fuse. Every time you're alone together, all our plans blow up." Serin massages her temples.

"Maybe if you shared more of the plan with me in advance, I wouldn't be such an *inconvenience*."

"She's right. The girl had ample opportunity to run to her prince last night, and she chose to help her friend instead. We need to start trusting her. And you need to focus. The side effects of the bond are making you lose sight of the target."

"What is your target? It's not just the egg. You could have stolen it at any point in the last three weeks and used it to hunt down the dragon yourself. What are you waiting for?"

"I don't need to hunt down the dragon. I already know where she is. She's being held in the dungeons beneath Tindlestone palace by Queen Isola. I can't get into the giant's stronghold without an invitation."

"Which Gideon has. That's why you staged the attack at the ball, to impress Serros so he'd send you on this quest. Which means you knew what Dagmara would demand."

"I may have suggested the idea to her."

"Are you working for her?"

"Not directly, but our goals are aligned. She wants her fiancé to hunt down a monster. I want the dragon and its egg."

"So you can slaughter the poor beast and steal the magic from its bones?" I clench my fists at my sides.

"What other reason is there?"

"The egg and its mother are the last of their kind. They need to be protected. Not hunted."

"I've watched you in the chart room, girl. Your entire body tenses up around the egg. It clearly terrifies you. Why would you want to protect something that tried to kill you?"

"Fear is a terrible reason to hate something. We know nothing about the way dragons reproduce and rear their young. That egg is an incredible opportunity to learn and understand more about a magnificent species. Serros wants to use it as a weapon. Gideon wants to destroy it, and you want to drain its power. I'm its only friend."

"It's unwise to befriend monsters," Silas says.

"So is swearing a blood oath to a reaver, yet here we are."

"Save your bickering for later," Serin says. "We have another complication to deal with. At breakfast, Landry made a big scene of accusing his protégé of stealing his dagger. He claims it's a priceless family heirloom. He made a big deal about having her room searched. When it came up empty, he demanded that Gideon search the entire ship before we disembark tonight. I think he's covering his tracks to deflect suspicion."

"How can you be sure?" Magic hums against my fingers as I study the blade.

"It's what I would do," Silas says. "Landry knows you have it. He'll make them search us before we leave the ship. Give it to me. I'll get rid of it."

Silas reaches for the dagger.

I clasp it to my chest.

"Give me the knife, Everly." The muscle along his jaw flexes.

"Stealing something this valuable is a hangable offense," I say. "Landry will ensure that anyone caught with the dagger is put in irons and transported back to Crecentis to be executed. After your little demonstration this morning, Gideon won't interfere. You'll lose whatever chance you had of getting into Queen Isola's palace."

Silas's gaze narrows on me. "Then open the fucking window and throw it overboard right now."

"It's goblin-spelled. We can't just throw it away. It might be useful if I can work out the magic. I have a secret warded compartment in my bag where I store my firebird feather. Jo-el searched me last night and didn't notice."

"That's because he was too busy groping your ass."

"I've searched through that bag myself when she was asleep. I never found the warded pocket," Serin says. "Let the girl keep the dagger. She might need a weapon to defend herself."

Chapter Twenty-Five

A caravan of oxen huff impatiently as storm summoners float crates off the ship onto wooden carts waiting on the docks of Port Hope's riverfront. No one notices the three of us slip from shadow to shadow under the cloak of Silas's magic as we sneak off the back in our civilian clothes to avoid being searched. Serin thought it best to not test our luck with Landry. Apparently, Silas's warning left the lieutenant with a broken nose.

My chest flutters every time I imagine Silas punching the entitled asshole in the face. The other part of me worries what a man like Landry might do in retaliation.

Silas jumps down to the dock five feet below. Serin follows as I gather my skirts and climb over the metal railing to the narrow ledge. There's a three-foot gap between the boat's hull and the low dock. They made it look easy. They're also wearing pants.

A prickling sensation runs over my skull. I ignore Silas's request to be let in. He reaches up with his shadows and lifts me off the boat without warning. I flail at the awkward sense of weightlessness until he catches me in his arms and sets me down slowly.

"Was that absolutely necessary?"

"It would be extremely inconvenient if you broke your leg." He leans down and whispers close to my ear. "The next time I ask you to open up for me, I expect you to listen."

"Keep your hands to yourself until we have an audience, reaver."

Silas backs away from me with that annoying smirk that sets my insides ablaze.

The trading port has doubled in size since the last time I visited with my parents five years ago. The limestone bluff above the river is dotted with more salt-box houses than I can count. There are buildings under construction on every street and entire blocks that weren't here before. Everything is new and clean. No horseshit to step around or mud to soil the hem of my skirt on the recently cobbled streets.

Silas orders three smoked meat sandwiches from a street vendor. I watch as a fire summoner slices three thick pieces of beef from the shank mounted on the spit of her pushcart.

The sizzling fat and smoke trigger a memory of my father roasting meat over our campfire. I shove it down before it unearths emotions I can't control.

"We ate before we left the ship. How are you still hungry?" I ask as the woman wraps up the sandwiches and hands them to Silas.

"He's always hungry," Serin says as she tears open the waxed-paper bundle he tosses to her.

"A piece of toast and two bites of beans isn't a meal. You're still starving."

"I didn't realize you were keeping track." My stomach growls as he shoves a warm, wrapped sandwich into my hand. It's not the first time he's known what my body needs before I do. I peel back the paper and take a bite, silently cursing him for being right.

He waits for me to swallow the first bite before dragging his gaze away and continuing down the street.

"I wish Nellie was feeling better. She wouldn't believe this," I say as I crane my neck to stare up at two industrial smokestacks stretching toward the sky above a factory.

"We don't have time for sightseeing," Serin says.

"What's the rush?" I ask around another mouthful of smoked meat and crusty bread.

"It's been three weeks since she's seen Thale," Silas says with a smirk.

"Is that why you were determined to win the game?"

She gives us a sour look.

"How did you do it? You didn't collect that many pieces of clothing."

"The officers made a show of collecting everyone's relics, but there was no rule against using magic. I caught three witches from each battle squad and warded them in their rooms before I set up the sanctuary in the showers. We won by forfeit after the Storm and Fire Squads were disqualified for lack of participation."

"Nellie and I didn't participate."

"Nellie got a pass for being in the infirmary and since you weren't technically in your room, you didn't break any of the rules."

"Stronger, faster, and smarter?"

"Glad to see you've been paying attention, girl. I hope you'll remember all my advice going forward." She glances between Silas and me. "Try to keep up."

Serin slows her pace despite the admonishment. Silas doesn't turn to ensure I'm following like last night. There's no hand at my back when he holds the door open and ushers me into a tavern sandwiched between two brothels. No more suggestive innuendos or accidental brushes of fingers when he hands me a glass of frothy beer as we sit at a table in the corner. He keeps both hands on his glass and watches the door as Serin and I talk about what to bring back for Nellie.

A sanguine smile breaks across her face as she lifts her gaze. "They're here."

Serin is up and out the door before I can ask who. It closes slowly, and I watch as she launches herself at Thale as he crosses the street. He lifts her from the ground, cupping her ass with his tattooed hands as she wraps her legs around him. The tavern door swings shut, and I glance around. There are no windows on the front wall of the building to explain how she saw him approach.

"Do Serin and Thale share a life bond?" I ask. It's the only other explanation that makes sense, even though she said she would never give anyone that kind of power over her.

"Serin and Thale are mated." Silas takes a deep swig of his beer. I watch his throat bob with each swallow.

"Mated?"

The door swings open, and the question at the tip of my tongue dissolves. I can't take my gaze off the statuesque woman who enters behind Val and Bas. She has to duck to get through the door. A swath of raven hair falls over her forehead, and she runs a hand through it, sweeping her short locks up and out of her face.

I'm not sure what's more striking, her imposing stature or her frost-colored eyes. Her crisp collared shirt and waistcoat are perfectly fitted to her muscular form. She wears a long-barreled pistol and coiled whip at her waist. The giantess has the nervous attention of every human in the room.

Silas keeps me behind him in a way that feels deliberate as I rise from my seat to get a better look at her.

"I'm Everly Thorne," I say, ignoring his grunt of annoyance as I scoot around him and offer her my hand. "I apologize for staring. I've never met a giant before."

"Fabienne Flint, but you can call me Tiny. The rest of these beasts do." Her gray eyes twinkle with amusement as her calloused palm swallows mine.

"Is that because you're only half giant?" I ask.

"Did Silas tell you that?" She shoots him a curious glance.

"No. The average height of a female giant is seven feet, nine inches. You're a foot shy of that."

"Silas warned you'd be perceptive when I saw him four nights ago." I catch a glimpse of her sharp flesh-shredding teeth as she smiles. "Most humans cower in my presence. I smell no fear in you at all."

Four nights ago. When Silas left the ship. A pang of jealousy knots my stomach. I'm not one to begrudge anyone their midnight rendezvous, but the thought of Silas sneaking off the ship to meet with a beautiful woman bothers me more than it has the right to.

"It's illegal for giants to hunt humans within Saracen's borders."

"You put a lot of faith in the law for a rogue witch cavorting with murderers and thieves."

"Not really. I do, however, trust Silas to act like an overprotective jackass. If he thought you were a danger to me, he wouldn't let me anywhere near you."

"Yes, well, his charm is an acquired taste." She winks at me as she pulls him into a tight embrace.

I force the image of them together in a tangle of sweat-slick limbs out of my mind as I turn to greet the others. "Hello, Bas."

The mop-headed young man grins from ear to ear and takes a step toward me like he intends to hug me. He glances at the grumpy wall of muscle behind me and halts, offering me a sheepish wave instead.

"Glad to see you haven't gotten yourself killed and wasted my alicorn powder." Val raises his arm to catch the attention of the barkeep and orders another pitcher of ale.

"Thank you for not letting me die the night of the ball. I know you did it to save Silas, but it's still appreciated."

"The fact that you know about the life bond and haven't used it to torture him yet is disappointing." He sweeps his mane of white-blond hair out of the way to avoid sitting on it as he takes a seat next to Bas.

"I'm not sure what you mean."

"We have business to discuss." Silas glares at Val as he slides onto the bench next to me. I'm all too aware of the way his thigh grazes my skirts. "How was the border crossing into the Northlands?"

"I'm afraid we may have ourselves a little hitch," Val says, eyes sliding to me. "King Otto shut down the border three days ago. Seems there are concerns about the increasing number of hunting parties reported along the border. Saracen soldiers have blockades set up along every road to stop humans from crossing into giant territory."

"Humans have gone missing off and on along the border for centuries. Saracen never seemed bothered enough to make a move like this before. This is Dagmara's doing. I may have underestimated her determination to ensure Krimore doesn't complete his quest. Are they sending out patrols?"

"I took a gander at their camps. Not yet, as far as I can reckon."

"Then we'll convince the prince to cross through Marshwood instead."

"That's a dangerous gamble," Val says.

My spine stiffens at the mention of the infamous reaver-infested forest that spans the border between Saracen and the Northlands. The place where my parents' bodies were found, throats slit, next to their ransacked wagon.

I'm suddenly in the foyer of our home in Crecentis, listening to the royal messenger read the report all over again. I shove the memory down, digging my nails into my thigh under the table as I blink back the sting at the corners of my eyes.

My scalp tingles as Silas tries to push through my wards. He shifts in his seat when I refuse to give him access.

"Drake's Pass is clear," Tiny says as she packs tobacco into a gentleman's burlwood pipe.

The giantess has my full attention. Baby Face Drake's pass is a two-hundred-year-old myth. No one's ever found it.

"That's not an option," Silas says, giving me a sidelong glance.

"I don't like it either," Tiny says, blowing smoke in my direction. "But news of Dagmara's betrothal gift has made its way north. There are whispers the egg left Perdanth with the prince. If he marches his army through reaver territory, every enterprising crew will try to take it. There will be extensive losses. Burying the dead and dealing with the injured will take precious time you don't have."

"That's a risk we'll have to take. Drake's Pass is not up for discussion."

"Every reaver will be looking for that damn egg," Tiny says, not backing down. "Are you willing to risk losing it, after all this time, to keep the pass a secret?"

"I've never lost a haul in my life. I can keep Krimore and the egg safe. The rest of his witches aren't my problem." Silas sips his beer slowly, as if he didn't just suggest sacrificing the lives of three hundred people.

Heat flashes through my body as I glare at the side of his head. "Half the soldiers in Gideon's army are children, most barely a year past their fever. How can you be so callous about whether they live or die?"

"Your anger is misplaced." He keeps his eyes forward. His movements seem stiff, almost forced, as if he's trying very hard not to look at me. "I'm not the one who conscripted them into the army and turned them into weaponized slaves. But go ahead, blame me if that makes it easier for you to digest when you defend your heroic prince."

"What is your problem with Gideon?"

"He's Serros's heir, is he not?"

"He's nothing like his father. Gideon is a good man. He'll do things differently when he becomes king."

Silas angles toward me, knees knocking against mine under the table. "Power is measured by its cost. The Krimore kings have built a legacy on the sacrifice and suffering of others. Ask yourself what your prince is willing to sacrifice to gain a second throne before you lecture me on being a monster."

A throaty laugh floats from the opposite side of the tavern, where Serin leads Thale up a staircase to the second floor, a room key dangling from a wooden ring clasped in her teeth.

"It was lovely meeting you," I say to Fabienne as I stand and nod my goodbyes to Val and Bas.

"Where do you think you're going?" Silas catches my wrist.

"To buy another firebird feather. I need to reinforce my wards."

"We're not finished here."

"I am."

The prickling sensation across my scalp intensifies into a sharp pinch.

"*Sit down.*"

The bastard broke through my ward.

"The only way I'm spending another second in your miserable company is if you tie me to the damn chair."

"*Is that a request?*"

"Go fuck yourself, Silas." I yank my hand free and stalk toward the door.

Chair legs scrape the floor behind me as they all rise, sending the bustling tavern into a hush.

"She took that about as well as you suspected." Fabienne's sultry voice carries across the room as the door clicks shut behind me.

Chapter Twenty-Six

My parents stopped in Port Hope to resupply every summer. Even if I'd paid attention to the location of the bone broker's shop on any of our visits, I'd be hard pressed to find it in the twisting maze of new streets. I keep a brisk pace, pretending that I know where I'm going. I'm pretty sure I've passed the same sandwich cart three times.

The huff of dragon's breath on the back of my neck isn't helping me concentrate. I don't need to turn around to know that Silas is following me. He's keeping his distance, letting me wander around until I'm forced to admit I have no idea where I am and ask him for help.

He's the most intolerable man I've ever met. I hate his demanding, possessive bullshit and the way he manipulates me with his seductive games. The way he seems to know exactly what I need without even reading my mind. I hate his cocky smirk and perfect lips and the way they feel so right against mine. I especially hate the way he makes me feel safe. Safer than I've ever felt.

I sigh with relief when I finally spot a bone broker's sign on the corner of a brick building. A set of soft bells chime as I duck inside.

The shop feels more like a museum with its black and white marble floor, polished mahogany paneling, and mirrored walls. It's lined with floor-to-ceiling windows on two sides and full of light, unlike Beaux's dark and dusty hovel.

There are no pixie wings or death masks pinned to the walls. No cloud of incense, stuffed beasts, or rush of magic to overwhelm my senses. The relics and an extensive collection of goblin-spelled jewelry are all on full display inside warded glass cases. I can't feel any of it.

"Can I help you?" a bird-faced woman in a crisp white pinafore asks, taking in my travel-weary clothing.

"I..." The words stick in my throat. Aside from my parents and Silas's crew, I've never admitted my abilities to anyone in public before. If I ask to see the firebird feathers, she'll know I'm a witch.

The bells jingle behind me as the familiar kiss of dragon's breath glides across my neck.

"There you are, darling." Silas smiles as he takes my hand. "When I told you that you could pick out a new piece of charmed jewelry for your birthday, I didn't expect you to run straight into the most expensive bone broker in Port Hope."

"*What are you doing?*" I ask through the bond.

"*Protecting your secret and keeping up my end of the oath. Is the clerk channeling any relics that you can sense?*"

"*No.*"

Silas wraps his arm around my shoulders and presses a kiss to the top of my head. "*Good. Distract her while I procure a new firebird feather for you.*"

"*I'm not helping you rob this woman. That's not part of the deal.*"

"*Are you hiding a license to channel magic in your secret pouch? Because that's what you'll need to purchase a relic in Saracen, where the magic trade is highly regulated and steeply taxed.*"

"*Then I'll manage without one.*"

"*You have two days, maybe three, of magic left. I can't afford for you to be any weaker or more vulnerable than you already are, so you can either drop your mind wards and conserve the magic you have left, or you can start pretending.*"

Silas doesn't take his eyes off mine as he lifts my hand and brushes his lips across my knuckles. "Pick out something nice, darling. Money is no object."

"*I hate you.*"

"Is there a particular spelled object you're looking for?" the clerk asks Silas, smile widening.

"You can direct your questions to my *wife*. She's perfectly capable of making her own decisions."

"*If I were your wife, I'd suffocate you in your sleep.*"

"Of course. Right this way, madam." The woman's smile thins as she steps behind a long case of amulets. "We have a number of pieces popular with young couples to enhance health, stamina, and fertility."

Silas meets my gaze in the mirror behind her. "*If I were your husband, I'd invite you to sit on my face and try every night while I pleasure you with my tongue until you beg for release.*"

My face and neck turn crimson as the cord between my navel and groin pulls taut with need. I squeeze my thighs together and clear my throat. "Do you have anything spelled to repel reavers? I hear the city is crawling with them."

"We're out of protection charms at the moment. They've been very popular in the last few days. The border closure has been good for business. Rumors about giants hunting humans have everyone up in arms. But you needn't worry. You're perfectly safe here in Port Hope, dear. Can I interest you in something for good health, perhaps?"

"That would be lovely." I watch as she unravels the ward, keeping my body between her and Silas as his shadows creep toward a case of firebird feathers. It's a lazy weave. Designed to be easily opened and closed multiple times a day, relying on repeated layers to slow down a would-be thief as they work it out.

"This one has three identical layers. Each pattern flips ninety degrees to the right from the one before it."

"Look at you, being helpful. I'll reward you later if you continue to play nice."

"Oh yes, here we go." The woman pulls out a necklace with a silver berry-shaped pendant, and my chest tightens. "This design is popular with travelers. It's a—"

"A rose hip," I say, voice weak.

"That's correct. You know your floriculture, madam. It's been spelled with a charm to improve immunity to disease, just like the tea. You know what they say, a cup of rose hip tea every day will ward illness away."

"I'm on the second layer now."

"My mother used to say the same thing. She collected the hips from wild rose bushes wherever we traveled." I reach out and let my fingers brush the delicate charm.

"Here, let's try it on."

"That's not necessary." I step back as she moves to slip it over my head.

"I need another minute. Try on the damn necklace and keep her busy."

"Perhaps something different, then," the clerk says curtly.

"Actually, I think I would like to try it on. My mother passed two years ago. It would be nice to have something that reminds me of her." I pull my heavy locks aside so the clerk can fasten the charm around my neck. "My mother brewed rose hip tea every day. The soft scent clung to her hair. I could still smell it on her when she tucked me in at night."

The visceral memory surfaces so quickly I don't have time to shove it down—my mother leaning over me, her golden curls falling around our faces as she kissed me good night. My vision blurs, and tears leak down my cheeks.

Silas is next to me instantly, folding me into his arms. The phantom ripple of heat radiating from him tells me he got the relic we need. I bury my nose in his waistcoat and take a deep breath, filling my lungs with his scent. Clove and peppermint. The hint of woodsmoke from a far-off campfire lingers in the fabric, reminding me of summer nights on the road with my parents. The tears come again, and my breath hitches.

What's wrong with me? I hate that I let my emotions spiral out of control.

"What did you say to her?" There's an edge to his voice. Serin's warning about the overprotective side effects of the bond has me worried for the shop clerk's safety.

"I'm so sorry, sir. I... didn't mean to upset your wife."

I will the frayed threads of my emotions into submission and peel myself away from him.

"It's all right. Can we just go?"

"Of course." Silas ushers me out the door, keeping a hand on the small of my back.

"Wait," the woman shouts. "You forgot to pay for the necklace."

"*Run.*" Silas grabs my hand and drags me down the street behind him.

I stumble, tripping over my feet, trying to keep up with his long strides as the clerk yells for help. Silas darts left and right around horses and ox carts for three blocks before he slows and hooks his arm through mine.

"We're safe," he says, glancing behind us. "No one's following."

He hasn't even broken a sweat, and I'm panting like a dog, heart racing. I tighten my grip on his arm and drag him into a narrow alley. Silas's mouth twitches with a seductive smirk as he allows me to shove him against the brick wall while I fish my hand up his waistcoat and pull out the feather.

"You could have just asked for it."

"And give you the satisfaction of making me beg?" I run my fingers over the deep red plume, pulling some of its magic into my body and reinforcing the hole he ripped in my wards.

"Don't ever break through my walls again."

"I warned you not to lock me out. Our ability to communicate across the bond could save your life."

"Why did you follow me? Landry is still on the ship. I don't need a bodyguard."

"Aside from the amusement of watching you wander in circles pretending not to be lost?"

"You're insufferable." I roll the crimson feather and tuck it into my waist pouch.

"And you have a habit of walking into trouble. I'm not letting you out of my sight."

"Trouble? You're the one who insisted on stealing from a bone broker."

"We make a good team when you play nice."

"We are not a team." I lean against the wall to catch my breath.

"You were impressive back there, using that story about your mother to throw the clerk off her guard."

"I told you I could pretend as well as you."

"You weren't pretending." Silas angles toward me. "Most, if not all, of that story you fed the clerk was true."

"Stay out of my head, reaver." I shove off the wall, ready to leave.

"I'll force myself through your ward to communicate with you if I must, but I won't touch the ward protecting your thoughts. No matter how tempting it is to read your wicked little mind. You have my word."

"You've been using my thoughts and desires to manipulate me from the moment I swore the oath. Now you expect me to trust that you're just going to stop?"

"I'll admit I was reluctant to teach you how to weave a mind ward. But I don't need to read your thoughts to know what you're feeling." Silas's smooth brow wrinkles. "You asked what Val meant when he said you could use the bond to torture me. I'm constantly aware of your body's physical needs. It's a side effect of the oath I swore to you. It ensures that I'm aware of your health and safety at all times, no matter where you are. It alerts me to any subtle changes so I can keep you alive. I know when you're hungry, dehydrated, and exhausted."

He lifts the silver pendant from my chest, rolling the charm between his thumb and forefinger. "I'm acutely aware of any pain or pleasure you experience as if it were my own. It's how I know the story about your mother and her rose hip tea is true. Your chest... my chest squeezed tight when you were talking to the clerk. I could barely breathe. I've been numb to those sensations for a very long time. The way you feel things intrigues me. The way you don't let fear or anything else stop you from going after what you want."

"It's probably just the burning eating its way through my brain. Inhibitions are the first to go. At least that's what my mother told me."

"Your parents didn't deserve what happened to them."

"Does anyone deserve to have their throats slit and their bodies left to rot in the woods and be picked apart by animals?"

"Would you like a list?" Silas asks, face hard.

"Do you ever consider the families of the people you kill? The parents and children left behind with shattered lives?"

"I turned that part of myself off when I watched a man murder my mother. Revenge and empathy make strange bedfellows."

"Maybe it's time to put that aside."

"Perhaps." He drops the pendant and studies my eyes.

"I've watched reavers hang every week for two years, convincing myself that any of them could have been involved in my parents' death. That they deserved to be punished. Watching them die never made me feel any better."

"Why did you keep going back?"

"I needed the money from the death portraits and..." I let my voice trail off as I toe a rock loose from the dirt with my boot. Silas doesn't push as the silence stretches between us. I've never admitted the real reason to anyone else. They wouldn't understand. "I imagined my parents' death every time I watched a reaver hang—forced myself to picture what they looked like or how they felt in their last moments. Did they try to fight or beg for mercy?"

"You tortured yourself because you believe it's your fault."

Even with my wards intact, he has an uncanny ability to see right through me.

"They were searching for a cure for me."

"Hey, look at me." Silas tilts my chin up and swipes the tears from my cheek with his thumb. "Don't go down that road. It's long, dark, and lonely. Their deaths are *not* your fault."

"Yes, they are. My symptoms started a year after my fever, long before I started summoning. The magic finds me whether I use it or not. There was never any question about whether I'd go mad. Only when. My parents were more determined than ever to find a cure when they realized what was happening to me."

"Have you experienced any other symptoms besides the headaches and tremors?"

"I'm in no danger of dying and taking you with me anytime soon, if that's what you're worried about. I've managed the headaches and occasional tremor with the tonic." I don't tell him the drug is useless in preventing hallucinations or that I've been seeing ghosts.

"Have you ever channeled from anything other than a firebird relic?"

"No. I don't see how that matters."

"Let me see your feathers."

I dig out the one we just stole and the one I bought from Beaux and hand them over without question. He takes a step back and sets them ablaze.

"You bastard. Are you mad? I can't maintain my shields without those relics."

"You don't need them anymore. Channel from me. I'm immune to the burning."

"No one is immune."

He twists the onyx ring on his thumb. "I guess I'm one of the lucky ones. If you pull magic across the bond, it will keep it from causing any further damage to you."

"I've never heard of witches sharing power," I say, keeping my voice low in case someone overhears.

"We're not sharing power. I'm giving it to you."

"Aren't you worried I'll deplete your reserve?" My throat goes dry as I watch him unbutton his shirt.

"I have more than enough for both of us."

"Why are you undressing?" I glance over my shoulder toward the busy street.

"Magic transfers more quickly with physical contact. If you want to pull enough power from the dragon scales beneath my skin to maintain your wards, you need to put your hands on me."

"What about the dragon flame I already have in my chest?"

"It's only a small seed of what I can give you." He takes my left hand and slides it inside his shirt, holding it against his tattoo. My palm throbs where it's pressed against his warm skin.

He's right. What I felt last night is nothing compared to the magic coursing through his body right now. There's no way all that power came from the single dragon scale he claims is inked under his skin. Why would he lie about how many ground-up relics it took to create the tattoo?

"Why didn't I feel that when I touched you before?" I ask, the accusation clear in my voice.

"I use a suppression ward to keep the magic contained until I'm ready to unleash it." He drops his hands to my hips. "Go ahead. Take what you need from me."

Every relic has a different resistance to being channeled. Firebird feathers are delicate and require a gentle touch to avoid pulling out all the magic at once. Dragon scales are nearly indestructible. I pull harder than I'm used to. His chest vibrates beneath my palm like a purring beast as I tug at the power inked under his skin. There's no resistance. The magic comes in an overwhelming rush without having to be coaxed.

The ground lurches beneath my feet, and I feel like I'm dropping off the cliff from my dream. I cling to Silas as I tip sideways. His fingers bite into the soft flesh of my hips, holding me steady until the world stops spinning. A familiar, seductive heat spreads through my chest the same way it did when I summoned his shadows. It warms my belly and settles in my core.

"How do you feel?" He dips his head to search my face.

"Like I just drank half a bottle of whiskey."

He presses the back of his hand to my cheek. "You're flushed with power. We should get you back to the tavern so you can rest while your body acclimates."

I force my attention away from the deceptive warmth of his gaze and remind myself not to get confused.

CHAPTER TWENTY-SEVEN

A single candle lights the dark room when I wake. My eyes automatically drift to where Silas sits in front of the window, watching me. The untouched tray of food on the table next to him makes my stomach growl.

"What time is it?"

"Half past nine." He stands and pours a glass of water.

"Why did you let me sleep so long?" I ask, stretching lazily.

"Your body needed time to process the magic coursing through your system. Drink this."

I gulp down the water and swipe my hand across my mouth.

"Have you been watching me the whole time?"

"Who's the boy you keep drawing in your book?"

My gaze darts to my sketchbook and open bag on the bedside stand. "Those are private."

"I was looking for pictures of the egg."

"Wait, who's keeping it safe while you're off the boat?"

Silas flashes me a cocky smile. "Are you saying I'm the only one you trust to protect it?"

"You know what I meant."

"I warded the chart room last night so no one could get to you while I dealt with Landry. You and I are the only two who can pass through it."

Someone knocks at the door. A sliver of light breaks across the floor as Silas opens it wide.

Tiny gives Silas a suggestive smile. "We're heading next door to the brothel if you'd like to join us."

"I'll be right back," Silas says to me. He steps into the hall, leaving the door open a crack.

The floor creaks as I pad across the room. I press my ear to the heavy wooden door. Their voices are muffled, but I can make out most of their conversation.

"It's been a long time since we've set a house of pleasure on fire together."

My stomach hardens at the silky persuasion in her voice.

"You know I can't leave her here unsupervised." The way he says it, like I'm some kind of burden, makes my chest burn.

"Thale and Serin are downstairs. Let them watch her."

"The way I let them watch you?" There's a thread of amusement in his tone.

"That was different."

"I'm bound to her, Fabienne. If something happens to her, all of this is over."

"She's no ordinary witch. I could smell it all over her. Queen Isola will too."

"Let me worry about the queen. Go have your fun and keep an eye on the kid tonight. There's a full moon in two days."

"If you change your mind, you know where to find me."

The doorknob turns. I rush to the table and pick up an apple from the tray of fruit, bread, and cheese. My heart pounds as I take a bite.

"Who was that?" I ask, feigning ignorance.

He stalks toward me and takes the apple from my hand.

"I didn't say you could eat yet, princess."

"I'm not a princess."

"You were named after a queen and groomed to sit on a throne."

"I don't need a reminder," I say, clenching my fists.

He holds my gaze as he brings the apple to his mouth and takes a bite from the same spot I did. Silas picks up a fresh one and tosses it up toward the vaulted ceiling of our attic room, catching it with a shadow hand as it falls.

"The food is a reward. If you want it, you have to earn it. You may eat when you can summon a shadow and catch this without using your hands."

<hr>

"Stop focusing on making the shadows appear and think about why you don't want the apple to fall. The shadows will respond to your instincts and desires. You can't force it. Try again."

Sweat drips down the back of my neck as he lobs my bruised apple into the air. I hold my breath as the dark flame in my chest flares. This time I manage to summon a thin haze. The apple passes through it and splats all over the floor with the others.

"My *desire* is to stop playing this game."

"You've been at it for less than an hour. It's too soon to give up. Try again." Silas picks up another fresh apple from the tray and lobs it into the air.

I catch it in my hands and set it on the table. "This exercise is pointless. It took me months to summon a flame. We set out for the Northlands tomorrow. I'm not going to master this, even if we keep at it all night. My time would be better spent studying Landry's knife and working out the goblin spell it's been cast with."

"There are other ways I'd prefer to spend my time too, but you need to keep practicing."

I don't have to ask him to elaborate. Not after Tiny's clear invitation. Which is none of my business.

"Why?" I ask, fisting my hands at my sides. "Are you planning on sticking around after the blood oath is fulfilled and feeding me your magic? Because as soon as I get back to my real life, I won't have access to dragon relics. I was doing fine with the firebird feathers. Now I don't even have those. When this is over, I'll be going home with nothing. So, no, I don't need to keep practicing. I need a bottle of rum and a long fucking bath."

"You summoned a shadow shield last night. Compared to that, this is a simple task. I've watched you train with Serin. No matter how hard she pushes, you never give up, even when you're injured or pissed off."

"Maybe I just prefer her company to yours."

"Perhaps." Silas steps closer, erasing the distance between us until our bodies are mere inches apart. "Or perhaps you're afraid."

He traces the line of my jaw, sliding his hand to the back of my head and fisting my hair.

"I'm not afraid of you." Heat coils low in my belly.

"Oh, I think you are," he says, tugging gently and tipping my face up to his. "I think you're afraid to admit you want this. The darkness. The danger. You've spent so much time suppressing your true nature you have no idea how good it will feel when you finally let go and accept what you are."

"I want you to leave."

"Do you? Or do you want me to stand outside your door like I have every night for the last three weeks while you pleasure yourself alone in the dark?"

Heat creeps up my neck. "How do you know about that?"

"I told you. I'm painfully aware of all your needs, Everly. When you need to eat and sleep. When you crave release. The way you ache for it right now."

Silas releases my hair, following as I walk backward until my ass collides with the table.

"Do you think of your prince when you get yourself off, or is it my company you crave?"

My vision flashes red. I don't realize my arm is moving until my fist collides with the underside of his jaw. "Get out."

"There she is." His mouth curls into a cocky smile as he rubs his chin. "Serin taught you well."

"Is everything a fucking game to you?"

"None of this is a game," he says, dropping the smile and backing toward the door.

"What are you doing?"

"Giving you what you asked for," Silas says, stepping into the hall and warding the doorway.

"You know that won't be enough to keep me in."

His gaze meets mine across the threshold. "There isn't anywhere you can go that I can't find you while you carry my magic."

"Is that why you gave it to me? So you can keep me on a short leash?"

"Keep practicing." Silas doesn't look back as he walks away. I resist the urge to slam the door behind him.

There's no point wasting time unraveling his ward. Where would I go? Back to the boat? Even if I could find my way to the river, the thought of being anywhere near Landry without my overprotective warden sends a tremor through me.

The bastard has been inside my head. He knows exactly how to push my buttons to prove a point. I hate that he's right. I am scared—of the magic and of him. Of admitting what I want and having it ripped away from me again. Of wanting something that isn't meant to be mine, no matter how much I crave it. Like a crown. Or the dark and deadly power to protect myself and everyone around me.

I toss an apple up toward the ceiling. The dark flame in my chest doesn't even flicker. The apple thuds against the floor and rolls under the bed. I try again and again with the same result until I run out of apples. Nothing. Not even a wisp of the haze I managed earlier. No matter how many times I repeat the process, I can't summon a shadow on my own. Not without Silas pushing me. I'm not sure what that says about my base desires.

"I don't want or need Silas Drake." I say it out loud, unsure of who I'm trying to convince.

I crouch down and collect the remains of my failed attempts. I toss the bruised and broken apples into the cold hearth and set them on fire. The room fills with smoke. I quickly grab the lever and open the damper, cursing under my breath. I can't even wield his flame without messing it up.

There's a soft knock. Serin doesn't wait for me to answer before stepping through the ward and holding the door open for Thale, who's carrying six buckets of water.

She sets a bottle of rum on the table and picks up a hunk of cheese, popping it into her mouth as Thale fills the copper tub opposite the window.

"Where's Silas?"

"Out. He said you requested a bath."

"Are you back on babysitting duty?"

"No. I have other orders. If you need anything, Thale will be standing guard outside your door until Silas gets back."

"Aren't you afraid I'll try to climb out the window?"

"We're on the fourth floor, girl. I know you're not that daft."

"When will he be back?" I ask, glancing at the tub of cold water.

"He's not likely to return until morning. You have the room to yourself for the night. Do you need me to heat the water for you, or can you manage?"

My stomach hardens. I shove the image of Silas and the beautiful giantess out of my head as I summon a flame. "I don't need any more *help*. Thank you."

Serin and Thale stare at the black fire dancing in my palm.

"He shared his power with you?" Serin asks.

"He torched my firebird relics and forced me to take it."

She shakes her head and moves toward the door.

"Is that bad?" The flame in my hand sputters out.

"That depends."

"On what?"

"On which one of you is dynamite and which one is the fuse. Enjoy the bath. It's the last one you'll have until we reach Tindlestone Palace."

Thale gives me a curt nod, pulling the door shut behind him.

I heat the water and gather the soap and towel from the washstand before dragging the table over to the tub so I can reach the food while I bathe. If this is my last bath for a week, I plan on sitting in it until my fingers and toes turn into prunes.

My breath hitches as I slowly sink into the scalding water. I pull the cork out of the rum bottle with my teeth and take a deep swig, savoring the warmth as it slides down my throat.

I lift the silver pendant from where it hangs between my breasts. The goblin magic it's spelled with hums against my fingertips as I recall what Silas said to me in the bone broker's shop about making me beg for release.

No one has ever spoken to me the way he does. He knows exactly what to say to make my pulse race. He warned me before we left Perdanth that he's good at pretending. I've seen the way he can misdirect a crowd, and I've been a victim of his manipulations firsthand. Everything the man does is calculated.

I didn't catch their entire conversation, but the giantess clearly wanted Silas to join her. He left the door cracked. He wanted me to overhear what they were saying. For all I know, he could have staged the entire thing to distract me from focusing too closely on his insistence that Gideon march his army through the deadly Marshwood.

I pull the dragon comb from my hair and slide beneath the water's surface. I need to find a way to tell Gideon there's a safer route across the border without betraying the oath. No one's ever found Baby Face

Drake's secret pass over the mountains that separate the Wastes and the western edge of Saracen from the Northlands.

Except Silas.

He's certainly not going to draw Gideon a map.

The map. That's it.

Water sloshes over the side of the tub as I sit up and grab the soap. I wash my body and hair and dry off quickly with the thin towel. I wrap it around my hair and pad over to the bed, leaving a trail of wet footprints behind me.

I grab my red leather sketchbook and plop down on the bed, not wasting time to get dressed. My fingers ache by the time I'm done recreating the map from memory. I can't leave it in my sketchbook for Silas to find. He can't know that I've seen his mind ward.

I rip out the page. My first instinct is to hide it in the warded pocket of my bag along with Landry's goblin-spelled dagger. Silas let me keep the knife, but there's better than good odds he'll demand I give it to him before we return to the ship. I can't risk him discovering the sketch.

I lay my skirt out on the bed and turn the pocket inside out, using the tip of the knife to enlarge the hole in the seam. I roll the map, careful not to crease the vellum, and slide it between the outer fabric and lining. It's not ideal, but the cotton fabric hides the stiffness of the paper well enough. I just need it to make it back to the boat so I can compare the sketch to the Dragon's Backbone Mountains in my map book. I have to be sure they're the same before testing the boundaries of the oath and showing it to Gideon.

Chapter Twenty-Eight

The familiar kiss of hot breath tickles my neck as I pace the room just after dawn. Gray light seeps in through the window, promising a day of heavy rain.

Silas's muffled voice filters in from the hall. I tiptoe to the door and listen.

"I had to be sure," Silas says.

"How much did you give her?" Thale asks.

"Enough to confirm my suspicions."

We don't have time for this. I open the door and glare at him. "Where have you been? I'm ready to go."

"Good morning, Everly. Sleep well?"

"Better than you, by the looks of it." His clothes are rumpled and damp, and he reeks of alcohol.

Thale grunts in amusement as he heads down the stairs.

Silas closes the door and starts undressing.

"What are you doing?"

"Taking a bath." He drapes his wet shirt over the chair. "You're welcome to join me."

"After you spent the night in a brothel? I'll pass."

"Ah, so you were eavesdropping."

"We need to get back to the boat." I stuff my hands in my pockets and pretend not to notice the scratches on his back while I tell myself he was clawed by a feral cat and not a beautiful giantess with sharp nails.

"Why the rush?" He eyes me skeptically as he unfastens the double rows of buttons at the front fall of his trousers.

I avert my gaze at the flash of dark hair as he lets them drop to the floor.

"I need to check on Nellie." My fingers graze the ripped seam inside my skirt pocket.

"Is that what's kept you up pacing all night?" Water sloshes behind me as he steps into the cold tub.

"Aren't you going to heat it?" I ask, stealing a glimpse of his incredible ass as he lowers himself into the water.

"The cold is invigorating after a long night with no sleep."

My stomach hardens at the thought. I have no right to be jealous. The bastard can fuck whoever he likes. It makes everything easier. A sobering reminder not to get confused. I drag my gaze away from his broad shoulders as he stretches and kneads the bunched muscles.

"Sounds like you got your money's worth from the woman that kept you up all night." The giantess is a far better woman than I am. If Silas Drake belonged to me, I wouldn't invite him to a brothel, and I definitely wouldn't share.

"The only woman who's kept me awake at night is you. I haven't desired another woman since I bound my life to yours."

My gaze snaps to his.

"You are extremely inconvenient, Everly Thorne."

I walk to the door and focus on unraveling the ward. I tell myself it doesn't mean anything. It's just a side effect of the bond. He's still my enemy.

"Absolutely not." I block the door to the women's latrine as Silas attempts to follow me inside.

"Landry made an attempt on your life. What part of me not leaving you alone did you not understand?"

"You left me alone last night."

He pushes past me. "You weren't alone. Thale stood guard at your door, Val spent the night in the alley under your window, and Serin came back to the boat to keep an eye on that sick fuck."

"Where were you?" I follow him inside while he inspects every corner of the empty latrine.

"Out." Silas puts his hands on his hips and nods to one of the stalls. "All clear."

"Am I not allowed any modicum of privacy?"

"You can shut the door."

"Silas, please. I have my courses," I cross my arms, hoping he buys the lie. My period is already over. It never lasts more than a few days.

"Yes, I'm aware."

My face heats with embarrassment. "Did Serin tell you I have a birthmark on my ass as well?"

"No, but I look forward to discovering it."

I ignore his attempt to bait me. "Are you seriously going to make me beg for this minuscule amount of dignity?"

Silas stares at me for a long moment. "I'll wait in the hall while you attend to your needs."

"Thank you." I shut the door in his face and triple ward it, hoping it's enough to buy me the time I need.

I drop to the floor in front of the ventilation grate on the opposite wall. The rusty screws securing the metal panel take a few minutes to remove with the tip of Landry's knife. My sweating palms don't help. The rectangular opening is just big enough to squeeze through on my belly to the cargo deck.

Silas is going to be livid. He'll never let me bathe or relieve myself alone again. A consequence I'm willing to accept if it means saving the lives of every witch on this ship.

———✦———

Gideon's head snaps up as I burst into the pilothouse, where he's standing around a map table with his navigation officers.

"Is there something we can help you with, Private Thorne?" Major Mattern asks.

"I need to speak to Colonel Krimore. It's urgent," I say, heart racing from my sprint through the ship to my room and then here.

"Everly, this is not the—"

I don't waste time with polite pretenses. "Dagmara closed the border."

The ember of magic binding me to the oath flares in warning.

"How do you know that?"

"A shopkeeper told me." I fiddle with the goblin-spelled charm around my neck, and the fire in my chest fades. "She said it's been good for business."

Gideon curses under his breath.

"It's fine," Mattern says. "We can cross through Marshwood Forest."

"No. Marshwood Forest is full of reavers. It's not safe." I can feel Silas's shadowy presence looming closer. He knows I tricked him. It won't be long before he comes for me. I just hope he makes it before I self-combust.

"Thank you for the report, Private Thorne. You may return to your regular duties. As you can see," Mattern says, "this meeting is for officers only."

I slip the map book off my back and flip it open on the table.

"March them over the mountains instead." I stab my finger at the rocky ridgeline that matches the sketch in my pocket.

"No one has ever successfully crossed the Dragon's Backbone Mountains," Mattern says.

"Baby Face Drake did it." I rush to get the words out before my chest flares again. "I've heard hundreds of stories about Baby Face Drake and his secret passage over the mountain from the reavers my parents treated."

They all stare at me as if I'm mad.

"Baby Face Drake?" Mattern snorts. "Tall tales passed around by mad witches are hardly credible. If there was a navigable passage over the mountain, someone would have mapped it by now."

My chest goes molten as my fingers brush the map in my pocket.

"They have." A huff of hot breath tickles the hairs on my neck as Silas strides into the room. "The first leg of Drake's Pass goes through the mountain, not over. The entrance is hidden in a cave."

I sigh with relief as I pull my empty hand out of my pocket.

"How did you find me so quickly?" I ask across the bond.

"It wasn't difficult to guess who you'd run to. The next time you want me to chase you, little spark, at least make it challenging."

"How do you know about the pass?" Gideon asks.

"I've been using it to move Ambassador Caron's gold out of the Northern Wastes. It's a two-week journey for a caravan on foot. We don't have that kind of time."

"I agree with the shadow summoner," the other navigation officer says. "Queen Isola's Menagerie opens in seven days. We need to go through the Marshwood."

"My parents lost their lives over a few crates of medicine and food in the Marshwood Forest." My voice cracks. "What do you think a reaver crew will do to get their hands on the egg?"

"I have three hundred soldiers protecting the egg," Gideon says.

"Half of the battle witches on this ship are untrained children. They don't stand a chance against a reaver raid. If they attack the caravan the way they attacked Fort Netherthorn or the ball in Crecentis, we may not even make it to Tindlestone," I say, refusing to back down.

"Give us the room," Gideon says, voice tight.

Mattern shuffles past Silas with the other navigator.

"Is there a problem, Drake?" Gideon asks when the shadow summoner makes no attempt to move.

"Not at all, Colonel Krimore. But it occurs to me that there might be a compromise to be had in the question of saving your soldiers and getting to Tindlestone on time."

"And what is that?"

"Leave your army here, in Port Hope, where they can keep the egg safe. Hire a teamster and crew of horses and let me lead a small unit on horseback through Drake's Pass. If we travel light, we can make the trip in five days with plenty of time to spare."

"I'll take it under advisement," Gideon says. "That will be all."

Silas dips his head and places a possessive hand against the small of my back, leading me to the door.

"Private Thorne, a word," Gideon says. "Alone."

Silas's body goes rigid behind me.

"Gideon isn't going to hurt me."

"It's not him I'm worried about." Silas tips my chin up gently. *"Give me one reason why I should leave you alone with your princeling after you tried to betray the oath and turn us both into piles of ash."*

"I'm just trying to keep everyone safe. I can't let anyone else die because of me."

Silas pulls me in as if he plans to kiss me. *"You told him about my secret pass."*

"I told him about Baby Face Drake's secret pass. You're the one who offered to lead him through it."

"To save your lovely ass."

"Silas, please. Let me speak to him. I can convince him to leave the army here like you suggested."

"And you just expect me to trust you?"

"Play nice, and I'll make it worth your while."

"Are we back to negotiating?" he asks.

"There has to be something you want from me."

"Shall I compose a list?"

Gideon clears his throat.

"Make me an offer. Your prince is getting impatient."

I know I need to give him something he isn't expecting. Something I said I'd never do. *"Give me this, and we can pretend in any way you like, as long as we have an audience."*

Silas's gaze darkens. I can't deny the little thrill that runs through me as he bends down and brushes his lips against my cheek. *"There's very little I wouldn't do in front of an audience."*

He steps outside and leans against the railing across from the pilothouse. I shut the door and lock it.

"Don't ever question my judgment in front of my soldiers again," Gideon says. "I'm the only person on this ship without magic, aside from you. If they lose faith in my ability to lead them, it puts every single life under my command in jeopardy."

The sharp reprimand catches me off guard, and I'm reminded again that he's no longer the boy I once knew.

"That wasn't my intent, but this couldn't wait."

"I no longer require your services as a spy."

"What?"

"I shouldn't have asked you to put yourself in a compromising position. It's too dangerous. Untangle yourself from the shadow summoner and focus your attention on the egg. I need to know if it's viable."

"You, of all people, have no say in who I choose to tangle with."

"Drake is lethal. Not to mention unstable. Landry came to me immediately after leaving the infirmary the night of the game. He said Drake attacked him and broke his nose without provocation. I had to promote him to captain and give him a spot on my Elite Guard to keep him from demanding satisfaction. Do you know how many problems it will create for me if Drake murders that entitled asshole in a magic duel?"

Maybe it's the madness seeping in, but I can't help the smile that breaks across my face at the image of Silas going after Landry with his shadow blades like a beautiful, brutal beast.

"Do you have feelings for him?" Gideon asks.

The ludicrous question makes my stomach drop.

"Don't be ridiculous. My relationship with Silas Drake is merely transactional. He offered me his protection in exchange for certain *services*." My chest prickles with heat. It's as close to the truth as I dare go.

"I should be the one protecting you. You don't know how much it pains me that I can't. I won't risk losing this alliance over rumors about my lack of fidelity to my future wife."

"A wife who would rather see you dead than in her bed. You're the prince of fucking Perdanth. Heir to the Krimore throne. You have an army of battle witches at your disposal and thousands of hero-worshipping subjects who will side with you if you go home and stand up to your father for once in your life."

Gideon glances around nervously, stepping closer and lowering his voice. "Don't ever say that out loud again. There are people on this ship loyal to my father who'd have both our necks in a noose for talking treason. There are things you don't know. Things I can't fix until I sit on the Saracen throne."

Ask yourself what your prince is willing to sacrifice to win a second throne.

Silas's words pierce my chest.

Gideon reaches for me.

"Don't." I step away from him.

"Let me send you home. Away from all this, where it's safe."

"I'm safe with Silas. He won't let anything happen to me."

"You were raised to be a queen, Everly. You shouldn't have to sell yourself for security."

"Neither should you."

"What's that supposed to mean?"

"Isn't that the whole point of this quest? So you can sell yourself to Dagmara in exchange for a second throne and the financial security of Perdanth?"

"It's my duty." Gideon's jaw hardens.

For a moment, I remember running hand in hand with him through the palace, being chased by guards after we knocked over the dragon skeleton and destroyed his father's throne. We escaped into the garden and collapsed under our tree, laughing until we fell asleep in the grass. It was the last time we were unburdened by the expectations of our future stations.

"You can't complete your quest or secure your alliance if you lose your life in the Marshwood Forest. Let Silas lead you through Drake's Pass."

"If he's Dagmara's spy, that's what she'll expect me to do. I'll take my chances in the Marshwood before I'll follow Drake through an unmapped route of the mountains into a potential ambush. She's been attempting to sabotage this alliance from the start. All she has to do is prevent us from making it across the border."

I open my mouth to tell him that Silas isn't working for the princess, but the words die in my throat. Partly because of the blood oath magic burning inside my chest and partly because an ambush sounds exactly like something Silas would do.

I close my eyes and think back to the conversation at the tavern. The way Silas's crew dropped hints about the pass. How Tiny didn't seem surprised by my tantrum, and the way Silas knew I'd run straight to Gideon and beg him to spare the lives of his soldiers.

Manipulative fucking bastard. I played right into his hands.

It's not the first time Silas has dropped breadcrumbs to lead me down the path he wants me to follow, making me believe it was my idea.

He could have snuck off the ship and met with his crew at any point. Why now? Why Port Hope? His crew didn't tell him anything he didn't already know at the tavern. Serin, his second-in-command, as far as I can tell, didn't even join the discussion. It's almost as if their plan was already a forgone conclusion and the tavern visit was simply a performance for my benefit, just like the night in the tomb.

Silas Drake is the master of misdirection. Everything he does is an act, using charm and bravado to distract from the details he doesn't want you to notice. When we swore the blood oath, he pretended to be torn about everything except the exorbitant sum I demanded, knowing full well he'd never have to pay it.

He distracted me with his seductive games at the ball so I wouldn't notice the reavers dressed as guards. He even got me to help him pull off his stunt in the training ring to get out of the unwanted task. *I see you, reaver.*

"Don't leave the egg in Port Hope. Insist that it comes with you to Tindlestone. The rest of your soldiers can stay here and pretend to be waiting for the border to reopen." It was the only part of the plan Silas didn't make a big deal about. His entire crew is here. Once Gideon and his Elite Guard are off the ship, they'll have no problem stealing the egg.

"I'm not leaving my army in Port Hope. I'll need every spare witch to hunt the dragon. I can't do it alone."

I pace the small room. The oath won't allow me to tell him the dragon has already been captured and is being held by Queen Isola.

Fuck. How do I convince him to make the right choice without all the information? He has no idea who he's up against. I rack my brain and think back to the tomb and the ball. The map Silas made me draw of the Menagerie as a test. Ambassador Caron whispering in my ear that the secret to Silas's success was that he only traveled under the cover of darkness. Silas disguising the reavers as guards and hiding them in plain sight before the attack.

"On the first day of training, you said reavers use unpredictability to their advantage. Everyone expects you to play the role of the heroic prince, to follow the rules. You need to stop thinking like a prince and start thinking like a reaver instead."

"How do you know how reavers think?"

"I'm a Thorne," I say, skirting around the truth. "The daughter of reaver sympathizers. My parents spent their lives studying them in their search for a cure for the burning."

Gideon runs his scarred hand through his golden curls. "What would you have me do? There are only two options here. Neither one of them good. If I leave my army behind, I could be walking into a trap. If I lead them through the Marshwood, it will draw unwanted attention, and I'll lose half of them before we get across the border."

My fingers brush the map in my pocket.

"Tell Silas you've taken his plan under advisement and that you need a guarantee. Ask him to draw you a map of Drake's Pass. Give it to Mattern for safekeeping and let her lead your army through the pass. Let Silas hire a teamster and livery, like he suggested, but don't tell him about Mattern or your plan until you have the map in hand and are ready to set out. Then announce that the shadow summoner has offered to lead you, along with your Elite Guard and the egg, through the Marshwood. No uniforms. No tents. No supplies. Just a small group disguised as reavers. Travel at night under the protection of darkness and Silas's shadows. Rest the horses and sleep in the woods during the day. If Dagmara or anyone else is planning an ambush, they won't have time to change their plans."

The ember in my chest is decidedly quiet. The oath won't let me repeat what I overheard from Silas and his crew, but apparently, the magic doesn't prevent me from plotting against him.

"And if he refuses to draw the map?"

"Lie and tell him you're taking your army and the egg back to Crecentis. That the alliance isn't worth the lives of your soldiers."

"I feel like there's more you're not telling me."

"The day you came home from the Wastes, when we were under the tree in the gardens, you told me you hadn't changed in any of the ways that matter. Neither have I. We still want the same things."

"And what is that?" He stuffs his hands in his pockets.

"Security and the promise of a better life for everyone in Perdanth. Let me help you protect the witches. Your mother was a battle witch before your father made her his queen. It's what she would want us to do."

Gideon sits on the edge of the table. "Once we're off the ship, you won't be able to pass me letters. We'll need a way to communicate. Do you remember the cues we used to cheat at the gaming tables during the balls?"

"I'm the one who came up with them so we could win all the peanuts."

"We're not playing for peanuts anymore, Everly. Drake is dangerous. If you're in trouble, scratch your nose like you would if you were dealt a bad hand. If you've got an ace and all is well, touch your eye. And if you need to talk, tug your ear, and I'll find a way to get you alone."

My insides twist.

I'm not sure who I feel more guilty about betraying. The man who's loved me since we were children and trusts me to help him save his kingdom, or the enemy who vowed to protect me with his life.

Chapter Twenty-Nine

I lean against a hitching post and gnaw anxiously on a hotpick as I watch Tiny, Thale, and Bas masquerade as a horse-for-hire livery crew in the fading light. Apparently, the only one in all of Port Hope available to leave at once. How convenient.

The stale hardtack I ate an hour ago sits in my stomach like a lead weight. Silas hasn't spoken to me since Gideon announced his change of plans. He just scowls in my direction every few minutes as he goes over the map he drew of Drake's Pass with Gideon and the navigators.

The silence is deafening.

Landry has given up the fake quest to find his knife, at least. The twisted, dark part of me gets a little thrill every time I see his swollen nose and blacked eyes. My stomach twists with guilt as he shouts orders at Grace while she secures their bedrolls and bags to their horses. The way she flinches every time he gets too close tells me he's done far worse than yell.

Craddock, a powerful fire summoner on Gideon's Elite Guard, makes eyes at Serin as she shows Nellie how to mount a horse. My guts twist again. Mattern and the senior navigators will be leading the army through the pass, leaving Nellie, Serin, and me to chart a course through the Marshwood Forest.

With Gideon's Elite Guards and Silas's crew, we're a party of twenty-five. A much larger group than I'd hoped for. It's hard to hide that many horses and a hay cart in the woods. We'll draw too much attention. Especially riding with a giant.

The only person missing from our ensemble is Val. The cadence of hoofbeats coming from the saddlebags on Tiny's dapple-gray stallion tells me the healer left his supply of unicorn relics with the giantess. Her horse tracks me warily with a pale eye as I approach from the side.

"He's beautiful."

"Did you hear that, pet? Everly thinks you're pretty."

"May I?" I ask, reaching for his white-blond mane.

"I wouldn't recommend it." She holds up a protective arm. "He's a bit testy right now. He has a wound on his forehead from scraping it repeatedly against a tree to get out of his bridle. This one doesn't like to be ridden. Do you, pretty boy?"

The horse chuffs at the giantess's placating tone.

"Do they ever stop staring?" I ask, nodding to the witches openly gawking at Tiny from the deck of the ship.

"You get used to it." She finishes securing a saddle to the horse's back. "My presence ensures that any attention we get while we travel will be on me and not on your prince. We can't afford for him to be recognized. If something happens to His Royal Highness, Silas will lose his invitation to the palace."

"How long have you been with him?"

She cuts me a wary glance.

"As part of his crew," I add quickly, all too aware of Silas's eyes on us from where he stands fifty paces away.

"On and off for twenty years." Tiny checks the fit of the tooled leather bridle that covers most of the horse's forehead and nose.

Twenty years? I attempt to make sense of the math in my head. Neither of them appears older than thirty. They would have been children when they met.

"You must be very close."

"We don't fuck, if that's what you're wondering. It's never been like that between us."

"That's not what I asked," I say as heat creeps across my cheeks.

"But you wanted to. I'm half giant. I can smell jealousy and desire. You reek of both, among other things."

"How does a half giant end up on a reaver crew?" I ask, eager to divert the conversation away from the way I may or may not feel about Silas Drake.

"My mother was a human slave owned by a brothel in the Northlands that catered to wealthy giants. Got herself in a bad way. I was too big to birth. She died when they cut me out of her. The madam kept me, taught me how to tease and please clients before I got my first bleed. I was the size of an adult human by the time I was ten. Silas found me when I was thirteen."

My stomach lurches. "He didn't—"

"No. Queen Isola's twin sons were frequent patrons. They were taking turns beating me. Silas heard the screams. He killed one of them, burned the brothel to the ground, and brought me to Shadow's Fold."

The gray stallion bucks his head.

"Easy, pet." Tiny pulls a beetroot from the canvas bucket at her feet and feeds it to him.

"What's Shadow's Fold?"

"A place for people like me." She strokes the horse's speckled coat. "Humans fear me because I look like a giant, and the giants shun me because they can smell my tainted human blood. Silas helped me find a place to call home. I'm not the only one. He brought Bas to us a few years ago. The poor kid was shot and left for dead in a swamp. He wouldn't have survived if Silas and Val hadn't found him."

"I've never heard of Shadow's Fold." I feel like a child staring up at her. My head is several inches shy of her shoulder.

"That's because we don't talk about it with outsiders."

"Why are you telling me?"

"Because Silas won't, and the others are oath bound to keep his secret. I have no magic in my bones. The oath doesn't work on me." Tiny moves to the next steed, a massive draft horse with a mahogany coat and black mane. "We've all done terrible things. Make no mistake, Silas Drake is a ruthless, vengeful beast, but he's not as unredeemable as he pretends to be."

"I don't think he was pretending when he told me he bound his life to mine so he wouldn't be tempted to kill me before I help him steal the egg."

"He said that?"

"I'm pretty sure he thought it was foreplay."

Tiny throws her head back with a sultry laugh. "I like you." Her eyes skate over me. "If I were him, I'd want to keep you all to myself too."

"It's just a side effect of the bond. I'm not naive enough to believe it has anything to do with me. Serin said it turned him into a possessive, overbearing ass."

"Trust me, he was all those things long before he bound himself to you. Blood bonds don't change your base instincts or desires, they just amplify them." Tiny rubs the gelding's muscular shoulder. "When I met with Silas the other night, I tried to convince him it was too risky to travel with the egg through the Marshwood. We argued about it and parted on harsh words. He's killed more than a few men to keep the pass a secret. You call him out on his bullshit, and he draws a fucking map and hands it over to his enemy."

I shift on my feet. Is it possible I was wrong about Silas's plans? The man has twisted the truth so many times I can no longer tell when he's manipulating me or putting on a show.

She pulls another beetroot from the canvas feed bucket and hands it to me. "You should spend some time getting to know Roan. You'll be spending the next few days on his back."

"I think I'd be better suited to one of the smaller horses."

"Silas insisted you ride this one. I've already packed your things in Roan's bags." She nods to the bedroll hooked behind the saddle. "He might look intimidating, but underneath all this brawn, he's a docile and loyal beast. Roan doesn't spook easily and won't run off from the group." She cuts me a knowing glance. "Even if you were to command it."

"I see."

Tiny leaves me alone with the huge animal. I'm not sure if I can mount him without the assistance of a block. My hand doesn't even reach the saddle's pommel.

"Hello, handsome."

Roan lowers his head and lets me stroke the white stripe that extends down the length of his broad nose.

"Please be gentle with me. It's been years since I've been in a saddle. I'm afraid I'm a little rusty."

"Congratulations on winning the game, Thorne."

My stomach curdles at the sound of Victor Landry's voice. I duck under Roan's muzzle, putting the horse between us as I pretend to check the fit of his bridle.

"What? No smart comment? You're not so brave without your bitch friend, are you?"

"I have a lot of friends. You'll need to be more specific." I smile sweetly as the familiar huff of dragon's breath slides down my neck.

Landry's gaze darts over my shoulder as Silas wraps a possessive arm around me from behind and presses a kiss to my neck.

"Fucking your way through the Elite Guard like you did at the Menagerie?" Landry asks with a smirk.

Shadows whoosh past me and whip around Landry's throat like a noose, lifting him up onto his toes. "Do not disrespect her again. That's your last warning."

Silas releases him, and Landry stumbles backward, falling on his ass in the dirt. He shoves to his feet and glances up at the crowd of witches watching from the deck of the ship.

"You'll get what's coming to you, Drake. Mark my words." Landry stalks off toward Gideon, face fuming.

"Was that necessary?"

"No, and neither is this." Silas tugs me against him and captures my mouth in a possessive kiss. It's all teeth and tongue and nothing like the other two times. I fist the front of his black tunic as need licks its way through my core.

Silas groans against my mouth before pulling away.

"What was that for?"

"Just setting expectations for our audience."

"You shouldn't have threatened Landry like that. Not with everyone watching."

"It wasn't a threat."

"Men like Landry don't take well to being humiliated. He'll come after you."

"I'm counting on it." Silas adds his bedroll to Roan's back with a scowl. "I'm going to enjoy killing that sick fuck once I'm no longer bound by the oath."

"What do you think you're doing?" I ask, ignoring the tightness in my chest at the thought of no longer being bound to him. "Find your own horse."

"Roan *is* my horse." He mounts the gelding in one graceful swoop and reaches down for my hand.

"It's not humane to make him carry two riders."

"You've run away from me twice in the last twenty-four hours. Do you really expect me to give you your own horse?"

"I'm not riding with you."

"You can come willingly, or I can truss you up like a doe after a hunt and throw you over Roan's back. The choice is yours."

"I'd prefer to not torture the poor animal."

"Give me your hand." The command makes my skin pebble. I'm not sure if it's from fear or something else.

I glance around. There aren't any other horses. I apologize to Roan for the additional burden and let Silas swing me up into the saddle in front of him. He tugs me back, seating me snugly against his hips, grazing his lips over the shell of my ear.

"Good girl."

CHAPTER THIRTY

Roan bucks his head and cants to the side as the hay cart in front of us lurches over an invisible rut in the dark. The full moon is high and bright, but I can't see anything past the protective wall of shadows that surrounds our group. We set out from Port Hope after sunset and have been traveling all night. Silas hasn't asked me about my conversation with Gideon or spoken more than a handful of words to me since we left. My ass is numb, and I have to pee.

"It's okay." I reach down and rub Roan's neck. Tiny said he wasn't skittish, but it isn't the first time he's tried to get away from the cart. I can only guess that he senses the hidden cargo buried beneath the bales of hay.

Roan settles, and I sit up in the saddle. The movement causes my backside to grind against the firm bulge that's been pressing against my backside all night.

"My beast likes you," Silas says close to my ear.

"Most animals do, except for my Pig."

"You don't own a pig."

"How would you know? I could have a whole pen of pigs at home."

"Because I made it my business to learn everything about you when I realized what you are." There's a thread of irritation in his voice. He's clearly still pissed about having to draw Gideon a map of the pass.

"Pig is a cat, and I'm pretty sure he owns me." I keep talking, hoping the innocuous conversation will distract me from his rigid cock. "He showed up one night in the middle of a thunderstorm and hid under my bed. I fed him a piece of toast in the morning. He bit me and ran off when I tried to pet him. I didn't think I'd ever see him again until he scratched at my window during the next storm. He still won't let me get close enough to touch him or comb out his fleas, but I keep the balcony window cracked so he always has a safe place to sleep."

"Most people would trap and kill a feral beast for attacking them. Yet you keep inviting it into your home."

"I prefer feral beasts to most people."

Silas shifts in the saddle, slipping a hand between us to adjust himself so he's not prodding me. It doesn't help.

I stare at the hay wagon ahead of me and count the rectangular bales I can make out in the dark. Anything to distract myself from the gentle rock of his pelvis against my backside in tempo with Roan's steady gait. I grab the pommel and shift forward to put space between us. The ridge of the saddle grinds against the bare bits beneath my skirt, sending a jolt through my core.

"Are you trying to torture me?" Silas asks, voice like gravel.

I bite back a smile, knowing he senses my arousal through the bond.

"You're the one who insisted on riding together to punish me for making you draw Gideon a map of the pass." I grind against the saddle again. This time I do it on purpose. He's been manipulating my desire since the day I swore the oath. He deserves a taste of his own medicine. Part of me thrills at knowing I have this small power over him.

Silas tugs me back against him, fingers splayed across my belly.

"You meddling little witch. I should have known this was your fucking idea. Silas takes a long, slow breath. "Do you know how long I've kept the entrance to the pass a secret?"

"I didn't force you to draw the damn map. You could have refused."

"It was that, or risk losing all the little battle witches you care so much about."

"What?" I twist to face him.

Silas has made it abundantly clear he doesn't care about the bodies he leaves in his wake. Why would he give up something this important to protect the lives of his enemy's army? I force my gaze forward, ignoring the fluttering sensation the answer leaves in my chest.

"You are extremely inconvenient." I can hear the dark smirk in his voice.

"Are you going to punish me?"

"Would you like me to punish you?" Silas inches his fingers down my stomach.

I gasp as he cups my center, sending a wave of throbbing need through me.

"Would you like me to tease and torture you until you beg me to let you come?"

"Yes." My response is immediate. I'm too far gone in my need to deny it. It's just bodies. It doesn't mean anything.

My skin pebbles as his shadows curl around my calf under my skirt, caressing me as if they were his hands.

"What if someone sees?" My gaze darts to the right, where Thale and Bas ride side by side ten paces away.

Silas brushes his lips over my ear. "Do you want me to stop?"

I slide my palms down my thighs and gather the fabric of my long skirt, lifting it slowly.

"No."

He grips my thigh and hooks my leg over his, using his shadows to spread me wide. The creaking cart and the other quiet conversations around us fall away as he slips his left hand beneath my skirt.

"Here?" he asks, slowly dragging his calloused palm up my knee-length drawers.

"Yes."

Silas traces the edge of the open gusset, his fingertips grazing my flesh. "And here?"

I bite back a whimper as he glides two fingers along my slick center.

"I love feeling the way your needy little cunt throbs for me. Standing outside your door every night while you touch yourself is the most exquisite torture I've ever known."

I throw my head back against his shoulder as his fingers and shadows tease and lick until I'm a quivering mess.

He grabs the saddle pommel with the hand still holding the reins as his shadows bracket my throat. Not enough to hurt, but enough to heighten my pleasure. The bastard has been inside my head. He knows exactly what I like without having to be told.

The thick tip of a shadow appendage presses against my entrance. I rock my hips, chasing the fullness I crave.

He grinds his erection against me. "Is this what you want? To feel what it's like to be filled and fucked by my magic?"

"Silas, please." I dig my nails into his thighs.

He pushes his shadow inside me, pumping slow and deep. My gasps for air come quickly as the prickling heat builds. I need this man to make me come more than I need to breathe.

The invisible string behind my navel pulls tight. I moan his name as my pleasure peaks.

"That's it, little spark. Tell everyone who you belong to." He releases my throat and uses his shadow hand to turn my face so he can claim my mouth. The kiss is possessive and unyielding and everything I want it to be. No softness. Nothing to get confused.

I melt into him as the orgasm rocks my body.

"*F-u-c-k.*" Silas's chest vibrates with a growl as his hips pulse against my backside once, twice, and he buries his face in my hair.

Roan bucks his head and quickens his step. Silas pulls back on the reins, coaxing the horse to settle. He holds me securely against him, heart pounding against my back in perfect cadence with mine.

We stay like that for a moment until our heartbeats peel apart, regaining their independent rhythms as we catch our breath. I untangle my leg from his and sit up in the saddle. He's no longer prodding my backside.

"Did you—"

"Like I said, very inconvenient." He presses a soft kiss to my temple. "Try to rest. We still have a few hours before we make camp."

Chapter Thirty-One

Bits of blue peek through the tree canopy. The way the dark branches move in the soft breeze makes the forest appear to be breathing. There are no bird calls or buzzing insects like I remember from my summers sleeping in these same woods with my parents. Just an eerie silence. I have a hazy memory of Silas lifting me off the horse and carrying me to our bedrolls sometime before dawn.

Every muscle in my body aches as I stretch out my arms to the empty space next to me where he should be.

I sit up straight.

My chest pinches as I scan the sleeping bodies around me.

Silas and his crew are gone.

I can't breathe.

I scramble to my feet and drop my shield. A familiar cold seeps into my bones. The egg is still here, hidden beneath bales of hay on the horse cart. Silas couldn't have gone far. I can't feel him, but I know he wouldn't leave. Not without the egg. My chest tightens, and I refuse to admit what it might mean.

A thick wall of shadows surrounds the rough campsite. I can't see, hear, or feel anything beyond it. I tiptoe my way to the perimeter, halting as a twig snaps beneath my feet. My gaze darts to where Landry snores softly atop a pile of hay layered with bedrolls and blankets. Grace is curled up on the bare ground at his feet like a dog. Part of me hopes he ignores Silas's threat and comes after me. If Silas kills the bastard, at least Grace will be free.

Something lands behind me with a soft thud. The ember in my chest flares as I spin, summoning a dark flame to my hand.

Bas holds a finger to his lips. I extinguish the flame before anyone else notices and glance up at the swaying branch where he must have been perched. He gestures for me to follow him through the wall of shadows. The ghost of a caress grazes my cheek, and I tell myself it's just my imagination.

"Sorry about that, Miss Everly," Bas says as we emerge on the other side to the scent of woodsmoke, tobacco, and roasted venison. "Didn't mean to startle you. Silas told me to make sure you got something to eat as soon as you woke."

Tiny, Serin, and Thale sit around a campfire, laughing and eating. Serin clears her throat when she sees us approach. Part of me is relieved that Silas isn't with them. I'm not sure if I'm ready to face him after last night. The other part of me wants to know where he is and when he'll be back. So much for not letting me out of his sight.

"She takes her coffee first," Serin says as she makes room for me on the log next to her and hands Bas her empty mug.

He refills it with a steaming ladle from a cauldron on the cold side of the fire and hands it to me.

"What time is it?" I ask.

Tiny holds her pipe between her teeth and pulls a watch attached to a gold chain from her pocket. "Half past one. The pixie dust should be wearing off. The others will wake soon."

I hold the mug up and look for the telltale pulse of magic.

"We didn't dose you, girl," Serin says. "Only the others."

"Why would you do that?"

"To help them sleep soundly," Thale says flatly. "These woods are full of unusual noises. Wouldn't want any of our new friends to go wandering off alone to investigate."

I don't miss the way they all glance at Bas.

"Can I make you a plate, Miss Everly?" the boy asks with a sheepish grin.

I nod, and he cuts a hunk of meat off the deer stretched over the spit and serves it to me on a plate with a handful of wild grapes and something that looks like a hunk of boiled potato.

"Thank you, Bas." I take the plate and inhale the food as they discuss the weather.

My pulse flutters annoyingly in my chest as the familiar huff of dragon's breath cascades down my neck. I glance past Tiny as Silas steps through the shadows.

My breath hitches.

The man is downright filthy—sweaty and covered in grime. I can't help but drink him in as he tugs his shirt off over his head, dunks it in a water bucket and drags it over the back of his neck.

"*It's rude to stare,*" Silas says through the bond, dragging his eyes over me.

"*Where have you been?*"

"*Did you miss me?*" The corner of his mouth twitches as he wrings the water out over his head. I watch as it runs down his body. The bastard knows exactly what he's doing.

"*Don't flatter yourself, reaver. I barely noticed you were gone.*" I force my greedy eyes away and catch Tiny watching me curiously.

The wall separating the two campsites dissipates as the others begin to stir. Nellie is the first to join us.

"How are you feeling after last night's ride?" I ask as Serin gives the girl her seat and takes my empty plate.

"My behind and lady bits are a little sore, but it's no big bother. Serin gave me some willow bark to chew on before we left. I got extra if you need some for yours, Everly."

"I think her lady bits are already well taken care of," Tiny says, winking at me.

Serin kicks Tiny's boot as she brings Nellie a plate of food. I sip my coffee and pretend not to notice the awkward silence that follows.

"This looks better than hardtack rations," Jo-el says as he, Gideon, and Craddock join us.

"Help yourself. There's enough for everyone," Tiny says.

Jo-el ladles coffee into an empty mug and adds a pinch of alicorn powder before handing it to Gideon.

"Who do we have to thank for the fresh meat?" Gideon asks as he inhales the steam wafting from the cup.

"That would be my groom," Tiny says. "Young Mr. Lowell here is a skilled hunter and forager. Bagged the doe after everyone fell asleep."

Bas blushes as Gideon praises him for his meticulous field dressing skills.

"I don't recall hearing any shots," Craddock says.

"It was just the one." The casual lie rolls off my tongue with a sudden protective instinct. "I heard it just after dawn."

"You always were a light sleeper," Gideon says softly, earning a dark look from Silas as he wrings out his shirt and spreads it out over a branch to dry in the sun.

"I'm on watch," Serin says to Nellie. "Stay close to Everly and don't leave the perimeter of the campsite."

"I have horses to feed and water." Tiny taps the tobacco out of her pipe and dusts off her black bowler hat.

"I'd be happy to help." I jump to my feet and smooth my skirt.

"That's quite all right, ma'am. My grooms and I can manage. It is our *job*, after all."

Right. I'd almost forgotten about the ruse.

She tips her hat to the group and strides away with Thale and Bas on her heels.

"Your skills are required elsewhere, Private Thorne." Gideon glances over my shoulder at Silas. "Is everything prepared?"

"I've cleared a section of the woods as you asked and set up a warded perimeter," Silas says. "There's ample room to un-cask the egg."

"Craddock, go rouse the Storm Squad. I want the egg moved immediately."

"I've already taken the liberty of moving it," Silas says.

"I give the orders around here, Drake."

"Of course. My apologies, Your Royal Highness. I assumed you'd want Everly and me to get started right away. We have six hours of daylight to study the relic before we ride out."

"Get some rest, Drake. You haven't slept yet. I need you to be focused and alert for the ride tonight."

"I'm afraid I must insist on staying with the relic while it's uncasked. I have no idea how my wards will react to its magic. We don't want a repeat of what happened at the ball," Silas says.

Gideon glances at me. I scratch the side of my nose. I don't trust myself alone with Silas. Not after last night.

"Take Captain Sanchez with you. His expertise may be needed to assess whether the egg is viable."

"Could I borrow Private Roy as well? There are a few things I need to collect before we get started. Her assistance would be appreciated."

"Fine. Now get to work. I want a full report from you in three hours."

"Thank you."

"Jo-el." Gideon flicks his gaze to me. "Take your medical bag. Just in case."

Snow catches on my lashes despite the summer heat as I circle the frozen ground. The egg is even more exquisite in the daylight. Each overlapping scale sparkles like a cut gem. I could spend hours drawing the minute details and still not capture its beauty. I wish Wallace were here. She'd do it far better justice than I ever could.

She'd love all of this—grumpy Serin and sweet Nellie, traveling with a real-life giant, and studying a dragon egg. She'd be drooling over Silas and his perfect teeth. My chest tightens. If she were here, I wouldn't be able to share any of this with her. It's hard enough lying to Gideon. I'm not sure I could lie to Wallace too.

"Serin said it killed three people the last time it came out of its box. Should we be standing this close?" Nellie asks nervously.

"You're safe as long as you don't cross the frost line," Silas says from where he hovers beside me, arms crossed over his bare chest, ribbons of shadow floating around him at the ready.

"How are we supposed to examine it if we can't get closer than thirty feet?" Jo-el asks.

"By experimentation and observation. Nellie, can you please hand me another pine cone?"

She picks one up from the pile we collected and tosses it to me. I roll it gently across the perimeter. It comes to a slow stop a few feet past the previous three. Frost creeps over its surface until every crevice is coated with a thin layer of ice. The same as the others.

"Another." This time I pitch the pine cone at the egg like a ball. It explodes in the air, sending glass-like shards of ice back toward us. Nellie and Jo-el duck, covering their heads as the shards hit Silas's shield.

"A little warning next time," Jo-el says.

"Sorry, just testing a theory."

"*What's your theory?*" Silas asks through the bond.

I ignore the question and roll another pine cone across the border, using a little more force this time. It goes a few feet farther than the last and explodes halfway between the outer circle and the egg.

"It reminds me of the double-layered wards used to secure the vaults at the Menagerie. There's a slow freeze zone around the outer edge—I assume to encourage other creatures or would-be predators to back off." I circle the clearing and roll five more pine cones across the line. They all explode at the same distance from the egg.

"And an instant kill zone to take out the ones who don't heed the warning," Silas says.

"We've established that someone warded it. Now what?" Jo-el asks.

"Silas, you have experience channeling magic from dragon scales. How many would it take for a witch to maintain a defensive ward around something that size indefinitely?"

"It would require constant daily maintenance, no matter how many scales they had access to. They'd have to travel with it."

"What if it warded itself?" I say aloud, mostly to myself.

"I've never heard of a magical creature that could set a ward," Jo-el says. "They'd need to possess a human-like intelligence to do that."

"Goblins and pixies have human-like intelligence. It's not that much of a stretch to think dragons might have been just as capable."

Silas lets out an incredulous grunt.

"You think dragons were sentient?" Jo-el asks.

"It's just a theory. I'd need to observe a living dragon to prove it."

"If the baby dragon inside the egg set its own ward, does that mean it's alive?" Nellie asks.

I can't help the smile that breaks across my face. "Yes, I believe it is."

She cocks her head to the side, deep in thought. "Why does it have scales?"

"All dragons have scales," I say.

"Yeah, but it's not a dragon. Not on the outside. It's an egg."

"Of course it's an—"

"Let her finish." I hold up my hand to cut Silas off.

"We have chickens back home. They're covered in feathers, but I've never seen one lay a feathered egg. Gators, snapping turtles, and snakes have armor and scales kind of like a dragon. Their eggs are smooth too."

"Wait. Say that again," Silas demands.

Nellie shifts back and forth between her feet. "I'm just saying it looks more like a giant pixie pod to me. You know, how their glow worm babies get fat and slimy and the pod hardens into a crystal shell so they can sleep through the rainy season? When they eat their way out of the shell the next summer, they got pretty wings and nasty sharp teeth."

"She might be onto something." I stare at the egg as every bestiary I've ever read flashes through my mind. "Every nonextinct magical species goes through some kind of transformation during its life cycle. Pixies pupate, like she said. Firebirds molt, self-combust, and regenerate indefinitely. Goblins have to venture out of the darkness of their caves to the daylight to burn their retinas before they can cast spells, and rougarous shed their hides every full moon."

"Are you suggesting dragons pupate?" Silas asks with a disgusted scowl.

"Paleontological evidence suggests that dragons were solitary creatures and rarely reproduced, despite their centuries-long lifespans. Birds are the closest living things we have to dragons, so we assume dragons laid eggs, but no one's ever found the remains of a nest or even a juvenile skeleton. This egg, if that's what it is, is the greatest discovery ever made. I need to talk to Gideon."

CHAPTER THIRTY-TWO

"I'd like to test its warded perimeter against different kinds of magic. If your witches can get past its defenses, Jo-el and I can study it up close and determine why it hasn't hatched. I just need a few volunteers—"

"No," Gideon says as we watch Craddock take on two storm summoners from his Elite Guard in a two-on-one magic duel. "If this thing is alive, I don't want you or anyone else near it when it hatches." He turns and orders Jo-el to oversee packing up the egg. "It stays inside its cask until we need to use it as bait to capture its mother."

"Gideon, please. We'll be in Tindlestone in three days. This relic is the discovery of a lifetime. I may not get another chance to study it."

"Watch your head, Weems." Gideon uncrosses his arms as he shouts the warning at one of his guards who's getting blasted by Craddock. "Don't want to lose all that pretty hair the ladies love."

"Are you even listening to me right now?"

Gideon cuts me a sidelong glance. "Jo-el said the pine cones you threw at it exploded like mini bombs. Is there any chance it could fight back if we start blasting its wards with magic?"

"Maybe, but Silas set up a—"

"Then my decision is firm. No more experiments. Don't ask me again." He nods to Silas, who's watching us intently from the opposite side of the training ring. "You're up next, Drake."

"Fine, at least let me observe it again tomorrow so I can sketch it."

"Thank you for the report, Private Thorne. You're dismissed."

I ball my fists and stomp away before I say something I'll regret. Thale and Bas dip their heads as I approach the communal campfire where Serin and Nellie take turns shooting flares at the doe's charred carcass.

"What are you two up to?"

"Serin is teaching me how to turn my enemies into charcoal," Nellie says with a gap-toothed grin that makes me smile despite my seething anger at Gideon and his stubborn refusal to listen to reason.

"Do you have many enemies?" I ask, unable to fathom her harboring malice toward anyone.

"Of course. I just haven't met them yet. Anyone who threatens my friends will face my wrath." She shoots simultaneous flares, one from each hand, at the carcass.

"The little fire witch needs no instruction," Thale says, his matter-of-fact tone leaving no room for debate. "She's a natural."

I tuck my sketchbook under my arm and clap vigorously. She's barely a month past her fever, and she's already throwing flames. It took me a year to teach myself how to summon a spark with my tattered old firebird feather.

"It's only on account of me being a Roy. Every witch in my clan has been a fire summoner except my Great-Uncle Quintus. He was a storm summoner. The madness took him real quick. Ma says it was comeuppance for him going against his blood."

"That's enough practice for today, girl," Serin says abruptly. "It's almost sundown. Let's let these gentlemen do their job."

A dark flame shoots into the sky with a loud boom, followed by a round of cheers.

"Like dynamite and a fucking fuse." Serin curses under her breath. "We're supposed to be keeping a low profile so we don't give our position away. This is what happens when you don't take my advice," Serin says, glaring at me. "Stay here. I'll deal with this."

Fire and shadows collide midair above the training ring, sending another boom across the campsite.

"What's going on?" Nellie asks.

"Silas is dueling with Craddock."

Nellie grabs my hand and drags me to the edge of the ring, where Craddock and the two other fire summoners square off against Silas.

"Craddock is the best fire summoner in Perdanth. He fought with Colonel Krimore at Fort Netherthorn. They say he's never lost a duel."

I flinch as a fireball narrowly misses Silas's head. The bastard smirks.

"Why isn't the shadow summoner using a shield?" Nellie asks.

"For the same reason he's not wearing a shirt. He likes to show off." I turn on my heel and stroll back across the campsite.

"Where are you going? Don't you want to watch?"

"If I wanted to see a bunch of swinging dicks, I'd visit the men's latrine."

The wagon wobbles beneath me as I scrub the heel of my palm against the sketch in frustration. No matter how hard I try, I can't replicate the play of light and shadow on the page. Every attempt to capture the relic's shimmering scales from memory comes out flat.

I rip out the page and let it flutter to the ground beneath my dangling feet and begin again. If I was in the Menagerie, with proper lighting and the egg directly in front of me, I could give the relic the artistic justice it deserves. I need to find a way to convince Gideon to let me keep studying the egg.

Its wards aren't like any I've seen. There are no threads of magic. No discernible pattern to unravel.

"I think you dropped this." Silas's deep voice pours through me, making my stomach flutter as if I've swallowed a pixie. I tell myself it's just a side effect of the bond as he uses his shadows to lift my disaster of an attempt to draw the egg.

"Throw it in the fire." I keep my gaze down as his dusty boots stop in front of me.

"I'm afraid the fire's already been put out. Besides, that notebook is made of the finest vellum money can buy. This won't burn easily, and we can't afford to leave any evidence behind." He folds the paper and tucks it into his breast pocket.

At least he's wearing a shirt now.

"I didn't realize you were a connoisseur of fine parchment." I focus on shading the sketch in front of me.

"I'm a connoisseur of many rare and beautiful things." He takes a step closer, and it takes every bit of willpower I have not to look at him. "The clerk at the print seller's shop assured me the parchment was top quality when I had it bound."

My gaze snaps to his and back to the sketchbook in my lap. I flip to the inscription at the front. Run my fingers over the tight, elegant script. *For your research.*

The sketchbook and new set of charcoals were on my bunk under the uniform and Gideon's letter that first day on the ship.

"You left it for me? I thought Gideon—"

"Of course you'd think it was from your prince." Silas shakes his head and turns to leave.

"Thank you." The words rush out of me. "It's the finest sketchbook I've ever owned. The charcoal grips the page beautifully. It's so much easier to get a deeper tone. Here, look." I turn the drawing around in my lap to show him.

Silas moves closer and studies the egg portrait in the fading light. This one isn't perfect, but it's better than my previous attempt at capturing the iridescent sheen. I point out the light and dark areas and explain how I used the negative space to give the impression of illumination and shadow.

When I look up, Silas is staring at me instead of the page.

"Do I have something on my face?" I bring my hand up to swipe away whatever it is.

"Don't." Silas catches my stained fingers and steps into the space between my knees. "You'll make it worse." The sun-bronzed skin around his eyes crinkles with a smile as he cups the side of my neck and uses his thumb to wipe away the smear of charcoal.

I've never seen him smile. Not like this. Not in the way that makes his brown eyes look like they've been underpainted with red ocher.

My throat goes dry.

"Are the others watching?" he asks softly as he slides his hand to the back of my neck.

I glance at the horses where Gideon and the rest of our traveling party are packing their saddlebags. Gideon's gaze darts away. He's not the only one staring.

"Yes."

"I've done my best to keep their attention off you, but I need to kiss you now to keep up the ruse."

My heart skitters as Silas bends down and presses his lips to mine. It isn't brutal or demanding. It's a slow and seductive claiming.

Heat floods my core as he snakes his fingers through my hair, tugging gently to tip my head back and deepen the kiss. My hand finds its way to his waist. A guttural sound vibrates from his chest as I slide my palm under the loose hem of his shirt.

Silas skates his free hand up my ribs, and I curse the tight corset under my clothes as he slowly traces the curve of my breast with his thumb.

My desire coils tight, and I have to remind myself it's a calculated and convincing performance. I pull away before I lose myself to the lie.

"Do we need to talk about last night?" he asks.

"What's there to talk about? It's just pretend. A means to an end for both of us," I say as casually as I can muster. Maybe if I keep repeating it, I'll actually believe it.

Silas brushes a strand of hair away from my face. "You've been trying very hard to ignore me all day."

"I've been busy." I lift the sketchbook clenched in my fist. "This may come as a surprise, but not everything is about you."

Silas's brow furrows as he glances down at my sketchbook. "None of this is about me, Everly. You should ride in the wagon tonight. There's room for you now that the horses have gone through a few bales of hay."

Chapter Thirty-Three

"Maybe it's just waiting for the right place to hatch? A spot where it feels safe?" Nellie says, riding behind the wagon on her brown and white painted horse. "If I was a baby dragon, I wouldn't want to hatch around a bunch of humans either."

"I would give anything to watch it hatch," I say.

"What would you do with a dragon, girl? Feed it toast and let it hide under your bed when it rains?" Serin cuts me a sidelong look from where she and Silas flank the wagon.

"It's better than being turned into a weapon or slaughtered for the magic in its bones."

"It probably won't like toast," Nellie says. "We'll have to feed it meat until it can learn how to hunt on its own. Do you think it would like wild hogs or deer better?"

"Venison braised in brown butter and herbs is always a good choice," Silas says.

"It's a wild animal. I'm sure it would prefer its meals raw."

"You are the expert," Silas says with a grin.

"I'm hardly an expert. We know very little about the habits of dragons. The first king of Perdanth is the only human to ever get close to one and survive. It's unfortunate he didn't have the foresight to take notes." I sit up straighter and tuck my legs beneath me. "Once the war was over, no one ever saw his dragon again. It was the last of its kind. Or so we thought. Now we know there are at least two left in the world."

"Don't you mean three?" Nellie asks. "The egg and both its parents."

The wagon jerks to a stop. I throw my arm out and grab the side as someone shouts from the front of our group.

"Don't let her out of your sight," Silas says to Serin as he urges Roan around the wagon to investigate.

"What's going on?" I lean over the side and try to get a look. I can't see anything past the hay bales in the dark.

"Stay in the cart." Serin scans the line where the dense woods meets the wall of shadows surrounding our travel party.

I climb over the bales to the top of the pile. A covered wagon like the one my parents traveled with lies on its side, blocking the path, its white top clearly visible under the full moon.

My stomach lurches. All the horrible ways I've imagined my parents during their last moments spool in my mind. Did they die instantly, or did they bleed out slowly in the dirt with no one to help them? I slide down the pile of hay and jump off the side of the cart.

Serin curses and snaps her horse's reins as I dart between Landry and Grace and the others to the front of the group, where Gideon talks to a middle-aged man and woman. Silas and Thale have dismounted and are assessing the wagon's broken wheel.

There are no bodies. No parents dying alone in the dirt. My shoulders loosen.

"We thank you kindly for stopping. We hit a rut. Spooked the horses and just went over," the man says, cradling his arm in a makeshift sling.

"Where are your horses?" Gideon asks.

"They ran off," the woman says flatly.

"*Do you sense any relics?*" Silas asks through the bond as he moves toward the back of the wagon.

"*Nothing.*"

"We have a trained medic riding with us," Gideon says. "He could take a look at your injured arm if you like. He may be able to fix it."

The man moves toward me, eyeing Gideon warily. I've seen the look before from people who don't trust medicine or magic.

"Where was that rut you said you hit?" Silas asks from the back end of the overturned wagon.

"Back yonder." The woman waves behind her. Her gaze snagging on Gideon's sword.

Silas nods to Thale. The storm summoner heads down the dark path as Silas lifts the canvas flap covering the back of the wagon.

"*Go back to the cart.*" Silas says across the bond.

Everything happens at once.

"It's an ambush," someone yells.

The man pulls a gun out of his sling and points it at my head.

Reavers in red death masks burst through the wall of shadows.

Gideon grabs my arm. A sharp crack splits the air next to my head.

Pain rips through my shoulder.

Silas roars my name across the bond. Shadows explode from his body, surrounding him in a swirling vortex.

Gideon shoves me to the ground behind him as he draws his sword. My ears ring as I scramble backward between the wheels of the overturned wagon, and the night erupts into chaos. All I can hear is my pulse pounding in my ears.

The man who shot at me slumps into a pile at Gideon's feet. His lifeless eyes stare at me.

Blood covers Gideon's shirt. I can't tell if it's his, mine, or the man's as he leaps over the dead body and enters the fray. I glance down at my shoulder.

"*He missed. The bullet didn't hit me.*" My voice is too loud inside my head. If Silas hears me through the bond, he doesn't say. It's just a sprain from Gideon twisting my arm and pushing me out of the way.

The hair on my arms rises as lightning flashes over the top of the wagon from behind. I scream Silas's name as it strikes the swirling vortex of shadows.

The ground rumbles beneath me. I can feel it vibrate my chest like the slow roll of thunder. The shadows evaporate, and Silas's limp body hits the ground.

The dark power inside me uncurls. I don't know who attacked him. All I know is that I need to protect Silas Drake.

I crawl to him on my hands and knees. He's not breathing.

"Don't you dare die on me, you bastard." Angry tears stream down my cheeks as I straddle him and pound on his chest.

Someone grabs my shoulders.

"*Mine.*"

I feel myself turn and snarl at Thale, but it doesn't feel like me. It feels like someone else is in control, like in my dream, when I jumped off the cliff. Like my entire body wants to crack open.

Thale backs away. "Easy, girl."

Silas sucks in a sharp breath. He flips me onto my back, a shadow blade pressed to my throat, baring his teeth.

I don't dare breathe. "Silas, it's me."

He blinks twice, studying my mismatched eyes. "Everly?"

I reach up slowly and curl my fingers around his wrist. "I'm not the enemy."

The shadow blade vanishes. Silas leans back and runs his hand over my shoulder and chest, looking for damage. "You were shot. I felt it."

"Krimore took the bullet," Serin says behind him. "Killed eight reavers before he fell. They took out most of our storm summoners, but we still have the egg."

"Gideon." My chest squeezes tight as I shove against Silas.

He rolls off me, and I'm on my feet and running to where Jo-el kneels next to Gideon, who is sitting on the ground. I drop to my knees as Jo-el cuts Gideon's shirt off.

"How bad is it?" Gideon asks, looking too pale.

"It went clean through, but you've lost a lot of blood," Jo-el says, face grim.

"What are you waiting for? Give him some alicorn powder," I say.

"I need to slow the bleeding first. Otherwise, his blood will flush it out before the magic has a chance to work."

"Tell me what to do."

"Put pressure here."

I take the scraps of Gideon's shirt and press it against the oozing hole in his back.

"Why did you keep fighting when you were shot? You could have bled to death."

"Because he was protecting you," Jo-el says quietly.

"I'm a soldier. It's my job to protect everyone under my command," Gideon says, swaying sideways.

Silas catches him as he goes over. "He's lost too much blood. You need to seal the wound now."

"I need a fire summoner and a piece of iron." Jo-el's voice goes tight with panic.

"He doesn't have time for that. Help me lay him down and give me room."

Silas hovers his hand above the wound. Gideon's blood sizzles as tendrils of dark flame crawl into the bullet hole, searing it shut from the inside out.

Silas rocks back on his feet, extinguishing his magic. "Lift his feet and cover him up. He'll have the chills when he comes to. We camp here tonight."

***

Serin recites a prayer as she circles the funeral pyre. It doesn't matter that we don't know the words spoken in the old language of her clan. We all understand.

The two dead storm summoners from Gideon's Elite Guard and Grace LeMay will be welcomed by the Mother of Fire when they cross into the Otherworld.

We take turns placing mementos around them. Gideon, still pale but otherwise recovered, thanks to a dose of alicorn powder, places their relics on their chests. Others add bits of hardtack for the journey or a generous pour of whiskey and rum from their flasks. I tuck a folded piece of paper into Grace's cold hand as I pay my respects.

Craddock and two other fire summoners light the bales of hay beneath them. I watch as the flames lick their bodies and wonder if the patrol that found my parents took the time to build them a funeral pyre. Did the flames carry them to the Otherworld, or are they cursed to wander as lost souls? I don't know if they'll get the message Grace carries with her.

Gideon speaks about each of his fallen soldiers not only as their commander but as their friend. He shares stories of their bravery. Of the sacrifices they made for each other and for Perdanth. A few others add stories of their own. The way Landry praises Grace for her loyalty makes me nauseous. Unfortunately, he didn't see fit to show her any kindness while she was alive.

I watch the flames dance and lick up toward the sky as people slowly peel away to find their beds for the night. I'm vaguely aware of Silas laying out our bedrolls behind me.

"I'm taking first watch of the perimeter with Craddock and Landry. You'll be safe here by the pyre with Serin and the little fire witch. They're on duty to make sure the flames don't go out tonight."

I nod, keeping my eyes on the three burning bodies.

"Promise me you won't wander off alone." There's no command in his voice. Only softness and something that feels like an unasked question.

"I'll be here until the fire dies." It's not a promise, but Silas gives me my space anyway.

Nellie and Serin take up their posts by the pyre. Only Gideon and Jo-el remain.

"You should lie down and get some rest," Jo-el says, handing Gideon a canteen. "The alicorn powder won't replenish the blood you lost. Your body needs time to—"

"I'm not lying down or leaving my fallen brothers until their bodies return to ash."

"Will you sit at least? Resting after an injury won't make you appear weak."

Gideon cuts Jo-el a sharp look. "Stop hovering over me. Go check on the others with injuries and make sure they have what they need."

Jo-el dips his head at the order before turning and walking toward me. "Make sure he keeps drinking water and try to get him to rest. We have a long ride tomorrow, and he won't listen to me."

Serin watches me as I move to Gideon's side. "He's right. You should rest."

"I'm not leaving them alone. As commanding officer, it's my responsibility to see every soldier home. When I fail, it's my responsibility to stay with them until they cross to the Otherworld."

We both stare at the flames. There's no point in trying to convince him that their deaths aren't his fault. Anyone can see that he carries the weight on his shoulders. The same way I carry my parents' deaths with me. My mother and father are just two people. Gideon lost hundreds in the siege at Fort Netherthorn alone. I can't imagine the burden he must bear.

"No one will think less of you if you sit." I let my fingers brush his.

Gideon pulls his hand away and grips the hilt of his sword. "Sitting is for idle kings on thrones."

"You're the prince of Perdanth. You'll be an idle king someday," I joke, attempting to lighten the mood.

"I'm not a prince, Everly. I'm a soldier." He keeps his gaze fixed on the flames.

"Are you angry with me?"

"We have three extra horses now. Pick one to ride for the rest of the journey. People are talking." Gideon walks away from me to stand on the opposite side of the pyre.

The bitter command doesn't sting nearly as much as the thread of disgust in his voice. I swallow my angry words and blink back the hot tears. We're supposed to be friends. He has no right to tell me how to conduct myself. Not when I'm doing everything I can to get around the oath to prevent Silas from stealing the egg. I refuse to let him make me feel ashamed.

What I need is a distraction. I yank the sketchbook from my bag and flump onto my bedroll to record images of the attack while it's fresh in my head. The overturned wagon, the man with the gun. Silas.

My hand trembles as I draw his limp body on the ground. I pull my flask from my bag and take a deep swig of the bitter tonic. If it was rum, it might be easier to shove down this bone-cleaving sensation in my chest I'm too afraid to name. Silas Drake isn't mine, no matter what the dark, feral part of me says.

Nellie plops down next to me. "Serin told me to protect you while she takes a piss. I have orders to torch anyone who tries to hurt you and to shoot a flare into the sky if you leave this spot."

"Are you my bodyguard now?"

"We're a squad. We're supposed to watch each other's backs. You don't have magic, and there might still be reavers prowling the woods."

"You're taking all this very well."

"No sense in wallowing in it. Life is like a rotten potato. You gotta cut out the spoilt bits and be happy with what you got left. If you don't, the whole thing will go bad, and you won't have anything to look forward to eating tomorrow."

"You're very wise for someone so young."

"Witches don't have time for regrets. We gotta do all our living while we have the chance." She glances at my sketches. "Did you give Grace a letter to take with her to the Otherworld?"

"It's for my parents."

"Do you think she'll pass along the message?"

"I believe she will." My stomach twists as I recall the warning she tried to give me about Landry.

"Will you help me write a letter to my sister to send the next time we build a pyre?"

My ribs tighten at how casually she accepts that we'll have to do this again before this is all over. Next time it could be either of us on the scaffold.

I swallow the dry lump in my throat and hand Nellie my sketchbook. I help her form the letters as she writes to her dead sister about Serin and me, about learning how to read and winning the rabbit hunt. At the end, she asks her sister to look after Grace, and I can't keep the flood of emotions in.

My vision blurs as I make an excuse about having to relieve myself and jog to the edge of the woods, away from the fire's light.

A silent sob racks my body. I can't stop the images from coming.

Grace being consumed by flames as her face turns into Nellie's.

My parents lying in the dirt with the same dead eyes as the reaver who almost killed me.

Fuck. Why can't I breathe?

I claw at the buttons of my blouse, yanking it off and flinging it to the ground as a huff of hot breath rolls down my neck.

Silas steps out of the shadows, flips me around, and loosens the ties of my corset.

"Breathe for me, baby." His breaths are as ragged as mine.

I suck in a lungful of air, then another, as he turns me to face him.

"You're okay." He slides his thumbs over my wet cheeks. "Do you want to talk about it?"

"No."

He tips my chin up so I can't avoid his searching gaze. A gaze that sees entirely too much. "Do you want me to walk you back to the campsite?"

"No." Fresh tears pool at the corners of my eyes as he wraps his arms around me.

He rubs my back and presses a kiss to the top of my head. I sob against his chest and take comfort in the arms of the brutal and beautiful man I'm supposed to hate—the bastard who tricked me into a blood oath and bonded his life to mine so he wouldn't be tempted to kill me. The man who can feel everything I feel and knows exactly what my body needs before I do.

"Do you want me to make it feel better?"

"Yes."

Silas pushes my hair over my shoulders, sliding his calloused palm down my chest. Heat throbs low in my belly as he traces his fingers over the swell of my breasts.

He pulls the front of my corset down and uses his thumb to trace a circle around my nipple, coaxing it to a hard bud. "I told myself I could handle the side effects of the bond. That I could resist my desire to claim you. When that asshole pulled his gun, I thought it was the end... that you were—"

"I don't want to talk about that. I just need you to fuck me and make me forget. Just this once."

Silas stares at me for a beat, then his mouth crashes into mine as he scoops me up in his arms and carries me to a soft patch of moss. It's all tongues and teeth and desperation as I hike up my skirts and he settles between my legs.

"Just this once? Are you sure that's what you want?"

He curses as I arch my hips and grind against him.

"Why are you still wearing clothes?"

"If I can only have you once, I want to take my time and do it right."

"Silas, please. I need you inside me. Don't make me beg." I reach down and stroke the rigid length straining against the fall of his trousers.

He makes a suffocated groan against my mouth as I undo the button and release his thick cock, stroking it from base to tip.

"I won't make you beg, love. Not tonight." He pushes my knees apart and reaches between us, dragging his tip through my wetness and notching himself at my entrance. "Tonight, I'll give you what you need."

A twig snaps behind him. Silas's chest makes a deep guttural sound as he blankets me with his shadows.

"Do you have a death wish, brother?" Silas growls over his shoulder.

"We have a problem," Thale says, keeping his distance. "Landry claims he spotted a rougarou in the woods. He's demanding the prince send out a hunting party."

"Fuck." Silas drags his hands down his face as I tug my corset up and tighten the laces. "Have Tiny ready the horses."

"Already done."

"A rougarou? This far north?" A shiver prickles down my spine as Silas helps me up. "That's not possible. They've never been seen anywhere outside the swamps of southern Perdanth."

Silas hands me my blouse. "Come on. I'm gonna need you to tell that to the prince."

Chapter Thirty-Four

"You're positive?" Gideon asks.

"Yes. I've studied them at length. Rougarous have never been reported in Saracen," I say.

"And you've never seen one in your travels?" he asks Silas.

"I've never seen one where it wasn't supposed to be. It was probably a bear. They look similar when they rear up on their hind legs."

"I know what I saw. Bears don't run on two legs like a man," Landry says.

"I'll ride out with the giant and one of her men. They're both experienced hunters. It shouldn't take long to sweep the surrounding area just to be sure."

"Then it's settled," Gideon says. "Landry and Craddock will reinforce the wards around the campsite. We can't afford to lose any more witches tonight."

Silas nods. His voice fills my head as he stalks away. *Get your sketchbook and meet me at the horses.*

I run to my bedroll, gather my things, and trot after him.

"Do you have the meat?" Silas asks Tiny as I approach.

"Yes, and the collar." Her gaze darts to me.

"It's not a bear, is it?" I ask.

Silas and Tiny exchange a knowing look as he takes the reins from her and swings up onto Roan's back.

"Promise me you won't kill it."

"Is there any manner of creature you *won't* try to save?" he asks, settling into the saddle.

"You say that like it's a bad thing."

"Having a soft heart in a sharp world just makes you more vulnerable to bleeding."

"Don't listen to him. Beneath his dragon scale armor, he's all soft underbelly," Tiny says, mounting her dapple gray. "A strong mind, soft heart, and sharp tongue are the three things every woman needs."

Silas reaches down for me. "Let's go. There's a storm coming. It'll be harder to track the scent when it starts to rain."

"You sure that's a good idea?" Tiny asks as Silas swings me up behind him.

"Everly swore the oath. She won't betray what she sees." He snaps the reins and goads Roan into a run before I can ask what he means.

I cling to Silas's back, arms wrapped tight around his waist. It's all I can do to hang on as we gallop through the woods, following Tiny.

"How do you know it's a rougarou?" I ask through the bond.

"Tiny can smell him. She's tracking his scent."

"How did it get this far north?"

Silas pulls back on the reins, slowing Roan to a walk.

"He's close. We'll set the trap here," Tiny says as we sidle up next to her.

Silas dismounts and helps me down. He ties the horses to a tree and sets out thirteen small moonstones in a circle around them as Tiny rubs them down with a hunk of salt pork.

"Stop. You can't use the horses as bait."

"We don't have time to hunt down a wild boar," Tiny says.

My stomach plummets. "How are we going to get back to camp if it kills them?"

"The horses aren't in any danger as long as they're within the stone circle," Silas says.

"How can you be sure? The stones aren't even goblin-spelled."

"Because we've done this before." Tiny glances at Silas. "Take her downwind. Her scent is overpowering the meat."

Silas takes my hand and drags me into the woods under a tree. I sniff my hair and armpits. "Do I stink?"

He grips my waist, pulling me toward him. "You smell like the darkest, untouched part of the forest at night. Like oakmoss, sweet rose, and wild, uninhibited things. It's fucking intoxicating."

"So... I don't stink?"

He turns me around and pulls my back against his chest, wrapping his arms around my shoulders. "Keep your eyes on the trees. He likes to attack from above."

"How do you know it's a he?"

A howl cuts through the dark. My heart kicks in my chest. Not from fear. I know, without a doubt, that I'm safe with Silas. No, it's not fear making the hair rise on the back of my neck. It's pure, undeniable excitement.

Silas traces a slow circle on my arm with his thumb as we wait. The silence seems to stretch, making minutes feel like an hour as I listen for the rustle of leaves or the snapping of twigs. All I can hear is the pounding of my pulse.

"*Don't move.*" Silas tightens his grip around me as the tree closest to the trap sways.

A dark form drops to the ground on all fours with a soft thud. Its yellow eyes flash in the moonlight as it lifts its long snout and sniffs the air. I don't dare breathe as its head swivels in our direction. It stands to its full height and stalks toward us on two legs, baring its canine-like teeth. It's bigger than the one in Beaux's shop. Seven feet tall, with elongated arms and clawed, human-like hands. Its copper-tipped fur bristles as it sniffs us.

Every muscle in my body twitches with the urge to run.

A shadow hand covers my mouth. "*Stay calm. He's just curious. As long as you don't make any sudden movements, he won't hurt you.*"

"Over here, pet," Tiny shouts from the center of the circle.

The beast drops to all fours and bounds toward her. It stops abruptly at the edge of the moonstone barrier and stalks around it, as if it's counting the stones.

Tiny unhooks the iron collar from her belt and jumps on the rougarou's back, snapping the goblin-spelled suppression device around its neck.

The rougarou yips as they tumble violently in the dirt behind the horses.

"Don't hurt him. We still need to hunt down a fucking bear," Silas says as he releases me.

"I don't understand what's happening right now."

He cups my face. "Look at me. Everything is fine. I just need you to trust me and wait here."

I cower under the tree, trembling and confused, as he strides over to Roan and pulls a pair of trousers out of the saddlebag.

Silas disappears behind the horses.

Tiny is the first to come out, brushing dirt off her clothes. "You don't have to hide anymore. The beast is subdued. Come see for yourself."

I swallow the dry lump in my throat. "Silas told me to wait here."

"Since when did you start listening to me?" he asks, stepping around Roan and holding out his hand.

I shake my head. "Tell me what's happening first."

"It's easier if you see."

I take a tentative step out of my hiding place. Silas meets me halfway and laces his fingers through mine.

My mind races through every fact and legend I know about rougarous. They only appear around a full moon. No one has ever found a den or litter of pups, despite the virile libido-enhancing magic in their bones. They're supposedly descended from a clan cursed with insatiable hunger after practicing cannibalism during a famine. They steal misbehaving children from their beds.

I step around the horses and stop, unable to process what I'm seeing.

"Hey." Bas gives me a bashful wave as I take in the iron collar hanging around his neck, his naked, bloody torso, the hastily buttoned trousers, and pelt of fur at his feet. "Sorry if I scared you. My head gets foggy when I shift, and my beast takes control."

"Your beast?"

"Yeah. He's not as well trained as—"

"What happened?" Silas asks. "We doubled your dose of bitter pepper. It should have been enough to keep it on a leash."

"I lost my flask in the attack. I thought I could handle it without the tonic. There was so much blood. I—"

"The curse is real," I say aloud as the truth settles. "You're... a rougarou."

"I don't know about any curse. I started shifting after I got my fever. Same as everyone else in my clan."

"I'm sorry. Can I... I need to sit down."

Silas grabs my elbow and helps me to the ground. "I'm sure you have a lot of questions. Ask them now. You won't be able to talk about any of this when we get back to camp."

Bas plops down across from me, bringing his knees to his chest as Tiny drags the pelt away and Silas sets it on fire.

"This happened to you after you came down with witch fever?"

Bas rubs the back of his neck. "We call it swamp fever, but yeah."

"And your body transforms into a rougarou every full moon?"

"Not as long as I take the tonic when I feel the shift coming on."

"Does it hurt?" I ask, trying to wrap my head around how it's possible for a body to transform without a pupation phase like pixies and... maybe dragons.

"Like breaking and regrowing every bone in your body, but it only lasts a few seconds. The longer I suppress the urge, the more it hurts the next time I shift."

"How many others are there like you?"

"Rougarous? I don't rightly know. In Red Stick, there's the Lowells, those are my people, and the Cormiers."

"Did you say Cormier? Do they have relatives in Crecentis?"

"I wouldn't know about that. The clans keep to themselves and protect their own."

I nod and shove down the sinking sensation in my stomach. Cormier is a common name. Wallace doesn't keep secrets from me. She'd tell me if she was a shapeshifting monster. Right?

My fingers twitch with the urge to draw as I study Bas's face for any traces of the beast. The ember in my chest flares at the thought of sketching him in his beast form. The magic binding me to the oath won't let me draw what I've seen.

"I think that's enough questions for now. It's been a long night, and we still need to catch a bear." Silas pulls a flask out of his saddlebag and hands it to Bas.

"Keep this on until sunrise, pet. Just to be safe," Tiny says, inspecting the iron collar.

"Yes, ma'am." He blushes and fiddles with the flask nervously. "I'm sorry I caused such a stink."

"Don't beat yourself up about it, pet. Even the best of us lose control sometimes," Tiny says, giving Silas a knowing look.

"You okay?" Silas gives me his hand and helps me up.

"Why did you bring me here?"

"Your secret isn't the only one I swore an oath to protect. I needed an eyewitness. One the prince trusts. He'll need irrefutable proof that Landry hallucinated what he saw. The bear carcass won't be enough. You're going to draw a picture of Bas killing the bear and you're going to be very convincing when you tell everyone how upset you are that we killed an innocent creature."

Chapter Thirty-Five

A reassuring kiss of heat slides down the back of my neck, waking me from the nightmare of snapping teeth and spinning shadows.

I pretend to be asleep as Silas stirs on his bedroll next to mine. He brushes the hair away from my face. "You've had fitful dreams, little spark."

I roll away from him and face the rising sun behind the smoldering pyre. Without its heat, there's nothing to chase away the damp chill seeping up from the ground.

"Do you want to talk about it?"

"No."

"Our audience is asleep. You can stop pretending to be angry with me about killing the bear."

"What makes you think I was pretending?" I pull my blanket up to my chin.

"Thank you for doing as I asked, even though you weren't obligated by the oath."

"I didn't do it for you. I did it for Bas. He can't help what he is. He doesn't deserve to be punished for it."

Silas tugs my bedroll toward him, covering us both with his blanket.

"I want to go home," I whisper.

"That's your desire? To return to Crecentis?"

I want to sit in silence with Adrian, who doesn't ask me to talk about my feelings. I want to laugh and relax in the chaos of a Cormier family dinner. I want to paint murals in the Menagerie where no one dies and the people I care about aren't in constant danger.

I don't tell him any of that.

"I want my old life back," I say instead.

"Try to get some rest." Silas snakes his arm under my blanket and pulls me back against his chest. "We have an extra-long ride tonight, and you and I are going on a little excursion when we make camp tomorrow at dawn."

"Are you going to introduce me to another monster?"

"No. We're going somewhere safe where you can practice until you can summon shadows on your own."

"What's the point? I can't openly wield magic without giving away my secret."

"There may be a time when you don't have a choice. The giants will be able to smell the magic in your blood. You'll be a tempting prize to collect. If we get separated, I need to know that you can protect yourself."

A foul scent clings to the low fog as we ride deep into the forest. There's no discernible path, but Silas seems to know where he's going. He didn't complain when I insisted on riding Grace's horse instead of with him.

Rain patters against the canopy of leaves high above. It's the only sound aside from the soft crunch of sticks and rocks under the horses' hooves. There are no tree frogs or birdsong, no skittering of small animals through the underbrush as we pass. It's not the first time I've noticed the lack of noise.

When the woods went silent like this, my father kept his rifle close at hand and built up the fire to ward off whatever predator was lurking nearby.

I scan the trees and thick brambles for copper fur and yellow eyes, even though I know Bas is back at the camp, cooking bear stew for everyone. That doesn't mean there aren't others like him who felt the urge to venture away from the swamps where they're hunted.

Wallace always talks about how she wishes she could get out of Crecentis. That doesn't mean she's like Bas. But what if she is? I've never sensed magic around her or seen her take the tonic. I don't sense it on Bas either.

"You all right?" Silas asks, interrupting my spiraling thoughts.

"I'm fine."

"Your heart rate says otherwise."

"I said I'm fine."

"There's no shame in admitting you're scared."

"Why does it smell like over-boiled eggs?" I ask, attempting to change the subject.

"There's a hot spring nearby. We'll go on foot from here." Silas dismounts and ties the horses off to a tree. He helps me down, gripping my hips as I slide down the front of him.

He tips my chin up and leans down to kiss me.

"We don't have an audience," I say, pulling away.

He lets me go and I follow as he cuts a path through the thorny underbrush with his shadow blade. The sulfurous scent gets stronger as we descend a steep hill toward a small, steaming lake surrounded by a muddy shoreline.

"Let's get started. We need to be back before nightfall."

I don't argue. The sooner we get this over with, the sooner we can return to the campsite with the others. I'm already annoyed with him. This shouldn't take long.

"We'll start with the basics. Use the power I gave you to summon a shield." There's no softness in the command. Good.

I widen my stance and shake out my limbs like I'm squaring off against an opponent in the training ring.

"Anytime you're ready." His gaze narrows on me.

"Aren't you supposed to attack me first?"

He flicks his wrist. I duck, covering my head as he shoots a dark flame past my right shoulder, singeing the sleeve of my blouse.

"First rule of dueling. Raise your shield before engaging with your opponent. Attacks happen fast in a battle. Your enemy isn't always the one standing in front of you. You need to protect yourself from all sides."

"Says the witch who likes to show off by not using one."

"I'll use one when I find a worthy opponent. Raise a shield, and we can get started."

I focus on the dark power in my chest. It uncurled inside me without having to call it when Landry almost caught me in the map room. Now it's decidedly quiet.

"You summoned a shadow shield once before. It's just like summoning a heat shield from a firebird feather. You can do this."

"I'm not used to having an audience. It's distracting."

"Didn't seem to be a problem when you asked me to punish you. Stop making excuses."

Heat creeps up my neck. "That was different. We were pretending."

"Felt pretty damn real to me. The next time you beg me to let you come, it'll be on my cock."

I ignore his attempt to bait me and tug at the borrowed magic. Unlike the firebird energy that flashed through my body when I called it, the dragon's flame is sluggish to respond.

"It's not working. The magic you gave me is more stubborn than my feral cat."

"Stop trying to coax it out so you can pet it. You need to show it you're in control. Yank it out by its fucking tail and make it comply with your intentions."

"You said it responds to desires, not commands. Which is it?"

"We don't have time for you to sort out what you want. We'll cross the border into the Northlands by this time tomorrow. If you can't summon and maintain a simple shadow shield, I'll have to ward you inside a barrel like the damn egg to keep you safe. Try again."

I clench my fists as anger flashes through me. "I hate you."

"I think we both know you don't mean that."

The dragon's flame in my chest flares. I bear down, focusing on expanding it outward. A tendril of dark magic curls over my shoulder.

A thrill runs through me as I watch the shadow lick its way down my arm. There's something mesmerizing and seductive in the way my body heats as it curls around me. Wielding a power like this could become addictive. Once I give myself over to it, I'll never be satisfied with any other type of magic again.

"That's it." His deep voice slides over me like a caress. "Unleash all those dark desires and let the power pour through you."

The shadow fizzles out in my palm.

"Try again."

"I am," I say through clenched teeth.

"Try harder." Three shadow daggers whoosh past my ear. I didn't even notice him throw them.

"Are you trying to kill me? If you keep throwing things at my head, you might actually hit me." I turn in the center of the muddy clearing as he circles me. "It'd be *inconvenient* if we both die here in the mud."

"If I wanted you dead, your swollen corpse would be floating in the swamps outside Crecentis."

"Does that mean you've decided not to kill me once the blood oath is fulfilled?"

"There are a lot of things I plan to do to you. Ending your life is at the bottom of the very long and wicked list."

My traitorous body flushes with heat at the insinuation. The bastard smiles.

"I know all your manipulative little tricks, reaver. Your attempts to seduce and distract me don't work anymore."

"You haven't seen half of my tricks yet, little spark."

Silas whips a shadow rope at me without warning. It cracks in the air, snapping a few inches from my face. I stumble back and land on my ass with a splat in the stinking mud.

"What is wrong with you? I wasn't ready."

"You'll get no warning from your enemies during an attack. Get up."

He wants to play dirty? Fine. I make a show of rolling onto my hands and knees, discreetly scooping my fingers through the thick mud. I shove to my feet and fling it at his head.

Silas flinches as the glob smacks him in the face. I bite back a smile as he slowly wipes a clump away from his eye.

"First rule of dueling," I say. "Erect your shield before engaging with the enemy."

"You're going to pay for that."

"Are you going to punish me again?" I tease as I clean my hands on my skirt.

"In every wicked way you've imagined. You have two choices. I'm going to count to fifty. You can summon a fucking shield, or you can run."

"What?" I swallow past the dry lump in my throat.

His gaze darkens as he crouches down and scoops up a handful of mud and starts counting across the bond. "*One. Two—*"

Fuck. He's serious.

My feet start to move before I have time to think it through. All I know is I *want* Silas Drake to chase me.

I sprint around the small lake and take cover behind a boulder the size of a horse. I press my back against the cold stone to catch my breath.

My skin pebbles when he gets to fifty. He's coming for me.

"I'm not afraid of getting dirty, reaver." I scoop up another handful of mud and peek around the edge.

My heart kicks in my chest. Silas is gone.

I glance up the hill, eyes darting from shadow to shadow as the huff of hot breath cascades down the back of my neck.

"Neither am I."

I spin toward the sound of his voice behind me. He must have sprinted around the opposite side of the lake. I lift my hands to block the clump of mud flying toward my face.

His magic pulses through my body. Shadows erupt from my hands, creating a solid wall between us.

The shadows dissipate as Silas steps through them.

"Are you satisfied now?" I collapse against the boulder, chest heaving, body thrumming with magic.

"Not even close." He tips my chin up and drags his thumb over my bottom lip.

Heat pools low in my belly, and I have to remind myself that he's the master of manipulation. Silas wields words and seduction as deftly as his shadows. He warned me not to get confused.

"You can stop pretending. We don't have an audience." I push away from him.

He catches my wrist. The ring he usually wears on his thumb is missing. "We need to talk about the other night."

"You mean when I asked you to fuck me?"

"No. We need to talk about what happened during the attack."

"I told you—I don't want to talk about that," I say through clenched teeth as the memory of his lifeless body flashes through my head. If I talk about it with him, if I even think about it, I'll be forced to admit that this isn't pretend anymore. Not for me.

"Then let me do the talking. You can walk away if you want, or you can listen."

I cross my arms and lean against the rock.

Silas paces in front of me, as if he's having an internal debate on how to say whatever it is he needs to get off his chest.

"When that piece of shit pulled his gun on you, I knew I wouldn't be fast enough. I was sure it was the end, that I'd failed to keep up my end of the oath." Silas's brow pinches like the thought of his own mortality is causing him physical pain. "I've never been that fucking terrified in my life. Not even when I watched my mother die. I lost control of my shadows. If Thale hadn't knocked me out, I would have done something I could never take back."

"I knew my life was over the moment I woke from my witch fever. I was terrified too. You get used to it. Death comes for us all. Even big, scary shadow summoners who think they're invincible."

I don't register his movements until he has me caged against the rock.

"I wasn't scared of dying."

"What are you saying?"

"That I'm not in control. Not when it comes to you."

I stare up at the man who claims he doesn't have a soft heart, that he's cut off his feelings. The man who handed his secrets over to his enemy and helped me save the lives of three hundred witches because I asked. The man who rescued a giant and gave a kid most people would consider a monster a second chance. I can't even be mad at him for tricking me into helping protect Bas.

My stomach flutters as he leans down and claims my mouth, teasing me open with a slow, languid kiss, as if we have all the time in the world. Heat coils low in my belly as he presses his thigh between my legs.

I work the buttons of his shirt, sliding my palms over his chest and pushing it off his shoulders as a pair of shadow hands makes quick work of mine.

"Turn around." He spins me so I'm facing the boulder.

I brace my hands against the cold stone as he tugs at the laces of my corset until he has it off.

"We shouldn't do this," I say, untying my skirt and shoving it to the ground with my undergarments.

"Tell me to stop." He pulls me back against him, cupping the weight of my breast as he slides his palm down my stomach, pausing so close to where I want him.

"Don't you even think about stopping, reaver."

"I'm going to give you everything you needed from me the other night. But first I'm going to take my time worshipping you until there isn't an inch of your body I haven't touched. When you're spent and you think you can't possibly take any more, then I'm going to fuck you."

I go wet recalling the feel of him at my entrance.

He groans as he presses his erection against my low back. "Is this what you want?"

"You know it is." I twist in his arms, hooking my legs around his waist as he grips my ass and lifts me.

I capture his bottom lip, letting it drag through my teeth as he uses his shadows to spread our clothes out like a blanket.

He lays me down and I let my legs fall apart. Silas rakes his gaze over my naked body from where he kneels at my feet.

"You're so fucking beautiful, spread out for me like this."

Silas glides his hand up the back of my calf, lifting my boot to his lap. He takes his time unlacing and removing it, as if he's forcing himself to go slow, drinking me in. When he finishes and moves to the next, I rub my bare foot against the outline of his erection.

He grabs my ankle. "Careful with that. If you make me come in my pants again, I'll have to punish you. Do you want me to withhold my cock from your pretty little pussy?"

I shake my head and pull my foot away.

"Good girl." His eyes darken as he spreads my knees and climbs over me.

Silas nips at my neck, alternating between soft kisses and gentle bites along my collarbone and across my chest. I arch against him as he rolls my nipple between his teeth and tongue. He presses his thigh between my legs. I groan his name as I lift my hips, seeking the friction that I crave.

I run my hands up his arms to his shoulders and attempt to push him down where I need him. It's no use. He's too heavy.

He grabs my wrists, pinning them above my head with a shadow hand as he kisses a trail between my breasts and down my stomach. I lift my knees as he dips his head and nips at the inside of my thigh. He hasn't touched me where I want him most, and I'm already aching with need.

"Are you trying to torture me?" I ask.

"I haven't even started yet."

I gasp as he wraps his arms around the back of my legs and tugs me closer, making my arms stretch above my head where he keeps them pinned. The bastard knows what he's doing, keeping me stretched taut so I can't move.

My breath quickens as I test the restraint.

"Look at me." Silas meets my gaze. "You're the one in control. If you're uncomfortable or if it's too much, tell me to stop."

The ember of magic in my chest flares as I flex my hips and unleash the dark part of me. The one that keeps whispering that this man is hers. Magic thrums through me as shadows curl over my chest and spill down my body, forming a shadow hand. I fist his hair and tug his head back.

"There you are. I knew I could get you to come out and play."

He growls with pleasure as he spreads me open and drags his tongue along my center. I arch against him as he licks and sucks until I'm writhing with need. Silas pushes two fingers inside me, pumping in slow, languid strokes. It's the best kind of torture. He presses down on my belly, pumping faster as his tongue rolls over my clit, bringing my pleasure to the edge.

Silas stifles a groan as he pulls away, halting my orgasm before it breaks. He drags himself to his feet and kicks off his boots.

"Why did you stop?"

"When I let you come, it will be on my cock while I'm buried inside you."

He releases my shadow restraints, and I push up to my elbows as he drops the fall of his trousers. He fists himself, running his thumb through the glistening bead of cum dripping down the head of his cock.

I bite back a smile as I drag my gaze to his face. He's going to absolutely wreck me.

Chapter Thirty-Six

"**Y**ou lied to me, little spark."

"You'll need to be more specific about which lie we're talking about if you'd like me to confess."

Silas runs his hands over my ass. "You do not have a birthmark back here."

"Are you sure? Maybe you should look a little closer," I tease, shifting back on my hands and knees where he's kneeling behind me. No point in playing coy now that the feral part of me is out of her cage.

"I should punish you for that." Silas pulls me back into his lap.

"It was a distraction technique. I learned from the best."

He sits me up so my back is to his chest and hooks one of my arms behind his head.

I suck in a breath as he cups my pussy, grinding the heel of his palm against me. I'm still sensitive and on edge from my unfulfilled climax, and the bastard knows exactly what to do to drag this out. He takes his time stroking my clit in slow circles. Shadows swirl around us as my body floods with heat. I can't tell which ones are his and which ones are mine as they twist around each other.

He releases his firm grip on my breast and tips my face toward him. Silas kisses me like he's never kissed me before. It's soft and deep and not for show. I whimper as his tongue sweeps through my mouth, caressing mine. There's no battle of wills, no desperation. Only the warmth of our shared breath and the overwhelming, terrifying sense of rightness.

I whimper as he pushes his fingers inside me, circling my clit with his thumb. The fire in my low belly coils tight as he brings me to the edge again. He flexes his hips, pumping his cock against my lower back.

I squeeze my inner muscles, holding back the orgasm as it begins to break.

He releases me, and I slide off his lap.

Silas growls as he squeezes the head of his cock and throws his head back, chest heaving.

A thrill zings through me as I watch the invincible Silas Drake struggle to regain control of his body. I love knowing I have this power over him. That I make him vulnerable in a way no one else can. That his life and his pleasure are tied to mine.

"I want you inside me." I push him onto his back and straddle his waist.

"Take what you need from me. There isn't a damn thing in this world I would deny you right now."

He grabs my hips as I reach between us and notch his head at my entrance. I slide down his shaft, taking him slowly, inch by inch, savoring the glorious stretch as he fills me.

Silas grabs my ass, fingers biting into the soft flesh as he spreads my cheeks, helping me take him fully. He groans as I brace my hands against his chest and rock my hips in a gentle, rhythmic motion, letting my body accommodate to his decadently thick cock.

I sit back and bring his hands to my breasts. My gaze doesn't leave his as I stroke my clit.

"You're the only one I crave when I touch myself."

His body tightens with need beneath me. I roll my hips faster, chasing my climax as it starts to peak.

Silas growls my name and my pleasure breaks in an exquisite full-body release. I feel a flood of warmth as he thrusts into me and we ride out the orgasm together.

He flips me onto my back, still buried inside me. I cup his face as he stares down at me. The way his eyes soften makes my ribs tighten. I squeeze my inner muscles and wrap my legs around him, not ready for the moment to end.

His cock twitches inside me as his mouth curls into a smile.

"We're not done yet, little spark." Silas kisses me as he moves inside me. The pressure of him against my oversensitive clit sets off a chain of mini tremors as my pleasure builds again. He doesn't have to touch me as he fucks me slow and deep.

My vision flashes red as my body flushes with a glorious, molten heat.

"Oh, gods. That's... I'm... going to cum again." I can hear the surprise in my voice.

"Fuck." Silas growls as I arch off the ground with the force of the second orgasm I didn't know my body was capable of.

I go limp beneath him, fully spent. He presses a kiss to my forehead and pulls out with a wet gush.

Silas rolls onto his back, tucking me against his side. We lie in silence, watching the swirling magic settle around us.

"Is that normal for you? To go twice?" I ask as my eyes grow heavy.

"Not before now, but I'm pretty sure I can go as many times as you need. My body is yours to command while we're bonded."

———※———

Silas hands me the tin plate of juneberries he gathered from bushes around the lake. Every part of my body aches deliciously as I sit on the log next to him while he tends the small fire.

I twist my wet hair into a tight knot and watch as he breaks up a hardtack ration and adds it to the salt pork stew. I'd offer to help, but I barely have the energy to move, despite the long nap. We fell asleep in each other's arms after the first time. He fucked me again when we woke. I'm still buzzing from the things he elicited from my body. I've never been with a man so intent on my pleasure or in taking care of me after.

As incredible as the sex was, I can't stop thinking about the way he carried me to the hot spring and took his time cleaning me gently and washing my hair, refusing to let me help. He gave me his shirt and made me sit on a rock while he washed my muddy clothes.

Silas glances at the plate of berries in my lap. "You spent a lot of energy today. You need to eat something."

"Do you take care of all your lovers so well?"

"I take care of everyone important to me," he says casually as he stokes the fire under the small cookpot.

I shove down the fluttering sensation in my chest.

"Do you take them to Shadow's Fold?"

He goes still for a moment and resumes tending the stew, ignoring the question.

"Tiny told me what you did for her."

"What else did she tell you?"

"How you killed the giant who was abusing her and burned down a brothel. How you helped Bas too."

"Did she tell you the giant I killed was one of Queen Isola's sons?"

"Is that why you aren't welcome in her court?"

"No, Prince Aeroc never saw my face." Silas drops his poker stick and dusts his hands on his pants and angles toward me. "It was a long time ago, but he may remember my scent. He'll certainly notice yours. You won't be able to hide the fact that you're a witch. It's why I was adamant about you being able to summon shadows."

"Why did you drag me on this journey if you knew I could compromise your life?"

"I haven't dragged you anywhere you didn't decide to go on your own. You volunteered as a scribe. I was going to send you with my crew to Shadow's Fold, where you'd be safe until I had the egg and its mother."

"You were going to kidnap me?"

"Ambassador Caron was going to offer your brother a job he couldn't refuse, leaving you alone in Crecentis, making it easier for you to go missing without being noticed. I underestimated your ability to undermine me, and my need to have you near me."

"You could've told me, and we could have avoided..." The words snag in my throat.

"This?" he says, tracing the hem of his shirt where it grazes my bare thigh.

"That's not what I meant. We could have avoided a lot of confusion if you'd just told me your plans."

"You've tried to thwart every plan I've made, especially when I let you in on the details."

"That's not true. I helped you with Bas."

"Yes, you did." Silas takes the plate of berries and sets it on the ground.

"I didn't argue when you made me bunk with you instead of Serin."

"You protested mildly." He smiles as he pulls me onto his lap so I'm straddling him.

"I've never heard of Shadow's Fold. It's not on any of my maps."

"That's because it's past the great mountains on the other side of the Wastes." Silas grazes his nose over the column of my throat, inhaling a deep breath. "The journey is long and treacherous. I've gone to great lengths to ensure no one can find it without an invitation."

"What happens when we get to Tindlestone Palace?" I ask, running my hands through his damp hair, breathing in the scent of him. Peppermint soap from our bath in the hot spring, woodsmoke, and a hint of clove.

Silas presses a soft kiss to my clavicle as he slides his hands under the loose shirt. "I plan to keep you away from Prince Aeroc, fuck you as much as possible, and fill you with so much cum that the only thing anyone smells on you is me."

———✦———

It's late afternoon by the time we get back to the campsite. I slide off the horse with a whimper and will my aching legs not to quiver as I walk him to the corral where Tiny waits.

"Rough ride?" she asks with a smirk.

"Vigorous." I bite back a smile and shove down the urge to say more. If she were Wallace, I'd tell her Silas wrecked me in all the best ways possible and that I'm pretty sure no other man on earth can go four times in a day.

"Here, you're going to need this." She hands me a small bundle of willow bark.

"Thanks."

She takes the reins from me and nods to the wagon, where Bas is fidgeting nervously. "The kid wants to talk to you."

"Hey." He gives me a sheepish wave. "I just wanted to give you this."

Bas holds out his hand. A little wooden wolf sits in his palm.

"Did you make this?"

"I whittled it out of basswood. The tree is a symbol of protection in my clan. I appreciate what you did for me. I hope I can repay the favor someday."

I take the trinket, running my fingers over the fine details. "You're very good. You could be a sculptor at the Menagerie."

His cheeks go pink as he raises his hand to scratch his forehead. Threads of magic trail the goblin-spelled ring on his finger.

"Is that Silas's ring?"

"Yeah, he thought... well, I guess he thought I could use a little extra good luck." Bas stuffs his hand in his pocket and looks at the ground.

I smile, recalling Silas's words earlier. "You're obviously important to him."

"We have work to do, pet," Tiny calls from the front of the wagon. "Come feed and water these horses."

Bas gives me a crooked smile, revealing a pearly white canine. His russet shoulder-length curls bounce as he jogs away.

I run my fingers over the carved wolf. How anyone could ever hunt or hurt such a beautiful thing is beyond me.

"Making friends?" Serin asks behind me.

I tuck the trinket inside the warded pocket in my bag with Landry's dagger. I planned to study it when Silas and I were away from the camp and forgot. It's probably spelled with the same magic as the guns Madam Faye's goons carry, guaranteed to strike true wherever it's aimed. Not that I'd know how or where to aim a dagger.

"Will you teach me how to fight with a knife?" I ask.

"Right now?"

"We'll be in Tindlestone tomorrow. I'd like to be able to defend myself, if it comes to that."

"Silas said you had a successful training session today," she says, lowering her voice. "When you can wield that kind of weapon, what more do you need?"

"I'd rather not give all my secrets away unless it's a last resort. Just show me how to aim. The charmed blade will do the rest."

She glances over her shoulder to where Gideon and Silas are going over a map. "Come with me."

"What are we doing?" Nellie asks, catching up to us.

"Serin is going to teach me how to use a knife."

"Oh, I'm good at knives," Nellie says. "When I worked on the farmyard, I learned how to skin rabbits and quarter chickens in less than two minutes."

Serin stops in her tracks and stares at the teenage girl with a disgusted look. "Please tell me you didn't pluck them while they were alive."

"Course not. Everybody knows you gotta scald them first."

Serin shudders as if the idea makes her skin crawl.

"I used to go behind the woodshed with some of the other kids and practice throwing knives at the wall. I was the best."

"Of course you were." I hook my arm through hers. "You're a smart girl. I have no doubt that you'll be good at anything you put your mind to. You'll be a lead navigator like Major Mattern before you know it."

"Or Fire Squad captain," Nellie says, summoning a flame and making it dance in her hand.

We spend the next hour taking turns throwing Serin's dagger at a tree. Nellie excels at the task. Not so much for me. Though the exercise does help ease my soreness into a delicious, dull ache.

"You need to relax your grip," Serin says. "Try holding it like a hammer."

I aim at the same spot and throw the knife as hard as I can. It hits the tree and bounces off into the underbrush ten feet away.

"At least you hit the tree this time," Nellie says.

I give her a little smile. As long as I have Landry's dagger, all I have to do is hit the target. The magic will do the rest.

Nellie fetches Serin's dagger, checking it for damage. "When we get back to Crecentis, I'm gonna buy one like this with my commission."

The familiar kiss of heat slides down the back of my neck, making my insides flutter.

"What are you going to buy with your commission, Everly?"

"I'm going straight to the Duck to see my friend Wallace. She'll be angry at me for leaving without telling her. She and I are going to have a long overdue conversation over a bottle of rum and as much fried dough as I can buy. I've been a terrible friend to her and an even worse sister to Adrian. They are the two most important people in my life, and I have some amends to make."

"I hope you're not planning on telling them all our secrets as soon as the oath is fulfilled," Silas says across the bond.

The way he says it, as if my returning without him is a forgone conclusion, makes my stomach drop. It's not like I'll be going to Shadow's Fold. Even if I was invited, I couldn't leave my brother to go that far, and Adrian will never leave Crecentis.

I swallow the dry lump in my throat and turn toward Silas, who's leaning casually against a tree with his arms crossed.

He gives me a strange look as he pushes off the trunk. "His Royal Highness would like to consult with his navigators."

CHAPTER THIRTY-SEVEN

"Give me your report, Private Roy," Gideon says to Nellie.

She beams as she flips her map book open on top of the goblin-spelled barrel. "We'll cross the border just after dawn. If we push through, we can make it to Tindlestone by midday tomorrow." Her voice rises with excitement as she traces the path she plotted earlier in the day with her finger.

"The edge of the Marshwood is here," I say, pointing to the map, "about an hour's ride north of the border. The terrain opens to rolling grasslands. There will be very few trees to provide cover during the day. I recommend camping in the Marshwood tomorrow and traveling the rest of the way after dark."

"I agree with Miss Thorne," Tiny says, packing tobacco into her pipe. "Giants can see thirty miles on a clear day. Our vision is terrible at night. You stand a better chance of making it there without being spotted by a hunting party if we travel when it's dark."

"I have an official invitation from the queen herself that guarantees safe passage from the border to the palace. If we sneak up on them under the cover of darkness, it may be perceived as a threat. We need Queen

Isola to trust us if I'm to convince her to give us permission to hunt a dragon on her land."

"Tindlestone is a six-hour ride from the border. The longer we take to get there, the more likely we are to be scented and tracked by a hunting party. We should ride straight through," Silas says. "I can cover our scent with a shield as we travel, but we'll need a storm to wash it away behind us. It will reduce the likelihood that we're followed."

"Lieutenant Landry, what do you need to summon a monsoon large enough to cover us for thirty miles?"

"A large body of water as close to the area as possible. Once I set it in motion, I won't be able to control where it goes."

"The Blood Lakes," Nellie says, barely stumbling over the words as she points to a pair of lakes on the map separated by a narrow peninsula.

A chill crawls down my spine as I watch her measure the distance.

"It's only an hour's ride northeast of the Marshwood Forest and then..." She takes another measurement. "A seven-hour ride to Tindlestone."

"That takes us two hours out of our way, not to mention the strain on the horses to ride all night and the next day," I say with a shudder as a familiar cold sinks into my bones.

No, no, no. Not again. I back away from the barrel and glance around the campsite. Gideon's Elite Guard are packing up, and Bas and Thale are saddling the horses. Everything seems as it should.

"How long will it take to create the storm?" Gideon asks.

"By myself? About an hour."

"The horses can rest then," Gideon says.

A shrill cry echoes through the trees. Grace LeMay appears behind Landry, his goblin-spelled dagger clutched above her head in her raised fist. She slams her arm down, through the middle of his back.

I cover my mouth to stifle a scream as it passes through him and embeds the knife in Nellie's book.

Everyone turns and stares at me as if I'm mad.

"Don't drink too much," Grace says in her haughty voice as her gaze flicks to mine.

My body trembles with cold. Her ghost and the knife disappear.

I push past Landry and run my shaking hand over the spot where the knife pierced Nellie's book in the center of the Blood Lakes. The ink morphs, and a black web spreads across the page.

"We shouldn't go to the lakes." The words stutter through my chattering teeth.

Silas wraps his arms around me. Warmth spreads through my body. "*What's going on with you?*"

"I think you rode your whore a little too hard and scrambled her brain, Drake."

Shadows whoosh past me and cram down Landry's throat. His eyes go wide as he clutches his chest.

"That's enough," Gideon shouts, pulling his sword and pressing the blade to Silas's neck.

He cuts Gideon a deadly look.

Serin summons a flame, and Tiny unsnaps the holster at her waist, hand on her pistol.

"Silas, please. Let him go. He's not worth it."

Landry sucks in a desperate breath, coughing up smoke as Silas retracts his shadows.

"I told you he was fucking unstable," Landry rasps.

"I won't tolerate derision in my ranks. If the two of you can't get along, I'll put you both in irons. Is that understood?" Threads of magic follow Gideon's blade as he sheaths his sword.

"I'm not the one going mad. You need to get yourself checked for the burning, Drake." Landry says, smoothing his hair.

"Dynamite and fuse," Serin mutters under her breath, snuffing out her fire with the flick of her wrist.

"Private Roy, plot a course for the Blood Lakes. We ride out in thirty minutes."

"Yes, sir, Colonel Krimore."

"Drake, load the egg."

Silas lifts the barrel with his shadows and carries it to the wagon.

"What happened back there?" he asks once we're out of earshot.

"You almost killed Landry."

"Not that. You had some kind of attack. Your body temperature dropped like it did in the Hall of Kings and every day on the boat before lunch." He slides the barrel onto the back of the hay cart.

"You felt all that?"

"I feel everything." His voice softens as he grabs my hips and tugs me toward him.

I don't know why it still surprises me that he's so in tune with my body. With me. This intense thing between us makes me feel closer to him than I have to anyone in my life. He knows nearly all my secrets.

I spit the words out before I change my mind. "It happens every time I see a ghost."

Silas pulls me behind the hay cart. "What do you mean every time you see a ghost?"

"I thought they were hallucinations at first. That I was going mad. Now I'm not so sure."

"How long has this been going on?"

"Since the ball. I saw Gideon's mother in the Hall of Kings right before you found me. The first queen of Perdanth came to me when we were in the ballroom before you took me out onto the terrace.

"The boy you asked me about, the one I keep drawing in my sketchbook. He came to me at the same time every day when I was in the map room. I think they were trying to warn me. Each time I see a ghost, something bad happens. Now Grace..."

"Landry's storm witch?"

"She had Landry's dagger and stabbed it through his back into the map. I think he might try something when we get to the lakes."

His jaw tightens. "I'll have Thale and Bas stay close to him. If he tries anything, he's a dead man."

"You believe me?" I ask hesitantly.

Silas's brow furrows as he traces a circle over my hip with his thumb. "I believe that you believe what you saw."

"That's not the same thing." I ignore the heavy thump in my chest as I pull away from him.

"I ripped you away from your life in Crecentis. You've been under a lot of strain. The side effects of the bond haven't helped."

"What are you saying?"

"You haven't been taking your tonic."

My throat goes dry. "You don't believe that I've been seeing ghosts. You think I'm going mad."

Silas brushes the hair away from my face, studying my mismatched eyes. "You've spent a lot of time close to the egg. Every time it comes out of its cask, your body is inundated with cold. You said before that it's the most powerful magic you've ever felt. I'm worried it may be having a stronger effect on your perception than other relics."

"I don't want to lose my mind to the burning," I whisper.

"Death has walked beside me my whole life. The only thing it ever taught me is that you have to take what you can from this life before it's taken from you."

I stare up at him. "I don't think we should go to the Blood Lakes. Something doesn't feel right."

"We don't have a choice. As much as I hate to admit it, we need Landry to summon a storm to cover our tracks. Hunting parties won't give a shit about Krimore's fancy invitation. Outside of Tindlestone, it's every clan for themselves. We need to get to the city where we'll be under the protection of the city guard as quickly as possible."

I rest my forehead against his chest. Every part of my body feels heavy and sore.

He presses a kiss into my hair. "You're exhausted. I may have pushed your body too hard today. There's not enough hay left in the wagon to hide the barrel. I'm going to strap it on the dapple-gray pack horse. You'll have plenty of room to lie down and sleep tonight while Serin and I ride beside you. Things could get complicated when we arrive at the palace. I need your mind clear and focused when we steal the egg."

"I'm capable of doing that myself," I protest weakly as Bas arranges a thick layer of hay on the empty side of the wagon and lays my bedroll on top of it.

"It's no bother." He gives me a lopsided grin.

"Let the boy do his job," Tiny says next to me. "He's clearly taken a liking to you. You can practically see his tail wagging."

"Is that going to be a problem?" I ask, glancing over her shoulder at Silas as he sets the barrel next to the grumpy dapple-gray pack horse. "I don't want anything to happen to Bas because of a little innocent flirtation."

"You've got nothing to worry about there, pet. Silas has a special bond with the kid. Bas was just a pup when Silas took him in. He's as loyal as they come and looks up to Silas like a big brother. Silas takes that responsibility seriously. He would never harm the boy or anyone else on his crew."

"Sounds like he has a habit of collecting wayward souls."

"Like I said, all soft underbelly with that one." Tiny takes a long drag on her pipe and strolls away.

The sweet scent of tobacco hangs in the air as I watch Silas place a thick blanket on the horse's back. He takes his time smoothing out the wrinkles before setting the cargo platform on top. The horse chuffs and shakes its head like they're having a conversation and reminds me of Posey, the executioner's grumpy mule back home.

My head throbs for the first time in weeks. I pull out my flask and take a sip of the bitter nerve tonic. Maybe Silas is right. We don't know anything about the egg or how its power works. My special perception makes me more sensitive to it than anyone. I need to learn more before I attempt to break its wards again.

The wagon creaks behind me as Bas hops to the ground with a soft thud.

"You're all set."

"Thank you, Bas. You're a true gentleman."

"No one's ever accused him of that before," Silas says, coming up behind him and capturing him in a headlock.

"There are two satisfied courtesans in Port Hope who would disagree." Bas grins ear to ear, throwing a playful punch at Silas's groin, missing narrowly as Silas shoves him away.

Watching them horseplay like this reminds me of Wallace's brothers. Thale's deep boom of laughter rolls across the campsite as he, Serin, and Tiny pass a flask back and forth.

My chest pinches. They're not just a crew. They're a family.

The realization that, once again, I'm an outsider looking in opens a cavern in my chest.

When are you going to give yourself permission to admit what you want?

My conversation with Wallace the day the egg arrived at the Menagerie rolls through my head along with images of chaotic Cormier family dinners and laughing and listening to tall tales around the campfire with my parents and Adrian.

I close my eyes, unable to stop the tears.

"Tell me what's wrong." Silas lifts me up and sets me on the back of the wagon so we're eye to eye.

"It's nothing. I'm just exhausted like you said. And a little homesick." It's mostly the truth. The part I'm willing to admit out loud anyway.

"It feels like more," he teases as he swipes the tears away with his thumbs. "Tell me what you need to make it feel better."

I force the tightness in my chest to loosen as I clasp his hands. What I want is impossible and too selfish to voice.

"What's so important about the egg and the frost dragon that you're willing to risk your life and the lives of your crew over it?"

His smile wavers. Silas takes a deep breath and looks down at our threaded fingers. He lifts my hand and brushes a soft kiss to the blood oath scar on my palm.

"Mount up," Gideon calls behind us.

"I don't have time to explain right now, but I promise I'll tell you everything when we get to Tindlestone and don't have an audience."

Chapter Thirty-Eight

"We're approaching the border." Silas's voice floats through the groggy haze, dragging me from my dream.

I rub the sleep from my eyes and sit up slowly. Beams of golden light cut through the trees, creating long shadows behind us.

"Why did we stop? Are we making camp?" I ask as Silas hands me his canteen.

"It's only for a few minutes. If you need to relieve yourself, do it now. We ride hard from here to the lakes."

The water eases the scratchiness of my dry throat. I keep drinking until the canteen is half empty and hand it back to him.

"Did you sleep at all?"

"I'll sleep when it's safe." Silas helps me down from the wagon. "We're leaving the cart here. It will only slow us down. Are you able to ride?"

I nod and straighten my rumpled clothes.

"Come, girl. Be quick and quiet," Serin says, leading me into the woods.

The trees are more spread out here, and there aren't any brambles to provide privacy. Serin keeps watch while I squat behind a tree and pull up my skirts to relieve myself.

"Can I ask you a question?" I say as we switch places.

"If you must." Serin gives me a sidelong look.

"Silas said you're *mated* to Thale. What does that mean?"

"We swore a unity bond to one another. It's similar to a blood oath and allows us to communicate without words and share magic."

"Share magic?"

"Can you share magic with someone you don't have a life or unity bond with?"

"Only mates can share magic." Serin stands and pulls up her trousers. "The others are waiting."

I follow her back to the clearing. Bas has already secured my bedroll to Grace's horse.

"This is the rendezvous point for the rest of the battalion," Gideon says. "They're behind us by a few days, but if you get separated from the group for any reason, make your way back here. Everyone will ride in pairs until we get to Tindlestone. You stay with your partner no matter what. Landry, you're with me."

Gideon goes through the group, pairing everyone off. Silas scowls when I'm stuck with Jo-el. He's partnered with Craddock and the horse carrying the egg.

We set out at a slow pace, riding in a line side by side to diminish the width of our tracks. Silas's protective wall of shadows is so glaringly obvious in the daylight, I'm not sure it matters. We'll be easy to spot.

Jo-el follows Gideon, goading his horse into a gallop as the Marshwood bleeds into open prairie. My thighs burn from sitting up in the saddle. If Serin hadn't pushed me to run every day for a month, I wouldn't be able to keep up.

The kiss of hot breath on the back of my neck tells me Silas is still somewhere behind me with the egg. I can't turn to check without falling off my horse.

My armpits are soaked with sweat, and I can barely feel my legs by the time we reach the narrow peninsula between the two lakes.

I sit back in the saddle with a whimper. My horse takes advantage of the slack in the reins and trots away from the group to the water's edge, dipping his head to drink.

A gunshot cracks behind me, followed by a shrill, ear-splitting scream.

The horse bucks, throwing me off its back onto the rocks. Shadows billow around me, protecting me from the fall. I scramble back as a water wraith claws her way out of the lake with her human-like arms, shrieking and spitting venom as she comes after me. Blood oozes from the hole in her scaled chest. Her cries become garbled, choking out as she collapses in the mud.

"I suppose that's how the lakes got their name," Tiny says, holstering her pistol.

"Do you believe me now?" I ask as Silas drags me to my feet.

"Any hunting party within a few miles will have heard that shot. We need to make the storm and get the hell out of here before they come to investigate."

"Landry, we need that rain. Now," Gideon says.

"I can help," Thale says, static crackling over his shoulders.

"Do whatever you can in ten minutes. Then we need to ride," Silas says.

"What are you waiting for, Landry? Start summoning that fucking storm," Gideon says.

Landry and Thale jog to the edge of the second lake, shooting lightning into the water.

Gideon turns to Silas. "Throw that fucking thing back into the lake. I don't want to leave any evidence that would suggest we've been hunting on Isola's land without permission."

I pull the sketchbook from my bag and start drawing the dead wraith. My fingers fly over the page, recording the spiny fin on her back, the dark gills along the sides of her ribs, her webbed fingers tipped in sharp talons and pointed teeth. She must be close to nine feet long with her featherlike fluke.

Silas runs his hand over the wraith's face, gently closing the solid black eyes that seem too big for her face. He picks her up in his arms and wades into the lake.

"Wait. It's not safe. There could be more."

Serin grabs my arm when I move to stop him.

Silas wades out until he's waist deep. He lays the wraith down on the surface and uses his shadows to push her farther out into deeper water.

My heart lodges in my throat as fins circle her floating body.

"*Silas, please, get out of the water,*" I plead through the bond.

"Don't you even think about getting near that water, girl," Serin says as I pull against her iron grip.

The sky darkens as the storm builds above us. Multiple pairs of webbed hands pull the wraith under. Silas turns and slowly wades back to shore as the body of water erupts into an angry frenzy behind him.

"Why aren't the other wraiths attacking him?" Nellie asks, holding my horse's reins steady as he paws at the ground nervously.

"Because like recognizes like. He's the only predator bigger and scarier than they are."

Silas stops in front of me, dripping wet, and glances at my unfinished sketch. "May I?"

I hand him the book as it starts to sprinkle. He rips out the page and sets it on fire.

"It's disrespectful to make pictures of the dead." Silas hands the book back to me and walks over to Roan.

"What was that about back there?" I ask, following him.

"Greif. Water wraiths mate for life." He pulls a flask out of his saddlebag and knocks it back as thunder rumbles above us.

"Why did you go into the water?"

"Returning her to her family was the only honorable thing to do."

"The storm is set," Thale says, coming up behind us. "Landry is informing the prince. We need to get moving before it outpaces our scent."

A horn blows before Silas can respond. He pulls me behind him as a riding party of giants atop massive draft horses gallops across the peninsula and surrounds us. My body tightens as I count fifty in black leather armor to our twenty-two.

"Stay calm. They're part of Tindlestone's City Guard, not hunters."

"What do we have here?" their commander asks, his nostrils flaring as he scans our group.

"I'm Gideon Krimore, Prince of Perdanth, and this is my Elite Guard." Gideon steps forward with all the confident superiority of a king.

The giant raises a dark eyebrow. "A prince and his Elite Guard. Smells like a bunch of rogue witches, a dirty half-breed, and a human to me."

"I have a personal invitation from your queen." Gideon pulls a red envelope from the pocket inside his travel vest and holds it in the air.

The commander motions for one of his soldiers to retrieve it. The second giant hops off her horse with a heavy thud and plucks the invitation from Gideon's hand. She towers over his head. Threads of magic float around the goblin-spelled crossbow strapped to her back. The others carry similar charmed weapons—rifles, bows, swords, and knives.

"This invitation is for Serros Krimore, King of Perdanth. Is he among you?"

"My father sent me in his stead."

"I met Serros once. You do not carry his scent. You're fifty miles east of the Marshwood Road that leads straight to Tindlestone. You ride with no banner or insignia, and you're dressed as common thieves. Tell me why I should believe that you didn't steal this invitation from its rightful owner."

"Because I have the dragon egg gifted to Princess Dagmara by your queen."

"That explains why you all reek of dragon. Let's see it, then."

"Drake, un-cask the egg."

"It requires a large perimeter," Silas says, moving toward the dapple-gray pack horse with Serin. "Your soldiers will need to move back."

"A word, Commander," a balding giant with an eye patch and burn scars on the right side of his face says.

"What is it, Cypherus?"

The older giant brings his horse around and whispers something in the commander's ear.

The commander eyes Silas, Serin, and Thale. "The three of you, come forward."

"*What's going on?*" I ask through the bond.

"*Stay close to Gideon. He's your only safe ticket home now, little spark.*"

I glance at Gideon. Landry and Jo-el stand next to him, bodies tight, ready for a fight. I step closer to Nellie and my skittish horse instead. If we have to run, I'm taking her with me.

The older guard circles his horse around them, nostrils flaring, and bends closer to sniff them.

"That's the one," he says, pointing at Silas, making my stomach drop. "Baby Face Drake. I'd recognize that scent anywhere. Bastard took my eye when he broke that fiery bitch out of Grislac prison sixty years ago."

The giant's head and shoulders slide off his body, severed by Silas's shadow blade.

"I should've killed you when I had the chance," Silas says with a dark smirk.

Chaos erupts around me. The giants pull their weapons. Their commander gets a shot off before Thale hits him with a bolt of lightning. Silas throws up a wall of shadows to block the bullet.

All I can do is stand and stare as the rain plasters my hair to my face. Silas, Serin, and Thale fight back to back as the giants close in around them.

Baby Face Drake? Sixty years ago? That can't be right. I must have misheard him.

A howl echoes behind me. I turn as Bas's body bends, breaks, and reforms. He leaps onto one of the giants, knocking him off his horse as he rips out his throat.

"I fucking knew it." Static crackles at Landry's fingertips as he aims for Bas.

I dive for Landry's legs, knocking him sideways. The bolt of lightning skitters across the ground, sending the horses into a panic.

Nellie loses her grip on my horse's reins.

Time slows as it rears on its hind legs, and Nellie cowers, raising her arms as if it's going to stop her from getting trampled. The dark flame in my chest flares. I hear my own voice scream her name as shadows explode from my hands and slam into the animal as its hooves come down on top of her. The horse stumbles, stomping and bucking as it careens away.

My body is moving before I take my next breath. I drop to my knees next to Nellie.

"I can't feel my legs." Blood trickles from her mouth as she takes a shallow breath.

"Don't move. I'll get Jo-el."

Nellie reaches for my hand. "Stay, please. I don't want to go alone."

"I'm sorry. I wasn't fast enough." Hot tears stream down my face.

"You're a witch." She smiles, taking in the protective dome of shadows around us.

"I am."

"Make sure my pyre burns all night." A wet cough rattles her caved-in chest.

I choke back a sob.

She squeezes my hand weakly. "It's okay. I'm not afraid. I know who waits for me on the other side." Her voice breaks as she struggles to take another breath.

"Hush, save your strength." I clasp both my hands around hers.

"The Mother of Fire knows my name. She'll look after me. I'll make sure she looks after you and Serin too."

"You are the best person I know, Nellie. Death doesn't deserve you."

Nellie's eyes flutter shut. Her chest shudders as it rises and falls. It doesn't rise again.

I pull her limp body into my lap. The shadows dissipate as I rock back and forth, holding her tight, as if I can selfishly stop her from dying. I choke back a sob.

"You're going to burn for attacking me, witch." Landry pulls me to my feet and drags me away from Nellie, static sparking at his fingertips.

Dead giants and witches cover the ground. Blood and rain spread in crimson puddles around their bodies. The kiss of hot breath on my neck is gone. I search frantically for Silas among the bodies. He's not there. Neither is his crew.

"Gather the horses. They took the egg," Gideon shouts at Jo-el and Craddock, the only other people standing.

"Let me go." I thrash against Landry's grip.

"So you can run after your reaver? I don't think so."

I slip my hand into my bag. Magic grazes my fingers as I fist the jeweled dagger.

"Everly, drop the knife," Gideon yells as I bring it up over my shoulder and attempt to stab Landry behind me.

Landry shoves me away from him. The threads of goblin-spelled magic stretch toward Gideon instead as I lose my grip on the dagger. It flies forward and embeds in Gideon's thigh.

"You traitorous fucking bitch." Landry grabs my shoulder and forces me to my knees, snapping an iron collar around my neck.

Chapter Thirty-Nine

"I'll ask you again, rabbit. Where did your reaver friends go?" Landry runs a static-charged finger over my swollen and cracked lips, sending an arc of pain down through the roots of my teeth. "All you have to do is tell me, and all this can end."

"Fuck you." The words feel like hot glass in my throat. I twist my wrists, attempting to loosen the rope binding me to the tree.

"I'm going to tame that vile mouth of yours." Landry presses his palm to my bare stomach, where he's cut away another section of my clothing to reveal flesh he hasn't already destroyed. My body convulses as the electrical shock rips through me. Not enough to kill me, but just enough to make me piss down my leg again as the sharp, needling pain crawls through my core.

A deep, guttural cry climbs up my raw throat. I shove it down and swallow it. I refuse to give him the satisfaction of hearing me scream.

Once the pain passes, I let my head fall back against the rough bark, counting backward from ten as my heart struggles to regain a natural rhythm.

"You've been torturing her for three days. She's not going to talk," Craddock says, washing his hands with soap and water from his canteen.

Landry's vicious touch is nothing compared to the sucking, hollow feeling in my chest threatening to devour me while I'm awake. Silas knows about the rendezvous point. He should have come for me by now. Part of me worries he's been hurt—or worse. But I watched him kill thirty reavers, walk into a lake full of deadly wraiths, and cut down giants twice his size. The man is unstoppable. He'll come.

"How's Krimore?" Landry asks.

"The same. Still delirious with fever. Jo-el's running out of alicorn powder. If the rest of the battalion with the Medic Squad and supplies doesn't get here soon, he might have to take Gideon's leg to keep the necrosis from spreading. I'm not a medic, but I don't see how he can survive a surgery like that in his condition."

I couldn't save my parents or Nellie. Now Gideon.

This time I wielded the weapon myself. This is what Grace tried to warn me about. I should have paid better attention to what she was trying to tell me. I shouldn't have used the dagger without knowing what it was capable of.

I close my eyes and call on the Mother of Fire, as I have every day for the last five days.

I, Everly Marlayna Thorne, offer my life to you in exchange for Gideon's. If it's your will to spare him, I will be your servant. I will devote myself in life and in death to your service.

"What, no tears for your dying prince today?" Landry asks.

The dark part of me thrashes silently against my restraints. I don't have any tears left. Only rage.

"If Gideon dies, we can add regicide to your sentence. Not that it matters. You're going to hang for treason when we get back to Crecentis."

"I wasn't trying to kill him. I didn't know your dagger was spelled to inflict an unhealable wound," I rasp.

"Do you think anyone will believe the jilted ex-fiancée turned reaver whore? Especially when your little sketchbook paints such an incriminating picture," Landry says, flipping through the pages. "Very clever of you to draw pictures of the wolf boy killing a bear."

"The kid did technically kill a bear. We all ate the stew," Craddock says.

"That hardly matters. We have four witnesses that saw her save that thing's life when it shifted and attacked us."

He has a name. I don't dare say it out loud. Not when it could have repercussions for Bas's clan. The less I say about any of them, the better. As soon as I give Landry the information he wants, I'm as good as dead. My silence is the only thing keeping me alive.

"At least we have all the sketches we need to print wanted posters of the man claiming to be Baby Face Drake and his band of reavers. It shouldn't take long to hunt them down and string them up by the neck."

Maybe it's the madness seeping in, but I can't help the smile that breaks across my face. "Silas killed fifty giants and got away with the egg, while you're here, stranded in the woods, waiting to be rescued and taking your sick little imagination out on me. You're too weak and afraid to even untie me. If you were half the man he is, you'd cut me down, remove this collar, and give me a fighting chance."

It's a bluff. I'm in no condition to fight him or Craddock. I don't even know if I'll be able to summon the magic Silas gave me now that the oath has been fulfilled and we're no longer bound. It doesn't matter.

That's not what I'm after. My words are my weapon now, and they strike true. Right in Landry's shriveled little ego.

Rage flashes across his face, and I know he's going to give me exactly what I want.

Oblivion. Landry can't torture me if I'm unconscious. I don't have to think about Nellie or Grace or Gideon.

He palms my stomach again, sending another jolt through me, stronger than the last. My teeth clench, and my vision goes black.

———◆———

"Drink some water, Thorne."

Silas? I'm not sure if I say his name out loud or just think it.

My ears ring as I struggle to force my eyes open.

I can't even lift my head.

The only thing keeping me upright are the ropes binding me to the tree.

Someone tips my chin back and holds a canteen to my mouth. I gag, unable to swallow.

"What the fuck did you do to her, Landry?" Major Mattern asks.

"Nothing she didn't deserve."

"Cut her down and put her in the back of one of the ox carts," Mattern commands. "And get a medic to look at those burns. We can't hang a dead witch. I want her alive and conscious when we hand her over to the prison in Crecentis."

———◆———

Birdsong cuts through the faint ringing in my ears. My eyelids feel heavy as I blink up at the curved white wagon canopy. I'm not sure how long I've been floating in and out of consciousness. A week? Two?

There's no hay or soft bedroll to dampen the rickety movement of the wooden cot as the medical wagon lumbers over the hard ground. Every bump and rut the wheels hit sends a burning pins-and-needles sensation through my body.

All I want to do is curl into a ball. I groan as I try to roll onto my side. The belts strapped across my shoulders and hips prevent me from moving.

"You're awake."

My vision blurs as I turn my head toward the medic sitting on a small bench across from me. I remember his face from the infirmary on the ship.

"How long have I been asleep?" I barely recognize the sound of my rough voice.

"Twenty-two days, plus the week you spent in the woods before we picked you up at the rendezvous point."

"A month? No. That can't be." I tug against the restraints.

"Major Mattern ordered me to keep you sedated during the journey to keep you calm. We just left the River District docks and should arrive at the prison shortly. The electrical burns on your face, chest, and stomach aren't fully healed yet. You're going to be in a good bit of pain once the laudanum wears off."

A month. The hollow, sucking sensation cracks open inside me. A month since the ember of magic in my chest went cold. A month since I fulfilled my end of the oath and set him free. Silas didn't come back for me. Hot tears roll down the side of my face and into my hair.

"You won't need to bear the pain much longer. Your execution is in three days."

"I want to talk to Gideon."

He gives me a somber look. "I'm afraid that's not possible."

I turn my face away and choke back a sob. I don't need to ask why. Gideon is dead. I killed him.

The driver at the front of the wagon yells at pedestrians to get out of the way. The wagon lurches to a stop, sending a fresh wave of torture through the places Landry branded me with his magic.

The medic's voice sounds miles away as he unstraps me from the cot and helps me stand on wobbling legs. I can't hear what he's saying past the ringing in my ears. He checks the iron collar around my neck to make sure it's secure before opening the canvas flaps on the back of the wagon.

I squint against the blinding light. The right side of my face throbs with heat as he hands me over to the waiting guards. They don't bother hiding their contempt as they drag me across Gallows Square to a chorus of angry slurs from the crowd gathered outside the prison gates.

They want someone to blame. Someone to hate for robbing them of hope. For killing their hero, who they thought would save them from wondering where their next meal is coming from. For leaving the country vulnerable without an heir to sit on the throne.

Up until two months ago, I wasn't any different from them, watching reavers hang, hoping it would bring me closure—hoping hate would somehow fill the void left by grief.

I can barely keep my feet under me as the guards drag me though the prison. They stop in front of an open cell. My stomach drops. I pull against them. A boot slams into my back, propelling me forward. Pain explodes across my cheek as my face hits the stone floor.

⁓ ❦ ⁓

Someone shouts in the hall outside my cell. My heart kicks like a mule behind my ribs. I lift my head, hugging my knees to my chest.

He's not coming. I know this. It doesn't stop me from staring at the door the same way I have for the last twenty-four hours, imagining a shadow blade slicing through it.

Silas's life is no longer tied to mine. He doesn't have a reason to care whether I live or die. He left me behind to take the fall as soon as the blood oath was fulfilled, and he had everything he wanted.

"Look alert, witch. You've got a visitor." I hate myself for the stab of disappointment that rents through me as the guard opens the door and ushers my brother inside. "You have thirty minutes."

Adrian watches anxiously as the guard locks him in with me. His dark blond curls look like spun gold in the narrow column of light from the small window up high on the wall.

My mind is definitely starting to slip. For a moment, he looks so much like Gideon it makes me do a double take. I can't tell if it's my mind playing tricks on me or if Gideon's ghost has come to torture me.

I shake off the hallucination as Adrian kneels next to me. He inspects the throbbing goose-egg on my right cheek and moves on to the burn that covers the right side of my face and neck.

"Have they given you anything for the pain?"

"It's fine. It doesn't hurt so much as long as I don't move."

"I can speak to the prison doctor to see if they can give you a numbing salve." His gaze drops to the collar around my neck.

"Don't waste your breath. I hang in two days for murdering the country's most beloved hero. They aren't going to give me any special treatment."

Adrian sits back on his heels. "You've been charged with theft, concealment of summoning abilities, treason, and attempted regicide. Not murder."

"*Attempted* regicide?" I sit up straighter. "Gideon's alive?"

"He's being treated in a Saracen hospital that specializes in magical wounds if you believe the papers."

I close my eyes and thank the Mother of Fire, biting back a whimper of relief. My body suddenly feels too light. Like I could float up the wall and slip through the bars in the window like smoke. Gideon is alive. I don't have to go to my grave with that guilt.

"The papers say you're a shadow-summoning witch that plotted against the crown to help the man masquerading as Ambassador Caron's security consultant steal the dragon egg."

I wait for the ember of magic in my chest to flare in warning, momentarily forgetting it's gone cold.

My dirty hair falls around my face as I hang my head in shame.

"Why did you do it?"

The last thing I want to do is relive the last two months. But my brother deserves the truth before I die. He deserves the closure we never got with our parents. I take a deep breath and tell Adrian everything. The gambling scheme I hoped would pay for my medical needs and my debts to Madam Faye. My blood oath with Silas, agreeing to be Gideon's spy, the game, the hallucinations, and Landry's dagger.

He listens quietly. By the time I'm finished, his eyes are glassy.

"I'm sorry I lied to you about the money and being a witch. I didn't want you to find out this way."

"I've always known that you're a witch. I suspected when you came back after the last trip you took with mother and father. You were different. They gave me vague answers when I asked them about it. You started showing symptoms of the burning shortly after, and I knew."

"You're not angry with me?"

"It's not logical to be angry about something you have no control over. You're the first witch in our family. You didn't ask to be inflicted with the fever."

"I love you. I'm sorry I didn't say it before." A burning sensation stretches across my stomach as I press up to my knees and hug him for the last time.

Tears spill down my cheeks with the realization that I'll never see him again.

"Don't come to the gallows. Let this be our last memory," I plead.

"We still have two days. I'm going to file a petition for a stay of execution on the grounds of coercion and cognitive impairment induced by the burning."

I grasp his hand. "Stabbing Gideon with the knife was an accident, but I'm still guilty of treason. I knew the consequences when I agreed to help Silas. I won't pretend to be insane so I can live out the rest of my life locked in a sanatorium for mad witches."

"I have to do something, Everly. I can't just sit by and let them kill you."

"There's only one thing you can do that will make any of this better. Stay alive. There's a bone broker in the Downriver District called Guy

Maynard. He's holding a bond on my life. You're the beneficiary. Take the money and leave Perdanth before they get around to charging you with harboring a witch. There's enough for you to sail across the ocean and set up a clinic somewhere far away and continue our parents' work. Find a cure for the burning."

The guard unlocks the cell. "Time's up."

"Tell Wallace I love her and that I don't want her or her family at the gallows. Promise me you won't come either. I love you, Adrian."

The guard grabs my brother by the arm and hauls him out of the cell.

Chapter Forty

"Get up, witch," the guard says as he sets a bucket of water by the door. "Full moon tonight. That means all the prisoners get to bathe today. You'll smell nice and pretty for the executioner tomorrow morning."

I ignore him and roll on my side to face the wall. I haven't moved since Adrian left except to relieve myself in the bucket in the corner.

"Did you hear me, you reaver bitch? Everyone bathes once a month whether they like it or not. You got ten minutes to scrub up before I come back and do it for you. And I won't be none too gentle about it."

There's no way I'm letting this asshole touch me. Every part of my body protests as I drag myself across the room and take off my shift. Angry red lines branch out across the right side of my abdomen. The lightning burn on my stomach is far worse than what I can see on my shoulder and chest where Landry touched me.

I grab the soap out of the bucket and try not to think about how many other prisoners used it before me tonight. I wash my body quickly. The grimy water stings my broken skin. The last bath I had was with Silas in the hot spring. He was gentle and attentive, taking his time as he washed my hair. I bite my lower lip to keep it from quivering.

I'm very good at pretending. That's what he told me the morning after the ball. After he saved my life. I scrub harder, as if the pain will gouge the memory of him out of my system. His magic, his touch, his beautiful fucking face.

The lock clicks. I slip into my dirty shift and back away quickly as the guard returns for the bucket. He leaves, and I slide down the wall to the floor.

My breaths come quickly as I clutch my chest, desperate to feel the spark of dark flame. I hate Silas Drake for making me want something that was never meant to be mine. For making me hope when it was all just pretend. I hate myself even more for falling in love with the lie and giving him this power over me. He warned me not to get confused.

I knew the consequences when I agreed to the oath. I knew what would happen if I got caught helping him steal from the crown. This time tomorrow, I'll be dead. My body will be added to a pile on the executioner's mule cart and burned in a shallow pit with the others.

No one is coming to save me.

———⬥———

The clang of metal jolts me awake. I don't even remember drifting off. It seems strange that I spent the last few hours of my life sleeping. I should have forced myself to stay awake. To listen to the birds announce the dawn one last time.

Two guards drag me to my feet while another secures shackles to my wrists and ankles.

"Make sure they're secure before you remove the collar. I helped clean up the aftermath of the Festivalla ball. If this shadow-summoning bitch is half as deadly as Baby Face Drake, you'll want to make sure those irons are good and tight."

"I have a name too, asshole."

"Which one would you like to be called, reaver whore or horny Thorne?"

"My name is Everly Marlayna Thorne." I square my shoulders, refusing to let these men strip away my last shred of dignity.

I say my name again as they push me into the hall, where more guards wait. I repeat it as we go down the stairs, raising my voice over the growing clamor of the crowd waiting outside. There are so many people the guards have to clear a path to the scaffold.

"My name is Everly Marlayna Thorne." I repeat it over the slurs and angry accusations.

"Mad witch."

"Reaver scum."

"Traitor."

I say my name as I climb the scaffold, my shackles clattering against the wooden steps.

The guards hand me over to the executioners in black hoods. I scan the sea of people as the smaller of the two tightens the noose around my neck.

I don't see Adrian. My gaze snags on every redhead in the crowd. There are too many to be sure Wallace isn't among them. I don't want my best friend or her family to remember me like this.

My stomach drops as I spot Victor Landry.

"Hello, rabbit." He mouths the words and flashes me a vicious smile.

"All right, Everly Marlayna Thorne. Do you want the bee or the honey first?" a familiar voice says behind me as the other executioner reads off my charges.

"Wallace?"

"Don't turn around." She grips my shoulder. "We don't have much time, so I'll give you the honey first. Adrian is safe. He's with my extended clan in Red Stick."

"And the bees?"

The scaffold vibrates beneath my feet as an earth-shaking roar rumbles across the square.

"It's just the one bee. One big, scary fucking bee."

The crowd erupts into screams of terror as dozens of rougarous shift in the crowd and attack the guards.

The second executioner pulls back his hood as Wallace unlocks my shackles.

"Bas?"

"He's going to need this to suppress his beast." Bas shoves Silas's ring onto my thumb and leaps off the scaffold, shifting before his feet hit the ground.

"I like your new friends," Wallace says, yanking the last iron cuff from my ankle.

Finally free of the goblin-spelled metal, the dark flame in my chest ignites. I yank a shadow shield around us as a bolt of lightning hits the scaffold. The wood explodes beneath us, toppling the entire thing to the ground.

Wallace helps me up and pulls the noose off my neck as fire rains down on the square.

My legs threaten to give out as I grab her arm and raise my gaze to the sky.

"That's not a bee. That's a fucking dragon," I rasp as its massive body blots out the sun.

"That's your dragon."

Iridescent black scales shimmer along its back and tail as it banks and comes back for another pass. It's the most terrifying and beautiful thing I've ever seen.

Sunlight bleeds through its leathery wings, highlighting the intricate network of veins and making them glow crimson.

Static sparks to my left, dragging my attention away from the magnificent creature. I watch as Landry raises his hands and takes aim at the beast.

My vision flashes red. I push Wallace behind me as I summon a flare and blast it at the side of Landry's head. It hits his shield and ricochets to the side.

I throw another flare as he turns toward me with a vile smirk. It slams into his shield, throwing sparks out in all directions.

"Looks like I'll get that fighting chance after all, asshole." I take a wobbly step toward him and fire again. The flare isn't as strong as the first two and lands short. Silas's magic is fizzling out.

"You don't have what it takes to end me, rabbit. I'm going to kill you, and then I'm going to hunt down all your feral friends. I'm going to enjoy carving them up and feeding them to my dogs."

The ground shudders as the dragon lands behind him with a thunderous noise. Its nearly as tall as the three-story prison. Its crimson eyes narrow on my face.

"*Who did this to our mate?*" a deep, unfamiliar voice booms in my mind.

My gaze darts to Landry.

The dragon throws its head back with an earth-shaking roar. Fire ignites in its throat. I watch as it unleashes the full force of its rage on the man who tortured me to the edge of death.

I squeeze my eyes shut as a blast of scalding air slams into me, knocking me on my ass.

The dragon grabs me with its talons, pumping its wings as it shoves off the ground with a tortured growl that reverberates in my chest.

My stomach goes queasy as I look down. The city shrinks away as the dragon soars higher. Wind whips at my eyes, making them water.

I should be terrified. I should not be memorizing the pattern of its scales or the deep grooves of the talons locked around me so I can draw them later. Something inside me knows this beautiful, brutal beast won't hurt me.

The goblin-spelled ring glints on my thumb as I caress the dew claw hooked over my shoulder.

"*I want to see Silas,*" I say in my head.

A defiant growl vibrates in the dragon's chest, setting off a ripple of motion along its belly scales.

I slip Silas's ring off my thumb and fit it over the sharp tip of his talon. My stomach drops as we dive for the swamp. It's just like the dream I had the first time I slept wrapped in Silas's shadows. Terrifying and exhilarating.

He spreads his wings, and we glide over an open area of water where the river flows through the swamp. He drops his tail, dragging it behind him like an anchor. Then he releases me gently as we slow.

The dark water swallows me whole. I kick for the surface and suck in a breath as my head hits the air. A swirling vortex of shadows slams into the swamp, throwing water and mud into the sky.

I swim against the current, muscles trembling from lack of use and near starvation. I can't remember the last time I ate anything. I'm not going to make it. My arms and legs are too weak.

My head slips under the surface. The water drags me away from Silas. Away from my beautiful, deadly monster.

No. I didn't come this far or survive reavers and giants and being tortured to within an inch of my life to drown in a fucking swamp.

My feet touch the mucky bottom. I shove off the mud and stretch for the light.

"*I'm not done with you yet, little spark.*" Silas's arm snakes around my chest, pulling me to the shore.

We crawl up the bank and collapse in the reeds. Silas rolls onto his side and pushes the hair away from my face.

"You came."

His eyes still carry a crimson glow as he drags his gaze over my fresh scars. "Not soon enough. I'm so fucking sorry."

"You really came."

"We will always come for you."

"We?" I ask tentatively.

"We're a package deal, I'm afraid, my beast and I."

"You're a dragon."

"I'm a monster, Everly."

"You're exquisite." I cup his face as the undeniable truth settles inside me.

"I've done terrible, unforgivable things. Things I regret. Things that will make you despise me."

"Let them stay buried in the past. I want to live in the present and squeeze all the joy I can out of the time I have left." Explanations about why I can still hear his voice inside my head now that the oath is fulfilled and what he did with the egg can wait. I'm not sure I want the answers to anything else. Not yet. Maybe never.

Silas presses a kiss to the scar on my palm. "I don't deserve you or your forgiveness for the pain that I've caused you. But I'll spend the rest of my life atoning for it, if you'll allow it."

"You're making it very difficult for me to be angry with you for not letting me kill Landry myself."

Silas's chest rumbles with an animalistic sound that's equal parts growl and purr as he brushes his lips against mine.

"I'll never deny you anything you desire again. I'm yours. You have possessed me, man, beast, and magic." He presses my palm against his chest, directly above his heart. "I've been dead inside for two centuries. You're the spark that brought me back to life. You're the flame that burns inside me. I will be yours until my dying breath."

Two centuries? The hollow sensation in my chest cracks open as I sit up. The average lifespan of a dragon is three hundred years. I can't even fathom what it might be like to survive another decade, much less another century.

"What's the matter?" Silas sits up behind me, trailing his fingertips down my arm.

"I'm scared. I don't know how much longer I have left before the burning destroys my mind and my body. I can't promise you a future or any of the things that come with it."

Hot tears spill down my cheeks. It's the most brutally honest thing I've ever said to anyone.

Silas pulls me into his lap and kisses them away. "All I want is you. Come with me to Shadow's Fold and let me help you squeeze the joy out of whatever time we have together."

"I'd like that."

"Good, because I'm a very selfish man and I was fully prepared to kidnap you if you said no."

I smile against the warmth of his lips. "Don't get too excited, reaver. I'm bringing my cat, my brother, and maybe a few stray wolves."

"Are we negotiating?" Silas folds his arms around me.

"Just setting expectations." I capture his bottom lip in my teeth.

A soft growl rumbles in his chest as his tongue sweeps through my mouth. There's nothing left to pretend. Just the heat of our shared breath and the familiar sense of rightness that reaches down through my core to the darkest part of me, telling her that she's safe. That she's enough and that she's home.

Also By J. Ember Hintz

J. Ember Hintz writes fantasy and paranormal romance because the real world has too many monsters and not enough magic. Follow her author life shenanigans by joining her No Damsels Newsletter.

For more stories about women fighting for agency in a dark world and the morally gray men who burn for them, check out her other works.

Dark Eden Series
Garden of Echoes and Ash
Scars of Seduction and Sacrifice

Masquerade of Bones Series
Last of Her Kind (Series Prequel May 2025)
Masquerade of Bones
Book Two (Spring 2026)
Dagmara and Gideon's Story (Holiday Novella Fall 2026)
Book Three (Spring 2027)

GLOSSARY

BITTER PEPPER: Drug derived from a plant native to southern Perdanth used to temporarily suppress symptoms of the burning.

CRECENTIS: Capital of Perdanth.

DRAGONS: Massive beasts hunted into extinction by humans for the powerful shadow and flame magic in their bones and scales.

FIREBIRDS: Peacock sized bird hunted by humans for the flame and heat magic in their feathers. Difficult to keep alive in captivity because of their tendency to self-combust under stress.

FIRE SUMMONER: Witch who channels magic from firebird feathers.

GOBLINS: Small cave dwelling creatures with the ability to imbue metal and stone with magical properties who are hunted and held in captivity by humans.

HEALER: Witch with medical training who channels magic from unicorn relics.

NYMPHS: Rare human-like, ocean dwelling creatures whose bones and scales are believed to bring good luck to those who find them washed up on shore.

PERDANTH: Southern kingdom, where witches are conscripted into military service and channelling magic is prohibited outside the military.

PIXIES: Small forest dwelling creatures hunted and bred in captivity for the sedative magic in the microscopic scales on their wings. Their bones are believed to a be good luck charm.

REAVERS: Gangs of outlaw witches who attack relic and supply convoys being transported in and out of The Wastes. A slang term for rogue, unlicensed witches.

RELICS: The bones, teeth, feathers, scales, claws, and hooves of magical creatures that contain residual amounts of the creature's innate magic.

ROUGAROUS: Rare, human-like swamp wolf hunted by humans for the libido enhancing magic in their bones.

SARACEN: Northern kingdom, where channelling magic is not prohibited for civilians.

SHADOW SUMMONER: Witch who channels magic from dragon relics.

STORM SUMMONER: Witch who channels magic from thunderbird relics.

THE BURNING: Degenerative neurological disease that shortens the lifespan of witches through debilitating cognitive and physical deterioration caused by channeling magic from relics.

THE NORTHLANDS: Lands beyond Saracen's northern border, ruled by the queen of giants.

THE WASTES: Lawless desert beyond Perdanth and Saracen's western borders, where the relics of extinct magical creatures and other coveted natural resources are excavated or mined.

THUNDERBIRDS: Massive, human-sized bird hunted into extinction by humans for the powerful lightning, wind and rain magic in their bones and talons.

TINDLESTONE: The capital city of the Northlands.

UNICORNS: Extremely rare horse-like creature hunted into extinction by humans for the powerful healing magic in their horns and less powerful healing magic in their hooves.

WATER WRAITHS: Human-like lake dwelling creatures hunted for their deadly venom.

WITCH: Gender inclusive term for humans with the ability to channel magic from relics.

WITCH FEVER: A deadly illness that affects teenagers and lasts several months. Those who survive gain the ability to channel magic from relics.